PRODIGAL SON

THE ORDER OF VAMPIRES 3

LYDIA MICHAELS

PRODIGAL SON
THE ORDER OF VAMPIRES 3
Copyright © 2022 by Lydia Michaels

Paranormal Romance
Fantasy Fiction
Horror Fiction
Thriller Fiction

Cover Design: Lydia Michaels

USA | CANADA | SPAIN | EUROPE | NEW ZELAND |
AUSTRALIA | AISIA

www.LydiaMichaelsBooks.com

READ WITH THE AUDIOBOOK!

Read along with the audiobook!
Download the audiobook on Apple or
Audible.
Listen Now!

PLAYLIST

DEDICATION

In memory of Ronda Joy Slager. Ronda was a significant woman in my life who always supported my endeavors. She was the first to order my books and promoted my stories to anyone who would listen. She was kind and loving and brought so much peace to other people's lives. She is the reason my middle name is Joy, and responsible for a lot of the confidence that still carries me through days when I doubt my skills. I'm so grateful her life touched mine. We lost her far too soon, but the impression she left will live forever in our hearts and souls.

Thank you, Ronda, for believing in me when I wasn't sure if I could do "this writing thing". Your

words influenced mine more than you probably
realized.

CHAPTER 1

A gush of hot blood soaked the fabric of Cain's shirt as searing pain shot through his chest. His knees crashed onto the cold earth as a grunt coughed out of him, the metallic taste of his own blood rising in his throat with his burning, now untethered, rage.

She truly shot him. That mortal terror of a female shot him. His stunned gaze lifted from the arrow protruding from his chest to the startled woman still angling the crossbow at him. Destiny Santos, star reporter for the Channel Six news, had finally gone too far.

"You must have a death wish," he snarled, and her dark brown eyes widened under the fringe of her black lashes.

"I…" Stark horror bleached the color from her face until her skin shined like white bone under the blue moonlight. "I told you not to move. Y-you didn't listen."

Her finger, still hooked around the trigger, trembled slightly. The scent of mortal fear filled the air in an inescapable sweet stench. The pain should have blinded him to the details, but he spared a second to wonder why any female would shape their fingernails as pointed claws. Hers were blood red—like his now drenched shirt.

He was going to kill her. Slice open her flesh and tear her limb by limb—as soon as he found his bearings.

Fluid filled his lungs and he coughed, choking as he drowned internally from the blood pumping through his punctured heart and lungs. The rattle of his cough no longer sounded hollow. Now, breathing felt more like waterboarding as he gasped in flimsy sips of air. Not enough.

Consciousness flickered. He needed to extract the arrow from his heart and feed before he lost all awareness. Falling unconscious as deep in the woods as they were, with a predator afoot, would leave them both in danger.

His stare latched onto her rapidly fluttering pulse. Mortals were a no-no, but the shrew shot him. He gripped the arrow, his mind reaching for Anna, as his concentration quickly severed by the unexpected pain. Gasping, he fell forward to his hands and knees.

"No, don't pull it! You need a doctor!"

His body wobbled as the blood drained from his chest, rushing faster as his heart pumped wildly around the hole. Too weak to access the cognitive link he and Anna shared, Cain waited, gasping. But the connection faded, fainter and fainter until he could no longer find the thread. He needed to heal before his injury spread to his sweet, pregnant… Annalise.

Stretching a hand in front of him, he forced himself to rise, wobbling precariously on his knees as life giving blood gushed from the open wound of his chest. His arm trembled beside the protruding arrow and he commanded the mortal female. "Come—"

Choking on the thick saliva crowding his tongue, he struggled to give the order. His mind scrambled with an effort to remain conscious, making telekinesis impossible, as his balance gave out and his heart went into a wildly agonizing spasm.

Collapsing onto the frozen forest floor, his shoulder took the brunt of his weight but the protruding arrow knocked hard into the solid earth, driving deeper into his chest and tearing at his back muscles. He rolled to his side, gasping and groaning, the mortal's ceaseless chatter blurring into a cricket's song lost behind the blaring in his ears.

The others were edging closer. He could vaguely hear their approach in the rattle of leaves overhead. They were outnumbered, and he was desperately in need of blood.

Slumber threatened to pull him into a deep sleep, tempting to release him from the horrific pain. His vision moved in trails of light and dark shadows as the mortal prattled on with her ceaseless chatter, worrying over her dead phone battery as he slowly died at her feet.

Silver stars blurred in the sky in an opaque smear of black as a scream tickled the back of his skull. A pool of heat cooled under his back as he stared up at the swirling sky.

"Anna…" he wheezed, desperate not to fail her, but fearful he might black out from the pain.

His shaking fingers, sticky with blood, wrapped around the arrow. He needed to get it out. Gritting his teeth, uncaring that his fangs were showing, he tensed and growled as he tugged at the shaft.

An ungodly roar of frustration escaped as the arrow refused to budge, the barbed tip shredding through the pulp of his organs as his blood pumped wastefully. Panting and sweating, chills took over as his heart thrust in an erratic assault, spilling more blood and causing his body to lock and tremble against the radiating agony.

"What have you done?" he snarled at the woman, frustrated with the endless assault that followed such a small intrusion. "You've impaled my heart—"

"I'm sorry!" her shrill cry tried to claim sympathy, as if she were the victim here. "I didn't mean to actually shoot you. I was scared!"

And so she should be, out in the woods with predators thirsting for her blood. Isaiah had nearly ended her. Cain wasn't sure what had chased him away. But he wasn't alone. By no means did Cain assume they were out of danger. They had to leave before the deranged army that served his uncle returned.

Gritting his teeth, he yanked the arrow. The barbed tip tore at tissue and his heart spasmed wildly. Pain knifed into his back and shoulders, exploding in an attack that would kill a mortal. He bore down, his body going into shock as he braced. Agonizing tremors jerked his focus and his grip loosened.

The offending spike wouldn't budge. So long as it remained, he'd continue to lose blood and weaken. He wrapped his bloodied hand around the shaft and heaved again, this time spewing the contents of his stomach onto the earth and crying out in pain.

A bouquet of store-bought perfume filled the air as brittle, fallen leaves crunched under the female's rushing footsteps. "Shit, shit, shit!" she babbled, her voice pitched with panic. "Wait! You're making it worse. Let me help."

His head snapped back and he hissed with unrefined venom. The mortal bitch doubled back, spewing a startled curse in a foreign language. Her words faded, sounding further and further away as the blackness of the sky flowed into his vision and he struggled to stay awake.

A strange numbness took over his body and

he could no longer feel his legs. How much blood had he lost? An unwelcome peace settled over him, the back of his mind weakly whispering for him to yank the arrow free. One or two more tugs should do it, but his body shivered and the numbness overtaking his limbs stole away the sting. Perhaps he could just rest…

Exhaustion pulled him gently into a tempting calm. Tranquility lured a sense of ease, inviting him into an eternal peaceful slumber immortals rarely found. Was this it?

He could simply…stop…fighting. Abandon this shallow, meaningless existence that had become his life.

But Anna… Would she come with him? What about Adam? Did he care?

Damn that unbreakable needle that guided his moral compass. He wanted to surrender and let go, stop fighting so hard to keep living this wretchedly lonesome life. Vision winking in and out, he glanced toward the sky and spotted something strange in the shadows of the canopy above.

A memory teased the tattered frays of his flickering conscience. He'd been looking for something. A creature. Not just a creature— his uncle, Isaiah. No longer recognizable as his kin, Isaiah had long ago turned *feeish*, living out the last century as *vampire*.

Cain's eyes squinted at the black branches overhead, his wavering vision making out the strange bundles. Several abandoned nests in the black shadows of the canopy. Bare branches cradled large clusters of twigs and scavenged scraps. So many nests, each one too large for hawks or owls.

They were cribs for *the others...*

"We must leave this place," he wheezed, wondering if he could trust the mortal to carry him. "Help me..."

"Oh, God, I don't think you should move. Where's your phone? We have to call—"

"Cursed female!" he snapped. "Do you ever listen?"

"I'm trying to help you!"

Her tedious reasoning drained him of effort and he sank weakly into the ground, catching his breath. A face filled his memory. Not Anna, but another female—innocent and young. Blameless eyes that spoke of horrors but a mouth that remained silent. Cybil. Should he perish in these woods, who would look after sweet, innocent Cybil?

He was here to avenge her mother's death. A mortal girl of ten, far too young to have seen what she'd seen when her mother had been murdered in these woods by his delusional uncle. And the mortal girl's mother had not been the only woman to lose her life at Isaiah's wrath.

Anger gnawed away his patience. *"Why are you here?"*

The foolish reporter lacked the sensibility to survive, which should have been a natural instinct. She reported on the deaths for her English news, knew there was something lethal hiding in these woods, yet here she was armed with stupidity and a weapon she could barely lift.

"Why are *you* here?" she snapped back.

An inhuman squawk chattered in the distance, drawing both their attention. Cain shut his eyes and called the wind. On the tail of a breeze, he scented *the others* moving in and surrounding them. If they reached them, surrounding them from all angles, he would not be able to defend himself let alone protect the mortal.

Cain's arm sagged limply onto the ground, his breath wheezing in and out of him in what seemed his final gasps. He looked at the woman, no longer hearing her panic, but watching her spiral. Why would anyone care so much if he lived or died? Perhaps it was a blemish on her conscience she wanted to avoid.

Mortals were not their responsibility. They were slow, foolish, and fragile, but this entire mess linked back to his kin. His family had a responsibility to end the murders taking place in these woods by tracking the source and ending Isaiah.

When the female turned, Cain frowned, noting the slashes that tore open her clothing and the dark stain of blood seeping from her back. His hunger rallied and his mind pushed through the haze. Survival instinct took over as the scent of her human blood called to him.

Cain had promised Cybil retribution. He swore he would find the monster that killed her mother and destroy it. Killing his uncle Isaiah would not undo the trauma little Cybil and her older brother, Dane, had suffered, but it might help Cybil find her words again.

"Blood," Cain rasped, curling his fingers as if the motion might lure her closer. His body was too weak to use compulsion.

He'd yet to fulfill his vows, not just the one he made to Cybil, but also his promise to Annalise. A promise he'd broken when he swore to his brother's wife he would not get injured on the hunt.

Scowling at the frantic female that just shot him in the heart, he reconsidered his stance on draining meddlesome mortal troublemakers dry. Blindly dragging his heavy hand to his chest, he gripped the rod of the arrow. The plunging throb spread through his back and shoulders and he screamed in frustration as the arrow twisted against the raw tissue of his spurting heart.

His insides revolted, a swirl of nausea lifting his shoulders off the ground only to have the agony in his chest thrust him back to the earth. Sweat beaded on his brow and he panted through clenched teeth as his mind fought to stay conscious.

He couldn't sleep. He needed to keep fighting. Needed to keep his promise to Cybil and stay alive for Anna—though his sister-by-law only required his safety and survival, nothing more. She had his twin brother, Adam, for all else.

He drew in a galvanizing breath and pulled again, gritting his teeth and screaming. Panting, he shut his eyes and tried to slow his breath so he wouldn't pass out. The continuous babble from the mortal female no longer registered, just a frantic pulse that played like a steady tribal beat in his ear. He should kill her. Feed, then snap her neck so he could think in silence.

His life's blood filled his mouth and he swallowed…choking…drowning. Blood loss weakened him. He couldn't think. Couldn't move as tremors raked his body and fluid suffocated him. Another attack seized his heart. Couldn't fight anymore.

The mortal's words volleyed between what sounded like Portuguese and English. *"Deus!* I can't go to jail for murder. Shit. Fuck." She moved as if searching for signs of salvation that didn't exist this deep in the woods. *"Meu Deus! Não sei o que fazer! Me ajuda!"*

Her gibberish grated on him as much as her modern attire and overdone eyes. "My phone," he panted, head back and eyes shut tight against the pain. "In my pocket." The lie lured her in as he expected it would. His finger twitched and he pointed to his hip. "Here."

Her pulse quickened, a fast-prattling harmony to his ears. The scent of her adrenaline laced sweat filled his ravaged lungs. He slowed his breathing, a predator lying in wait, as thunder rumbled low in the distance.

"There's so much blood," she blubbered, as if she'd been the one injured.

"Yes," he rasped, hardly able to open his eyes. "Thanks to you."

She crouched low. "Try not to move. Oh, God, I never meant to actually shoot you. Just...keep breathing. Please don't die, okay?"

A twig snapped under her boot, close to his ear, and instinct took over, the last of his strength jolting him forward, too fast for any human to escape as he latched onto her with claws and fangs.

A sharp scream of shock pierced the night, quickly silenced as his fangs lanced into her jugular and hot, enriching mortal blood flooded his mouth—laced with the drugging effect of her adrenaline as her fight or flight response kicked in.

She fought, and his mind reached for hers, but her struggles did not subdue. Gurgling screams bounced off the trees and prey scrambled deeper into the brush. He used the last of his strength to hold her, his mind too overwrought to compel her into calm.

Her booted foot dragged over the dirt as he yanked her closer, kicking and blaring an earsplitting cry. Nails scratched down his face, and she grabbed hold of the arrow, jerking and ramming it deeper in his heart.

He screamed and viciously bit into her throat, ravaging her vein as blood gurgled from her artery and her body went limp. The warm nourishment replenished his strength and subdued the pain, but an astounding amount still remained as the arrow stayed lodged in his heart.

The wind kicked up and he scented cold blood. He sniffed the unconscious mortal and frowned. Like any once living food, blood was prone to rot. The breakdown of the hemoglobin on her flesh dried into an indigestible compound, turning his stomach.

Yanking his fangs free, he scowled at her unconscious form and examined her torn clothing. Lifting the tattered layers of her coat, his eyes widened. Deep grooves scored her flesh, exposing pink muscle in five long gouges. Dried blood and dirt crusted each wound as fresh blood leaked profusely, scoring her caramel flesh. The marks would likely scar, forever marring an otherwise flawless body.

Mortals could only sustain so much injury and blood loss. She, too, had been injured and needed help. Unsure how much he'd taken from her vein or how much she had already lost, he snatched her wrist and felt for a pulse. It was weak but there.

The offending arrow still remained, draining all that he'd just replenished. He couldn't think from the pain as his arteries pumped and popped. He needed to stop his blood from spilling before taking any more of her blood to heal.

Fangs dripping, he lifted his head and searched the forest, listening for nearby creatures that might tide him over. But his presence, and that of *the others*, kept small prey at bay. Irritated by the unwanted need for conservation, he shoved the female's unconscious body away and scented the cold winter air.

He should rip out her throat and bleed her dry, save himself and save Anna from possibly suffering his pain. But there still remained some misguided hope for his abandoned soul that floundered about in his confused mind, a conscious part of him that inconvenienced his life on a regular basis.

He'd been branded a cursed immortal without honor. Yet, here he was, hesitating to take what he needed to heal in order to save the she-devil who shot him.

Yanking her closer, her upper body draped

weakly over his legs. Soft swells of feminine curves caught his eye, just as a twig snapped in the distance. Blood would strengthen him and he needed to be strong.

Gripping his fist in her wild, dark curls, he lifted her face and growled. Loathing the wafer-thin honor that protected the mortal female and greatly inconvenienced him, he jerked her close and licked the wound on her throat shut. His saliva would rapidly heal her tissue and prevent infection or scarring, but it couldn't replenish the blood he took. Without a transfusion, her feeble human body would need time to recover and weeks to regenerate red blood cells.

Forcing himself to rise despite the pain, he stretched his mind and searched for another option. They would have to move, travel somewhere far away from the stench of evil and danger if he intended to lure smaller prey close enough to sustain him.

His body struggled to stand upright and he questioned if he had the strength to carry her deadweight. There was no doubt in his mind that this specific mortal female would tell the world what she saw tonight. Still too weak to penetrate her mind or wipe her memories, he decided he couldn't leave her.

He also couldn't kill her—although death would ensure her silence.

A tremor skated up his spine as he felt the urge to retch. Stretching his mind over the distance, he tried to reach Anna again, but found nothing but blackness, all threads of communication cut without a trace. Maybe his sister-by-law found a way to protect herself from sharing his pain. He hoped so, for the sake of not just the babe she carried in her womb, but for her own protection as well.

The mortal's blood helped anesthetize his pain, but the arrow still skewered his chest and his body couldn't heal around the intrusion. Getting it out would be…unpleasant, so he took a moment to galvanize his nerves.

Had he been human, he'd already be dead. The blood he stole from the woman slowly worked its way through his system, the tissue of his heart mending. Torn sinew sewed together around the muscle, as regenerated cells reconstructed capillaries. But that damn arrow remained.

He only had minutes until another attack would strike. Once more glancing at the many nests in the trees, he debated the best course. Cribs, constructed of pine and mud, large enough refuge for a primate, but apes didn't inhabit these woods. The meddlesome woman passed out at his side would be dead by morning if he left her here for when *the others* returned.

His bloodied hands closed around the arrow and he pulled hard. His insides rolled in objection, the contents of his stomach spewing from his lips in a surge of blood and energy. Consciousness flashed in and out as black oblivion threatened his mind. All that he'd just drank from the mortal now lay wasted in the leaves and dirt at his side.

The arrow needed to come out. Clawing at the earth, he coated his bloodied hands in dirt and gripped the protruding arrow. His scream sent night birds flocking from the trees and owls screeching as his howl broke the illusion of peace. He gripped the hilt of the arrow with his right hand. Molars locked, he bared his teeth. A deafening roar ripped out of him. Not giving himself a chance to stop, he extracted the arrow with a slow, agonizing slurp and fell back as the excruciating pain sent his body into shock.

The buried, barbed tip tore open his freshly mended tissue and he gasped under the pain. The earth swayed as a wave of dizziness struck, turning his stomach and sending more blood spewing from his lips.

He threw the offending spike on the ground and caught his breath. Blood spurted from his chest as his heart pumped hard.

His arteries clotted and spasmed, pumping hard in an unnatural way as incredible pressure built in his chest, bursting like an explosion through his back and shoulders and down his arm. His heart pulsed painfully, hammering against his ribs as if under another attack, giving him no choice but to wait out the pain as his muscles tensed and his living cells died off.

Through the delirium of agony and the rush of blood clotting the corners of his eyes, he stared through blurry vision at the branches above. The sky looked peaceful and he could scent snow in the air. His ravaged body begged his mind to rest, but he needed to move. Despite the sense of calm, the woods were a very dangerous place to be—especially injured as both he and the mortal female were.

Her weak pulse pounded in his ears. A beat of silence passed as he called the wind, glad some of his power remained. He scented *the others* nearing in the distance. They were out of time.

His uncle Isaiah might appear a weather-beaten wild animal, but his ancient bloodlines and diet left him strong. The memory of his dark black hair trailing in snarls behind his filthy, naked form reminded Cain just how savage and lost an unanswered soul could be. Cain's own fears threatened to destroy his remaining calm, the cloying suspicion that his fate might someday resemble that of his deranged uncle.

He glanced at the unconscious woman at his feet. If his uncle got ahold of the battered female, he wouldn't simply kill her. He'd toy with her like all the others. Vampires liked to torment their prey the way cats tormented mice. Isaiah would take his time and drag out her suffering.

"Foolish English woman. You should have never returned to these woods." He grunted, bending to grab hold of her arm. The stench of her dried blood held hints of an oncoming infection.

Understanding what he needed to do to save them both, he lifted her limp arm, drawing her wrist to his lips where her pulse beat weakly. "I promise not to let you die."

His fangs punctured her smooth flesh and her body flinched, not stirring from unconsciousness but still spiking her blood with added adrenaline. The warm rush of renewing fluid down his throat took immediate effect, thwarting the start of another chest spasm and restoring his strength enough for him to at least think straight. He drank heavily, her sluggish pulse slowing with each strong pull. So long as her heart didn't stop, he could revive her. Right now, he needed strength to get them out of the woods or they would both be worse off come morning.

The approaching chatter of *the others* rustled the leaves in the distance. He was too focused on salvaging his strength to use his powers. A small tornado could have scrambled their scent and confused *the others* about their location, but he couldn't spare the energy. Besides, the wind might only lure *the others* faster once they scented her spilled mortal blood.

Cackles echoed, as their bodies swung from distant branches, surrounding them and closing in from all directions. They had less than a minute before they would be completely enclosed by predators. He'd been able to fight one, but by the screeches coming from the trees, there were more than twenty out there. Add Isaiah into the mix and…

He forced his fangs to retract from her vein and licked her wound shut. "We have to go."

Scooping her into his arms, he stood on shaky legs. A screech echoed from the west, met by a resounding shriek in the east. They were closing in on them, surrounding them from all angles.

His grip tightened on the plump little blood bag pressed to his aching chest. They needed to move.

Crouching low, preparing to leap into the trees, his muscles bunched and he staggered, falling off balance as claws scored his back. A distant scream pierced his brain, dropping him to his hands and knees. The mortal's body broke his fall as he gripped his skull and roared.

A flash of blood filled his mind. Pale, feminine legs. Horrific cries.

"Anna!" he snarled, another wave of dizziness holding him down as the vicious *other* at his back snarled and snapped her fangs, clawing to get to the unconscious mortal under his protection. Cain bared his fangs and pivoted. The chaotic vision ripping through his mind knocked him back with dizzying speed. Anna's horrific screams told of excruciating pain, but he couldn't reach her without losing focus on the now.

The *other* sprung, knocking him back and ripping open his throat as she bit into his face. Cain roared at the fresh pain and flung her off. His gaze shot to Destiny, her unconscious body laying limp and helpless in the dirt. The *other* crawling into a crouch, following his stare and bared her filthy fangs.

"No!" Cain snapped, lunging for the mortal and throwing his body over hers in protection as the *other* landed on his back, ravaging his newly regenerated skin and clawing open the tender wound from the arrow.

Cain screamed in agony and twisted, feral and untethered from his sanity as pain knifed through his back into his heart. He grabbed hold of the *other* and snapped her neck with a sharp twist. Panting and seething, he searched the shadows for more only to recall the mortal. He had to get her somewhere safe.

Anna's cries filled his head with chaos, hysterical and distant, nothing like their usual connection. Her voice was weak and...fading.

Cain hoisted Destiny into his arms. Anna's

screamed plea punctured his mind as fresh blood tunneled through the gaping hole in his heart. The faint echo of Anna's cries as she called his brother's name tore open the scars that would forever mark his soul. Even in death, fate would torture him.

Staring down at the flaccid body in his arms, his ears followed the hissing of the approach of more *others*. With no time left, he had no choice but to sever the mental connection to Annalise and focus his remaining strength on escaping the present threat.

Staggering forward, he yanked the limp female's body higher onto his shoulder and opened his stance, spreading his claws for battle. Red eyes bore through the shadows, their shrieking cackles now surrounding him. There were so many. More than he expected. Getting out of the woods alive no longer seemed like an option. He was going to need divine intervention.

Cain circled in place, certain he was about to die but determined to go out with honor. "Let's go, you rotting waste of human flesh."

The others, all female, prowled closer, hissed with sharpened, gnarled fangs, and lunged.

 ybil dropped the corn husk doll as a scream pierced the air, traveling from some distance over the hill. Her mind instantly returned to the night in the woods when she saw her mother's dead body draped in the arms of—

The screen door ripped open and Gracie tore out of the house. Her dress whipping at her ankles as she raced toward the gate.

Cybil stood and Gracie looked back at her with panicked eyes. "It's Anna. I have to go."

Anna was married to Adam. Adam was Cain's twin, but not a fair substitute. It had been weeks since Cain left the farm, and every day Cybil played out front, watching the distant hills, staring at the nearby woods, and waiting for him to return.

"Cybil, are you coming?"

Abandoning her dolls on the porch, she stood, but Gracie was already gone. More screams shrilled from the valley where Adam and Anna lived.

Cybil's leather boots carried her over the frozen ground, her arms chilled from the cool air as it wafted beneath her wool cloak. Since moving to the farm, she no longer dressed like a regular kid, but dressed like the other children who lived among the Amish. She hoped to fit in, but none of the other kids accepted her as one of their own.

Perhaps it was because she didn't speak. Or maybe it was because she and Dane weren't Amish. But deep down she knew it was something else.

Secrets were whispered in silence, and many times things were said around her without thought, on account of her staying so quiet. She crept into homes as smoothly as a spider and silently stayed in shadowed corners so not to get in the way. Often times, they forgot she was there.

Except Grace. Grace never forgot her presence and always seemed to know exactly what she was thinking. Cybil didn't mind. She was used to not having privacy in her mind. Her brother, Dane, often plucked ideas out of her head. It was a gift he'd always had, one she'd grown used to over time.

Deep down, she feared Dane fit in on the farm more than she, and sooner or later they'd make her leave. But she had nowhere to go. Her mother and father were gone. Her grandmother wasn't coming back. She only had her brother, and there seemed something very fleeting about their time left together. She sensed it in her bones, a ticking time bomb that followed the beat of her heart.

Anna's screams penetrated the walls of the towering home and rattled the rafters. Cybil slipped across the threshold without making a sound as something shattered on the second floor. Clinging to the wall, she sidled deeper into the house. Chaotic voices crashed together like thunder upon thunder in the eye of a storm. Whatever was happening upstairs was bad.

Another scream from Anna and Adam yelled, "Do something? What's happening to her?"

Gracie sped down the stairs and raced into the kitchen, moving past Cybil so fast the hair hanging free of her bonnet lifted in the wafted breeze. She only knew it was Grace because she could smell the rosemary soap she used in her hair. A second later, she raced back up the stairs, holding what looked like a basin of water and towels.

Doors slammed and more screams followed. By the time Cybil made it to the second floor, the tension vibrated through every pore of her body and rattled every crack of the house.

The bedroom door stood open, and Cybil stared in horror. An expression of searing pain stole across Anna's face as she breathed raggedly. Her bloodied hands gripped her protruding belly as her knees crashed into the planked floor. She thrashed, her body buckling backwards as the screams continued.

Gracie held a compress to Anna's chest, but she wouldn't still. Blood spilled from her eyes, nose, and mouth as she screamed with unrefined agony.

"Do something!" Adam shouted, his white shirt soaked through with blood as he cradled her on the floor.

Cybil's shoulders pressed into the cold plaster wall. It was as though an invisible attacker ravaged Anna's body.

"My baby!"

Her devotion to her unborn child was both startling and beautiful. Cybil wondered if her mother had fought so honorably in the end. Was this Anna's end? The sheer abnormality of the situation warned it might be, and she was suddenly sad for Adam.

"What's happening?" he shouted, smears of his wife's blood marring his skin as panic welled in his eyes and his strength waned to that of a little boy's.

He reminded her of Dane when they found their mother in the woods. She didn't blame her brother for his fear. She had been equally afraid and learned that day that boys don't contain panic the way girls do. Cybil swallowed hers down. At first it was deafening, then immobilizing, then repressing. Her sense of responsibility in the matter became a ubiquitous crime that would sentence her for life.

"I can't get through to her! She's blocking me!" Gracie screamed, pressing sheets between Anna's legs. "There's no blood here."

Anna's back bowed, her feet pointing and her limbs stiffening as more blood gathered on her skin.

"I don't understand!"

There was a rare cold comfort in seeing adults confused by life. A disturbing hint that she might never make sense of it all, but also a reminder that Cybil wasn't alone in her confusion.

"We have to protect the babe," Adam shouted. "*Ainsitch,* hold on to me. We're doing everything we can for you. Tell us where there's pain."

"It burns!" Annalise gasped as scrapes ravaged her skin and blood pooled at her chest, soaking her clothing and weakening her fight. Her arms protectively cradled her protruding stomach. *"My baby!"*

"It's not the babe, Anna. You have to stay calm." Gracie ripped open Anna's gown. Blood bloomed on her skin as she arched off the floorboards and screamed. "The blood is coming from somewhere else! Tell us where it hurts, Anna."

"Everywhere! Make it stop!"

Adam's face paled, whiter than bone. "Dear God…"

Anna's voice cut off with a gurgle as if she were drowning. She wheezed and choked for breath. The absence of her screams caused more alarm than her words ever could.

"Breathe, Anna! Breathe!" Adam gripped

her shoulders as more blood spilled from her chest and her face went pale.

"Where is it coming from?" Grace pressed her hands to Anna's chest, trying to stop the flow of blood.

Cybil's vision blurred as she pressed her spine into the wall, shrinking as far back as she could. Why had she followed Gracie here? Why wasn't she leaving? She couldn't pull herself away from the horror. Everything inside of her needed to stay and see that Anna lived. Or know exactly how she died.

Their fear spiked the air with palpable adrenaline as the brutal attack went on. Anna thrashed and screamed as if her soul were trying to break free.

She clawed at the phantom attacker, unable to stop the assault. Choking on blood, she tore at her throat, her eyes dilated and glowing, her words garbled and hissing. The room spun into delirium as their frenzied aid did nothing to help poor Anna.

Cybil's stomach knotted. Her affection for Anna now overshadowed by a desire for mercy. They had to make it stop. The torture of watching Anna's pain grew unbearable, and Cybil had to look away, curving her shoulders into the wall and covering her face.

"We need a healer!" Adam screamed through the hysteria.

"I can't leave you like this!" Gracie cradled Anna's face in her hands, trying to still her shaking head. "Anna, let me in. Let me in so I can help you."

The scent of blood overwhelmed the room as it spilled onto the floor. "My baby…"

"You need to let me in so I can reach the babe."

Anna's voice, now weak and ravaged, struggled to speak as she gasped and choked. Her fight was fading.

Cybil peeked through her fingers, watching as blood red tears welled in Anna's eyes. The metallic stench of this room would stay with her forever.

"Give her your blood, Adam!"

Cybil's hand clamped over her mouth as her stomach ruptured in repulsion as Adam bit open his wrist and pressed it to his wife's mouth. Cybil's mind screamed, but she could only watch in silent horror.

"She can't swallow! Help her!"

"I'm doing my best! I don't know what's wrong!" The wound on Anna's chest swelled and contracted as if healing and opening like a tear in the ocean floor. "Dear Lord… How is this possible?" Gracie snatched the bloodied sheets and pressed them to Anna's chest. "Hold this here, Adam. She needs pressure. Her heart is losing too much blood too fast."

Anna's body tensed as a flood of crimson spewed from her lips. "Do something, Grace! *Now!*"

Gracie shut her eyes and gripped Anna's temples. *"Sleep!"*

Anna lost consciousness as her body spasmed uncontrollably. Grace remained still and silent, her hands holding Anna's head as Adam wept over his dying wife, begging her to stay with him.

Though there were four of them in the room, Cybil felt like an intruder. She shut her eyes, but could not block the sound of Adam's words as he pledged his eternal heart to Anna and divulged every secret fear a man would never speak to anyone but his wife.

Anna's body jerked as a seizure took hold. Her body pulled taught, rattling tighter than an earthquake's tremors, and then her muscles went slack.

Grace jerked back, her body knocked to the floor. She gasped, as if coming awake. "I saw dark woods. Trees. Red eyes. I could feel her panic, and the incredible pressure and pain." She panted. "Adam…I've never felt anything like it. I could feel the capillaries bursting in her brain."

"What is it?" He swelled with uncontainable rage.

Sorrow and regret flooded Gracie's eyes as she shook her head. "I don't know. She pushed me out."

"Well, get back in there. Tell me what's hurting my wife!"

She gripped her brother's bloodied fists as he shook her. "I'm sorry, Adam. Everything went black."

Destiny's mind awoke from the jolt of what she hoped was the residual shock of a nightmare. As the pain in her back and skull registered, adrenaline chugged heavily through her veins sending a surge of dizziness that assured this was no dream. She was too cold and weak to move. Her body felt like she was kicked down several flights of stairs.

Where was she? Her mind struggled to fully awaken as the crackle of burning wood stirred a sense of nostalgia. Was she camping?

The recognizable scent of earth filled her lungs, but the air seemed thin. Flashes of irregular recollections danced through her memory, indistinguishable as dreams or reality.

The woods—claws—running for her life—the crossbow—no... What had she done? She focused on the now, and the pounding in her head intensified. Flashes of an attack had her tensing. She needed help. She was badly injured and unsure of the extent she'd suffered, afraid to take a full inventory of her body's aches and discover what damage might have been done.

The piney scent of balsam filled the air, but it was still dark. Unsure if she was alone, she carefully kept her breathing calm and her body still as she listened for clues to her surroundings.

Sleep threatened to pull her back under. Her body was uncharacteristically heavy and weak, like a nightmare when she needed to run but her feet felt encased in cement. Maybe she was still dreaming.

Her eyes seemed the only part of her that didn't hurt, though her vision was gritty and her head pounded. Carefully, she tried to look over her shoulder, but the angle twisted her muscles so painfully her stomach trembled and she swallowed back bile.

Her back burned with excruciating sharpness. She attempted to roll, her mouth watering and the urge to vomit derailing the impulse to move.

Too traumatized to even cry, she searched the silver shadows. Nothing looked familiar. The wavering horizon of trees was off—low and not at eye-level. She frowned. Or was she high? Not high like on drugs, but literally higher than the trees. She was far above the tree line of what she hoped was the Pennsylvania mountains.

Or maybe she *was* stoned. Maybe she'd been drugged by that thing in the woods. Was it a thing or a man? Or both? Maybe they were two separate things? And where was the guy she shot?

Too much thinking made her head hurt.

Her temples pounded as if her skull had shrunk three sizes and she suffered from the worst hangover of all time. But she hadn't drunk anything.

She was so tired.

Her head lulled in what smelled like damp leaves. Bugs. She could only think about bugs, hating the thought of any creepy crawly thing climbing on her, but even that terrible possibility wasn't enough to make her move.

A tear rolled from her eye just as it started

to snow. Snow? Yes, it had to be. The flakes were peaceful and mesmerizing against the sapphire sky. The warm saltwater of her tears mixed with the press of cold flakes melting on her skin.

Staring up at the falling flurries, she frowned and noticed part of the sky was blocked from view. She was under some sort of shelter. She could see it now, where the gray clouds swathed the black moonlit sky and where the ceiling of what looked like a cave blocked the view of falling snow. Had someone left her here, in the mouth of some cave? She had no recollection of getting to this place.

This had to be a dream, because it was way too trippy to be real.

She needed to turn and look around, but her back hurt so badly she couldn't find the strength to move. Standing would be better. Just a few minutes and she'd get up. Just a few…more…minutes…

Her thoughts drowsed on a drug like wave, ebbing and flowing in and out of consciousness. She wasn't blinking enough. Time slowed and her fear drifted further away, a whisper tucked in the back of her mind she could almost ignore if she just kept watching the tranquil snow as she tried to block out the pain.

The longer she stared at the skyline the less she could see. Her blinking had turned to miniature blackouts. Each momentary nap jolting her awake with a need to stay conscious. Time to move.

Taking a deep breath, she rolled to her stomach, swallowing the moan of pain and bile that threatened to escape as she braced on her hands and knees. The vapor from her breath formed a cloud as she stared at a heap on the ground several feet away. Then it moved.

Not a heap, but a body! It was the man from the woods. She'd had nightmares about that man, yet some part of her recognized him with endearing, obviously misplaced, emotions. Why?

She moaned, her skull pounding and brain still too tired to think clearly. Had he saved her? Brought her here to this place? Or captured her? Maybe even drugged her, because she was definitely under some sort of tranquilizer.

With the flickering flames of the fire separating them, she could now see they were in fact in a cave. Steam rose from his form as he breathed slowly. The air was cold enough to make her teeth chatter and the scent of ice on the wind reminded her of a childhood memory when her father took her and Vito ice skating.

Thinking of her brother brought more stress. Was Vito out there searching for her? He was probably worried sick. How could she have been so selfish to endanger not only herself but also involve others. Speaking of…

Her stare returned to the man sleeping on the other side of the fire, struggling to make out his features. How was he still alive? She'd sworn she'd shot him in the chest, but everything was now a blur and her damn head hurt too much to think.

Flames sliced through the shadows playing over his broad chest. Flickers of light caught on the tiny ripples of muscle like sunshine catches on a lake. Golden swells of muscle glistened behind the licking flames as the cave was cast in the dancing glow of firelight. She sort of liked this dream.

Shutting her eyes, she lowered her forehead to her arms and breathed in the scent of earth and burning wood, stirring visions of gardening with her grandmamma outside of their family's villa in Portugal. The memory brought her peace and she reveled in the distraction for a moment, taking her mind off the searing cuts on her back and the throbbing headache radiating down her spine.

She pictured the brightly tiled buildings butted together along the sloping, pebbled streets of Reiros. The warm August sun glinted against the monuments of idols as blackbirds and tourists crowded the stone walkways. Warmth spread through her, as clothing draped over strung lines connecting balconies and simple dresses and sheets danced in the wind.

Something nudged her side and she winced, her mind jolting from the dream into the now.

"Stay still." The low rumble of a predatory growl interrupted her peace and her body tensed, no longer in a crawling pose but sprawled out on the dirt floor of the cave. She must have fallen asleep. Her heart hammered against her ribs as she realized the man who had been sleeping on the other side of the fire now knelt directly behind her.

The pull of material peeling away dried blood made her gasp. Her back had been slashed open from shoulder to hip and the cuts burned. She needed a doctor or at least something to clean the wounds.

Her teeth chattered as he lifted her shredded coat, the high-altitude cold winds cutting right to her bone. "Don't," she whimpered, arching away from his touch as he gently probed at the raw flesh of her back.

"You've lost a lot of blood."

He prodded at the tender pulp and she hissed, curling away from his probing touch.

"Easy now. Don't tense. Just relax."

A slight tickle along her scalp triggered more apprehension, but her muscles softened. She didn't know this man or trust him. She shouldn't let him touch her.

"It would be better if you slept."

"Better for what?"

"You need to heal."

"I need a doctor."

He grunted and continued to examine her wounds.

She didn't fight him or struggle. She shivered, her unblinking eyes staring at the flames as her mind went somewhere else. Maybe she'd wake up in a hospital bed with her brother, Vito, frowning over her with hard-earned relief.

The thought tempted her closer to sleep. She just wanted this to be over.

Her lashes fluttered and she curled her fisted hands under her breasts in an attempt to keep warm. Flashes of amber danced over the jagged stone walls of the cave. She remembered learning about the old railroad tunnels throughout Jim Thorpe, Pennsylvania. Maybe they were inside such a tunnel.

The shadows moved and the walls lightened as the sun slowly rose. A vulture or eagle flew overhead, cawing and reminding her how high they were.

"Wha' d'you give me?" she slurred. The high-altitude winds stole what was left of her tentative voice.

"I gave you nothing. You're dehydrated, and you lost a lot of blood."

She turned her head toward the opening of the cave, the slight motion pulling the tight skin at her back and causing her to wince. Dropping her cheek to the cold dirt floor, she caught her breath.

Green peaks stacked across the pale horizon. The forest floor lay miles below, and the mere thought of escaping took more effort than she could currently spare. The sky changed color every time she found the strength to look at it. Black, purple, gray, sometimes blue and then black again.

"Careful. It's best if you stay still. Save your strength." His voice warned from far away.

She turned her head again, now finding him back on the other side of the fire which had burned low. Had she fallen asleep again? Her brain wasn't tracking time.

Her heart beat out of rhythm, speeding then slowing as she licked her dry lips. She needed water but asking seemed a daunting task. Her hands and feet were numb and the walls were spinning. She was going to be sick.

"What are you doing?"

She struggled to rise to her hands and knees. A wave of dizziness pushed her dangerously close to the fire and her breath halted and held as she met his stare. His eyes appeared too bright for the shadowed cave, as if they were glowing. It had to be the reflection of the fire separating them.

He sat in the glimmer of the low-burning flames. His face mostly hidden, except for those startling eyes. The sparks of rising embers cast an amber glow over his heavily muscled chest. Flashes of red and orange licking over every bulge of exposed sinew and—was that blood?

Facts jumbled in her memory, blurring the line between reality and fiction once more. She shot him. She remembered the arrow sticking out of him, but now…

Not a single imperfection. Just a few smears of red, but even that didn't seem enough. Where was the wound? How was he sitting there without a single cut on his body?

Alive. He was alive. *She* was alive. None of this made sense.

Her gaze searched the cave floor. "Where's my phone?"

He pushed off the wall, rising with startling agility, as he stepped out of the shadows. His face came into full view as he towered over the flames appearing ominous and powerful. No mistaking that nasty glare or the wide breadth of his shoulders meant to threaten her.

Okay, so they weren't friends. That made sense if she'd shot him. But he appeared uninjured. She frowned. Just…bloody. Was that *her* blood? It tinged the gold stubble along his jaw making it appear darker. How had her blood smeared over his chin and face?

His boots scraped over the dirt floor of the

cave as he approached, a leather canteen dangling from his fingers. "Drink."

The moment he gave the command her thirst registered once more, undeniable and desperate. With shaky hands, she took the cask and awkwardly tried to open it. She was so weak, even the simple act of twisting a metal cap depleted her.

He yanked it back and loosened the cap. "Not too much." He shoved it back in her hand.

The water was warm but clean enough to wash away the dust in her mouth. It soothed her raw throat.

"Not too much, I said. You haven't eaten in days. It's a waste if you throw it up."

Days? She swallowed hard, the gulp stretching her throat painfully and causing her to wince. She coughed and pressed the back of her hand to her mouth. "I'm sorry, did you say days?"

"This is our third morning in the cave." He took the cask, moving back into the shadows and lowering to the dirt floor.

She thought of Vito, her heart sick for how much her stupidity must have cost him in unnecessary worry. He probably had the police out looking for her, and God knew who else. "I need to find my phone and a charger—"

"Your phone is gone."

"We have to backtrack. My phone is my life."

"Quiet."

She shut up and the silence stretched between them as he stared daggers at her, now back in the shadows.

Once again, she looked at his naked chest. This made no sense. While her memories were messy, she was certain she hadn't dreamt shooting him. "Were you wearing Kevlar?"

"Kevlar?"

"A bulletproof vest."

"No."

But she shot him. His blood was still on his skin and in her hair. She looked around for her crossbow. What if the cops found it in the woods and it was cataloged as evidence? Her fingerprints were all over it but it was licensed to Vito. What if that made her brother a suspect for the murders in the woods? What if they already had him in jail? This was a mess. "We have to go back."

"I said quiet," he snapped, the lash of his voice stifling her words.

He shut his eyes as if in deep concentration. His brow furrowed, knitting his face into a frown.

Her brother could be in jail right now, being questioned for murder. She rubbed her filthy hands over her knotted hair and massaged her temples. "You don't understand—"

"I understand fine." Then under his breath he mumbled, "Stupid English female."

"First of all, I'm not English or even American for that matter. I'm Portuguese. Second of all, I'm not stupid, you dumb jackass."

His eyes set in a cruel, intolerant expression that spoke of his deep dislike for her. Civilization seemed a thousand miles below. She was alone with a man who looked hungry for revenge and fully blamed her for their current predicament. A man who outweighed her without an ounce of fat on his chiseled body and could probably snap her neck in one quick, military-Kung Fu-paid assassin move. Who was this guy?

"Look," she said nervously, softening her tone. "You're obviously all right. I'm sure I can find my way back—"

"Unteachable fool."

She stiffened. "Excuse me?"

"I've wasted more time explaining that

what is out there is dangerous, and you refuse to listen."

"I've listened. I'm just not going to let what's in those woods stop me from doing my job or finding my way home. I'm a reporter. I go where the story takes me."

"The *story*," he snarled, practically spitting the word into the air. "Those *stories* are human lives."

Insulted that he would think her so callous as to not recognize the lives lost, she snapped, "I know! That's why I'm doing my part and trying to catch whatever's out there."

"Your part? You've only made matters worse. You care nothing for the victims. I watched you intrude on that woman's funeral while her children mourned the loss of their only remaining parent. You don't even know their names."

"Yes, I do. Their names are Dane and Cindy. Reporters like me help apprehend killers, so kids like them can find peace in the midst of their grief."

He scoffed. "Cybil."

"What?"

"The girl's name is Cybil."

Damn it. She really wanted to get the kid's

name right. "Regardless, I'm trying to help them."

"All you've done is interfere."

"I—"

"Enough! I need to concentrate."

She snapped her mouth shut as he once again closed his eyes. Massaging his temples, his frown deepened. He whispered something, but his voice was too low to hear. A mantra or a name, perhaps. Then she remembered the name he cried out in the woods the second she shot him.

There was no doubt she shot him. She just couldn't figure out how he wasn't injured.

Her mind replayed the events on a loop of hazy memories. Chased by that thing in the woods. Her back was clawed open and she fell. Then he was there—approaching—and she pulled the trigger on the crossbow. He collapsed to his knees and hissed a name.

"Who's Anna?"

Her head slammed into the cave floor as he lunged. The weight of his body crushed her, knocking the breath from her lungs as his thumb pressed hard into the soft flesh below her jaw, cutting off her airway. She never saw him move.

"What do you know of Anna?" he growled, eyes flashing silver.

Thunder rumbled with a crashing bang over the trees, rolling closer as a gust of wind cut into the cave, sending sparks dashing from the flames and skittering up the stone wall. Tears sprung to her eyes as her wounds tore open and her shoulders rammed into the unforgiving floor.

Terror took hold as his pupils dilated. He bared his teeth, her eyes widening, as his grip tightened around her throat.

"Wh-what…are you?" she wheezed.

Saliva strung from his sharp teeth as his jaw unhinged, opening wide.

"Wait," she blurted, covering her face.

He stilled and cocked his head, a slight frown crimping his brow. His face lowered to her neck, and he breathed in her scent like some sort of deranged animal. "Relax."

If it were only that easy. "Please don't hurt me."

His weight sank deeper into her, his hard body settling over hers as he pulled her wrists apart and lowered her clenched fists to her side. His body was a wall of heavy muscle. He held her immobile, glaring into her eyes, pinning her to the earth.

"I could snap your neck if it pleased me."

"Please don't." Her back burned and the base of her skull throbbed. There was no relief with his body crushing hers the way it was.

"Stay quiet." His hips rocked forward and he growled.

Her eyes closed, tears soaking her lashes. "Just don't hurt me."

His nose pressed to the slope of her shoulder, nuzzling away her loose hair as a low purr rumbled from his chest. She couldn't breathe, couldn't catch her breath. Fear paralyzed her, and tension locked every muscle.

He gripped her hair, angling her head back as his tongue licked over her pulse. Her whimper broke the silence.

"Stay quiet and still and I won't hurt you."

"I…" She didn't know what he was doing, but she had an idea where this was going. "Please…I can pay you. I have money."

"Silence," he snapped, his fist bunching in her shirt and yanking her closer. His hips shifted and there was no disguising his arousal as it pressed against her.

"I'm sorry. I'll stop talking. You're right. I'm just a stupid girl. A selfish reporter. Pplease, don't hurt me. I just want to go home—"

Her words cut off as his strong hand cuffed her throat, squeezing so that no oxygen could pass to or from her lungs. "Stop talking, or I will make it so you can't speak." He shoved her away and snarled, "You're breathing because I allowed it."

She nodded tightly, tears welling in her eyes, as she gasped and choked.

"You're alive because I saved you."

"Th-thank you. I'm a big fan of living."

"Shut up!"

She snapped her lips closed and whimpered.

"I'm the only voice you listen to from here on out. You don't speak or question or argue or breathe without my permission. You *obey,"* he growled the last order, looming over her and forcing her shoulders to press into the unforgiving earth. "Understand?"

A tear rolled from her lashes. She didn't understand any of this. "Please don't hurt me," she whispered, realizing too late that she'd just broken his rules. "I'm sorry. I'm sorry. I'm just scared and my back—"

Before she could finish the frantic thought, he'd flipped her to her stomach, knocking the wind out of her. The weight of her clothing lifted, pulling at her lacerated flesh. Cold air touched her back and a tear slipped from her eye. She was at his mercy now.

"Your cuts have opened." He seemed bothered by this, despite his desire to hurt her.

"I'm sure it's—"

He palmed the back of her skull and shoved her down when she tried to rise. "Stay still."

A startled sob, trapped in her throat, escaped when her cheekbone hit the hard ground. He ripped her torn clothes out of the way, her body pinned beneath him and trembling. He leaned close and at the first touch of his lips to her battered body, she bucked wildly. "Get off me!"

"Be still!" His fist locked in her hair as he clamped his knees around her hips, holding her helplessly to the dirty ground. "I'm trying to help you."

Her mind spasmed like a taught rubber band let loose too quickly. Survival instinct blotted out all other thoughts and she went ballistic, shoving and kicking, doing anything in her power to loosen his hold, but he was so strong.

The material of her coat tore with a sharp rip as he yanked the wool apart. "No!"

"You're doing more damage to yourself by fighting me."

"Don't touch me!" She kicked and thrashed, desperate to escape his unbreakable hold. "No—"

Then something cool and soothing traced over the burning cut on her back and she stilled. Her body shook with shock as she tried to understand if he was assaulting her or actually helping her. Trembling uncontrollably, she sucked in a breath and silently sobbed as relief soothed the burning scrapes at her back.

Her hair covered her face and sweat and tears burned her eyes. He held her head against the cave floor, making it impossible to move.

He applied some sort of numbing salve to her cuts and the pain quickly subsided. Her jagged breathing calmed but remained uneven as his firm touch turned tender. She stopped fighting, a strange but fragile truce taking hold as she accepted his care.

She understood then how hostages could so easily fall under the spell of Stockholm syndrome. She was at his mercy, and in that moment she would do anything for kindness over cruelty. The relief the medicine brought terrified her, because it endeared her to him, and he was not a good man. Why was he trying to help her?

He carefully treated each gash with a gentle touch, but then she felt his mouth and squeezed her eyes shut. Her raw muscles were torn and exposed. She needed a doctor. Hopefully whatever salve he applied would prevent further pain or possible infection.

The mood of the cave shifted, her cold terror sliding into something warm and comforting as if under the influence. A balmy wind pushed through the arctic air, and his touch lowered, his body pressing against hers as he quietly growled.

Safe feeling gone.

His lips trailed over her exposed skin and she trembled, fear mixing with shame as some part of her curiously wondered if there was a way for him to take what he wanted without hurting her. Could she bear it? Struggling was futile and would only make matters worse.

Perhaps it was self-preservation that so desperately wanted to romanticize this nightmare into something redeeming. He was a vicious mercenary of some kind, and she was at his mercy, but if she cooperated, she might avoid some degree of suffering.

With great effort, she forced her body to unclench. As she softened beneath him, he stilled. She closed her eyes and loosened her fist, laying her palms flat on the ground in a show of surrender. His arousal rested heavily against his clothing, pressing firmly into her curves.

His weight disappeared and he sprung to his feet, leaving her abandoned and confused on the ground, trembling with fear. Worry kept her still. Had she upset him? She hadn't meant to. She only hoped to prolong her life and avoid more unnecessary pain by cooperating.

"Get up. We're leaving."

The warmth of the cave evaporated as cold gusts of wind howled past the grotto. With shaky arms, she lifted her head and looked over the horizon. Thick black clouds rolled in from the north as thunder rumbled over the treetops. A choking sense of foreboding took hold.

How was she ever going to make the walk back to salvation? Her back felt better from whatever he'd applied, but she still ached from everything she'd been through, and she was sure the anesthetic wouldn't last.

Should she run? How far would she get? She had no water or supplies or even a clue where they were in relation to civilization. There was no sight of a nearby road or houses anywhere in the landscape below.

He was stronger—by a lot. No doubt he could catch her. But instinct told her not to go to the second location. Or was *this* the second location? What did they say about the third?

"People will be looking for me," she said, trying not to sound oppositional as she struggled to sit up and adjust her ruined coat. "If you let me leave, I'll never mention you to anyone or this place. I'll just say I got lost—"

Her words cut off as he glared over his shoulder, eyes narrowing with unmistakable threat.

She immediately realized two things. He likely killed before and he wouldn't hesitate to kill again. She needed to shut the fuck up and cooperate, no matter what that meant.

"Never mind. It's cool." She climbed to her feet and took a step back, but felt no safer. She was at his mercy until someone else found them.

Her DNA was on the cave floor. Was that enough for the police to track her at least to this point? She pressed the sole of her boot into the dusty ground, hoping the UGG imprint might help identify the footsteps as her own. Vito bought her the boots for Christmas and should recognize the logo if he was working with the cops.

Turning, the man kicked sand and dirt over the fire, dousing the cave in shadows. Destiny fished in her pocket, her fingers closing around the waxy wrapper of a cough drop. She squeezed the paper tight in her fist, holding her arms at her side.

He moved through the shadows and gathered any traces of their belongings. Shouldering the leather strap of the canteen, he lifted something else.

Destiny's breath ceased at the sight of Vito's crossbow. Relief tunneled through her at the sight of the weapon. That, at least, would keep her brother safe from becoming a suspect.

The man then picked up a bloodied rag. *Dear God it was his shirt!*

He stormed past her and snapped, "Come. We must walk while the sun is high."

What else would they do, call an Uber?

She opened her fist and the cough drop fluttered to the cave floor.

A shallow breeze stole past her knees, gathering grit and ash from the fire as it spun into a squat tornado. Her eyes widened as it traveled from one side of the cave to the other, smudging out all footprints and sifting the granules of dirt back to earth in an undisturbed surface. Her boot prints were gone. So was the wrapper.

"Don't make me shoot you with your own weapon," he barked, already out of the cave and hiking down the steep terrain.

She looked back. All traces of their presence had been erased by nature in less than ten seconds.

With absolutely no survival skills or knowledge of the outdoors, she had no choice but to follow him. Her knees locked, as she stood at the mouth of the cave overlooking the mountains. They were literally standing on the edge of the earth at the highest possible point. How did they get up there?

The wind whipped at her clothing, her hair trailing across her face. The man hiked into the tree line without a word, his steps navigating the incline with a confidence she couldn't match. Then she spotted her purse hanging from his large hand.

Her feet kicked into gear as a breath of hope stole into her lungs. Did he have her phone? She always kept a charger zipped away in the inner pocket. If she could get into her bag and find an outlet—possibly at a rest stop or a charging station—she could call for help and send Vito her location.

She reached for a spindly branch jutting from the rock and set her foot on the slope to climb down the foothill after him, only to slip on a spot of moss and land on her ass. Tears rushed to her eyes as pain shot up her tail bone.

"Careful, the ground's slippery with morning dew."

Lips pressed tight, she scowled at the trees where he'd disappeared. The arrogant bastard was so certain she'd follow. Either that, or he was unconcerned if she stayed there to die. Who was she kidding? She couldn't even start a fire. She had no knowledge of the wilderness, and he had her only weapon.

"Wait up."

He kept moving, vanishing in and out of the pine trees, giving her little chance to mark his path before having to race after him. Bears and God knew what else lived in these woods. They assumed it was a wild animal killing the women, but now she wasn't so sure. Whatever attacked her felt *human*…but not. Sort of like her captor.

He didn't slow, but he whistled and she was able to track the sound. The trees blocked the morning sun and the temperature plummeted below the twenties.

The longer they walked the more injuries she endured. Scratches from branches tore at her cheeks and hands. Her ankles twisted unnaturally as she miscalculated several steps over mossy rocks and uplifted tree roots. He never slowed to check if she was okay and didn't wait for her if she stopped to catch her breath. After two miles, it became clear that he didn't care if she lived or died.

By what felt like the tenth mile but could have been the fourth, she no longer believed he had a plan of escape. He seemed to have a specific destination, but made no mention of how long they would be walking or even if he planned to make it there by dark. As she traveled at breakneck speeds to keep up with him, she wondered if their destination would be the last place she ever visited.

Where would they find her body? What

kind of condition would she be in? How long would it take? Would the snow preserve her flesh or would she eventually bake in the upcoming seasonal heat? They were so deep in the woods there was no beaten path that would lead others this way. She might be nothing more than bones when this was all over.

The irony of her life whittling down to a mere statistic wasn't lost on her. How many times had she given a report and referred to a human life as only a *victim?* She'd been trained to use terms like *John* or *Jane Doe*, but never expected someone might refer to her as such.

"My name is Destiny Santos," she whispered, even if she was only saying it to hear herself speak. She needed to affirm that she wasn't dead yet. She still had time. So long as she existed, she wasn't a statistic.

"I know who you are."

Of course, he did. He had her purse. But what would the authorities go by when they only found her remains? How much more pain would she suffer before this nightmare ended?

A tear rolled down her cheek. She didn't want to die.

CHAPTER 4

*J*uniper's gaze lifted from her phone as the bell above the door chimed and a tourist stepped into the shop. Frankincense and other herbs snaked into the hazy air, forming a smoky trail from the altar in the corner. A purple tapestry tinted the sunlight seeping through the window, which wasn't much, due to the store entrance leading underground.

"Crystals are twenty percent off today, and incense sticks are buy one get one," she told the man. It was the same speech every customer got.

"I'm looking for the owner of this shop, Mabel Tempest."

Juniper glanced up from her phone again,

raising a pierced brow at the sight of the man's clothing. Was he Amish? Unimpressed, she called, "Aunt Bel, someone's here to see you." Her attention returned to her phone as her thumbs swiped quickly to the next screen.

At the back of the store, the beaded curtain rattled as Mabel appeared, still chewing whatever she'd just taken a bite of. She coasted a hand over her dark curls in an attempt to tame her long mane, but the wiry silver coils never settled. Aunt Bel claimed the gray hairs were the bane of her youth and the badge of her wisdom, a prized sign that she'd officially reached the rank of crone.

"Can I help you?"

"I hope so." The man crossed the store slowly. "Are you Mabel Tempest?"

"Who wants to know?"

Mabel's guarded tone was unexpected. Her clothes might be sewn of tattered rags in too many patterns to count, but Juniper's aunt was no flake. She read people better than most people read books. And she accepted all walks of life into her store. So why was she eyeing this man with such disdain?

"My name is Jonas Hartzler. I'm—"

"I know what you are." Aunt Bel's arms crossed over her chest. The long crystal pendant hanging from her throat glinted against her freckled skin. She sniffed the air and frowned. "You're ill." Her plain, oval face tilted, surrounded by a spill of salt and pepper curls. "How is that possible?"

"Is there a place we could speak privately?"

She studied him for a moment, reading something from his presence, then nodding concisely. "Juniper, keep an eye on things while I'm in the back."

"I'll do my best," Juniper said dryly, swiping her finger over her phone, then mumbling, "First customer all day, but whatever."

Mabel parted the beaded curtain and waved Jonas toward the shadowed back room. The temperature dropped and the skin on Juniper's neck prickled as the curtain swished shut behind them.

Losing interest in her phone, she left the register and grabbed the feather duster. Sweeping off the crystal displays, she worked her way closer to the back room.

"We don't get many of your kind around here," Aunt Bel said.

"Amish?"

Mabel chuckled. "Sure."

Through the beaded curtain, Juniper could

see the wooden cabinets that traced the perimeter and the soapstone countertop cluttered with various plants and jars. Herbs hung from a ladder suspended from the ceiling. Juniper planned on stealing some of her aunt's herbs for later tonight.

"Have a seat, Jonas."

A small round table nestled into the corner with two simple chairs tucked underneath. The trickle of the fountain in the corner of the shop broke their silence, accompanied by the quiet melody of Native American flutes streaming from the speaker at the front of the store.

Hardened wax dribbled from the mouths of wine jugs where candles burned throughout the back room, making it difficult to see through the shadows. It was an intentional, shrouded vibe that made palm readings that much more convincing, according to her aunts.

Juniper dusted the mortar and pestle that sat by the spell station. A chalice of crushed flowers and seeds made an offering beside Aunt Bel's book of shadows. Runes scribbled across the thick, aged parchment made sure her notes stayed safe from wandering eyes.

"How did you sense my illness?" the man asked.

"There's a smell."

"A smell?"

"A rot. Your kind typically carries the scent of death, but this is…stronger."

Juniper paused, startled by her aunt's insensitive words. Sick people came into the store all the time, searching for healing spells and customized talismans. Aunt Bel was usually more openhearted to those customers, so why was she being so insensitive to this man?

"Is that how you recognized my kind?"

"We have many ways to identify our enemies."

Again, Juniper paused from dusting the displays. Enemy? She sensed none of the darkness her aunt spoke of.

"I have no enemies."

"That may be true, but druids have been wary of the undead since the stone age. Old habits die hard."

Undead? Abandoning her housekeeping, Juniper crept closer to the curtain and listened.

"Is that how you identify—druid?"

"My ancestors have been called many things—druid, pagan, witch, Wiccan. We prefer to think of ourselves as healers and herbalists. That's why you're here, is it not?"

"I'm in need of wisdom. I'm told you hold the ancient mage of a crone."

Juniper rolled her eyes. If that was true, why did the IRS have her aunts registered as merchants and the town directory labeled their goods as souvenirs and knickknacks? People were so gullible—including her aunts.

"You claim you're Amish. Are there more of your kind hiding in plain sight?"

The man hesitated. "Yes. Many more. We have an order just an hour north of here, but we are a peaceful, God-fearing sect that does not follow the ideals of our European ancestors. We are, in every sense of the word, Amish."

"So, you believe in a Christian god, or is that part of your cover?"

"I believe in one eternal God that rules over all creation."

"Has your god failed you? Is that why you're seeking the wisdom of The Goddess?"

"I seek only knowledge and mercy."

"But you asked for a mage. You want access to the crone, which is only one part of the trinity. Much like your god takes shape as the father, son, and spirit, our Triple Goddess has three forms. The crone holds the knowledge, but the mother bears all mercy. And what of the maiden? Is it not youth and salvation you seek?"

"I only wish to heal. The source matters little at this point."

"You're rather humble for an undead."

"Immortal."

"I'd say that's up for debate."

Juniper had no idea how her aunt kept a straight face through such role playing. They actually expected her to do the same, taking a larger role in the store after graduation, but there was no way. Juniper was fine with manning the register and stocking the shelves, but she wasn't dedicating her life to the role of small-town hippy witch like her aunts had. They were literally one cat whisker away from being as bad as carnie freaks.

"Can you help me?"

"I am only a portal between The Great Cosmos and The Great Goddess. I have no power beyond what she gives me."

"Will you try?"

"For a price."

Ah, there it was. The old sales pitch. Had to keep those florescent lights burning, because the electric company apparently couldn't be charmed.

"How much?"

"First, I must understand what it is you will need. You'll tell me your story and I'll listen—for one thousand dollars."

Juniper's eyes widened then she silently chuckled. Her aunt didn't mess around.

"To listen?"

"My energy has value, Jonas. I'm careful about permitting access to the wrong clients, and you are not, exactly, what I'd call my ideal client."

Squinting through the beaded curtain, Juniper watched in stunned amusement as the man withdrew a leather wallet and counted out several bills. "How soon can you start?"

Her aunt held out a hand. "We've already begun."

CHAPTER 5

"My wife, Abilene, no longer recognizes my scent," the man, Jonas, explained. "Six decades together and I now feel like a stranger to my own partner."

Juniper studied him through the beaded curtain, taking in every detail. There was no way this guy was over forty, and even that was a stretch. But her aunt kept a straight face and humored him, playing her role of concerned witch to perfection, as she should for a thousand bucks.

"Many couples experience a disconnect when fidelity is broken."

"I'm not an adulterer."

"Perhaps there's been an emotional break. There are more than carnal affairs, Jonas.

Sometimes, the bonds of the heart carry more threat than physical bonds."

"I've never loved anyone more than I love my wife."

"Explain how the bonding works."

Juniper's phone buzzed and she pulled it from her back pocket. Trent's text hit a second after Zoey's, both of them asking if she had finished work. She quickly texted back, telling them she would need a little more time.

"The longer an immortal goes unanswered, the more they risk losing their humanity," Jonas finished. Juniper pocketed her phone, unsure what she'd missed.

"*Feeish.*"

"Correct."

"And you were suffering some of these symptoms in the end?"

"Yes. I'd…wake up in the woods with no recollection of arriving. I would find…carnage in my wake."

Juniper's nose wrinkled. Her gaze shifting to the athame display on the wall. This guy better not try anything. They might have knives in the store, but her aunt was a total pacifist who couldn't even kill a spider. That left Juniper as the heavy, and she really didn't feel like breaking a sweat today.

"Human?"

"No. Not that I know of. Mostly small woodland creatures. But our order makes a point of preserving life whenever possible. It's frowned upon to bleed an animal dry."

"And it harm none through what thou wilt."

"Pardon?"

"It's one of our most ancient vows. Witches are healers. Despite the lies *his*-story likes to tell, we rarely practice in blood magick or sacrifice. Our power is three-fold. Whatever we send out into the cosmos will return to us stronger. We must do no harm if we wish to avoid harm upon ourselves."

Jonas lowered his voice. "I've harmed."

"I'm not a priest. I have no need to hear your confessions."

"I…I attacked her."

"Your mate?"

His gaze cast downward and shame overtook his voice. "Not my mate, but Abilene, my wife. After months of neglecting her needs, I brutally attacked her."

"You were *feeish,* under this dark spell?"

"Nevertheless."

"Pagans believe in a shadow-self, a dark

part of the soul where secrets and shame grow. That's why shadow work is so important. It nurtures the balance within, assuring we are no more darkness than light, no more evil than good. Even in yin, there must exist a spot of yang to maintain this balance. One cannot exist without the other. If you seek to absolve all darkness inside your soul, I'm afraid that's impossible."

"I only wish to be normal again."

"Ah, but you were never *normal.*"

Juniper's breath held as she waited for his response. Mabel might play along with these kooks, but she didn't go easy on them. It was a skill.

"When immortals ignore God's call, evil takes hold, erasing the good until there is nothing left," Jonas finally muttered, His voice heavy with shame.

"Are you suggesting you waited too long?"

"I waited longer than I should have, but acted soon enough. However, I don't think I stopped the process. I'm afraid I've only slowed it."

"Can that happen? Has anyone else of your kind gone through something similar?"

"Not that I know of, and I'm fearful to ask.

If I become a danger to others, our laws require my death."

"Do you feel dangerous?"

"I feel evil creeping inside of me. There's an ache in my bones, a brittleness that rattles my lungs, as if my insides have been loosened by time."

"Aging."

"Dying," he corrected. "It's pushing out the good, stealing away my life. My soul. What happens when there is nothing left of me? What will become of my body? Who will take care of my wife?"

"Existence is a give and take, Jonas. A balance. Joy cannot exist without pain. Good cannot exist without evil. We arrogantly label something evil when it no longer feels like it's serving us, but what if *this* is exactly as you were designed to be?"

"I am not evil."

"No living creature is completely good. We are all capable of evil when survival is on the line. Faith, true faith, requires surrender and trust. Relinquish control and let the Goddess work. Nature is self-healing, self-correcting. If She wants to save you, She will make it so."

"I'm immortal. Our kind is not meant to

die."

"But half of your soul is gone. It died with your mate, Clara." Despite Jonas's rising frustration, Aunt Bel remained composed and kept her voice calm.

"There has to be a reason why I'm still living even though she is not."

"Are you living or are you stuck in the *In-Between*? We all exist in Mother Earth's cycle, though some of our cycles last longer than others. But in the end, we all come full circle. Ashes to ashes. Death is but a new beginning."

"Immortals do not die."

"Don't they?"

He held his words for a long pause. "We can be killed, but it's difficult."

"Even gods die. There's no shame in it. You think you're somehow entitled to eternity, but your arrogance has misled you. The Goddess gives life and takes life. That is how She maintains balance. You surrendered half of your soul when your mate passed on."

"But I'm still here."

"For now. If I cut down a tree, the roots will eventually die. If there is a rot at the roots, the tree will wither away. Decomposing might take thousands of years, but every living thing will eventually die. It's just a matter of time and circumstance. Half of you is already gone."

"There has to be a way—"

"I'm careful with my words, Jonas. I did not call you *immortal*, because mortality has you. Whatever that woman gave you, it was not enough."

"You must help me."

"I can't. The Great Goddess has already decided your fate."

"I reject such a fate," he snapped and the candles flickered.

A cool chill stole through the air. Her aunt was taking this too far. This guy was obviously unstable. It was all fun and games until the customers got nasty.

"Careful," Mabel warned. "My niece is just outside that door and she's holding a charged blade.

Juniper looked down at her hand, surprised to find she was in fact gripping one of the athames from the wall, yet she had no recollection of grabbing it.

"My God would not forsake me this way. I'm an honorable male."

"Your Judeo-Christian ego is overreaching again. Your mythology was written by man, recorded in a book that has been weaponized against your kind and used to label your species as demons. It's a story told by man, written by man, embellished by man, and swallowed by man. It's all myth, a tale that has stayed alive long past its characters or creators, a mere legend with no tangible substance anymore."

"The men mentioned in the Bible were not immortal."

"Neither are you."

Energy sizzled from her aunt's aura as she no longer disguised her dislike for his kind. Regardless of their play-acting, there was something personal passing between them, something Juniper couldn't fathom.

"I kept my word and listened to your story, Jonas, but now it's time for you to leave."

"You must help me."

"I can't."

"Can't or won't?"

"What you desire from me goes against The Goddess's plans. Surrender your soul to The Summerland and be reborn. Use the time you have left to be with your loved ones. That's the only option you have left to save your soul."

The chair screeched against the tile floor

as he stood in a rush. Juniper's back pressed into the wall as he flung back the beaded curtain and left the store. Her eyes went to Aunt Bel's as she looked down and blew out a shaky breath, all bravado gone.

Juniper entered the back room, her nose twitching at the scent of rot she'd missed before. "Um, what the hell was that?"

With shaky hands, Mabel pressed a bundle of sage into the flame of a candle and softly whispered her intention. "Lock the door and flip the sign." When Juniper hesitated, Mabel snapped, "*Now.*"

She did as instructed, startled by her aunt's nervous energy. She never saw her so frazzled. "Did you know that guy?"

"No." Mabel waved the bundle of sage, extinguishing the flame. Setting the smoking herbs inside the marble mortar, she selected a black feather from the jar and wafted the smoke in the direction of the abandoned chair, cleansing the air. Fanning the smoke, she directed it around the table, purifying the space and back door. "He's born of the devil."

Juniper paused. "Excuse me?"

"He was exactly as he smelled—vampire."

She choked on a laugh. "You're joking."

Mabel cleansed the air where Jonas had

been. "We never joke about such things. Find me the Florida Water."

"Holy fuck, are you serious?" Juniper rushed through the beaded curtain and plastered herself to the front window.

"Juniper, get away from the window! He hasn't gone far."

Distracted by curiosity, Juniper retrieved the herbal cologne from the shelf and spritzed the doorway. "Does he really drink blood?"

"Among other things."

"Gross. How could you tell that's what he was?"

Mabel stilled and stared at Juniper, her eyes brimming with enough worry to remove any humor. "This isn't a joke, Juniper. That man is dangerous. Pour some black salt at the threshold."

She did as she was told. "What did he want?"

"Something I can't give."

That never stopped her aunt from making a sale before. Maybe the guy was really dangerous and that's why she didn't try to scam him with some moon water or energy charged crystals. "What can't you give him?"

"Salvation. He wants to evoke dark magick. That sort of sorcery can be deadly."

"Right." There was no masking the sarcasm of her concern.

Aunt Mabel grabbed her shoulders and turned her to look into her eyes. "I'm serious, Juniper. If you see that man again, I want you to get as far away from him as you can, and tell me immediately. Do you understand?"

"He's Amish—"

"Do you understand?" she asked more firmly.

"Y-yes. Jeeze."

"Good. Now, put away the salt and go do your homework. If you get another D in algebra, I'm taking away your phone for a week."

Juniper scoffed. If she had any sort of real witchery hiding in her DNA, she wouldn't be flunking math. She gathered her backpack, which hadn't been opened since leaving school and disappeared through the beaded curtain into the back. Aunt Bel drew back the purple tapestry curtain and peeked out the window. While she was distracted, Juniper pulled the black jar off the second shelf and silently uncorked the top.

Thick, green buds filled her palm and she quickly stashed them in the pocket of her schoolbag. Predictably, the chime of a Facetime call sounded and Aunt Venus's voice broke the silence. "Do you think teal is pretentious or pretty?"

"Are we talking underwear, cookware, or jewelry?" Aunt Bel asked.

"Hair. I'm tired of purple."

"Teal's fine. But we have a bigger problem."

"What? Is it June? What did she do, now?" Juniper rolled her eyes and Venus continued, "I told her she better get her act together if she wants—"

"A vampire came to the shop today."

"What?" Venus croaked. Aunt Venus struggled to take anything serious, which made the sobriety of her concern that much more alarming. "Are you certain?"

"One thousand percent. And, Venus…he knew my name."

"Fuck."

CHAPTER 6

The mortal female navigated the woods as if walking was a second language. Even through the dappled shadows of the forest, Cain could see how out of sorts she was in nature.

Beyond the earlier damage to her clothing, mud caked the treads of Destiny's boots, grass stained her legs, and small scratches nicked her skin. She was a walking disaster.

"Ah!" Once more she tripped, landing awkwardly on the ground. A short chuckle slipped past his lips.

Her eyes narrowed on him with the venom of a viper backed by the strength of a toothless barn kitten. He laughed again, possibly out of fear that this might be his last chance for any hint of humor. Or maybe he was delirious from blood loss and he was losing his mind.

He hated her. His injuries were her fault. Yet, watching her flail about in mud as she struggled to navigate a simple hill stirred something endearing. She was helpless, pathetically so, and he took pity on her. Or maybe it was just satisfying to watch her struggle because he wanted to see her punished but lacked the energy to do it himself.

Once on her feet, she glared at him, gave a furious huff, and marched east. He allowed her to stomp away only because there was still a hint of sunlight in the sky and she needed to blow off steam. But as she stalked further and further away, he glanced upward at the fading light and sighed. They were running out of time.

"Destiny?"

Her right arm shot out, bent at a ninety-degree angle, as her middle finger spiked toward the sky. He arched a brow. The finger gesture was not an endearment.

"You're heading east."

Her steps halted and her shoulders bunch in frustration. She flinched as the motion pulled her skin tight, likely angering her injuries. Pivoting, she swiftly marched back in his direction, chin high, stare averted, and her unwavering pride still intact.

They walked another mile in silence. Although he was too weak to get into her head, her hunger and thirst beat at him. He had nothing to offer her aside from the water in his nearly empty canteen.

He could only assume her occasional tremble came from pain or fear. She was sweating profusely, so he doubted it was the chill in the air. Unless she was ill. He knew very little about mortal illness, but instinct told him a hot body with chilled skin was a bad sign.

Damn her mortal fragility. He had too much on his mind to spare her a single worry. Her constant moaning and griping was only distracting him.

Cain needed to get home. Too much time had passed since he last heard Annalise. The silence that followed their severed link was maddening. He could rest and try to reach her through a dream, but he didn't want to chance closing his eyes. He also didn't trust the mortal female in his company. She'd already tried to kill him once.

His chest tightened, this time not from his

injury, but from guilt. Anna was hurt. He knew it. And it was his fault. He could blame the mortal, but he'd been the one to place himself in harm's way.

Hopefully, Anna's immortal blood and Adam's presence was enough to stabilize her and the baby, but without a telepathic link he had no way of knowing for sure. He only had his fury and guilt.

Although the mortal female played a part, Cain had been the culpable one. He had promised not to endanger Anna and broken that vow. His foolish actions plagued him with shame, and it was too easy to make Destiny the target of his blame when he was the one at fault.

Her blood atonement would have to be retribution enough. However, his human blood bag wasn't strong enough to provide what he needed to properly heal, and he hadn't spotted a single animal worth feeding from since they started their trek. His equilibrium was so off from blood loss, he doubted he even possessed the speed and agility to catch a deer at this point, let alone wrestle a bear.

Destiny paused and shut her eyes as her fingers pressed into her temples. Rather than keep walking, he held back and waited. Her olive skin held a greenish hue. There was no rosiness to her cheeks, despite the glaze of sweat.

His head tipped as he glimpsed the puncture wounds at her throat. Had he been so out of it at the cave that he forgot to close his bite mark the last time he fed? She seemed unaware of his thievery, which had undoubtedly contributed to her suffering. Perhaps he took too much. Signs of anemia and dehydration showed in her unstable posture and lethargic motions.

Yet part of his mind demanded he hadn't taken enough. Forget this mortal. Annalise was in trouble. So long as he remained weak, Anna remained weak. He needed to fortify his strength for the sake of Anna and the baby. Destiny was merely a mortal, a weaker link in the food chain. Her cursed fragility was her own fault. He had to keep his focus on Anna and the baby.

The baby...

His gut clenched hard with regret. "Enough stopping. We have to keep moving."

"I need a minute," she barked, still massaging her temples.

"You've taken several. We must go." The

sun was setting and they had yet to find a safe place to bed down. The safest choice was to keep traveling toward the farm.

"I'm not fucking moving," she snapped then winced. "My head is throbbing."

Cain pressed into her mind only to hit instant resistance. A strange sting prickled along his scalp, and Destiny's face scrunched tight as if sharp pain stabbed through her temples. He scowled at her stubbornness, but she seemed unaware she was deflecting him. Maybe she wasn't. Perhaps he was simply too weak.

Mortals need constant rest to survive and heal their feeble bodies. If he could compel her to sleep, he could carry her, but attempting to do so only sapped more of his energy. Depleted as he was, he wasn't sure he even possessed the strength to lift her for more than a few miles.

Furious with such unusual limitations he snapped, "We're moving. Let's go."

"No. I want to go home."

He spun and growled in her face, "Do you think I care what you want? We're in this predicament because of you!"

"Me? You're the one who—"

"Enough!" He snapped, gripping her

shoulders tightly and ignoring her whimper of pain. He shook her roughly. "I decide, not you. We must get back to my family. No more stopping. No more lagging. No more crying. Shut your mouth and obey—"

The slap came out of nowhere. Stunned she'd been able to sneak in such a blow he staggered back a step.

She blew up like a rooster about to rouse the world. *"Fuck off!"*

His molars locked and he barreled forward, but she didn't stagger back as expected. Nose to nose, he glared at her. "Listen here, little girl. I'm bigger, stronger, and you do not want to disobey me."

Fury exploded as she shoved him back. "I'd intentionally catch myself on fire before I'd ever give obedience to an arrogant prick like you! I'm not a fucking dog, and you're certainly not my master! Your privilege doesn't work with me, got it?"

He wanted to throttle her. Bend her. Break her. Prove he could soften all of her hard edges and have her following him like a kitten chased a string, but he didn't have time for any of that. Nor did he understand why her outburst impressed him on some level. If she had enough spark to yell at him, she surely had enough energy to keep moving. In a strange way, he was starting to like the stubborn brat.

"Walk."

"No."

They scowled at each other, neither one backing down. He scoffed and pivoted away, calling her bluff. "Fine. Stay here and die. The sun's setting and you won't make it past dawn on your own." He purposely bumped his arm into her shoulder as he marched toward home.

Mortal women were the death of immortal men, and he should have never gotten tangled up with this one. He was a fool for trying to help her. Had he left her for dead, he could have easily found another blood source on his own. She was not his priority. Anna was his only responsibility.

His mind instantly wrapped around his sister-by-law, hating that he'd trained himself to label her as such. Annalise was so much more than a sister to him. She was a fraction of his soul—but she also shared the soul of his twin brother, Adam.

Never had there been a recorded case of two males sharing a call to one female until both he and Adam experienced their calling to Annalise. Adam would have never been able to successfully bond with Anna had Cain not permitted it. It was his life's greatest sacrifice.

Without a mate, an immortal had no purpose. Hunting the creatures in the woods seemed an honorable cause, but it was far from satisfying in comparison to his brother's life. And look where Cain's foolish cause landed him.

He glanced back at Destiny who grudgingly followed several yards behind. Her palpable disdain wasn't a new concept. Females tended to resent him long before ever entertaining softer emotions toward him. Anna also didn't love him, at least not the way he'd hoped she would. Not the way she loved Adam.

He should be grateful he maintained his brother's affection, although that might be gone now. Was the baby gone? Why couldn't he feel Anna?

His speed doubled. He wanted no woman who loved another man, yet he could not shut off his affection and loyalty toward Anna. It had grown more platonic with time, but somehow more intense as well. Her safety meant everything to Cain, and he'd jeopardized that.

For all of Adam's noble traits, Cain knew his brother dreamt of a simpler life without him, one where Anna wasn't sharing another man's dreams or endangered by Cain's choices. The moment Cain's destiny had been forsaken he should have ended his unfulfilling life, but death wasn't an option, not while Anna suffered all of his injuries the same.

He was cursed. There was no other way to explain it. Cursed by an endless, bleak, lonesome eternity. The loss of his soul mate would likely require an eternity to accept, though he might never fully understand why fate had overlooked him.

There were so many peculiarities he still struggled to comprehend. Such as why had he not lost his mind when he surrendered Anna to Adam? Cain suffered early symptoms of *feeishness,* but they faded the moment he shared his blood with Anna. A blood exchange was only part of the bonding. Adam had fulfilled the rest. Yet here Cain was, sane enough to process the ongoing agony of his circumstances. Insanity would have been a welcomed sign of God's mercy.

He inwardly sneered. What kind of god allows such suffering? Certainly not a merciful one. With his mate, he surrendered the dwindling scraps of his faith.

Cain was a loner. Loners didn't need a partner and they certainly didn't need a god.

Incensed with only his own choices to blame, Cain seethed as he marched over the twisted roots of the forest floor. At the moment, anger seemed an easier emotion than worry so he reveled in his spiraling, bitter thoughts.

Adam might have Anna's body and access to her awakened mind, but he no longer shared her dreams. Only Cain could share her unconscious mind. A selfish part of him enjoyed that he and he alone knew such an intimate, unguarded part of his brother's wife. If he lost that link…

"Hurry up," he barked over his shoulder.

The crunch of the underbrush filled the silence and he paused, registering the absence of Destiny's following footsteps. He looked back, squinting through the gathering shadows but didn't see her.

"Destiny?"

Silence answered and he huffed, retracing his steps until he spotted her body heaped on the ground.

"We don't have time to rest. The sun is setting."

She didn't respond. Her lashes formed dark shadows over her pale face and her breathing was uneven. An air of malaise surrounded her like an aura. He touched the back of his fingers to her forehead and winced. Her skin burned to the touch yet she shivered.

Pressing a finger against her pulse he frowned. The accelerated thrum wasn't a good sign.

"What do you need?" he whispered, unwelcome concern twisting his focus.

She moaned, her expression tight as her eyes remained shut. "*Cansada.*"

Cain didn't know what *cansada* meant. Destiny spoke a different language aside from English. She often mumbled this native tongue in her sleep.

"What is *consada?*"

"Tired," she weakly mumbled. "*Eu estou com fome.*"

"English, Destiny."

She moaned, her body doubled over as she curled her arms over her stomach. "I need to eat."

He pressed his lips together. She was

barely conscious. Her body slumped into the earth, all signs of resistance gone. He pulled her onto his lap.

Cupping her chin, he pried open one of her eyelids and sighed. She was out cold. "I'll carry you."

He stood and cradled her slack body to his chest. Once more he tried to press into her mind. This time there was little resistance, but he could not see more than images. Strange words whispered and then the connection was gone. He'd never experienced such a slippery mortal conscience and wondered, had he not been so injured, if he might have more control over her mind.

He called a warm wind under the trees in an attempt to warm her. She continued to shiver despite the burning heat of her skin. He wasn't sure how to help her, but feared she might die. Having taken so much of her blood, he felt responsible for her safety.

"Just rest. I'll find you a healer." Shifting her weight, he ran toward home.

CHAPTER 7

The last harvest had passed months ago and the fields were empty. Unbroken land under the glow of a snow moon patiently waited for the dawn of spring and new seeds to sew. If Cain thought his return to the farm might stir some sense of homecoming in his heart, he'd been mistaken.

The door to his parents' house opened before he reached the front gate. His youngest sister, Gracie, greeted him with a glare that said she'd been expecting him.

"I could hear you coming from a mile away."

Of course, his intuitive sister would have sensed him. His mind hadn't stopped and he was too weak to guard his thoughts. "Get the door."

"You can't—"

"The door, Grace."

She rushed to hold it open as he marched into their home. Ready to collapse, he dumped Destiny's unconscious body in an unceremonious heap on the wood floor.

"Dear Lord." Gracie's hand rushed to her mouth. "Is it dead?"

"I don't know," Cain caught his breath, then corrected. "No."

They had been traveling for hours without rest, half of which Destiny had been unconscious and dead weight. He was ready to collapse from exhaustion.

His sister turned her gaping stare on him then gasped again. "Cain, your…" She drew back. "You're hurt."

"Of course, I'm hurt. Where's Anna?"

She glanced away and shook her head. "You can't see her."

"I don't have the patience for your games. Where is she?"

Gracie flinched at the lash of his voice. "She's home, with Adam, but you can't—"

He was out the door before she could finish her thought.

"What am I supposed to do with the mortal?" she called from the porch, but he couldn't be bothered worrying about the mortal another second.

There was no steeling himself for the inevitable wrath that awaited him. The moment he reached Annalise and Adam's home, he sensed his brother's rage and knew Adam felt him coming. Similar to Gracie's telepathic gifts, Adam was a powerful empath. If anything, he would feel Cain's deep regret for putting Anna in harm's way.

He entered the house without knocking and waited, certain his brother would appear.

"What do you want?" Adam hissed from the staircase above.

"I came to see Anna—"

"My wife," he sneered between clenched teeth, "does not want to see you. You're not welcome here. Go away."

His words gutted Cain. Without a link to Anna, he had no way of knowing if Adam was protecting her with lies or speaking the truth. "Let her tell me to go and I will."

"Don't you get it? She can't tell you. She has no strength because of you. Leave. And leave us alone to live our lives in peace."

As Adam turned away, Cain panicked.

"You cannot shut me out, Adam. I need to speak with her. You owe me that much—"

"*I owe you nothing!* Everything I have—*everything*—you nearly destroyed it!"

Remorse choked him. There was no apology worthy of forgiveness. His grief and worry crippled him. "I just need to speak to her. I haven't dreamt of her."

"You haven't dreamt of her because she hasn't slept, you selfish animal. Do you have any idea what you've done?"

"I won't know until I see her! I nearly died, too, Adam. I haven't fed on more than a few drops in days. I'm weak and sick with concern. I know that doesn't excuse my actions, but I did everything I could to survive for her. I'm here for her."

"You're here for yourself. Your selfish actions nearly cost her her life and the life of our child!"

"Believe me, none of this is for me," he rasped. If Cain had his way, he would have given up in the woods and let himself die, but that wasn't an option, not without risking the lives of Anna and the babe. "My existence continues for her. Do you think any of this is what I wanted?"

"Don't pretend that you were thinking of

her out there. You were thinking of yourself, thinking of how you could redeem your reputation in the eyes of The Elders."

Cain scoffed. "Fuck The Elders and fuck you for thinking so low of me." His chest hurt from more than the blow of the arrow. He'd done the most selfless thing of all for his brother. "Your memory is short."

Adam's jaw twitched, but he didn't rescind his words.

"Was I selfish that night? Was I thinking of The Elders? No! I was only thinking of *you*, my twin." Cain seethed, still weak from injury and lack of blood, but refusing to rest until he saw her. "She's yours, Adam, isn't that enough? Must you keep punishing me more than God already has? I can't die, because it will kill her, so I must go on suffering, knowing exactly where peace and salvation lies, but forbidden to take respite in her arms. My distance isn't out of ease, it's out of respect for you and Anna. Every second I deny myself, I suffer all I've lost again. So go ahead, call me selfish. Look me in the eye and say it as if you truly mean it and you're not simply speaking from an insecure place of fear."

"I should kill you," his brother growled.

"I know the feeling, but you can't, not without killing your sweet wife."

"She's my *mate*," Adam growled through clenched teeth.

"Do you want my response to that?"

Adam snarled and lunged, his fist knotting in the tattered shreds of Cain's shirt. "She will never be yours the way she's mine! You only bring her pain! You can't conceive of the horrors you've wrought. She nearly bled out! A true mate protects his female at all costs. You only put her in harm's way!"

"I didn't do it on purpose!"

"Excuses! That's all you have to say for your thoughtless actions. How many more apologies should we expect before this nonsense ends? How far will you go before you learn? What price will the rest of us pay?" Adam's composure slipped and true fear flashed in his eyes. "To be rendered impotent in the grip of an enemy I cannot see..." He panted. "Curse this hold you have over us, Cain. The enemy is *you*."

Adam's restraint was for Anna's benefit alone. There was no mistaking his desire to hurt Cain, and he'd accomplished the task without compromising Annalise. Adam understood any blow to Cain would be a blow to his wife. But he didn't need to hit him. His words destroyed him, cutting deeper than any physical injury possibly could.

"You're right," Cain wheezed. His campaign to stop Isaiah was a foolish cause led by his ego that placed Annalise in grave danger. Shame sapped the rest of his strength. "I'll go."

Adam released his grip and stepped back. "Get out."

Cain nodded and turned toward the door.

"Wait." Her fragile voice cut through Cain like a bolt of lightning, and he pivoted to face the steps, searching the second floor landing for the relief that always accompanied the sight of her.

"Anna." She stood just inside the door, cloaked by shadows. Her copper hair hung rebelliously loose over her shoulders and her small hands cradled her rounded belly protectively through her shift.

"You should be in bed—"

"And you should not speak to your brother that way."

A furious growl purred from Adam's chest, his frustration also with his mate. "Five minutes, and you will sit, not stand. Your body is still weak."

"Fine. But you will give us those five minutes to speak privately."

Adam's eyes lit with fury and he growled, shoving past Cain to leave the house.

"He's angry," she admitted, without meeting Cain's eyes.

Her hand gripped the molding and he rushed up the stairs. "You need to rest."

She flinched away from his touch and her distrust cut deep, but she was too weak to refuse his help. Escorting her back to the bed, he gently helped her recline and covered her with a blanket. The room smelled of blood and soap.

"Are you in pain?"

She glanced up at him. "You know I am."

"I'm so sorry, Annalise."

She sighed and looked away.

He grasped her arm gently and led her back to bed. "Do you hate me?

"No, but I'm angry." She finally met his gaze. "I nearly lost my baby, Cain. I could feel his soul being pulled from my womb." Her normally pink lips were white as she forced the words out, fighting dearly to hold onto her composure, as tears welled in her eyes.

"Please don't cry."

"How could you have been so reckless? If I

lost my child because of your actions, I'm not sure I could ever forgive you. Do you understand what I'm telling you, Cain? *Never*. And we both know that Adam would not."

Her declaration was a hot blade cauterizing the hollow part of his soul. He was empty. He understood that having a mate meant putting her safety above all else, including his own. Adam was right. He needed to leave them in peace. "I understand."

He had sacrificed everything, the highest honored gift among immortals, for his brother and Anna, but that wasn't enough. An eternal life sentence of a lonesome existence where he was a pariah among his own family was all he had left. Cain had no one waiting on him, nor would he ever.

His heart constricted. If not a mate and if not a warrior dedicated to protecting The Order, then what was he? What purpose did he serve? Such a useless existence with no sight of a hopeful future was enough to make a male want to end it all. Yet, there again, he could not give up on life, for fear of taking innocent Annalise with him.

There was nothing more for him to say. "Just tell me you'll be all right and I will leave you in peace."

"I will be, but I'm not yet."

"What will it take for you to forgive me?"

"Cain, it felt like a thousand heart attacks paired with the fear of having my unborn child ripped away from me. The horror of not knowing what was hurting me or how to stop it…" She shut her eyes as a tear slipped past. "That sort of trauma takes time to heal."

"I'm so sorry, Anna. You didn't deserve any of this." Any acceptance of his apology would have been forced and false at that time, so he stood, emotion clogging his throat. "Rest and be well."

He would not contact her again, not even in his sleep. From here on, he would leave her be unless she decided otherwise.

He didn't see Adam as he left the house, but he was sure his brother sensed him go. Cain's quick, heavy steps carried him toward the barn. The first act of contrition would be fully healing himself so that Anna no longer suffered his aches and pains.

As he ducked into the shade of an empty stall, he slammed his fist against a heavy support beam, rattling the structure. His head came up quickly when a soft feminine gasp sounded from the shadows. Could nothing go right for him?

"Cain? Is that you?" a delicate voice called.

He squinted through the shadows. "Hope? What are you doing here?"

"My father sent me to retrieve a tool that Adam said he could borrow, and I got side tracked with the animals." She held the device in her petite hand. "I didn't know you were back."

Her pale skin held no imperfections, her hair the color of wheat. She was typically pleasant company, but he didn't feel like being social. "I just got home."

She set down the tool and closed the distance, pressing her palms into his chest. "Was it dangerous out there?"

The disquiet of his mind needed silencing. Taking her wrist in hand, he tugged her further into the shadows. She followed willingly.

The tight space reeked of sawdust and hay. He jerked her narrow hips to his and yanked the fastenings of her apron loose. He needed a distraction from his terrible thoughts.

He wanted to think of anything but Anna and the baby. He needed to mute his guilt and shame. Hope's mouth opened under his demanding kiss, and her daring tongue darted past his lips. He didn't like her willingness, which he usually appreciated.

His kiss turned punishing and his fingers quickly pulled the fabric of her dress down her front until her pale breasts were exposed. He bunched her skirts, seeking the ties of her undergarments. When she giggled, he growled. He didn't want her to enjoy his touch. He wanted her to hate him like everyone else. No point in the tiresome masquerade when they all knew how lost he was.

"Turn around." He shoved her toward the wall and bent her down. She spread her legs apart, too eager.

Reaching around her slender waist, he gripped her small breast and she moaned. How was she enjoying this? He was using her. He gripped a fist in her hair and tugged.

"Mmm," she moaned. "I missed your touch."

He shoved away from her body, enraged by her enthusiasm. His erection flagged. He wanted to hit something.

Hope was not his enemy, but his rage blinded him to her innocence in this. "Get out of here."

Shock stiffened her spine and she stood up, holding the front of her dress to her chest. "Cain, what's wrong—"

"Go!"

She flinched and tears welled in her eyes. "Did I do something wrong? Show me what you want and I'll—"

"I want you to leave! Get out of here and don't come back! I don't want you anymore!"

She sucked in a sharp breath and ran out of the barn, clutching her apron to her front.

He cursed when he saw the tool she'd come to borrow forgotten on the shelf. He was a monster.

Hope hadn't deserved his cruelty, just like Anna, yet he hurt them both. He hurt everyone who dared to interact with him.

Enough. There was no room in his life for sadness or self-pity. Sadness was for victims and he refused to be a victim when his only job was to survive. A life sentence that would last all of eternity. No need to drag it out with defeatist emotions. From here on, he'd shut everything off. He'd keep himself and Anna safe, deal with the Destiny dilemma, and find someplace quiet to be alone until the baby was born. Then he'd disappear for good.

But first, he had a stop to make. There was one other female he needed to see.

CHAPTER 8

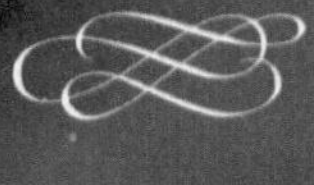

"*Y*o, yo, yo, check it out!" Trent grabbed the hairspray from Zoey's hand and pumped it at the flame of his lighter. A blaze exploded in the air. "*Dracarys*." He laughed and pumped the flammable spray into the flame again.

"Don't waste it." Zoey snatched the hairspray from him and stuffed it back in her bag. "What the hell was I looking for?"

"Your manners." Trent flicked his zippo shut and sulked. "June, how long's it take to pack a fucking bowl?"

"Don't rush me. This is good shit. I stole it from my Aunt Bel."

"Man, your aunt's weed is killer," Zoey said, using her bag as a seat as they sat around the bonfire tucked deep in the woods. "I wish I knew where she got it."

Juniper sprinkled the last bit into the bowl and twisted the jar shut. "She grows it."

Trent tossed her the lighter and laughed. "That's not all she grows. We could be smoking some voodoo up in here." He playfully tugged Juniper's jacket off her shoulder, exposing the crocheted weave of her sweater. "I can see your bra through this shirt."

"That's the point." She lit the bowl and puffed until it glowed, releasing her finger to suck in a deep inhale. Voice tight, she handed it to Zoey and said, "It's hot."

They passed the bowl around, each one taking a few puffs, as the effects of her aunt's high-quality cannabis quickly kicked in.

"So is this *magick* pot?" Zoey giggled.

"Fuckin' right it is." Trent laughed. "It magically appears and we never have to pay."

"Aren't you afraid she'll find out you stole it?"

"No." Juniper held the lighter over the bowl, but it was mostly resin at that point.

Trent snorted. "Mabel's probably watching us right now through her crystal ball."

"Yeah, right." Tapping the ash onto a

nearby rock, Juniper stuffed the bowl into the pocket of her torn jean shorts. It was too damn cold for shorts, but she liked the way they looked with her black tights and boots. "Throw another stick on the fire." She burrowed deeper under her wool coat.

"I'll keep you warm." Trent nestled closer, nibbling her shoulder and neck.

She shoved him away, preferring the warmth of her coat. "Quit it."

"But I'm a vampire. *I vant to drink your blood!*"

"A second ago you were imitating an insane dragon queen." Zoey poked the fire with a long branch.

"It's this magic weed. I can be whatever I want."

"I'm not even high." Juniper wondered if she accidentally grabbed some kitchen herb instead of pot.

"Did you guys hear about the bodies they keep finding in the woods by Jim Thorpe?" Zoey had a penchant for ghost stories whenever they stood the chance of feeling extra paranoid.

"What bodies?" Juniper's aunts didn't own televisions. They also believed the news on social media was full of conspiracy theories and fear mongering bullshit, so Juniper rarely paid attention to anything out of her small, unbearably boring, suburban teenage world.

"*All* women's bodies. There have been, like, eight of them or something. They're completely drained of blood and some of them have even been sexually assaulted—post mortem."

Juniper drew back in disgust. "Ew, gross."

"Is just my fellow vampires," Trent said in a heavy Transylvanian accent. "Ah, ah, ah!"

Zoey rolled her eyes. "You sound like that puppet on Sesame Street."

"*You sound like that puppet on Sesame Street,*" Trent sneered, mimicking Zoey in a whiny voice. "Lighten up."

Juniper ignored their bickering, her mind returning to the man who visited her aunt's store earlier that day. "What if it actually *is* a vampire out there?"

Her stare locked on the mesmerizing flames as she recalled every underwhelming detail of the guy. Talk about a legendary let-down. Nothing screamed Dracula like suspenders and an Amish hat.

Trent snickered. "The weed's hitting her now."

Juniper's stare snapped to his. "I'm serious.

What if vampires really existed? Maybe that's what's been killing those women."

"After 2020, nothing can surprise me." Zoey flicked some fallen ash off her jeans. "A global pandemic, killer hornets, and the government finally acknowledges aliens, sure, why not throw vampires into the mix?"

The wind whistled through the trees. A swirl of ember and ash floated skyward. Usually smoking pot relaxed Juniper, but after bailing on studying to hang with her friends, she knew she was going to bomb her algebra test tomorrow and her aunt was going to murder her.

She couldn't unwind. Not that studying would have helped her relax. She was already failing her math class beyond redemption. Why did people need algebra anyway? Who gave a shit what X stood for?

"Is it raining?" Zoey looked up at the trees. "I swear I just felt a drop."

"An owl probably just peed on you." Trent flicked the lid of his zippo open and shut, open and shut. *Click, clack, click, clack,* the continuous snapping disrupted the tranquil crackle of the fire and only added to Juniper's irritation.

"There it is again! It's definitely raining!" Zoey stood. "I'm done."

"Oh, come on, it's just a little drizzle," Trent argued. It really didn't matter what Zoey wanted. If she said black, Trent automatically said white. The two of them together were a constant headache.

Zoey gathered her belongings. "I just got my hair done. I'll meet you guys at the car."

She marched off and Juniper frowned. "Do you hear that?"

"Zoey's drama? Yeah, it's a little hard to miss."

"No. The fire." Juniper leaned closer. The crackling flames hissed softly, building into the low roar of a wave, louder and louder until it sounded exactly like the surf of the ocean, ebbing and flowing with a rhythmic static.

"I don't hear anything. You wanna fool around before we go back to the car?" He pulled his zipper down.

Juniper rolled her eyes and turned her attention back to the fire. A steady drizzle fell through the branches, tapping softly on the leaves overhead. The wind pushed through the trees. The flames breathed to the measure of a conch shell whispering into her ear.

"Watch it, Juniper!" He yanked her back. "You're gonna catch your hair on fire."

She looked up, finding the sky strangely clear for rain. It was a new moon, so it should have been darker, but twinkling stars peeked from above the dancing branches as the leaves curled upward as if catching the droplets. Yeah, maybe she was pretty high.

She could feel the energy of the moon pulling her as much as it pulled the tide. Usually, she hated any tingles of pagan instinct or symptoms of her weird gene pool, but at the moment she felt calm and compelled to feel whatever this was.

Typically conflicted by her family's faith, she was oddly at peace in this moment. At peace and strangely attuned with nature. It was enough to remove her usual resentment for being raised a witch.

Her upbringing didn't consist of an early education like other little kids might experience. While most toddlers played with blocks and mastered their ABCs, Juniper's aunts taught her about herbs and crystals and all the reasons they celebrated the pagan sabbats.

She used to love her aunts' stories about the Oak and Holly Gods and all the powers of the Goddess, until she went to kindergarten and realized other kids worshipped some guy named Santa. No one knew who Odin was, and they all looked at her like she was crazy when she tried to explain their family's strange holidays.

Aunt Venus said Christian holidays were all originally pagan holidays before the burning years, but that didn't stop Juniper's classmates from ostracizing her. Aunt Bel told her to be proud of their heritage, but Juniper just wanted to be like everyone else. She wanted to be accepted and asked to birthday parties and sleepovers.

Zoey was her first friend on account of their unifying diversity. In their private grade school, they were given free-choice art projects while the rest of their classmates colored pictures of easter eggs during Ostara, a spring sabbat when Juniper's family celebrated the goddess Ēostre. Zoey's relatives only observed Muslim holidays, so she would often get paired with Juniper. By high school, she and Zoey accepted they would likely always be outcasts and stopped giving a shit what others thought.

"It's really starting to come down, June. We should head back."

And then there was Trent, the first guy to

ever see past her dorky reputation that followed her since kindergarten. Switching to a public high school helped, because it was bigger and she wasn't the only weirdo. Boobs also helped. Trent actually made her feel pretty, and the more she let him compliment her, the more she began to see her own beauty and embrace her authentic style.

He hung out with the cool jocks, a clique Juniper found outwardly obnoxious, but she envied their social status all the same. Having sex with Trent wasn't so much an act of desire as it was a social experiment. She and Zoey got an instant upgrade and found themselves invited to parties and lunch tables that never spared them a passing glance before.

But Zoey didn't trust Trent or his jock buddies. She didn't want to be like the kids that spent years making fun of her and could give a shit about their acceptance, which was why she never cut Trent any slack and the two of them bickered constantly. Zoey tolerated him simply because Juniper was her best friend.

"June, are you coming? Zoey's waiting in the car."

Ignoring Trent, she spread her palms over the earth, her fingers splayed wide. All the elements were present: water, air, fire, earth. She could feel the spirit awakening around her. It wasn't usually this obvious. Typically, it was subtle.

The hair rose at the nape of her neck and goosebumps prickled her skin as the flames hissed in a tempo that matched her heartbeat. She shut her eyes, feeling the vibration of earth below her and her connection to every root and tree.

"Juniper, I'm getting drenched."

The rain fell in a steady stream but it wasn't bothering her. Nor was the cold. On the contrary, her insides felt warm and her skin alive, sun kissed by the warmth of the fire and replenished by the fresh air.

She kneeled on the ground, fingers forked through the earth, turning her face upward to the sky. "Can you feel that?" The clouds opened and the rain fell harder, soaking her hair and face like a baptism.

"You're high as a kite and getting soaked. You're gonna get sick. Come on." Trent grabbed her arm and she flung his touch away.

"No!"

"What the fuck, Juniper?" He cradled his wrist, his brow kinked in disbelief.

Startled out of her trance, she looked at him. He pulled his hand away, revealing his fingers, one twisted unnaturally at a gnarled angle.

Startled, she gasped. "What happened?"

"You hit me."

"I didn't hit you. I just..." She shook her head, unclear on how she hurt him. "I'm sorry. I didn't mean to touch you." Mortified, she stood, brushing the dirt off her palms and legs. "Trent, I'm sorry."

"Whatever. I'm heading back to the car." Protectively holding his injured fingers, he marched back toward the road.

"Trent, wait."

He ignored her and kept walking. The familiar sting of rejection awakened old pains. Her newfound confidence wavered and something ugly filled her in a rush, tears brimming at her eyes. "Fuck you, then," she muttered, putting up walls as a defense mechanism to protect her from further rejection.

"I guess I'll take care of the fire..." She glanced over her shoulder and her voice faded away.

The flames shrank into a small flicker, no bigger than a candle on a birthday cake. She frowned and stepped closer. A second ago it was a raging inferno.

She inhaled and the wind stopped, the rain pulling back into the sky. Her breath held in her lungs as if time and nature stood still, waiting for her to exhale. Her eyes widened. Nothing moved. Not the wind, the rain, the trees, the earth, or even the fire.

"Whoa." The whispered word expelled her breath and a gust of wind cut through the woods lifting her hair off her shoulders as the fire burst back to life. Flames stretched six feet high with the roar of a blowtorch, knocking her off her feet onto her ass. She crab-crawled backward, afraid her clothes might catch fire.

"Holy fuck!" As she sucked in a breath the flames shrank back to a flicker. "That's not possible." Her frantic stare searched the shadows, wondering if Trent was messing with her. Maybe he was playing with Zoey's hairspray again.

"Trent? Zoey?"

No one was there.

Heart pounding, she stared at the little flame. Tightening her lips, she blew out a small breath and flinched when the fire blazed upward. Rather than sticking around to see how that was possible, she twisted and scrambled to her feet, racing back to the street.

Both Trent and Zoey waited inside the car, out of the rain. She ripped open the passenger door and clamored inside.

"Watch the mud," Trent warned.

Juniper panted. "Just go."

Zoey frowned at her. "You okay?"

"Fine. Just way too fucking high."

Trent didn't do his usual chuckle as he started the car, and she remembered his hurt hand, unsure where that left them as a couple.

CHAPTER 9

A soft drizzle accompanied Cain on his walk home. His thoughts replayed the exchange at his brother's house, gnawing away at his insides until even the act of breathing rubbed him raw.

The houses were dark and silent, supper resolved and many already retired for the evening. The moon glowed low behind the trees, long shadows crawling over the earth. Candles illuminated the windows of his grandparents' home as he crossed the prairie. Only then did he spot Cybil playing on the dark porch with a corn husk doll.

And there it was. He shut his eyes for the briefest moment, savoring the innocent sense of nostalgia he'd longed for. Although Cybil had not lived on the farm long, Cain had taken a great liking to her and often worried over how she was adapting. Now, in her traditional Amish clothing surrounded by the safety of the farm, he felt great relief that she'd been adjusting fine in his absence. Perhaps part of his worry was actually the unfamiliar longing of missing someone.

Cybil sat on a quilt, no shoes on her stocking-clad feet, and her wild blonde hair uncovered, not a single part of her seeming to mind the cold, despite her rosy red cheeks. The gate hinge creaked and her gaze snapped up, fixating on him.

Such a haunted stare shouldn't belong to a child, yet she had seen unnamable horrors for a girl of only eleven years, and her eyes wore the wisdom of such trauma.

He lifted a hand. "Remember me?"

Her intense stare softened the moment she realized it was him and not his twin brother Adam. She breathed in a silent gasp and the doll fell forgotten to the planked floorboards, as she barreled down the walk and launched herself into his arms.

Her bunched gown and long cloak smelled of cold weather and tree sap. Warmth spread through his chest as he shut his eyes and breathed in the familiar scent of her fine hair.

"You've grown." She was too old for dolls, but small enough that others might mistake her for much younger.

She hugged him with a ferocity that couldn't be faked, and he thought … *this* is love. He needed a welcome like this after the week he had.

As she pulled away, she looked at him, tears of joy in her baby blue eyes. Her cool fingers cupped his jaw, frowning at the stubble, her palm brushing over the prickles.

"Should I try to grow it in?" he asked, not expecting an answer.

She scrunched her nose and shook her head.

He laughed, setting her back on her feet.

She took his hand, walking him to the porch and tugging him toward the quilt.

"Do you like your new clothing?" Last he saw her she wore English street clothes.

She curled her lip to one side and stuck out her tongue.

He chuckled again.

Her expression grew serious, and she pointed to his chest and then slowly opened her fingers and lowered her palm toward the ground and held it still. She looked at him again and made two fists, with her thumbs and pinkies pointing outward and thrust them toward the ground. He tried to understand what she was saying.

"Am I staying?" he asked, and she nodded. "For a bit, yes."

An unguarded smile transformed her face, and she threw her arms around his neck, squeezing tight.

She was part of the reason he left. After the attack and murder of her mother, Cybil stopped speaking. Cain had hoped she'd find her words by now, hoped he'd have news of justice to share, but he was wrong on both accounts.

Someone obviously found a different solution and taught her sign language. That was good, he supposed, but he wanted more for her. Dane and Cybil Foster were Clara's grandchildren, and Clara was his father's mate. Cain had promised to watch over them for as long as they needed watching.

After Clara passed away, his father reunited with his mother. His father claimed they needed time away from the farm to reconnect. He left Cain in charge of the children. When duty called Cain to the woods, he passed the responsibility to his grandparents.

Clara hadn't survived the bonding, but had completed part of the transfer. Cain often wondered if his father truly felt normal or if he struggled with the aftermath of losing a mate the way Cain did. Their situations were different but shared enough similarities for Cain to hope they might be able to share some insight as to why life was so unfair.

Regardless of Clara's fate, his father had made a vow to watch over her grandchildren. Cain was a part of that promise, and like his father, he did more than keep his word. He moved them to a safe home and tried to avenge their mother. It was too early to say he failed, but for now, he could not tell either mortal that he'd succeeded.

Dane understood more than Cybil and sometimes showed a defiant, oppositional side, but it was healthy for a young man to question his circumstances. Cybil likely had questions, too, but she lacked the words to ask them.

Eventually, they would realize what Cain and the others were. He just hoped they were wise enough to realize that they weren't anything like Isaiah. They were a gentle, immortal species. Isaiah was vampire.

Dane had likely figured out what they were by now. The boy had impressive intuition for a mortal. Beyond instinct, he had telepathic gifts. Nothing like immortal telepathy, of course, but Dane could read innocent minds, mostly children's. Adult thoughts were lost to him. Still, it would be enough for him to glean the children of The Order were different than he and his sister.

"Cybil, where is Dane?"

She shrugged.

He wished he could visit with her longer, but it was getting late and he needed to return to Gracie and Destiny. "I'm glad I got to see you, but I have to go now."

She frowned and gripped his arm.

"I'm not leaving the farm. I can visit you again in the morning."

She rapidly signed several gestures and he laughed.

"You'll have to teach me how to do that." Righting her cockeyed bonnet over her messy blonde hair, he grinned. "No more growing. Understand?"

She smiled up at him, her eyes laughing.

When he returned to his parents' home, he

halted at the sight of a buggy. It was getting late for visitors, and he wasn't sure how to explain the presence of another mortal on the farm. He rushed up the walk and called for his sister as soon as he entered the house. "Gracie?"

"I'm right here." She appeared, carrying a trough of dough to the counter.

He searched the kitchen floor. "Where is she?"

"I moved her to your bed."

"Who's here?"

"Larissa."

Cain inwardly cursed. He loved his sister, Larissa, but she was mated to the bishop. He didn't need Eleazar involving himself or The Council with Destiny. He just needed someone to feed her, fix her up, and wipe her mind. Then they could take her to the nearest town and dump her.

"Is she alone?"

"Yes." She flipped the dough onto a floured surface, paying him little mind.

He sighed with relief. "Thank God." He rushed down the hall to his bedroom only to hear Gracie call after him.

"The bishop knows you brought another mortal here."

Cain winced. He'd deal with Eleazar later.

The moment he entered his room, Larissa looked up and smiled. "You're back."

"For a bit."

"Are you healed?"

"I'm mending. I'll be fully recovered by morning." He had a chance to feed from the animals, knowing it wasn't safe to take any more from Destiny. Once the blood worked through his system, he should be back to normal.

"And Annalise…"

"Anna will be fine."

"Gracie said you went to see her." Unspoken worries showed in her perceptive eyes, but his sister had always been too polite to come out and ask tough personal questions. "And Adam?"

"Your manners are killing me, Larissa. Just say what you want to say."

Her lips twitched. "There was so much blood, Cain."

"You were there?"

"Afterward. When she calmed. Every time she fed, she vomited. Adam couldn't sustain her. Gracie even fed her, but I could not." Her hand curved softly over the front of her gown and Cain rushed forward.

"Are you…?"

"It's early, but yes."

"And mother?"

Larissa smiled, a breathy laugh crossing her lips. "Mother, too. Father is beside himself with joy. It's a miracle."

"You've spoken to him?"

"He sends letters. They're enjoying their time away together."

Hesitantly, he took another step closer and placed his hand over hers. His heart swelled with joy for his sweet sister. Although he had never been too fond of the old bishop, Eleazar treated Larissa well and cared for her greatly. That was more than her first husband had done.

"I'm happy for you, sister."

"Thank you."

They let the emotion-laden moment play a while longer until Cain stepped back. "The bishop knows I'm here?"

"We don't keep secrets from each other, Cain."

"You kept secrets from Silus."

"Eleazar is my mate. There's no comparison."

Between Eleazar and Silus? There certainly wasn't.

The bishop was well over five centuries old and possessed gifts far beyond Cain's comprehension. Silus was a privileged windbag now buried somewhere only he and the bishop knew how to find.

In a million years, he wouldn't have paired his sister with a male like Bishop Eleazar King, especially after the abuse she suffered at Silus's hand, but God had chosen well for her. For all the bishop's older ways, he seemed eager to please his sister's young heart.

Larissa glanced at the mortal sleeping on the bed. Cain's nose wrinkled as Destiny breathed out an unladylike snore.

"What do you plan to do with her?"

He sighed. "I don't know. She's sick or something. I took a lot of her blood, probably more than I should have. She's impossible to control."

"Really?"

"Yes. I've no idea how she does it, but every time I push into her mind, she somehow kicks me out. I can't compel her."

"Then how did you feed?"

"She was delirious with fever. I took what I needed while she slept, careful never to take too much."

"You're sure she didn't know?"

"I can only hope. Like I said, I can't compel her. It's like she has me blocked."

"It's not as uncommon as you may think. I can block Eleazar, and he's much older than I am."

"Honestly?" That surprised him, being that Eleazar had incredible power. "Well, nevertheless, you're immortal. She's nothing but a weak little human."

"She's pretty."

"She's a nuisance. As soon as she's awake and well, her mind needs purifying. That's the only reason I brought her here. One of The Elders will have to attempt it. After that, I care not what becomes of her."

Larissa gave him a skeptical glance. "Are you sure?"

"Trust me, the sooner I'm rid of her the better." If anyone realized Destiny had been the one to shoot him, thereby causing Annalise such trauma and pain, there would be no protecting her. "She's someone else's problem, not mine."

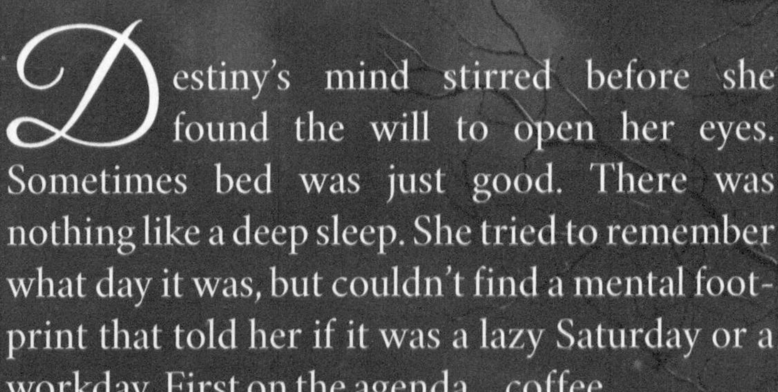

CHAPTER 10

Destiny's mind stirred before she found the will to open her eyes. Sometimes bed was just good. There was nothing like a deep sleep. She tried to remember what day it was, but couldn't find a mental footprint that told her if it was a lazy Saturday or a workday. First on the agenda...coffee.

Languidly extending her legs under the covers, she groaned happily then stiffened mid-stretch. Her eyes opened wide and she stilled. *Not her bed.*

Jackknifing upright, she gasped and gathered the blankets to her chest. Boobs everywhere! Where the fuck were her clothes? Where the hell was she?

Her heart hammered wildly. Unfamiliar pale mint-colored walls surrounded her, accented by antique furniture. A pitcher sat within a porcelain bowl on the plain bureau. The large rustic bed looked hand crafted, as did the quilt covering her naked body.

Seriously, where were her clothes?

Wrapping the quilt around her like a toga, she slipped off the bed and went to the window. "What the hell…"

Beyond the plain green curtain, a cool draft seeped through the old marble glass of a paned window. Fields of brown and green shaped patchwork strips of land over the rolling hills as far as the eye could see. No sign of familiar civilization anywhere—just colonial style homes with tall chimneys and split rail fences and barns.

The trotting footfalls of a nearby horse had her searching for roads, but only a few dirt paths wove through the land. No pavement. No cars. No people.

Last she recalled, she was being forced to hike through the freezing woods for miles. Her hand went to her back, but she couldn't reach or see where she'd been injured. She searched the room for a mirror, but didn't find one. Her back actually felt better. How was that possible?

She remembered stumbling through the woods and fighting with that jerk—where was he?

"Oh, my God?" She looked at the wood paneled door, her fingers covering her mouth.

Did he dump her here? Abandon her? Was this his house? It didn't look like a house a guy his age would own. Maybe they were at a primitive old Airbnb.

Unsure if she was safe, panic set in. She once again searched for her clothes. Sliding open the dresser drawers, she found several men's shirts and plain black pants. "Jeeze, starch much?"

The stiff cotton fabric smelled of hard work and outdoors. The pants were too long for her short legs and too tight for her thick waist line, but she could probably make one of the shirts work.

She shook out a cream shirt and frowned at the strange way the buttons were hidden. Glancing back at the closed door, she dropped the quilt and quickly shouldered on the shirt. Luckily, it hung below her hips, but it was ridiculously tight over her chest. Still, it was better than nothing.

Climbing back onto the bed, she covered her legs with the blanket and waited. Why couldn't she remember getting here? She examined the quilt covering her lap. Such intricate needlework could only be handmade. A serial killer wouldn't put that much work into a blanket, would he? Maybe a nice, old grandmother lived there.

Should she look for someone? Underwear would have been helpful.

The door opened and Destiny tensed, pressing her back into the headboard. A woman in a bonnet appeared and paused. "You're awake."

The beautiful young woman, garbed in a loose-fitting black dress, entered the room. Was she a nun? Was this a convent? The woman smiled, transforming her already pretty face into something stunning as she carried a tray to the dresser.

"I brought you some chicken broth."

Parched and hungry beyond measure, she silently watched the woman set the tray aside. She laid a cloth napkin over Destiny's lap and then brought the soup to the bed.

"You must be hungry. I didn't want to make anything too heavy after all you've been through." She handed her the ceramic bowl. "Careful, it's hot."

Destiny accepted the warm offering and stared at the woman. "Who are you?"

"You may call me Sister Larissa."

Sister. So, she was a nun. "Thank you, sister."

"Take a sip."

She watched the nun as she brought the bowl to her lips, not expecting the broth to be so flavorful, she hummed with appreciation. "It's good."

Sister Larissa's smile widened. "Your clothing was a mess, so I washed it. I tried to mend your shirt, but I'm afraid there was no fixing it." She touched the cuff of the shirt Destiny stole. "But I see you found something."

"Is that okay?"

"Of course. If there's anything you need, just ask. You're our guest."

This nun was way nicer than the nuns that taught at her grade school. "Thank you."

Despite her hunger, her empty stomach could only handle so much broth. When she had enough, Sister Larissa carried it back to the tray and poured her a glass of water from the pitcher.

The room was cold with exposed hard-wood floors, aside for one braided mat, yet the nun's feet were bare. She didn't look like a traditional nun. Instead of a habit she wore a bonnet. Maybe she was in that casual stage Julie Andrews was in just before she was shipped off to the Von Trapps—an apprentice nun.

She moved a wooden chair closer to the bed and sat. "How did you meet Cain?"

Destiny's focus jerked from the nun's bare feet to her face. "Cain?"

"The male who rescued you." She smiled fondly.

Was it a rescue or a form of kidnapping? Her memories jumbled. "Where is he?"

"He'll be back soon."

She didn't seem afraid of Cain, so Destiny supposed he wasn't a threat. "Is there a phone I can use?"

The nun tilted her head, but the rapid tempo of approaching horse hooves distracted her. She glanced toward the window then adjusted the quilt over Destiny's legs. "We have company."

The clip-clop halted and a door opened and closed, followed by heavy footfalls. Sister Larissa stood just as the door opened and a tall, black haired man with onyx eyes ducked into the room.

Destiny shrank into the pillows. There were just certain people who were imposing without speaking a single word.

"This is Bishop King," Sister Larissa introduced.

The man took a menacing step toward the bed and scowled down at Destiny with clear disapproval. "What do they call you?"

"Destiny...Santos."

His lips pressed into a firm line. "Where is Cain?"

"Visiting Cybil. He was anxious to get out this morning,"

Who was Cybil?

The bishop's jaw tightened. "He can't keep picking up strays, especially when he has a habit of abandoning his responsibilities and saddling others with the chore."

Was he calling her a stray? "Um..."

"Hush."

Destiny's mouth snapped shut. She wasn't the sort to obediently keep quiet for domineering men, but she suddenly lost the will to speak. She frowned as the bishop drew the nun aside and whispered something into her ear. The nun smiled, her expression softening and her lashes lowering as his large hands curled around her petite waist.

Destiny frowned. What sort of convent was this? The possessive way he touched Sister Larissa was completely inappropriate and unmistakably intimate. He nuzzled her ear and she laughed softly, his possessive hands traveling higher up her ribs as he held her with absolute entitlement.

It was so very wrong, but Destiny couldn't look away. No one had ever touched her like that or looked at her with such unashamed hunger. They weren't even trying to hide it. Talk about sexual corruption. But Sister Larissa seemed all for the bishop's attention.

Did they even care that Destiny was there?

When the bishop spoke again, he used a different language. It sounded German, but she wasn't sure. Sister Larissa blushed, staring up at him with crystalline eyes, and responded in the German tongue. Both appeared completely fluent and speaking as if aware Destiny was there, but believing the language barrier gave them ample privacy, which she supposed it did.

He took her hand and tugged her toward the door. Only then did the nun look back. In a jumble of German words, Destiny caught her name.

The bishop scowled and set his intimidating stare on Destiny. "You will not move from that bed until I grant you permission."

They left the room. *Hey!* She meant to call after them, but no words came out when she tried to speak.

She wanted to get off the bed and find a phone, but a mixture of fear and discomfort held her in place on the mattress. She just sat there, wanting to call for help but inexplicably silent and still. She wasn't sure if she wanted to get off the bed now or not. She couldn't seem to make a single decision in that moment so she waited until the bishop returned and told her what to do next—no matter how little sense that made.

CHAPTER 11

The kitchen still smelled of breakfast meats and cinnamon when Cain entered the house with Cybil in tow, her small hand entwined around his much larger one. He had not been included in the breakfast meal that morning, or much else since returning home last night.

As soon as Gracie saw him, she rolled her eyes. "You can't keep disappearing, Cain. I don't have time to watch your mortal." Shifting her attention to Cybil, she smiled. "Good morning, sunshine. I was just about to come get you for our lesson."

Cybil's hand tightened on Cain's, and she shouldered closer to his hip. Gracie frowned.

"What's this about?" Gracie made a

clucking sound, likely nosing around in the child's thoughts, and lowered herself to Cybil's eye level. "Don't you worry about that. Brothers and sisters sometimes disagree. That's all this is, a disagreement. Isn't that right, Cain?"

Cain looked down at Cybil. She must have picked up on the tension between him and his siblings. How sweet of her to be so protective of him.

"That's right." He shot Gracie a snide glance and looked back at Cybil. "Just like Dane sometimes bothers you, Gracie can also be extremely annoying."

Cybil silently laughed with her eyes. She understood perfectly.

Gracie pursed her lips and stood. "I'm sure that's what it is. Why don't you go check on your ward. Larissa's been watching over her all morning. Come along, Cybil. We have a lot of work to cover today."

Cain gave Gracie a suspicious look. "What kind of work?"

"I found a book at the shop in town on American Sign Language . I'm teaching Cybil, so that she can communicate."

"She isn't deaf, Gracie."

"I'm aware," she said with superiority as

she pulled out a chair from the table for Cybil to sit. "She's mute."

Cain scowled, disliking either label. Cybil could talk, and she would when she was ready. She'd already suffered enough. She shouldn't have to also suffer through Gracie's tedious lessons. She should be free to play and explore the farm.

"Stop it, Cain," Gracie said with a warning glance that reminded him to guard his thoughts. "Cybil needs to go to school with the other children, and she can't do so if she has no way of communicating."

"Who says? She communicates just fine."

Rather than answer him, his sister collected a book from the shelf and set it on the table for Cybil. Reluctantly, the child took a seat.

Gracie occupied the seat across from her. "Now, let's begin with the alphabet."

Cybil mimicked Gracie's hand movements as she recited the letters. Intrigued, Cain took the other seat at the table.

"Very good," Gracie praised, motioning with her fingers from her chin down to her open palm. Her hands moved quickly as she spoke, "Now, can you tell me what month we're in?"

Cybil held up her left hand, made a circle with her right thumb and index finger, keeping the other fingers straight, and glided it up and over her left palm.

"Good," Gracie signed again and then repeated the motion Cybil had gestured. "That's right, it's February."

Cain slid the book in front of him. "How long has she been practicing this?"

"For a few weeks. She's very good at it. It's quite easy. Watch." She turned to Cybil and signed as she spoke. "Talk to Cain so he can learn. Tell him whatever you want."

Cybil tapped her chin for a moment, and then her hands began moving rapidly. Cain had no idea what she was saying. He laughed nervously and looked at Gracie for help.

His sister smiled. "I think he needs you to go a little slower."

Cybil's hands moved as if she were conducting an orchestra. Her fingers twisted with ease and her expression was tense as she focused on making him understand. At one point, she screwed her lips to the side and looked at Gracie.

His sister read the child's mind and then said, "Oh, like this." Gracie held up her hand, fanning her fingers wide and then folded down her middle and ring finger. Cybil faced him and repeated the gesture.

"What did she say?"

Gracie blinked, as if surprised by Cybil's declaration. She looked at Cain and signed through the monologue as she spoke. "She said she doesn't want you to leave again. She missed you and has bad dreams when you're gone. She asked, why don't you stay here if this is home?"

He had followed the signs closely, but Gracie left something out. "And what does this mean?" He held up his palm and folded down his middle and ring finger, leaving his index finger and pinkie extended.

Gracie hesitated. "It means 'I love you.'"

Cain's heart constricted. He looked back at Cybil and held up his hand, two fingers folded down. "I love you, too, munchkin."

And there was the reason he always felt lighter in her presence. No matter how complicated Cybil's situation was, she was easy to enjoy. He liked that she was sweet and sarcastic in her own silent way. Although she was just a kid, she had an old soul and a quick wit. She trusted Cain even when most of his relatives did not.

He believed the farm would be a good

home for her, a safe place where she could explore and grow. A place where she could heal at her own pace, but what did he know? He wasn't an expert on children and he could hardly manage his own life let alone anyone else's.

"Are you happy here?" he asked, using his fingers to point to his smile.

Gracie chuckled and showed him how to sign happy. He was way off.

Cybil signed and Gracie translated. "She said she's happy when you're here."

He affectionately brushed a hand over her bonnet. "I'm staying for a while."

When she smiled, his heart pinched. At least one person wasn't angry with him.

He sat quietly through the rest of her lesson and tried to pick up as many expressions as possible. Cybil was quite fluent, as was his sister. When the lesson was over, Cybil left to return to his grandparents' house, and Gracie moved on to preparing food for lunch and supper.

"Will you be eating with us, Cain?"

He looked up from the sign language book. "Yes. Can I borrow this?"

For the first time since he'd arrived, his sister smiled at him. "I think that would be nice." Then she frowned. "I can't fathom why that child adores you so. You barely spent any time with her."

"Some people do like me, Gracie."

She shook her head. "There has to be more to it. She's suffered a trauma. She probably bonded with you as some sort of coping mechanism."

"Thanks a lot." He stood, not wanting to risk further insult.

"You should know, sometimes I find her sleeping in your bed. For whatever reason, she feels safe around you, Cain. Try not to spoil that."

Her words offended him, and he almost said something snide in response, but the truth was, he could very easily ruin Cybil's trust. He didn't want to but also never wanted to betray his brother, hurt Anna, or disappoint his family. "I'll do my best."

Before she could make another hurtful comment, he took the book to his room so he could check on the headache that waited there. He really didn't want to deal with Destiny, but it wasn't fair to keep dumping her on his sisters.

CHAPTER 12

"I hope you remembered your graphing calculators, because you're going to want them for this next problem. If we're trying to find the solution set for a system of equations, to solve the equation, we have to substitute five x plus y, expanding to fully represent the intersection of these two points…"

Juniper rolled her pencil back and forth over the surface of her desk as Mr. Weckle droned on and on about mathematical bullshit she'd never actually use in real life. The only thing more irritating than sitting through algebra II was knowing she'd have to sit through it all over again the following July in summer school.

Everyone pulled out their calculators. Juniper silently cursed. Hers was at home on her dresser.

Trent, sitting in the next aisle over and wearing a splint around two of his fingers, clumsily rummaged through his backpack. Their gazes crossed and she smiled, lifting her hand in a subtle wave.

He saw the gesture but only turned away. He hadn't answered any of her texts since dropping her off last night after the incident in the woods. He could have at least had the decency to dump her if he was that angry. Anything would have been better than this awkward stage of not knowing what was going on with them.

"Are you getting this, Juniper?" Mr. Weckle asked and several classmates stared at her.

Nothing like being singled out. Her jaw locked and she picked up her pencil, doodling a flower rather than copying the equation into her notebook.

"Where's your calculator?"

She shut her eyes for a brief moment, preparing for the lecture that would undoubtedly come. "I forgot it at home."

"Unprepared again." Mr. Weckle shook his

head. "See, folks, this is exactly what's going to make or break you when it comes time for those college applications. How are you going to get to the next step if you can't remember the tools needed to meet the basic requirements at this stage of the game?"

Her fist tightened around the pencil, but Mr. Weckle wasn't finished.

"What month are we in?"

"February," the class mumbled.

"Almost March. We've been at this for seven months and some of you still don't have it together." The longer he spoke the further and further away his voice carried.

Her fingers rubbed over the wood of the pencil, creating friction as her blood slowly boiled. Why did teachers feel the need to pick a sacrificial lamb? Why couldn't they just deduct the damn points or whatever and be done with it? They weren't happy until they completely humiliated a student for something as stupid as forgetting their school supplies.

"Now, the whole class will have to wait for Juniper and anyone else who forgot their calculators to solve the equation the long way. And that's not going to help you on the SATs, people. How many times can I say it? Technology is your friend."

The pencil snapped and, with that subtle crack, Mr. Weckle doubled over and grunted, his tirade cut short mid-sentence. The class erupted with noise as students angled forward in their desks and gasped.

"Dude," Laurence, a basketball player sitting in the front row, hollered, "Look at your arm!"

Students yelled as Mr. Weckle cradled his forearm. Juniper's eyes widened at the unnatural angle of the bone. Chaos erupted as some students rushed to the front of the class and others started talking all at once. Mr. Weckle rushed out of the room, giving no instruction as to what they were supposed to do next.

Trent looked back at her, his mouth tight and his eyes suspicious. She scowled at the clear accusation in his stare. Then his gaze dropped to the surface of her desk where her broken pencil lay split in two. Beside the flower she'd doodled was the bold letters A R M.

Juniper slammed her notebook shut and gathered her things, quickly exiting the classroom. She didn't stop to catch her breath until she was outside on the path, her back pressed into the trunk of an oak tree.

"What the fuck?" she whispered. Could she have done that?

Her heart pounded and she felt sick to her stomach. She compulsively swallowed, the memory of Mr. Weckle's broken arm making her want to vomit. She disliked algebra and thought he could be a dick, but she never meant to hurt anyone.

*You didn't do it...*a voice in her head demanded.

She couldn't have. There was no way.

Too freaked out to return to school, she hoisted her bag over her shoulder and walked toward the tow path of the canal that led home. The cold wind did nothing to settle her nerves, and by the time she reached the foot-bridge, she was completely disturbed and ready to confess all.

She crossed the bridge and—"Holy fuck!" Juniper jumped back, her heart lodging in her throat as a man emerged from the shelter of the trees.

"Did I frighten you, child?"

She instantly recognized his plain clothing and the black hat. It was the guy who visited the store a few days ago. The...

Even her mind rejected the possibility and refused to accept such reality. No way was this guy a vampire. He looked straight up hokey with his old-fashioned boots and simple black jacket.

"I recognize you," he said, before she could confess the same. "From Mabel's store. You were minding the register."

She didn't find him frightening. He honestly appeared so unthreatening she didn't know what her aunt was afraid of. He looked like a guy who might run a fruit stand on some back country road or have his picture taken for a canister of Quaker Oats. "Yeah, it's my aunt's store."

He cocked his head. "So, you're Mabel Temperance's niece?"

"Yeah, and she's expecting me, so I better go." She side-stepped him on the path and walked briskly toward the store. School still wasn't over and she'd have to come up with some explanation for skipping last period, but there was no way she was hanging out on a vacant trail with Cotton Eyed Dracula or whoever this guy was.

He kept pace with her. "If you're her niece, that would make Venus your mother?"

Thrown that he knew her other aunt's

name, she frowned and walked faster. "Um, no. Venus is my other aunt."

"Your aunt. So that would make you the daughter of—"

"Look, dude, I don't know what your deal is, but I'm not Ancestry dot com, and I don't share my personal business with strangers, so how about you go back to your little troll bridge in the woods and leave me the fuck alone?"

He drew back, a look of such offense on his face she almost took pity on him. "I apologize if I've made you uncomfortable."

Okay, maybe she overreacted. "Just…back off."

He held up his hands in a peaceful gesture. She stepped around him, then turned and continued walking on her way. It would help if someone else showed up. Even a dog walker or an eighty-pound jogger would be a comfort at this point.

That guy was just a creep. *Vampire my ass,* she thought, shifting the weight of her backpack and—

A scream screeched out of her as his hand covered her mouth and gripped her throat without warning. He lifted her booted feet clear off the ground and she kicked wildly, her hands grasping his arm so he didn't choke her.

"Silence."

Panic welled in her chest, breath after breath, until her lungs were painfully full. She couldn't scream, couldn't breathe. Tears of panic made it hard to see as the tree line blurred.

"I want you to convince your aunts to help me. Have them meet me here, tomorrow night at midnight, with whatever they need to make my problem go away. If they're not here, their little secret won't stay safe much longer."

Juniper kicked her legs and threw her elbow back, hitting him hard enough in the ribs that he dropped her to the ground. She landed on her hands and knees, coughing and gasping, as she stared up at him, no longer finding him unthreatening.

He glared at her with elongated pupils and distended fangs.

"What the hell are you?" she rasped.

"Tell them. Tell them I know what they're hiding, and now," a trickle of blood slid down his finger and he licked it clean, "I can track your coven anywhere."

Juniper's hand jumped to her throat and

she felt the burn of a fresh cut. Red smeared her palm. The sick fuck was licking her blood. "What the hell?"

"I can find you. Anywhere you go, I can follow. Tell them that. Tell them I said tomorrow at midnight, or there will be consequences."

Heart hammering, she scrambled to her feet and ran as fast as she could toward home.

CHAPTER 13

Cain entered his room and paused at the threshold, surprised to find Destiny awake. "You look better."

Her brow furrowed, but she didn't say a word. For a girl who always seemed to get the last comment, he found her silence odd.

Setting his hat on a peg, he glanced at the tray on the dresser. "I see you ate." When she remained silent, he looked over his shoulder and frowned. "And helped yourself to my clothes."

Glancing down at her body, her frown deepened. Why was she being so quiet, and why did the sight of her in his shirt bother him so much? Rumpled and strangely tempting, unlike Hope, Destiny had a full figure with thick thighs and round hips, and breasts that he should not be admiring.

Irritated by her appearance, he shifted to antagonistic. "Problem?" This time when she didn't answer, he frowned. "Where's Larissa?"

Destiny pointed toward the door and made several hand gestures that, in comparison to Cybil's tidy sign language, looked like sloppy charades.

"For the love of God, use words."

She pointed to her full lips and swept her hands apart in a universal signal for *no*.

Cain cocked his head. "You can't talk?"

She nodded, her frown looking more angry than confused at this point. She pointed to the door and returned to her wild gestures.

He shook his head. "I'm never going to understand what you're trying to say." He opened the door and yelled for his sister. "Larissa!"

She looked up at him with relief, and it was his turn to frown. What changed that he was suddenly her ally?

The door pushed open and the bishop, rather than his sister, appeared. Destiny shrank back on the bed.

"Oh, you two met." That explained a lot. Cain glanced at the bishop, his newest brother-by-law. "Did you do this?"

"I found her questions tedious." He waved a hand at Destiny. "You may speak."

"What the fucking fuck?" she blurted.

Eleazar lifted a brow. "A hopelessly unrefined species, the English."

"I want to get out of here! I need a phone. Now."

The bishop ignored her. "This is becoming a habit, Cain. If you keep bringing home strays, I'll have no choice but to rescind your welcome. You know the rules."

"I'm not some dog he picked up off the street! I'm a human being with rights!" Destiny rose to her knees, but didn't get off the bed. "Hello? Is anyone listening to me?"

"I didn't bring her here to stay. I can't compel her."

Eleazar frowned. "Perhaps because you were injured?"

"I tried again this morning while she was sleeping. She's completely blocked to me."

"Hey, bozos! Do one of you want to point me toward my clothes so I can get the hell out of this *Little House on the Prairie* nightmare?"

Cain continued to ignore her. "You had no issues?"

"None."

The bishop was much older than Cain. That might have been why he could get into Destiny's mind. Cain tried again, only to draw back in defeat. "I don't get it."

Destiny scoffed. "I don't get why you're ignoring me to talk to that pervy bishop."

Cain arched a brow, swallowing back a laugh. Very few were able to insult the bishop without consequence. Destiny's defiance was a mixture of courage and audacity he found utterly amusing.

She glared at the bishop and accused, "FYI, he's banging the nun."

At that, Cain's laughter escaped, both amused and impressed by her feisty accusation, he looked at Eleazar. "Care to explain that?"

Destiny pointed at the bishop. "He was groping the nun. I saw it."

Cain's mouth curved with interest as he cocked his head. "And who is the nun in this scenario?"

"Sister Larissa."

He smothered another laugh with his hand. "Oh my, we had better alert The Elders." He glanced back at Eleazar who was scowling at Destiny with a mixture of disdain and pity.

Larissa walked into the room, rumpled at just the right moment. "Is everything all right?"

"Ah, there's our little nun, now," Cain greeted.

His sister frowned. "Pardon?"

"Go ahead, Destiny, tell her what you told us." When she remained silent, he teased, "Bishop got your tongue?"

She scoffed and flushed. "I just want to get out of here, you ass-hat."

Larissa stepped further into the room, taking sympathy on the mortal. "Whatever fun you two are having, that's enough. Your clothes aren't dry yet, but I'm sure I can find something for you to borrow. Why don't you come with me?"

Destiny moved to follow Larissa, then hesitated. Cain realized the bishop had done more than silence the mortal. After all the trouble she caused, he couldn't resist tormenting her. "What's wrong?"

"I…" She hovered by the edge of the bed, a look of confusion on her face.

Cain smirked. "Go with Larissa, Destiny."

She scowled at him. "I am. I'm just getting off the bed."

He waited a few seconds but she made no progress. "*Can* you get off the bed?"

"Of course, I can." She scooted closer to the edge, her legs dangling as she stared at the floor as if it were lava.

He crossed his arms. "Show me."

"No."

"Why not?"

"I … I don't want to get off the bed."

"I thought you wanted to leave."

She huffed in frustration. "What the hell is going on?"

Cain laughed and Larissa tsked. "Stop toying with her. Eleazar, fix this right now."

The bishop waved a hand and Destiny lost her balance and clamored to the floor. As she scrambled to stand up, Cain caught a glimpse of her juicy hips, round bottom, and thick thighs.

Her face darkened with fury and embarrassment. "Look, I don't know what you gave me or what games you're playing, but I need to get to a phone. I need to call my brother and go home."

Cain looked at the bishop. "Perhaps it was nicer when she was silent."

Destiny ripped the book out of Cain's hand and threw it at his chest. "Are you listening to me? I. Want. To. Leave."

"Enough!" Eleazar snapped. "I want her gone as well. She is not to return. Do we have an understanding, Cain?"

"No problem. I just need some assistance *correcting* the facts for her and she can be on her way. She's a reporter for the English news, and we don't want her spreading rumors about us or what she might have seen in the woods."

"I'll handle her." The bishop turned toward the mortal.

Destiny's anger shifted to fear. "Wait!" She backed into the corner and held out her hands. A stream of foreign words spilled from her lips before she switched back to a heavily accented English. "I just want to go home! I don't want any trouble! You can't keep me here! I have rights! Don't do this—"

"Stop talking." The moment the command left Eleazar's mouth she fell silent.

She tried to make a sound, but failed and her hysteria doubled. Her dark brown eyes welled with tears of panic and frustration as she looked to Cain, her face a desperate plea that he intervene.

"Not very nice, bishop," Cain reprimanded, knowing there were ways to calm mortals when compelling them.

Eleazar pinched the bridge of his nose. "I find the English utterly exhausting."

"You could at least relax her nervous system."

Destiny snatched the book off the floor and flipped rapidly through the pages. She slammed it down and formed a half circle with her right hand and tapped it over her heart. They all frowned at her.

"What is she doing?" Larissa asked.

Cain leaned forward and turned the book then looked back at Destiny. "She wants us to call the police." He sighed and gave her back the book and then in a raised voice said, "No police."

"Let the poor woman speak, Eleazar. You're being cruel. The both of you."

The bishop once again gave into his wife, restoring Destiny's voice, and they all flinched at the shrill screeching of threats that followed.

"You're all crazy! What the fuck is happening? How are you doing that? Don't come near me! *Help!* Somebody, help me!" Frantic, she ran toward the door. "Let me out of here!"

The bishop caught her shoulder with a gentle hand and said in a soothing voice, "*Calma mulher.*"

Destiny stilled, her frenzy subdued as her eyes glazed with an unfocused stare.

"It will be more merciful my way, my lioness. Trust me." The bishop turned Destiny's shoulders so she faced Cain. "She thinks in Portuguese. I suspect that's why you can't compel her. But she is controllable, I assure you. See how docile she is now?"

Despite obedience being his goal, Cain didn't like seeing Destiny's eyes so vacant. He didn't like knowing the bishop, or any immortal who spoke her native language, could have such control over her. He waved a hand in front of her face. "She's completely nonresponsive. Is that necessary?"

"At this point, the simplest solution is necessary." Eleazar looked into her eyes and spoke softly.

"*Quando você said daqui, você vai esquecer o que viu. Vai esquecer as pessaos e essa. Você vai esquecer o que viu na Floresta.*"

Cain took a protective step forward, but Larissa caught his arm. Without knowing what the bishop said, he found it difficult to trust him. He owed Destiny nothing, but he'd witnessed her fear and she'd suffered enough in the woods. He didn't want to see her unnecessarily punished.

The bishop stepped back. "She will obey now."

Cain scowled. "What did you say to her?"

"I told her you were a man of the law and you were going to escort her home. Come dawn, she will have no memory of you or this place. She will only recall a nasty fall in the woods and believe that a doctor tended her wounds. I've also left an impulse to avoid the woods."

"How am I supposed to lead her home when I don't know where she lives?"

"I was able to extract her address with a few other details."

Cain didn't like the idea of leaving her in this condition for more than a few minutes. "Release her. I can get her to calm down and follow me without taking away her free will."

"You can't, and I won't. My decision is not up for debate, Cain. Her address wasn't the only memory I saw. I know what happened in the woods. This mortal is not a friend of ours."

And now they were even. Eleazar despised

that Cain knew the secret location where he buried Larissa's abusive ex-husband alive. But the bishop now knew that Destiny shot Cain in the heart, thereby endangering the life of Annalise and the baby. Adam would be within his rights to seek justice if he found out, and Cain couldn't let that happen. If he wanted to protect Destiny, such information must remain a secret. He had no choice but to do as The Elder commanded.

"How long do I have?"

"Until dawn."

He glanced at Destiny. She stood in a waking coma, no light in her flat brown eyes and no animation to her pretty face. "She'll be fine after that? Back to normal?" She was annoying, but she had a right to be however she wanted. He worried such overwhelming control of her mind might have lingering effects.

"She'll be just as she was."

"She needs clothes."

Eleazar glanced at his wife. "Larissa, find her something appropriate to wear." She left the room to find her clothing and the bishop looked at him. "Put your attraction aside for this one, Cain."

He drew back. "There is no attraction."

Eleazar cocked a dark brow. "The subconscious is often more honest than our words. Your thoughts are unguarded around her, and that's dangerous. For the sake of your family, take closer care of yourself."

CHAPTER 14

$\mathcal{A}$ cold tingle raced up Cybil's neck as her breath clouded in vapor in front of her. All familiar surroundings faded away, replaced with dark, endless shadows.

It was always the same place, but each time was a little different. She squeezed her eyes shut and tried to slow her breathing, not wanting him to hear her. A low purr crept closer, and she held her breath. She could sense the dripping saliva on his fangs and feel the weight of his stare. Without ever really looking at him, she knew every detail from the jagged edges of his claws to the silver glint hidden in his blood-red eyes.

When they were here, she recognized him more than she recognized herself. Her body was not her *own here. She was older, different, but still a scared little girl inside.*

She trembled, huddled on the ground with her arms wrapped protectively around her knees. A potent discomfort filled her belly as he moved closer. She wasn't sure what held him back when it was clear he wanted to consume her. His hunger beat at her, and she whimpered with fear.

Her life was his decision. She had no power here. But he never touched her. It was as if he recognized something delicate and innocent inside of her that needed to mature, something he craved so deeply she hoped she'd never grow up. He saw her fragility and protected her, even when the enemy she needed protecting from was himself.

She sucked in a breath, and he stilled. She wiped her eyes, silently praying he'd go away. He didn't intentionally scare her but sensed she feared him. He didn't like her fear. It angered him, which only made her more afraid. But deep down, no matter how unsafe she felt, she believed he wouldn't hurt her. He always placed her safety above his own.

He only came to her at night, in the dark, beneath a moonless sky. She looked different here. Her baby-fine hair was fuller and her body thicker. She sometimes caught glimpses of flesh, blood, teeth, entwined limbs, and writhing bodies entangled in ways she didn't understand. Ugly flashes she didn't want to see. And those glowing eyes...

Her breath came fast when the images wouldn't stop. They weren't spontaneous chaos, they were prophetic visions of a far-off, inevitable future she dreaded.

He hushed her, wanting to come closer, but she cowered further away. She wasn't ready. Not yet. His impatient growl echoed in her ears, but he backed off all the same.

He never spoke to her, but she heard his voice in her mind. "When you recognize what I am to you, you will say my name..."

Cybil bolted upright, heart pounding as she awoke, tucked safely in her bed. Shoving away the blankets, she looked down at her small hands and knobby knees, finding great comfort in her familiar childish build.

She wanted to scream as recollections bombarded her, even if just to whisper that it was only a dream, but worry kept her silent. She would not utter a sound for fear of accidentally speaking his name.

Curling into her body, she burrowed under the covers and stared at the plain walls. There was no distraction from her thoughts, and she couldn't stop thinking about her nightmare.

Her labored breath disrupted the silent house as her stare darted to every corner of the dark bedroom, tears slowly gathering along the curve of her nose.

She was alone. It was only a dream. Another nightmare. So why didn't she feel safe? She felt like he could still reach her.

She shut her eyes and tried to imagine anything else. The farm animals. The barn kittens. The cake she helped Gracie make that evening. Cain's face filled her mind, and she smiled as she wept, remembering his deep laugh and the way he lifted her through the air the day he returned.

Dane used to play with her like that, but hadn't since their mom died.

She shoved the thought away. Nothing had been the same since that night in the woods, and she wished she could go back. At the same time, she wanted to forget the past, but it kept haunting her.

Unable to fall back to sleep, she wiped her nose on the sleeve of her nightgown and slipped out of bed. Her bare feet touched the cool floor then she quietly padded into the hall, pausing at Dane's room. One bony foot poked out from the covers and his mouth was open as he snored.

She went to the kitchen where the wood stove still burned, and she slid her feet into her loose boots, not bothering to tie the laces. Her black cloak hung from a low peg by the door and she wrapped the heavy wool over her shoulders. Silently, she unlatched the front door and raced down the walk.

Her dreams wouldn't follow her to Cain's room. For some reason, she always felt safe there, safer knowing he was home again.

Rushing through the garden gate, she crept onto the dark porch and climbed through the unlocked kitchen window. Gracie had moved a table below the window after the night Cybil accidentally fell and woke the whole house up.

Once inside, she shut the window and took off her shoes. Tiptoeing down the hall, she went to his room and quietly opened the door. The hinges creaked and she paused, surprised a fire was lit in the hearth. Brow furrowed, she looked at the empty bed. No Cain.

Her jaw clenched in anger, and her eyes burned with tears of disappointment. Where was he? Why wasn't he here like he promised he would be?

She couldn't accept that he left the farm again, especially without a goodbye, so she crawled onto the bed and waited. But the longer she sat alone with her arms wrapped tightly around her knees, the more it became clear he wasn't coming back.

His betrayal sliced deep, over and over again until she could hardly feel the ache anymore. She didn't know why she drew so much comfort from his nearness, she only knew that in his presence she felt safe. How foolish, when his abandonment hurt most of all.

CHAPTER 15

*D*estiny's shoulders propelled off the bed as her body flung upward with a startled gasp. Air filled her lungs as if she were breaking through the icy surface of a lake she'd been drowning under for days. The sudden shock of waking so abruptly left her shaken. Heart punching hard, her chest vibrated with inexplicable panic.

Home. She was home.

Disoriented, she searched her bedroom for anything that might have startled her awake. Brain still foggy, she wasn't sure if she'd had a nightmare or some outside source woke her so brusquely.

Was there a bang? Perhaps thunder? Was someone breaking in? Her panic didn't immediately subside when her brain recognized she was safe and everything looked normal.

Blowing out a breath, she reached for her phone but came up short. Where was it? She glanced at the floor, thinking it might have fallen off the nightstand, saw nothing but a dirty sock and a few novels she'd been trudging through.

A golden haze backlit the blinds, but she wasn't sure if it was dawn or dusk. Grabbing the remote, she flicked on the television. 7:15 am—still morning.

"Wow." She fell back into the pillows, her heart finally slowing and her equilibrium returning. She hadn't slept that deeply in years.

Pushing her unruly curls away from her face, she stilled. *Wait...*

She looked around her bedroom again, sensing something was off. Memories teased the fringe of her mind like a thought when one suddenly forgets what they wanted to say. She was supposed to do something or be somewhere. She couldn't remember. Something about Vito.

"Shit. I need my phone." She stumbled out of bed and froze. "What in the mother of Rosemary Rogers am I wearing?"

She looked like she either escaped from a

psych ward or a Victorian novel. Gathering up the cloth nightgown, she frowned, thinking over her last insomniac shopping episode. No, she definitely wouldn't have ordered a nightgown like this no matter how sleep deprived her shopping habits tended to be. So where did it come from?

She rushed toward the door to find a phone, but stalled out again at the full-length mirror. "Holy Medusa." Her hair was in a full-blown, bride-of-Frankenstein frizz.

She shook off the distraction. "Phone."

Darting into the hall, she froze again at the sound of a toilet flushing, something that shouldn't happen when one lived alone and wasn't using the bathroom. Her back hit the wall, and she searched for a weapon. The nearest object was a metal water bottle so she lifted it like a club— "Oh, Jesus!"—Water spilled down her front. "Great," she hissed, swiping a hand down the billowy front of the hideous nightdress.

The bathroom door opened and she sucked in a breath, drawing back her water bottle club, ready to attack. A large shadow fell on the adjacent wall and Destiny swung.

"What the fuck, D?" Her brother stumbled

into the door frame, a hand holding his head where the water bottle hit.

"*Vito?* What are you doing here?"

"Looking for you. Christ, I'm seeing Tweetie birds. What the fuck did you hit me for?"

"I thought you were a burglar. Why are you in your underwear in my house?"

He wobbled to an upright position and growled at her, wrenching the metal water bottle out of her hand and flinging it down the hall. "Where the hell have you been?"

"I was…" She couldn't remember what she did last night or who she'd been with. Had she gone out? Stayed in? Ordered bad Chinese food and passed out? There had to be alcohol involved for this level of amnesia.

Startled by the blank spots occupying her mind, she looked up at her brother. He must have recognized the confusion in her eyes, because his scowl abruptly shifted to concern. "Are you okay?"

"I think so." Disoriented and oddly re-lieved by her brother's presence, she wanted to throw her arms around him but hesitated on account of the underwear. "Can you please put some clothes on."

He rolled his eyes and ducked back in the

bathroom. "You should have woken me the moment you got home."

"I've been trying to reach you for days," she said, then frowned. The words felt true, but she had no recollection that fit the conviction.

"You've got a lot of nerve. I had the cops searching for you. I've been going crazy. I thought you were dead!"

"What?" *Cops?*

Her brows drew tight as she had the strangest impulse to form her hand into a C shape and place it over her heart. She shook it off.

"Yeah. You've been MIA for days," he said from behind the bathroom door.

"I was…here." Her frown deepened, a sharp wave of nausea churning her stomach. No, she wasn't there. She'd been…

I had a nasty fall. The thought surfaced with zero memory, but her certainty felt as solid as plastic. Synthetic and unlikely to biodegrade with time. Planted like pollution among the soft gray matter of her mind.

Vito emerged from the bathroom in a pair of jeans and a wrinkled Phillies T-shirt. "D, I've been here for days. The least you could do is be honest with me."

Moving into the living room, she tripped over a pizza box on the floor. "What the…"

Papers were everywhere. News articles pinned to the wall, sticky notes with masculine scribble, maps, brochures, highlighted reference books scattered across her coffee table, empty beer cans, pizza boxes, and, most frightening of all, a handgun.

"What is all this? My house is trashed."

"Me first. What happened in the woods?"

"The woods?" *Pine needles. Mud. Roots. Trees. Moss. Snow. Running. Ripping. Fear. Searing pain. Panic.* Images and emotions flashed through her mind too fast for her to analyze. She sucked in a sharp breath. "I *was* in the woods."

"No shit. You're lucky you weren't killed."

"I had a nasty fall." The words came out of her like a compulsion without memory. Yet, she was certain she had a nasty fall. Maybe she hit her head.

"How did you get home?"

She dropped onto a couch cushion. Her memory sliding through one gaping hole into another. "I don't know. I lost track of my crew and… I must have fallen and hit my head or something."

"Destiny, you were gone for days. *Days.*

You have to give me something more. Did someone find you? How did you get home?"

She'd gone back to Jim Thorpe to investigate the recent murder scenes and... Jim Thorpe was quite a commute. She'd been all alone in the woods, of that she was certain. Then she had a nasty fall. "I woke up in a convent."

He snorted. "Come again?"

She shook her head. "A convent. You know, where nuns live. A nun named Larissa took care of me, and a very nice bishop helped me get home." She pursed her lips as a bitter taste filled her mouth like a lie.

"Wait, did you just say a nun named Larissa?"

"Yeah, why?"

He shrugged. "I don't know. That's kind of a weird name for a nun."

"Who cares what the nun's name was?"

"You're right. What else do you remember?"

"She fed me soup and...I think there was a bishop."

"What convent? St. Elizabeth's?"

"No."

"St. Clare's?"

"No."

"St. Mary's?"

"No, Vito, jeeze! And why do you know the names of so many convents?"

"We do a seven deadly sins night at the club and the girls dress up like nuns. We name drinks after the local nunneries."

"You're going to hell."

"Tell me about it. If not one of them, what convent was it?"

"I don't know. I can't remember. There were pale green walls."

"That's all you got?"

Frustrated with her own shortcomings, she snapped, "Yes, that's all I got, so back off. I had a nasty fall."

"Hold up. This doesn't make any sense. First of all, how would a bunch of nuns find you in the woods? And why was a bishop at a convent? Don't they usually stick to the fancier places like the Archdiocese or the Vatican? Is there even a big church in Jim Thorpe."

"There are churches everywhere. Why are you so obsessed with the church? You should be concerned with my health. I had a nasty—"

"Fall. I know." He waved away her reminder.

She drew back. "Hey, I could have died out there."

"But you didn't. You got lost in the woods and fell down. You should be more concerned with the fact that you can't remember how you got home."

"It was a nasty fall."

"Did you break a leg or sprain anything? It couldn't have been that bad for you to be standing here perfectly fine." He looked at her suspiciously. "You better not be lying to me, D."

"It was a nasty fall!"

"All right, all right, I get it. Nasty fall." He held out his hands in a calming motion. "Did anyone at the convent notify the cops? I had an MPR out on you."

Cops. Once again, she had the urge to form her hand into a C and place it over her heart. *No police...* A male voice drifted through her mind like a shadow, but the moment the thought occurred, it was gone. Irretrievable. "Why would you put out a missing person report?"

"That's what you do when someone goes missing. I was worried sick, D."

Her head lowered, unsure why she was being difficult when he'd only acted out of concern. She should be grateful. "I'm sorry I scared you."

"Well, you're home now. Where's my crossbow?"

She scrunched her nose. "How the hell would I know where your bow and arrow is?"

"Crossbow," he corrected. "And probably because you took it."

"No, I didn't."

"Yes, you did. It was my Barnett Buck Commander Crossbow, and I'm telling you right fucking now it better be here or you're reimbursing me the five hundred I paid for it.

"Vito, why *the hell* would I take your"—using air quotes she emphasized—"crossbow?"

"I want my key back. You don't steal people's shit and leave it in the woods. And don't tell me you had a nasty fall. You shouldn't have been there in the first place!"

She didn't have time to listen to his ridiculous accusations. She probably had hundreds of notifications awaiting responses.

"Where are you going?"

"I need to find my phone in this pigsty!"

"For what?"

"Because I lost it!"

"Maybe it's with my crossbow."

"I didn't steal your stupid crossbow!" Her phone was usually attached to her hip. "Can you call it?"

A generic ring came from her bedroom, but it wasn't her typical ringtone. She followed the sound to her nightstand and pulled open the drawer. Not her phone, but her iPad. At least now she could use the Find My Phone app.

She sat on her bed and sent out a signal to locate her linked devices. The last known location of her phone wasn't too far off the hiking trail where her crew usually parked, but the battery was dead. "Great. My phone's in the woods."

"So, put in a claim with your provider and get a replacement. You're not going back there—at least not alone or unarmed."

"You're being ridiculous." Yet some part of her agreed with him, and she suffered an instant aversion to the thought of returning to the woods.

He pointed to the wall. "Open your fucking eyes, Destiny! Whatever's killing women in those woods is far from finished." He swept his arm across the mess in her living room. "I read all your clippings. I don't think it's human, and it ain't some animal."

"What are you talking about?"

"Look." He rushed over to the wall where he'd hung a map. "Here's where all the bodies were found over the last twelve months, each one suffering similar lacerations and abuse. But get this, I found records of women who were murdered in Jim Thorpe dating back all the way to the last century, each victim bearing similar markings, all basically left unsolved."

"The woods are dangerous, and good little girls should stay in safer places."

They both froze. The words shot out of her as though triggered. She had no idea what made her say something so out of character.

Vito's eyes bulged as he blinked at her in confusion. "Uh, do you fuckin' hear yourself? What the hell was that?"

Her face scrunched. "I have no idea. It just came out."

"Whatever. Look, I need you to be normal for a second, okay? See, here, on the map?" He lifted a paper with dates scribbled on it. "Here's where the first victim was found last year. Here are the next four. Nothing special, right? But then look here. There's a pattern. The ones that were sexually assaulted were all murdered in this vicinity, up by these higher altitudes. The ones that were more or less tortured and drained were done more sporadically. These two were found within two days of each other, but the autopsy estimated the time of death to be the same date and roughly the same time. There's no way that thing could have been in two places so far apart at once."

Destiny recognized bits and pieces of her own notes, now overwhelmed by her brother's. He'd taken this to a whole different level. "Did you buy red yarn to do this?"

"That's how you do it."

"Do what?"

"Track. I saw it on *Homeland*."

She laughed, picturing him making a special trip to the arts and crafts store just so he could play detective. "All right, settle down, Agent Starling. Why don't we focus your investigator skills on finding my phone."

"Enough with the fucking phone. Don't you get it? There are two killers out there."

The moment he said it, she could see it in the patterns and dates. How had they not realized that before. "Two?"

"Yes! This one is definitely male, but the ones responsible for the deaths out here..." He circled an area on the map with his finger.

"No sexual assault, just blood loss and some pretty fucked up dismemberment."

She cringed, recalling the pictures.

"Except…" Vito gripped his chin and cocked his head.

"What is it?"

"This one, the Sharon Foster chick… Her body wasn't destroyed like the others. She had blood loss, but then she was just sort of dumped according to the police report."

"The killer was interrupted. Her children found her."

His eyes widened. "Seriously? Did they see it happen?"

"The son said it was a wild animal, and the little girl wouldn't talk."

"At all?"

Destiny shook her head. "It's called selective mutism. It's a form of PTSD caused by anxiety after a trauma."

She tried to get a statement from the son after the mother's funeral, but some guy gave her a hard time. She frowned, her memory of the man who approached her wilting from her mind as if it never happened. But it had happened. She even knew his name. It was…

"What's wrong?"

"I… Nothing. I must have really whacked

my head. Did you see my log book?" She was sure she would have written down the guy's name in her notes. And she would have definitely taken a picture of him on her phone.

She unlocked her iPad and opened her photo library.

"I don't believe this is a wild animal," Vito said, sorting through crime scene photos as Destiny scrolled through her own personal shots. "Here, look at this. Natasha Price. She was one of the ones that were defiled. See that mark on her leg?"

"Yeah." She only glanced at the grotesque image, having studied each body before. Her attention went back to the screen of her iPad, her mind playing such tricks on her, she wasn't sure if there was a guy at the cemetery that day or she dreamt the whole episode up.

But it wasn't a dream. The man had a name. She just couldn't remember it at the moment.

"What does it look like?"

Destiny hated looking at the crime scene pictures, but did so for her brother's sake. "It looks like a bruise."

"Look closer. See here, these small spaces where the blood vessels are still intact?"

She stopped scrolling through the iPad

photos and gave him her full attention. Her stomach twisted, and chills raced down her arm when she saw what he was trying to point out. "It's a handprint."

"Yes!" Vito cheered, a little too detached. "Now, look at this one." He spread several photos out on the cluttered coffee table.

Destiny set down her iPad and squinted, trying to blur some of the carnage. This was one of the victims that had been tortured. The sight of what looked like claw marks made her back tingle.

"See there?" He pointed with the tip of a pencil. Another handprint. "Now, look at them side by side. What do you notice that's different?"

She swallowed. "I don't know." Her hand went to her shoulder as phantom pain knotted up her back.

"Look at the handprints. Look how this one wraps around the girl's hip and how the other barely fits around this girl's arm."

"It's smaller."

"Exactly. Like a girl's hand."

"You think this…*thing* is working with a woman?"

"Maybe several. What if it's a cult?"

"I doubt there's a secret cult hiding in the woods that's murdering women."

"I know it sounds crazy, but when I searched the public police records from Jim Thorpe, I came across a lot of missing person reports—most of them young women. Did you know there was a massacre there around the 1930's? They never caught the killer and several missing victims went unfound."

"That was almost a hundred years ago. Do you think we have a copycat killer?"

Vito shook his head and pushed all the photos off the coffee table, revealing a collection of books tossed in a messy pile, *Salem's Lot*, Bram Stoker's *Dracula*, and several by Anne Rice and other science fiction writers. "What the hell's this?"

"Vampires, Destiny. I think they're vampires."

"Okay, we're done here." She pivoted toward her bedroom. For a moment there, she thought her brother was wasting his time working as a bouncer at a strip club and should maybe look into a job in forensics, but now she just felt sad for him.

"Come on, Destiny, think about it."

"I've thought about it. Now, I'm done."

"They were all drained of blood. And

those were human handprints, not animal prints—"

"Enough, Vito! These are *real* people who lost their lives. Mothers and sisters and daughters. This isn't Twilight and we aren't living in Forks. For God's sake, show the dead a little respect."

"But what about the women who are still missing?"

"I'm done with this conversation. When I get out of the shower, I want all this crap cleaned up." She shut the door in his face before he could say one more stupid thing.

CHAPTER 16

$\mathcal{T}$he police station was a complete disaster. Vito insisted they stop by the station to close out the MPR, but Destiny should have known he wouldn't leave it at that. The experience went from slightly embarrassing to completely humiliating once her brother shared his supernatural mumbo-jumbo and vampire cult conspiracy theories.

They spoke to an officer named Odessa, who incessantly tapped the tip of his ballpoint pen on the rim of his coffee mug.

"Aren't you that weather girl?" Odessa asked, rubbing the calloused edge of his thumb along his lower lip.

Destiny winced, not wanting her professional image tainted by anything her lunatic brother said. "I'm a reporter."

"That's right. A reporter. Not exactly an investigator, though, is it?"

Her mouth firmed into a thin line.

"You see, Miss Santos, when women like you start this vigilante stuff, it usually ends up costing citizens hard earned tax dollars in the end. A lot of time and resources went into searching for you."

And yet they hadn't found her. Her eyes narrowed at his chauvinistic tone, but she pasted on a fake smile. "Like I said, I appreciate the effort."

"And we appreciate you staying out of the woods until we apprehend or put down whatever's out there."

"The woods are dangerous, and good little girls should stay in safer places." She jerked back in her chair, her mouth twisting as if she'd just bit into a lemon.

What the fuck was wrong with her? Words kept shooting out of her mouth as if she had Tourette's.

Vito's lip curled at her peculiar behavior, and she shrugged, unable to explain why she kept saying dumb shit.

"That's right," Odessa agreed. "It would be

best if you kept away from the woods." He gathered the paperwork into a manilla file. When the phone on his desk rang, he held up a finger telling them to wait and answered the call. "Odessa."

Vito shoved her arm with his and hissed. "Double your dosage and stop saying creepy crap."

She shoved him back. "Like I'm the one who sounds crazy. You're a one-man army suggesting a vampire hunting to the local police force. Don't judge me."

He stuck out his tongue mocking her like he used to when they were kids, then he made a moon-eyed expression and mimicked, "Good little girls stay out of the woods."

Oh, God. Was that what she sounded like? "Shut up, doofus."

Odessa hung up the phone. "Before you go, I'll need a statement."

She didn't have much to share. Every time she tried to explain more than her nasty fall, her head started to ache. By the time they left the station she was exhausted and wanted to go to sleep in her bed.

On their way out of the station, they passed two officers taking a smoke break on the brick steps out front. "Take care, now," one said.

"And be sure to keep on the lookout for Teen Wolf and *Nosferatu*."

The officers snickered in an exhalation of cigarette smoke. "And watch out for any unlicensed broomsticks in your travels."

She wanted to crawl under a rock and hurl one at her brother's stupid head. As soon as they got in the car, she snapped, "I told you *no* vampire talk!"

"The world needs to know!"

She hit him in the arm. "There's nothing to know, you moron! You just humiliated me!"

"Who cares?"

"I do! I'm a reporter. People talk. Your idiotic theories could erase all of my credibility."

"I think you're being a little over dramatic. I mean, come on, Destiny, you don't even have ten thousand followers on Instagram. Who's going to talk about this?"

She gaped at him. "I can't believe you just said that. At least I'm not holding doors and staring at fake tits all day!"

"Hey! Some of the dancers have very real tits."

"Oh my, God." She rubbed her temples. "Just drive."

"Where are we going, now?"

"The mall. I need a new phone."

She didn't speak to her brother the entire drive, nor did she talk to him while they waited for the pimple-faced tech assistant at the electronic store to program her new phone. As soon as the device was in her hand, she called the station to speak to her boss.

Vito had notified her crew that she hadn't come home, and they were relieved to hear she was safe and sound, but that didn't erase the fact that she'd pissed off her team before heading back into the woods.

"What were you thinking, Destiny?" her boss asked.

She winced at the censure in her supervisor's voice. "I'm really sorry, Bob. I realize now that the woods are dangerous, and good little girls should stay in safer places." She slapped a hand over her mouth. What the hell was wrong with her? Why did she keep saying that?

An awkward chuckle crossed the line. "Well, that's one way to put it. Why don't you take the week off to recuperate? It sounds like you've been through quite an ordeal and you're still a little shaken up."

"I'm fine—"

"I insist. Come back in a week, ready to report."

He framed it as personal time, but it felt more like a suspension. She could only imagine what the crew told him. Whatever. She was on salary, and she could use a vacation anyway.

"Then I'll see you in a week." Her lips hardened around the false sincerity, recognizing that she'd just been manipulated and passively penalized.

"Sure thing. Get some rest." Bob ended the call, and she threw her new phone in the back seat of the car.

"They seemed cool." Vito said, shoving a cheese doodle in his mouth.

"Just...be quiet."

He twisted in the driver's seat to face her. The cheese doodle bag crunching against the steering wheel. "Look, I know you're pissed. But maybe your boss is right and you just need a few days off."

"Just take me home." Remembering the condition of her home, she dropped her head back and groaned.

"What's wrong now?"

"My house is a pigsty."

"Forget about that." He put the car in reverse and backed out of the parking spot. "How about a drive?"

"Whatever. I don't care."

Ten minutes later, they were cruising down the Pennsylvania Turnpike.

Vito's phone was hooked up to the Bluetooth, and his playlists consisted of strip club music and heavy metal. Neither were helping her mood.

The gaps in her memory grew more concerning the longer the day went on. She'd assumed something would jog her memory by now, but nothing had. It was as if she'd been drugged. She worried she might have permanent brain damage from her nasty fall. What if she started forgetting other stuff? Maybe she was concussed.

"I think I should go to the hospital."

"Now?"

She shrugged. "Don't you think I should have a scan or at least speak to a doctor?"

"I thought you already did."

Her brow pinched. She thought so, too, but she couldn't actually remember sitting in a doctor's office or having any sort of exam.

A vision of a cave flashed in her mind, triggering the familiar scent of wood burning. A tingle shot up her back and she shivered, vocally, the way a child does after sobbing.

Vito glanced at her. "You okay?"

She shook her head. "I keep getting these weird flashes that don't make any sense."

"Memories?"

"I don't know."

They drove in silence for a few miles. "If you go to the ER, it'll cost an arm and a leg. Just call your primary and see if they can get you in later this week."

He was right. She called her doctor's office and they said they could see her the following Friday. Maybe by then she'd remember what happened to her and be able to at least answer some basic questions.

While they drove, she reclined in the passenger seat and used her new phone to search every convent in Pennsylvania. There were only a couple close to Jim Thorpe.

"None of these convents look familiar."

"Did the nuns wear any special pins or stitched symbols on their clothes?"

"I can't remember."

"What about the building? Was the exterior stone or stucco or did it have siding?"

"I just remember pale green walls." She clicked on a map, following each pin to a specific listing. "Who knew convents had websites." She chuckled. "And ratings. This one has four stars."

"That's commercialism at its finest."

"I give up." When she looked up and noticed how far they'd driven, her brow creased. Signs for the Northeast Extension passed overhead. "Where are we going?"

Vito kept his eyes on the road, both hands tight on the wheel.

"Vito?"

"What?" He shrugged. "I just figured we could take a quick look—"

"I told you I didn't want to go back to Jim Thorpe!"

"Come on. You're Destiny Santos, star reporter. You're always sticking your nose where it doesn't belong."

"I said no!"

"I'm already on the exit."

"So, get off of it."

"I can't."

"Damn it, Vito, stop the car! Pull over!"

He grudgingly pulled onto the median where the exit ramp forked off the highway. She slapped him in the arm.

"Stop hitting me! I'm sorry. I thought you might change your mind."

"Well, I'm not going to."

He sighed and merged back onto the Turnpike taking the exit toward Lancaster.

Feeling maneuvered and helpless, she glared out the window. An annoying ringtone filled the car. "Are you going to get that?"

"It's not my phone, it's yours."

"Oh." She should probably program a better sound for her notifications. Scowling at the screen, she cursed. "Why the hell is Adrian calling me?"

Vito winced. "I might have contacted him when I was looking for you."

She tsked. "Seriously, Vito?"

"I didn't know where you were! I thought you might have hooked up."

"Give me a little credit." She sent the call to voicemail. "I can't believe you called him."

She had given Adrian three years of her life and, in the end, he emptied her savings account to cover his ass from getting fired after embezzling money from his job. She hadn't known he was a criminal. She especially wouldn't think he was a thief. Thieves typically acquire assets or money. Adrian was always broke. Turned out, he never had any money because he spent it all on his *other* girlfriend. Destiny was just the fool funding their relationship and unknowingly paying back his stolen loans to save his ass from jail.

She should have turned him in, but she didn't. Vito wanted to kick his ass, but she stopped that from happening, too.

She gave three years of her life to a man who never truly loved her. Adrian used her and made a fool out of her. Retaliating would have only drawn out her pain and exposed her ignorance to more people.

In the end, she was so shaken she just wanted Adrian to go away. He destroyed her trust, not just for him, but for all people. She'd become so cynical, she swore off men all together. It had been three cold years, and her heart still hadn't healed.

"Ah, you know you've arrived in Amish country when you can smell the horse shit."

She ignored her brother and continued to stare out the window as the pretty farmland rolled by. Even in winter, when the grass had hardened and the earth faded to brown, she found peace in the country.

The sun caressed the gray clouds, casting golden shadows on the fields below. Red barns dotted the hillsides and smoke billowed from chimneys on farmhouses. The primitive countryside reminded her of an old oil painting—*"Stop the car!"*

She shot up in her seat, and Vito startled, jerking the wheel and veering off the road. "What is it?"

Destiny's head whipped around as they passed a barn tucked away on a spread of open farmland. "Get off the next exit."

The turn signal clicked, and Vito edged the car back onto the road. "Why are we getting off?"

She didn't have a rational explanation. "I need to see something."

"Could you be less cryptic?"

"There was a barn back there. I recognized it."

He frowned and pulled off the exit. "This is Amish country."

"Just turn right and follow that road."

He did as she instructed. Destiny searched the area for any landmark that looked familiar. "I've been here before."

"When?"

"Recently. I've been on this road. I know it."

"You mean this week? We're like two hours from Jim Thorpe."

Geographically, it didn't make sense, but something in her gut felt right. Or she was going crazy. Great, now she was losing trust in herself. "Pull over."

He barely had the car stopped before Destiny jumped out. Small houses dotted the property, and colorful quilts flew in the breeze like sails sewn of rainbows.

Vito got out of the car and hustled after her. "D, wait up."

She stood on the edge of a gravel path meeting the paved road they had been driving on.

"I've been here." She turned in a circle. "Here. I stood in this exact spot." The memory was slippery like a fish under murky water, but she was sure of it. She followed the path walking at a clipped pace.

"Where are you going? This is somebody's private property." Her brother huffed after her.

She couldn't slow down. The deeper onto the property she traveled, the more familiar it felt. "It's like déjà vu. I can't place it, but I recognize it." Not the buildings or the land, but something else. An essence or a feeling. Inexplicable fear and nostalgia rolled into one.

"Destiny, will you hold up a second?" Vito

speed walked beside her, huffing under the extra weight he'd put on recently.

Her eyes searched the land. "I need to talk to someone."

"Who? Look at the clothes lines. Only the Amish do laundry like that in the dead of winter. They don't speak English. They speak some Dutch Pig Latin German." The path sloped up a large hill, and he grabbed her arm. "Will you listen to me? We can't bother these people."

He was right. She knew it was wrong to trespass. The Amish were extremely private people, but she needed some answers. She wasn't even sure what questions she might ask, but something told her she needed to find someone.

"I have to do this, Vito. Go back to the car if you want, but I'm not leaving before I speak to someone."

Distant voices traveled over the land from the valley below, and she continued up the hill. When she reached the summit, she froze.

"Whoa." Vito caught his breath at her side. "Destiny, we don't belong here. Look at them."

Amish children dressed in black, blue, and mauve scattered around a quaint schoolhouse with a copper bell by the door. The girls were cloaked in black and the boys wore wide brimmed hats.

Vito sighed. "I really don't feel right about this."

She hesitated. There was something sacred about this place, something completely contrary to her and her strip club bouncer brother. "I…" She didn't know how to explain the pull she felt. It was like something was literally calling to her. "I feel like this is right, Vito. In my bones and my blood. That's the only way I can explain it."

He looked unsure. "Fine, but I'm not letting you go down there alone."

"They're Amish."

"So? Remember that big coke ring they busted a few years back. Amish clothes could cover a world of sin if you really think about it."

She rolled her eyes. "You need to start watching something other than crime shows. It's making you weird."

She crested the hill and headed toward the homes. The moment they shifted downhill she felt exposed. The children returned to the schoolhouse and all signs of life disappeared, but she sensed people watching them—like the first time Dorothy arrived in Oz when all the munchkins hid in the gardens and closed the shutters.

"That house looks impressive. Maybe we should start there."

They were all large and beautifully crafted in a colonial style. The one Vito pointed to didn't strike her as familiar, but it was bigger than the rest, attached to a meeting house of sorts that looked official. Maybe someone important lived there—someone with answers.

The sun was getting close to the horizon, and it would be dark in an hour. There were no phone lines or exterior lighting on the houses. Everything was simplified down to the bare essentials.

The wood of a large wrap around porch creaked underfoot as they approached the door. She glanced at Vito, now feeling foolish for having dragged him there with no real plan. She knocked on the door and they waited.

When no one answered, she knocked again, strongly considering if this was a mistake. Finally, the door opened and a striking woman in a bonnet appeared.

"Hi, I'm Destiny Santos and I was wondering if you could—"

"Oh my heavens," the woman gasped, her slender fingers covering her full lips. "Vito, is it really you?"

Confused, Destiny looked back at her brother, who looked equally caught off guard. "Uh…Yeah?"

The woman smiled and laughed, the sound melodic and enchanting. "Don't you recognize me? Oh, of course you don't. Not dressed like this, anyway." She gripped his arm with unmistakable familiarity. "It's me, Larissa."

Destiny's jaw dropped and she and Vito both blurted, "Larissa the nun?"

Cybil handed Cain the pliers and he tightened the last wire on the bull pen. The sun passed overhead long ago, falling behind the tree line and painting the land in hues of gold, making it harder to work in the growing shadows.

"That should keep the beast in for a while." Of all their bulls, this one was the least tame. Clive had plowed into practically every foot of fencing along the corral, tangling the lines into a sure mess over the past few months.

The Elders were considering putting the brute down, but Cain shared a sort of kinship to the old bull, a sort of sympathy for his misunderstood life that set him apart from the more gentle creatures of the farm.

Cybil pointed to the ornery animal and tapped two fingers of her right hand over two fingers of her left hand.

"What's his name?" Cain had been studying the sign language book at night. He was far from fluent, but it was nice to have a means for communicating with Cybil.

She nodded and pointed to the bull as he huffed and stomped at the ground.

"Clive."

She shaped her hands like claws, palms toward her face and dragged them down to her belly. He didn't know what that meant, but her scrunched face gave him a clue.

"Is he angry?" When she nodded, he said, "If he rams this fence one more time, *I'm* going to be the angry one. Let's go find some supper."

He gathered his tools and checked that the lock on the gate was secure. Cybil caught his wrist and looked up at him, rapidly signing then pointing to a scrape on his hand.

He looked at the wound. It would be gone in a matter of minutes. Stuffing his hand in his pocket, hoping she would forget about it, he pointed to his parents' house. "I'll race you. Winner gets a slice of Gracie's pie."

Cybil took off, and he ran after her. Colby barked and trailed after them.

The fading sun lit the sky in radiant shades of purple and gold. The air smelled of incoming snow, and he wondered if he should have Dane help him haul wood from the shed.

"Where the devil are you two racing in from?" Grace greeted then scalded, "Good grief, your boots are caked with mud! Go put them by the door."

Cain's head lifted when he noticed Dane standing by the door. "I'm thinking we might want to add to the wood pile tonight, Dane. The air smells of snow."

"Later. I have a message for you." Every day Dane's voice grew deeper. He held up a folded slip of paper with the bishop's wax seal.

Cain rose, leaving his boots on his feet. The bishop only sent messages when he required someone's presence or had private business to share. He tore open the seal.

"What is it?" Gracie asked, Cain's thoughts no longer susceptible to her nosey ways.

"It doesn't say." All the note contained was a heavily scribbled order that he report to the bishop's home immediately.

"Is it Larissa? The baby—"

"I'm sure Larissa is fine." He put Gracie's worries to rest. "If anything was wrong, he would have sent for you or the healer. It's probably just council business."

Cybil clenched his hand in a tight fist. Sometimes her eyes said more than her hands ever could.

"Sorry, munchkin. You can't come with me this time, but you can stay here and get that first slice of pie. Fair is fair."

Cybil smiled and released his hand.

The bishop was the last male Cain wanted to see. But he also didn't want to leave him waiting. They were equally strong-willed males, both stubborn and committed to their values, but he and Eleazar didn't always see eye to eye.

The Elders were wise and powerful. They controlled The Council which dictated the rules of The Order and upheld their many outdated laws. Cain racked his brain wondering if he'd broken any lately.

Depositing his tools in the barn, he headed toward the safe house to find out what his pompous brother-by-law wanted. Since making his promise to Anna, he'd done little more than fix fences and shovel dung, trapped on this oppressive farm until the babe arrived—another joyous celebration for his prideful brother indeed.

He sometimes wondered if Adam truly understood how much Cain continually sacrificed for him. Did his twin ever consider how easy his life was in contrast to Cain's?

He climbed the pretentious steps to the bishop's front door, and David greeted him.

"Is he in his office?"

"Yes. He is expecting you." The male waved Cain toward The Council's chambers.

An ominous knot tied in his gut as he traveled down the long corridor that led to the Council Hall and the bishop's office. Beneath this building hid several holding cells, some of which Cain had passed the most agonizing hours of his life at the mercy of his dear old bishop. It was difficult to always look kindly on the male now that he was mated to Larissa.

As he knocked and let himself into the bishop's chambers, he tensed, spotting his sister's willowy form perched on the edge of a wooden chair, spine stiff and an unmistakable trail of tears trailing down her cheeks. His brow hardened. "What's this about?"

"We have a situation."

"I can see that. Mind telling me why my sister is distraught?"

"She isn't distraught. She's merely upset with me."

He turned to his sister. "What is it? What's happened?"

Before she could find her words, another tear slipped past her lashes and the bishop said, "Your friend, the reporter, is back."

"That's impossible."

"I would have agreed with you, had I not witnessed her presence—in my home—for myself." His hard jaw twitched. "And she's not alone."

Cain's shoulders stiffened. "Who is she with and where is she?" He couldn't explain the protective worry coming over him.

"Not so fast, Cain. The mortal reporter is acquainted with an old friend of your sister's."

Cain looked at Larissa and then scowled at the bishop. "What have you done?"

"I have done nothing outside of protecting our order."

"Then why is she crying."

"Pregnancy—"

Larissa scoffed before he finished the word. "I am not crying because I'm with child.

I'm crying because you're behaving like a superior windbag."

Cain smothered a laugh. He needed to teach his sister how to swear like the English if she ever expected to intimidate a man like Eleazar King.

"Insult me all you like. That man has intimate knowledge of you, and I will not have him in my home."

"Hold on." He shot Larissa a confused glance. "You know the man with Destiny?"

"His name's Vito. He was my friend. I met him when I was…living among the English."

Cain smirked. She meant dancing at the club. It had to destroy the bishop that others had seen his sister in such a state of undress. "Right. And this friend of yours knows you intimately?"

"Enough!" Eleazar snapped. "The mortal male is aware that what's in the woods isn't human."

All levity left the room. "How do you know this?"

"I read his thoughts. He knows what Isaiah is."

Cain frowned. "How? He wasn't even there."

"Are you certain?"

Destiny chattered a lot on their journey, and he tried to recall any mention of others. "It's her brother?"

"Yes," Eleazar agreed. "If he wasn't in the woods, then she must have told him what she saw. That means the compulsion didn't last."

It made sense that Cain couldn't penetrate her mind once he discovered her thoughts were a jumble of English and Portuguese, but the bishop spoke both languages. He was an elder more than half a millennium old. He should have had no issue taking control of the mortal and wiping her memories. "How is that possible. She's just a mortal."

"So you did not tamper with her mind?"

"I couldn't," Cain reminded. "I did exactly as you asked."

"She does seem rather confused about why she's here," Larissa said.

Perplexed as well, Cain asked, "How did she get here?"

"They have a vehicle. I had David move it into the barn."

"She drove here but doesn't know why?"

"So it seems."

"Where is she?"

"That is not the issue at the moment."

The hell it wasn't. Cain opened the door. "I want to see her. Where is she?" The door ripped out of his hand, the bishop's telekinesis stronger than his grip.

"Sit down, you fool," the bishop growled. "You and your bleeding heart have caused enough trouble—"

"Tell me where she is or I tear this place apart brick by brick." The thought of her locked in one of the holding cells had him seeing red. "She's been through enough."

"You're out of line."

"You are. Unlock the door before I break it!"

"They're in the den under compulsion," his sister blurted, disobeying her husband's demand for control.

"Larissa!"

"I won't stand for this arguing between you two. As my mate and my brother, I insist the two of you find a way to get along."

Cain jiggled the knob. "Unlock the door."

"We're not finished talking."

"Vito was good to me," Larissa snapped. "He was my friend. What we shared happened before you and I were mated, and I needed to feed. You're being completely unreasonable."

The bishop pinched the bridge of his nose. "Larissa, we will discuss this later. Right now, we need to focus on a solution. There are two confused mortals sitting in my den, and I want them gone."

"When we mated, you swore I would be allowed to have friends."

"He's mortal. My loyalty on the issue resides with the safety of The Order."

"Well, I hope your stubborn loyalties keep you warm tonight."

"You're behaving like an irrational female."

"You're behaving like a domineering warthog!"

"I will not have you speak to me in such a way!" The bishop crossed the room, but instead of throttling his wife, he took hold of her and hugged her tight. "My beautiful lioness, you must trust me in this."

She leaned into him but thumped his chest with her small fist. "I will not be bossed and ordered around like your inferior."

He kissed her head and stroked her back with a calming touch. "You are my wife. My equal."

Cain jiggled the knob and the door clicked open, the bishop's focus now elsewhere. He drifted through the bishop's private home, prepared for the onslaught of Destiny's questions, oddly anticipating her demands. But when he reached the den, his gut clenched.

Destiny lay supine on an upholstered bench, her eyes in a trance and her limbs lifeless. A larger man—Vito he supposed—occupied the nearby chair in a similar state. He kneeled in front of the bench and swept a finger under the curtain of her dark, curly hair.

"Destiny?" He waved a hand in front of her face, unsure how she could be under compulsion now yet somehow retrieved her erased memories from before. "Can you hear me?"

Full, soft lips drew his gaze. He didn't trust her.

"I know you can hear me, woman. Tell me how you found your way back here."

She stared blindly at him, neither blinking or flinching when he snapped his fingers in her face.

"Stubborn."

He gripped her jaw and studied her face. Glancing over his shoulder at the unmoving heap of her brother, he looked back at those tempting lips.

"Let's see if this gives you away." He

pressed his mouth to hers, taking everything he could taste of her with one stroke of his tongue. It was no surprise she didn't kiss him back, but she also didn't shove him away.

Drawing back, he frowned. "Destiny?" He shook her shoulders but got no response. "Wake up."

"She's dreaming."

Cain's gaze jerked to the bishop, as his body filled the doorway. "How can you tell?"

"Her thoughts."

Cain stood defensively, unsure what the bishop saw in her dreams and envious that mortals could enjoy such things so casually. "Do you plan to wake her?"

"In time. First, I must speak with The Council."

"You can't leave her like this."

"What do you suggest?"

Cain glanced at her helpless form. As much as she infuriated him, he preferred her spitting and fighting to this lifeless display. "Let me take her to my house. I'll watch over her. My parents are still out of town so she won't be in the way."

"Very well. As long as she's in your care, I'm holding you responsible for her. As far as they're concerned, we are just simple Amish farmers. And let me make this clear to both of you," the bishop said, alerting Cain to his sister's shadow on the other side of the door. "Neither is staying."

"Of course, my love." Larissa's tone had softened from what it was minutes ago. He sensed she was hiding because her hair had come undone.

"And you will *not* be in this male's presence without me. Understood?"

"Yes."

"Good. Cain will take them both back to your parents' house."

"Both?"

"You volunteered."

"To take the female—"

"I'm afraid they're a set."

The bishop planted a memory of a warm welcome in both mortal's minds and instructed David to load the male onto a carriage. Cain lifted Destiny into his arms, an unexpected warm nostalgia surrounding him as he held her close to his chest.

"I expect you to be back here tonight for the meeting, Cain. We have concerns regarding your uncle to discuss. Enlist Grace to watch over them while you're occupied with council business."

Cain tenderly cradled Destiny's soft, sleeping form close to his chest. Tonight's meeting had been his highest priority until a few minutes ago. Now there seemed a more pressing issue that commanded his attention.

CHAPTER 18

"What's she doing back?" Grace did a double take as Cain entered the kitchen, Destiny's sleeping form cradled in his arms.

"We're not sure, but she's not alone."

His sister looked over his shoulder at the door and frowned when she found it empty.

"In the carriage. I'd appreciate it if you could lug the big one inside."

"The big one? You're creating quite the collection, Cain. Whatever will Mother and Father say when they return from their trip to find a menagerie of mortals roaming about the house?"

Ignoring her, he carried Destiny to his room and lay her carefully on the bed. His parents wouldn't be back for another week or so, and the mortals would be gone by then. He hoped.

Unsure how long the bishop's compulsion to sleep would last on a mortal of her strength, he studied her for a moment. She looked harmless enough.

She was peaceful in her comatose state. The sight of her thick, coiling curls against his pillow pleased him. He never brought females back to his bedroom. The illusion of permanence had his heart reflexively savoring such an impossible idea.

She really was quite lovely when she wasn't complaining or infringing on others' privacy. Her body was soft with full-bodied curves a male could hold onto. Somehow, her build suited her feisty personality perfectly. His cock twitched as his attention followed the slope of her ass down to her thick thighs where black cotton pants clung to her like a second skin, leaving little mystery.

Softly, he traced a finger down the long slope of her nose. Her eyelids rippled ever so slightly, and a soft sigh formed in her throat. He watched her with open curiosity and fascination.

Was she dreaming again? From what he

understood, mortals dreamed regularly about anything and everything. Their dreams held no life-altering meaning but impressed him all the same.

His desire to make her comfortable should have alarmed him, but he didn't give it much thought. Removing her wool lined boots, he set them by the door and grinned at the sight of her bare feet. Her toes were chubby and short, curling ever so slightly.

He touched the soft arch of her bare foot, and she reflexively pulled it away and moaned in her sleep. Was she ticklish? He wanted to find out, but now was not the time to risk waking her.

Drawing the quilt over her legs, he studied her a moment longer. Snapping his fingers in front of her face, he tried to rouse her. A snuffle escaped her nose as she softly snored.

"Charming," Grace said, startling him to her presence as she watched him from the bedroom door.

Cain scowled, feeling slightly exposed. "Did you get the big one?"

"Yes. He snores, too. What are you thinking, bringing them here? If the bishop finds out—"

"The bishop knows. He's the one who told me to bring them home."

"Why?"

He smirked. "So you could watch them."

"Oh, no." She held up her hands. "I'm not babysitting any more mortals for you. My plate is full."

"Too bad. The bishop insisted. I have a council meeting to attend."

"Cain, council meetings can take hours."

He swapped out his damp jacket and hat for fresh attire. "They're mortal, Grace. You'll be fine. I'll return as soon as The Council meeting's over."

She followed him into the kitchen where the male slept like a corpse on the table. "I can't believe you're leaving me alone with them."

Cain glanced at the rather large stomach hanging over the mortal's belt. "If it wakes up…feed it."

"Yes, that's all I'm good for, I suppose. That and mortal sitting."

He paused at the door and gave her a genuine smile. "I appreciate this, Gracie."

"Don't thank me. I'm doing this because our bishop demanded it of me, not because

I'm inclined to show you kindness. Perhaps at some point during my eternity, this patriarchy we live in will get flipped on its rear. Then all of you entitled males can return the many favors us taken-for-granted females are owed after our many years of servitude."

He chuckled. "That'll never happen."

She scoffed and rolled her eyes. "Get out."

He looked at the sleeping male mortal once more, then back at his sister's petite size. All of the males would be attending the meeting for the next few hours. He went to the gun cabinet in the hall and removed an old musket and quickly loaded it.

"You can't be serious. I'm way more threatening than that old relic."

"Mortals fear guns. All you have to do is point it at him if he tries anything." He placed it in her hands. "Point the right end at him."

"Cain…"

He sensed her warning coming. "You'll be fine."

"I know that, but…" She waved a hand toward the mortal heaped on their kitchen table. "*This* endangers us."

"I didn't bring them here. They came here on their own."

"You brought her. You brought Dane and Cybil."

"I brought the Foster children here for father, and do not pretend you don't enjoy having Cybil around."

"Well, she comes with Dane, and I find him as irritating as a flea. I'm sure this one will be no different."

"They're mortals, Grace. That sort of bother is beneath us. All of this is temporary." He pointed in the direction of his bedroom. "Keep an ear open for that one. When she's awake, she babbles like a brook."

"Great."

Cain's attention was distracted as he returned to the safe house with the bishop's buggy. He had been anticipating this meeting for days, but his mind was now elsewhere. He hoped the agenda would move quickly so he could be on his way.

Males filled the pews of Council Hall as The Elders gathered at the bench. Tonight's meeting held great importance as it would determine the next action in regard to hunting his uncle. Cain would not return to the woods, not until he could assure there was no risk to Anna or the babe. He wondered if he'd ever have that sort of guarantee.

His attention leapt from council business to the mortal in his bed. The meeting began, but his attention remained divided. Had she woken? He wanted to be present the moment she did.

Bishop King's heavy footfalls echoed down the center aisle, his stature and power evident in each confident stride. He took his seat at the center of the bench among the other eight elders on The Council and silenced the room full of males with a slight lift of his hand.

Cain's gaze caught on his brother, Adam, for a moment. The stern set of Adam's jaw and spine amplified the effort he put forth not to spare Cain a single a glance. The sense that he'd become a pariah made him long for his father's return.

His grandfather's gaze caught his, and the male gave a subtle nod. The corner of Cain's mouth lifted. At least all of his relatives did not look upon him with contempt.

The date was given by the clerk with a review of the agenda so matters could get underway. After several announcements regarding common practices and upcoming events, the meeting moved on to graver matters.

The bishop sat stiffly at the bench, the earlier softness Cain had glimpsed in the male while in Larissa's presence now replaced with something hard and unforgiving. "I call Brother Cain Hartzler forth to discuss his recent findings in the woods of Jim Thorpe."

Cain stood from the pew and approached the bench. Eleazar nodded at him in greeting, no impression of kinship or dislike in the bishop's cold, inert stare.

"Please share the details of your last hunt."

Cain reported his sighting of Isaiah and *the others* in the woods, leaving all details about Destiny out of his retelling. As he spoke, his grandfather's stare grew more distant. Cain couldn't imagine a similar situation without feeling ill. Isaiah was his grandfather's brother. If it had been Adam out there in those woods, Cain would have done whatever necessary to save him.

"It is understood that you're rescinding your offer to continue the hunt for Brother Isaiah. Is that correct, Brother Cain?" Eleazar asked.

Cain looked at Adam only to have his brother look away. The cold, detached way his siblings saw him now cut deep. Resentment bubbled, and he wondered if he should say to hell with them all and do his duty without apology, but then he thought of Anna and his calling to always protect her. "That's correct."

Adam's expression remained indifferent. Another great sacrifice from Cain gone unrecognized.

"We will need volunteers. If Isaiah is not alone, it would be wise to ban together. How many were there, Brother Cain?"

"It's difficult to say. *The others* moved quickly. There were swarms. They behaved like rabid primates and screeched like banshees. They're vicious and deranged, but they speak."

"Strong?"

"Very."

"How large were these other males?" another elder asked.

"They're not male. The ones I saw were all female."

"You say they speak?"

"Yes. One claimed Isaiah was her mate."

A rumble of deep whispers rolled from the pews and the bishop clapped the gavel. "Did Isaiah show favoritism to the one that made this claim?"

"No. I assume he sired them, but… If he

found his mate, wouldn't the bonding repair him?"

"At this point, the damage is likely done," Elder Abraham Gerig stated. "How many would you assume are in the woods?"

"Close to one hundred." More male voices rumbled with concerns and doubts. "They're not as strong as Isaiah, but they're fast and they're reckless."

"You have fought these abominations?" Elder Christian Schrock asked, appalled.

That was one way to describe the perverse creatures. "They attacked me. They're quite strong."

"They're an affront to God," someone yelled.

"How would you describe them, Brother Cain?"

Thinking back to the woods, a shiver teased at the base of his spine. "Their foulness is a result of an atrocity. They did not choose this life, Isaiah chose it for them. They speak as though their throats have been abused beyond recovery. Their eyes shine with crimson. They reek of ruined innocence, orphans that are now the devil's children. They're territorial and protective of their sire."

"They must be put down," Elder Abraham

demanded. "There is nothing human left when an unmated soul is stolen. It would be merciful to end their suffering. We must exterminate all of them."

"I call forth a band of brothers prepared to hunt our lost elder and exterminate the mess Isaiah has created. We are responsible for his crimes," Cain's maternal grandfather, Elder Thaddeus Christner, announced. "We must act swiftly, so that no more mortals are brutally harmed."

Cain's attention shifted to his other grandfather. Ezekiel's head lowered. His brother's suffering transcended to his own over the years. Isaiah's resurfacing had taken a great toll on his grandfather once more. As an elder, Ezekiel would have a say in how The Council voted.

"Let us not allow ourselves to become monsters simply to save the world from one," the bishop announced. "Isaiah's sins are not ours to judge, and we will show him mercy in the end so that he might find redemption at the hand of God Himself."

After countless murders and heinous acts of brutality, Cain wasn't sure Isaiah deserved mercy. It surprised him that the bishop would make such a request. Perhaps his marriage to Larissa stirred a sense of loyalty to their grandfather, thereby making Isaiah his kin as well.

Ezekiel, Cain's grandfather, kept his eyes downcast and his face devoid of emotion, but his pain was evident.

"What if there were enough males present to safely incapacitate Isaiah and return him to the farm where he could be locked in seclusion and studied?" Cain asked and the hall silenced, pews creaking as every male body twisted to gape at him. He shrugged. "There has to be a reason why he still breathes. All of our teachings claim an unanswered mate will die without the bond. If his mate was mortal, she must be gone by now, yet he still lives. Shouldn't we try to understand why?"

A strange kinship toward his uncle had his heart pounding. What if Isaiah was like him? Cain feared he, too, would eventually wither away without Annalise at his side, but he was still here. Perhaps his survival was tied to Anna's. Yet his father survived the death of his mate, so where was the actual science behind their theories?

"There seems to be much we still don't

understand," Cain argued. "If we could protect the outside world from Isaiah and still study him, wouldn't it be in our best interest to do so?"

"We are already asking our brethren to endanger their lives. Capturing Isaiah would make this mission all the more perilous."

"Then send more males. There are hundreds of us and only one of him."

"But there are *the others*, the abominations."

Cain believed they were worth studying, too, but he didn't want to press his luck. "If God wanted Isaiah dead, he would have killed him by now. What if it's God's will that we keep him alive?"

His grandfather's head lifted and Cain held his stare. No hope hid in Ezekiel's eyes, only fear.

"You make a strong point, Brother Cain." The bishop clapped his gavel. "Let it be done. We will send more males, and if Isaiah can be captured, we will bring him home. Males not attending the hunt will reinforce a cell below. However, if the dangers prove too great and Isaiah is in fact too strong, then he is to be destroyed on the shadow of which he stands. You will attack at night and transport him during the day when the sun has him at his weakest. Do not expect him to recognize you as anything other than a male trespassing on his territory. Every volunteer will be risking his own life." The bishop stood. "Who is brave enough to take this burden upon their shoulders and bring this evil to an end?"

A male in the back stood. "I shall go." Then another male and another. Soon enough there were over twenty large, imposing males forming the band of brothers vowing to bring Cain's uncle home.

When The Council meeting was dismissed, Cain waited for his grandfather. Ezekiel appeared grave and deeply troubled by tonight's decision when Cain hoped he might feel relieved.

"You spoke well tonight, Cain. Your father would have been proud to see it."

"You don't seem pleased with the verdict." They left the safe house and walked slowly through the dark. Insects chattered, and owls called in the distance.

"I'm grateful for your mercy, but there is no saving my brother."

His grandfather had gone on the first hunt and nearly lost his life when Isaiah tried to decapitate him. Though their kind rarely scarred, his grandfather had returned with a stripe of white hair that never turned black again.

"We don't know all there is to know about mating, Grandfather."

"I suppose you make a good argument for that, but I know my brother. That thing is not Isaiah."

They walked in silence for several steps. "Will you tell me about him?"

A sad smile curled his grandfather's mouth. "If not for my brother, none of us would be here. Isaiah had heard whispers of the New World. Another plague had unleashed on Europe, making it impossible to feed without risking suffering every time we ingested putrid blood. We were mostly starving. I didn't want to leave *Maman* or *Pére*, but Isaiah had a premonition."

"Uncle was a prophet?"

"He had visions from time to time. Perhaps they were dreams, but our kind did not dream. He called them *aperçus de Dieu*, glimpses from God. He saw a great ship transporting us across the sea and warned of many deaths."

"From Europe?"

"Yes, but he had other visions as well. I had

been enchanted by a female called Vashti but scorned when she married Caleb. Isaiah told me not to be bitter, as another love was destined to come my way. He also warned that Vashti would suffer the loss of a child on the journey. She did. And soon after we arrived in Philadelphia, I was called to your grandmother. The more his premonitions came true the less I questioned him. But one night he came to me, and we had a terrible fight."

Their steps were unhurried. "What did you fight about?"

"Isaiah told me he would disappear. He said I would lose him forever, and I must not think of the past but do whatever was necessary to protect my family in the future, even if it meant ending him. I refused any such fate and we quarreled. I told him his visions were wrong, and we would live millennia as brothers. He became so frustrated with my refusal that we didn't speak for months. I'd give anything to have those months back now."

"Because he was right."

"I should have trusted him," his grandfather said, voice heavy with remorse. "Isaiah was different. Special. He saw things the rest of us could not. But I could not see how any male could fear themselves so deeply. He claimed a monster hid inside of him and it would eventually break free. He begged me to kill the monster before others were hurt, but I could not make such a promise."

"Because killing the monster would mean killing your brother."

"Do you blame me?" His grandfather looked at him through shimmering blue eyes.

"No. As much as Adam angers me, he'll always be my brother."

"Adam reminds me a lot of Isaiah. My brother was a charitable male, always helping others, protecting the females, and gifting the children with whimsical finds. His presence was sought after and his spirits were always high, even during the lowest of times."

Cain considered all his family had built since arriving in America with nothing but the clothes on their backs. While some might see an Amish farm as lacking, The Order had sustained and stood the test of time. "It's easy to overlook the hardship we no longer face."

"Those hardships strengthened our values and helped us appreciate what graces we were given. *The Charming Nancy* had been a tomb upon the sea, but we survived better than most. The nine families that traveled over still exist today. We've worked together like a family for more than a century, been blessed by many callings, and celebrated almost as many matings."

"Except Uncle Isaiah's."

"He, and your father, and you."

Cain frowned. "Do you think it's some sort of abnormality in our bloodline?"

"I think it is God's will."

Cain struggled to understand a God that would cause such suffering. "How long after Uncle Isaiah's ominous prophecy was he called?"

"More than a decade had passed. I believe he knew before it happened. I found him in the barn one afternoon, sharpening a metal rod. He later impaled himself."

"Intentionally."

"Yes, but my brother was strong and the wound kept healing. He was distraught. He asked if I planned to permit your mother and father's marriage, and I told him I would. He warned that Jonas was not your mother's true mate and great heartache would come."

"Why didn't you stop the union?" Of course, had his parents not married, Cain and his siblings would not exist, so he was grateful the marriage was permitted, but confused by the logic nonetheless.

"Isaiah said there was no stopping it. Your mother and father were in love and would marry one way or another. He saw you and the others—three sons and two daughters."

"Three sons?"

His grandfather grinned and nodded. "Perhaps now that Jonas has faced his calling and dealt with the matter, this babe will survive. Your mother has suffered so much loss."

"I hope so."

Ezekiel caught his arm and they stopped walking. "Your father hindered fate, Cain. Every choice we make carries a consequence. Isaiah saw something that day that scared him close to death. When he tried, again, to injure himself, I fought him."

"Did you win?"

"There are no winners when violence is chosen. An oil lamp was kicked over and flames the size of ten men engulfed the barn. Isaiah begged me to leave him there to die, but I could not." He gripped Cain's arm and looked at him with solemn eyes. "I'll never forget what he said to me as I wrestled him through the clouds of black smoke."

"What did he say?"

"He said, 'It is better that I die here tonight

than live to sacrifice a hundred innocent souls.'"

"The others."

"Yes. He knew what would come of him. He made me promise I wouldn't wait too long, that I wouldn't hesitate to end him, but in the end…"

"He was your brother."

His grandfather turned his head in shame. "I waited too long. When we finally found him in the woods, the stench of blood and decay was suffocating. I thought there was still hope. If we could find his mate and possibly sedate Isaiah. But it was too late. My brother was gone. The moment he saw us, he fell into a rage. I hesitated and he nearly killed me. I was nothing to him. His mind and memories and all that we shared was gone."

"Why are you telling me this?" Cain knew the story of the day The Elders tried to hunt his uncle.

"Because I want you to understand that there is no bringing my brother back. I appreciate everything you said at the meeting tonight, but my brother is not in those woods. A monster is out there, and Isaiah was no monster. He was kind and good, and that is how I intend to remember him."

"You don't want them to bring him back here?"

"If bringing him here serves a purpose without endangering The Order, so be it. But do not expect me to celebrate his return. I grieved my brother many years ago, and I only want to move on in peace now."

They had reached his grandfather's gate. "I can talk to Eleazar and tell them not to bring him here."

"God will guide them to do what is best. I appreciate you walking with me."

Cain stood by the gate as his grandfather walked the path to the door. He wasn't like the others. He didn't feel a connection to God or sense when he was being guided.

"Sleep well, Cain."

"You as well, Grandfather."

As Cain walked home, he considered the situation in the woods and what the band of brothers would face. He wished he could go with them, but his vow to Annalise kept him honor bound to the farm. Isaiah was a grave threat, a danger to anyone who approached him. *The others* were a danger as well. They would die protecting their sire, and kill for him as well.

It had to be a blood exchange that made

the others the way they were. Elders told many tales, indoctrinating members of The Order since birth to believe that bonding was strictly for called mates and sharing such a unique blood exchange with non-mates would carry lethal consequences. Was this why?

The other's acted on two channels: conflict and lust. They were aggressive in every motion yet conscious of their loyalties to Isaiah. He worried for the males heading into the woods and wished them a fast and safe return to the farm.

The longer he walked alone the more his mood had soured. He couldn't shake the sense that he was missing something. His mind replayed his grandfather's story, searching for any significance or overlooked area of hope.

How was Isaiah a monster, but his father seemed fine? He wanted to speak to his father and hear his assurance that all his symptoms from the calling had disappeared.

Cain still dreamt with Anna. Did that mean his soul was still in danger? And if *the others* in the woods were a result of a mutated blood exchange, there would be no hope for Cain to ever share such intimacy with a wife.

Anna was his called mate. There could be no other.

The black sky was brighter than his bleak future. Eventually, Grace would be called, and he'd be the only one left. Alone. Why had God forsaken him?

When he reached the house, he felt reckless. If this was his life, his eternity, he had nothing left to lose. His mind was so twisted around his own turmoil, he forgot about the curvy female waiting in his bed but thought her a pleasant surprise after such a trying evening.

Destiny lay in the same position he left her. He approached the bed slowly, tracing a hand up her leg. Her warm body created a direct contrast to the cold and hollow space of nothingness in his chest.

If he could pretend, just for a minute, what it might be like to have a female waiting for him at home…

The sensation was so sweet it stung, and he had to shove it away. He would never know such a reality, and it was masochistic to fantasize of foolish impossibilities.

Cain removed his hat and shirt. His lips firmed when he realized he'd put her on the side of the bed he preferred, but he didn't want to disturb her. Rounding the bed, he paused.

Her shirt had slipped down her arm leaving her shoulder exposed. Lush curves swelled under the blanket and his hands itched to touch her. She'd been sleeping for a while. Would she wake if he kissed her? Would she yell at him? Slap him? He wanted to find out.

He eased into the bed, trying not to disturb her. The honorable side of him believed he should let her sleep, but the other side— the side that always lost and still paid every penalty—told him to take what he wanted, consequences be damned.

She was mortal. Lower on the food chain. His sense of refinement shackled his desires to give in to his animal nature and take what was so readily available to him. She wouldn't be able to stop him. He was a natural predator of indomitable strength.

Why keep up the charade that he had any redeeming qualities left? Without his soul, he was nothing. Forsaken by God, shunned by his brother. It would be liberating to give up this fruitless campaign for redemption and simply take whatever the hell he wanted. And he wanted her.

He wanted to bury himself in her curves, sink his teeth into her flesh and gorge on her spicy blood. What harm was he causing if he sought such pleasure? Anna would be safe, and he would see that Destiny enjoyed herself. The moment he admitted his pleasure would cause no risk to Anna, there was no going back.

His cock lengthened with need as he pulled the covers off of her. Thick, luscious thighs begged to be stripped. His pulse pounded through every vein as his mouth salivated with hunger. He'd had her blood before. Remembered the taste and craved it.

He breathed her in, savoring the heady blend of jasmine mixing with the natural musk of her skin. He touched her cheek, the soft set of her features giving her the face of an angel sleeping in moonlight. Her satin skin was a shade darker than his, her lips a deep pink like the center of a ripe berry.

He remembered her exotic eyes, flecked with onyx and gold. He wanted her to look at him now. Coiling a silky black curl around his finger, he brought the strand to his nose, breathing her in. How selfishly he could use her to slake his desires. She inexplicably tempted him, and he wanted to know her in the most carnal ways.

He wanted those full lips around his cock. He wanted to feed from her full breasts. Shutting his eyes, he inwardly groaned. He was tired of waiting, tired of asking permission. He tugged her curl. "Wake up."

A soft moan and a gentle stretch, then her eyes opened and she stilled.

CHAPTER 19

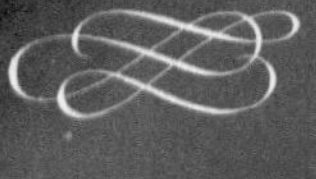

*W*ith a deep gasp Destiny stilled, eyes wide, a look of confusion on her face. "Who are you?"

His brow twitched. She was here, yet she appeared to have no memory of him. "I'm Cain."

Her frantic gaze searched the room. "I… Are we…" She frowned. "Is this a dream?"

"Do you experience dreams so frequently and vividly that you sometimes confuse them with reality?" Then he had a thought. "What if this was a dream and there were no consequences to any of our choices?"

She felt her head as if searching for an injury. "I had a nasty fall."

"Did you now?"

"Yes, I…" Her stare snagged on his chest. "Where's your shirt, and why are you in bed with me?" She scooted back toward the headboard, drawing the quilt over her body like a shield.

He caught the blanket and she stilled. "Do I frighten you?"

"That depends. Do you want to hurt me?"

He chuckled. "Quite the opposite."

Her mouth opened with a response but no words came out. She snapped her lips shut.

Cain caught her ankle and dragged it out from under her. "I was watching you sleep, and thinking of all the things I could do to you." He pulled her other foot toward him and crawled between her knees.

She stiffened and he paused. "Don't be frightened. I have no intention of harming you, but I need your word you won't make any attempt to injure me."

"Um…What?"

"You see, I have this pesky little deal with God and my brother's wife. I won't bore you with the details, so let me skip to the end. I've decided I want you, and I want you to give yourself to me."

He tugged her ankles to his hips and she slouched lower on the bed, her body shifting to the space beneath him, her brow twisted in confusion. "Wait," she squeaked, but she didn't fight him. "I don't understand."

He bent low and nipped at those full lips with a teasing kiss. She looked up at him with dazed eyes. Caging her in with his arms, he grinned. "Are you frightened now?"

"A little."

"I'd offer to ease your worries, but you're more complex than most females so you'll have to trust me."

She placed a staying hand on his chest. "I don't trust anyone."

He chuckled. "Neither do I, so this should be interesting." He tugged at her shirt, teasing beneath the fabric.

"Who are you again?"

"I'm Cain. I'm in charge and here to protect you. And please you. Let's just leave it at that."

He kissed her again, distracting her, but then she pushed him away. "Where's my brother?"

"He's safe. He's under the care of my sister. I assure you nothing will happen to him. You have my word." Pulling her beneath him again, he ground his body against hers and she gasped. "I want you to play a game with me, Destiny. Tonight, we're going to forget how to worry and let instinct drive us." He flexed his hips forward, dragging his hard length between her parted thighs. "Have you ever done something for the pure, self-serving satisfaction of it?"

"I don't…Not in a really long time." She stumbled over her words when he pulled her shirt lower, exposing the dark plum lace of her undergarments.

His tongue licked up her throat landing on an exceptionally sensitive spot and her toes curled, her knees tightening around his hips. "Oh, my God." Her head tipped back as his mouth teased along her jaw.

He chuckled. "You were saying?" He tugged the loose shirt to her hips, exposing her and fully intending to have her nude in a matter of minutes. His fingers went to the fitted waistline of her cotton pants.

She sighed as he stripped her clothing away. "This is crazy," she gasped, his touch trailing up the inside of her leg. "I don't know you."

True, yet she no longer resisted. On the contrary, she was the one pulling him close.

He kissed her deeply, driving her wild and teasing her into a frenzy. "We met months ago when you were doing a story on the Foster family."

"That was you?"

So she didn't have her memories back. "Yes, and then we crossed paths again in the woods." He dragged his nose along the satin of her skin and shut his eyes, inhaling her scent.

"I had a nasty fall." She frowned as the words pelted out and her back arched, positioning her body for his open perusal.

"Of course, you did." He teased his nose over her hip, trailing little nips and licks along her soft belly—marking her with his own scent. He lifted her arms, pressing her hands into the pillows. "I'm the one who helped you get home—safe and sound."

"You won't hurt me," she stated, more for her benefit than his.

The mingled fragrance of their arousal awakened a deep hunger inside of him. Rising above her, he pulled a nipple into his mouth and discretely suckled the sharp tip between his fangs. "I could easily show you my cruelest side, but that wouldn't benefit me. Tonight, I'm purely focused on seeing *my* needs met. Mine and yours, of course. I'm going to use you for my pleasure, Destiny. And you're going to use my body for yours."

His fingers hooked around the lace covering her hips and she locked her knees together. "Wait."

He paused and when she didn't say anything, he said, "Don't overthink it. Take whatever you want. We're just two warm-blooded animals who find each other attractive."

"I…"

He shoved his nose between her thighs and inhaled deeply, spearing her with a slow lick. "No use denying it. I can smell and taste your arousal. Be a brave girl, one who denies herself nothing when presented with an opportunity." Rising on his knees, he stared down at her and stroked himself. "Do you want me inside of you, sweetness? Because I *really* want to get there."

Her olive skin flushed and a smile trembled to her lips as her gaze skittered away.

Cain caught her chin with a delicate finger, his gaze holding her prisoner. "No need to be shy with me. The door's there and you're free to leave at any time. You just have to tell me what you want."

"I… You know you're attractive."

"I know no such thing." He pressed a

teasing kiss on the soft curve of her stomach. "I find you fascinating and delectable." He dragged his mouth upward and her heartbeat went wild.

"Oh, God." She shut her eyes.

"I've been called worse," he teased. Their bodies aligned and he held himself suspended, drawing out the intense anticipation to sink into her. "Why did you come back, Destiny?"

"I…I don't know. I can't remember."

"Perhaps, I can help you." He pressed a kiss to the curve of her throat where her pulse rapidly danced. "Just relax. Let's see if anything comes back to you."

He slid the tips of his fingers through her arousal and her head tipped back. The sweetest gasp escaped her throat as she arched into his touch.

"Be yourself with me, Destiny. Show me who you really are. Use me the way I intend to use you." His tongue swiped over her speeding pulse as he parted her. Another gasp met his ear as he sank a finger into her heat.

Her body came alive under his touch, arching and sighing into every stroke. He could sense her desire, hear it in her moans, and taste it on her skin. He licked and nipped at her throat, fighting back his hunger.

Sinking his teeth into her as she came apart in his arms would be indescribable bliss, but he had to be careful. Without the power of compulsion, he mustn't do anything out of the norm.

Her nails dug into the muscled flesh of his back and shoulders. He dragged his cock over her slick flesh, teasing and tormenting her until her body silently begged to be filled.

"Please," she reached between them, curling her fingers around his solid length.

Every raw nerve soothed and he inwardly preened as she encased his hard cock in a tight fist. "That's it. Take what you want."

She rubbed her sex against him, stealing pleasure. His aching body swelled and wept for more. The scent of her arousal called to him and he lunged forward, sliding the swollen tip between her delicate folds, stabbing deep and holding her for a moment under his command. "You fit me so well."

She whimpered at the intrusion, startled by his demanding length.

"Shh." He kissed her throat and traced a hand over her hair as he whispered softly into her ear, "That's all of me, sweetness. You can fit me just fine, but take a moment to adjust if you need one."

Her breath came fast and her nails embedded in his skin. "It's just…been a while."

Seated deep inside of her, his cock pulsed. Her confession lent a sense of potency to his position. "How long?"

"Years."

Surprised and pleased by such a revelation, his chest filled with a satisfied purr. Without compulsion, they were on equal ground. He wanted her to bend to his will—not because he commanded it, but because his powerful presence earned it. His autonomy had been slowly stripped away over the past few months, and he needed to take back a sense of authority. She could give him that.

Settling his weight on his knees, he hauled her closer to him, keeping his body deep within hers. She gasped and arched, her body malleable as if under his spell, yet she moved according to her own free will. He dragged his palms over her, cupping her breasts. Every inch of her was full and curvaceous, the body of a goddess.

He thrust into her, taking his time and driving her to the brink of madness with lust.

Breathy cries filled the room as he pulled her closer, cradling her body to his and driving into her without restraint.

She spoke in foreign tongues, as he devoured every inch of her. His fingers traced where smooth rivulets of scars should have marked her arching back, but her skin had fully healed. That surprised him, but assured him she was fit and healthy again.

He thrust hard, driving into her with uncensored lust. He'd been deprived of true pleasure for too long. Wet with arousal, wild with unconstrained lust, she washed away his loneliness like a storm clears a drought.

Sinking deep inside of her, she shattered, her screams of pleasure crashing into the walls like black ocean waves break along the jettied coast. Her body writhed beneath his, nails scraping and teeth nipping. For the briefest moment, he no longer felt trapped. He was free.

Harder he drove into her body, seeking respite from his reality and longing to be someone else. He wasn't a disappointment or a pariah here. He was a god, taking everything he wanted without apology, and she saw him with unpolluted preciseness, exactly as he was, a male desperate to escape from life's pain and find respite in a mild impression of love.

He wanted more of her. All of her. He wasn't letting her go until he was certain she had nothing left to give. He needed everything she could offer, needed to bury himself alive in her, end and begin in her, disappear in her.

Pounding his hips forward, he slammed deep, his strokes almost punishing, but his anger was not with her. His fury had been solely aimed at himself, his blunted circumstances. She was merely his escape.

His choices landed him here, alone with a desolate future. He would never find the satisfying end his brother found, the conclusion he provided through great sacrifice and love. And what thanks did he get for his devotion to family?

His anger at God's cruelty heightened his emotions, and he rode her harder, taking out his frustrations in ways he never thought to try. Or was it that no other female had ever successfully stripped him of the façade so completely and driven him to such a brink of hunger and desire?

Greedily taking out his pleasure to hide his pain. He thrust into her with strong, punishing strokes. Tired of the rules, sick of pretending to live without sin when those he tried to protect most saw his attempts as wicked betrayals that might threaten their otherwise peaceful lives, he relied only on his sense of pleasure and lost himself in this hedonistic moment.

No more trying to please those who didn't appreciate him. He was through living in the shade of Adam's shadow. Let them call him wasteful or extravagant. They could accuse him of abandoning his duty. He knew the true score. They saw him as the prodigal son, but it was *his* honor that saved their family from ruin time and time again. *His* sacrifice. *His* devotion. *His* love.

Gripping her wrists, he shoved them into the bedding above her head. She surrendered so easily to his desires, and he found himself equally wanting to fulfill hers. "Tell me what you want from me."

Her breathy moans increased as her body came apart in his arms. "Just don't stop."

He lost himself as her greedy hunger fed his. She took everything from him and he relished in her uncensored lust. He gave her all but his final truth. And in the end, he desperately wished he could show her that as well.

He wanted to let himself go, bare his fangs, feed from her vein, and face his actuality. This was his reality, and he was tired of living in secret, tired of hiding and praying to a God that ignored him when all he'd ever wanted was acceptance.

The purpose of his existence had been spent the day he gave Anna away. He had nothing greater to lose. Nothing of real value to gain. No mate to call his own, no hearth to call home, no beneficiaries or loyal lover waiting in his bed.

Pleasure would be his respite and he would shamelessly indulge himself as often and as brutally as he pleased. Judgement be damned.

He licked the swell of her breast. His heavy length sliding in and out of her tight sex. Her nails scraped down his arms and back as their bodies locked as one. Skin slick, flesh gliding against flesh, they moved like poetry, rhythmic and anticipating, satisfying, every sway and thrust, teasing out every measure of desire.

They shared an intimacy he couldn't explain. It was as if she understood his pain and carried her own. Drawing back, he met her stare and everything stilled.

She'd so neatly convinced him they shared indifference, that this was merely a physical exchange, but as he looked down into those dark, wavering eyes, he recognized a flash of vulnerability.

He couldn't fathom why he'd feel so protective of her. A few days ago, he didn't even like her. But she was helping him now, in ways no one else could.

"Who hurt you, Destiny?"

Her expression instantly shuttered, her body noticeably cut off to him. He understood the desire for privacy. He was an incredibly private male when it came to matters of the heart, but he wanted to know her secrets. Wanted to help her heal.

"Tell me."

Her body stiffened with tension. "My ex."

"How?"

Her shoulders tensed and she tried to look away, but they were too entwined. She had nowhere to go. She was at his mercy.

"He betrayed me."

He could have pressed for more, but her eyes glistened with unshed tears, delaying his curiosity in favor of meeting her needs. "I'm sorry someone hurt you like that." Rather than pry further, he did something he'd never done to a female before. He kissed her on the nose.

She looked up at him. That small kiss on the nose somehow more intimate and personal than anything else they'd done tonight. "Me too," she whispered.

"He was a fool." Cain spoke the truth. Anyone who would hurt this female would fail to fully appreciate her.

He understood her. Saw her. Not the ball busting, do-anything-for-a-lead reporter on the job, but the vulnerable, inquisitive, shy yet brave woman who hid her battle scars well. He wanted to compare stories so they could comfort each other and move on. But they were alike in that they carried every tear and felt every fracture so long as their heart still beat.

An unsure smile trembled to her mouth, gone a second later. There was something sweet and innocent about her, something he valued and wanted to protect, even though he couldn't. Tomorrow she would return to her regularly scheduled life and have no memory of him or this place.

A bitter sense of urgency burned inside of him, demanding he learn as much from her as he could, while he had the chance. "Tell me how you found your way back to the farm."

"I didn't come here on purpose. My brother was driving. I… It felt familiar. That's all."

Perhaps it was because he had healed her. He'd already burned off her blood, and he'd been too weak and unable to compel her to offer any of his own, so there would be no bond or instinct shared between them, but perhaps his actions left an imprint of their own. Something the bishop couldn't see to remove. Something private and solely theirs.

He glanced down at her body. The rough scrape of his jaw had marked her tender flesh. Rosy blooms showed where his mouth had suckled, and spatters of purple tinged her hips where he'd gripped her too hard. All of which reminded him she was merely a fragile mortal. She wouldn't have the power to override the bishop's compulsions.

Perhaps she truly returned by coincidence. Disappointment wove through him like a delicate thread and he wanted to snap it away. Whatever possessiveness he felt toward her was misguided and dangerous. He knew better. He needed to worry less about protecting her and more about protecting himself.

"Did you love him?"

She frowned. "Who?"

"The ex that betrayed you." He held his breath, fighting back the unwelcome sense of possession that took an instant dislike to this male of her past.

"On some level—regretfully."

"How so?" He couldn't make sense of loving someone halfway.

"Everything we shared was a lie, so I loved someone who wasn't real. In the end, that makes my feelings fake, too, I guess."

But those feelings hurt her all the same. Mortals had such a short time on this earth. How did they find time to heal from the pain of heartache?

"I also lost someone recently." Why was he telling her this?

"Oh?"

He nodded, desperate to unburden himself. "She fell in love with my brother. I'm forced to witness their happiness every day."

Her lips parted. "How do you stomach it?"

"I try not to feel anything anymore."

Her hand flattened on his chest as if to comfort his broken heart. "Except pleasure."

He met her stare, understanding that she was giving him an escape from the emotional bludgeoning he started. "Yes. Pleasure." As much as he wanted to share these emotions, acknowledging his feelings came with a great deal of pain. There was no way around it.

"Let's not do the personal thing, Cain. I think we're better off the other way."

Perhaps she was right, but he couldn't evade the sting of rejection. One more person uninterested in his pain. It was nice to have a choice. He lived with the pain every day, without choice. A solid reminder that he had no one and could only rely on himself.

Whether in agreement or not, he wanted to punish her. He needed to give her exactly what she requested, intercourse without feeling, pleasure without pain. Were such things even possible?

Fisting his hand in her hair, he yanked her head into the pillows, exposing her neck. He licked up her throat. Her heels dug into his back as his tongue found her pulse. He could show her how little he cared by sinking his teeth into her and allowing her fear and panic to take over, but that animalistic side of him remained in check.

Deep down, he feared letting it escape.

Feared becoming like his uncle. No one, including him, knew what his future held. There were absolutely no guarantees.

Her fingers raked through his hair. He captured her wrists once more, prying her hands open and pinning them to the bed beside her head, so his fingers could intertwine with hers.

She surrendered to him, arching invitingly and rocking her hips to take him deeper. He smirked, pressing her wrists harder into the bed, and her body tightened around his.

The transient need rushing through him screamed how temporary her presence was. They only had this moment in time, and tomorrow she would be gone so he had to take his fill while she was still in his arms. Yanking her body closer to his, he slammed his cock deep inside of her and she moaned. He wanted her cries of pleasure and her body wild beneath him. His mouth crashed over hers, a blatant display of dominance, but she met him bite for bite. They mated like animals in hedonic disorder so untamed and unguarded that instinct took over.

Her nails clawed down his back. Cain growled, exerting his strength as his fangs punched through his gums. His self-control trembled. Just one taste of her and he'd explode.

He buried his face in her neck, his fists coiling in her wild hair as he bucked into her, greedy and wanting. His jaw opened, releasing a natural anesthetic as his tongue traced her pulse, but he couldn't drink from her.

Biting into his own lips, he tasted his blood. His body rammed forward, frustrated by yet another consequence he needed to respect when he so desperately wanted to drink the hot, life-giving blood from her veins.

He sucked her flesh hard, marking it with bruises as he resisted the urge to bite down. Fucking her into the bed like a greedy animal, he took what he could brutally, angry that he could not consume all of her.

Her moans gathered and collided as her body tightened. Quick pulses clenched his cock and his seed rushed free, filling her. It was uncensored ecstasy and exactly what he needed. Exactly what *they* needed. So why did he want more?

His weight sank into her, his head resting on the pillow as he let the moment live a while longer, reveling in each little aftershock that tremored through his bones.

"We forgot a condom."

He scowled as reality intruded once more. And in such a ridiculous worry. He practically laughed. As if God would ever bless him with children.

CHAPTER 20

"*D*on't you walk away from me. I want to talk about this."

Juniper dodged her aunt's persistent questioning and went into the bathroom. She didn't have to pee, but she'd pretended just to escape this ceaseless inquisition. Shutting the door, she sat on the toilet, rubbing her temples.

"Juniper, you can't just bury your head in the sand like an ostrich and hope this goes away. It's a required class. Failing means summer school. Is that what you want?"

Frustrated that her aunt assumed she hadn't already considered how shitty it would be to bake in an air-condition-less building all summer while relearning algebra, which she hated, she flushed the toilet and turned on the sink.

"I don't see you putting any effort into this. If you need a tutor, we can get you one, but you have to take some accountability and tell me what you need."

She needed a moment to think. The quiz Aunt Bel was bitching about felt like something she'd taken a lifetime ago. Since then, she'd been silently dumped by her boyfriend, possessed by the spirit, cornered by some Amish blood drinking freak, and possibly broken her teacher's arm. She couldn't give two shits about algebra and solving for X when so much other crap was going on.

After brushing her teeth, she spit into the sink and rinsed her mouth. Mabel was scowling on the other side of the door when she exited the bathroom. Juniper walked past her to get to her bedroom.

"Juniper, I want answers." She followed.

"What do you want me to say? Algebra sucks. My teacher's a dick. I'm never going to use that sort of math in real life, so what difference does it make?"

"What about college? You can't have an F on your transcript, June."

She rubbed her temples, ready to burst

into tears or hit something. Overwhelmed, she dropped to the bed and shook her head.

"Hey." Aunt Bel sat beside her and rubbed her back. "What's going on with you? You know you can talk to me about anything."

Not this. She'd been raised by her aunts, right here in their apartment above the store, celebrating sabbats and learning about herbs. While her friends read tabloids, Juniper's aunts insisted she read the stars. They said witchcraft was in her blood, a birthright that couldn't be ignored. But as far as magick went, it was all bullshit.

However, it was also their faith and she didn't want to disrespect their belief system, but she was sick of living on the frays of society. They were always the weird ones at school functions. Sometimes classmates would come into town and visit the store then whisper and gawk at her at school the next day. She just wanted to fit in.

"I don't want to run the store after graduation," she blurted.

Aunt Bel didn't have time to curb her shock which quickly transformed into hurt. "Oh. Well, we can talk about that."

"I'm sorry. But if I'm really going to college, I want to go for something I can use. I don't want to take astrology or theology, mysticism, or anything else having to do with the store. I want to take classes *I* enjoy. I want to figure out what interests *me*."

"Of course, you do, sweetie. I want that for you too." She rubbed a hand down Juniper's back. "Listen, the store is our livelihood. It's not who we are."

She gave her a disbelieving look.

"Fine, it's a little of who we are. Our family has practiced witchcraft for generations. It's what we know. Why wouldn't we capitalize on it in an age when witches are no longer persecuted?"

Aunt Bel's words reminded her of what the Amish freak had said about telling their secret. Why the hell would they care if he told people they were witches? The burning age was over.

"I just think it would be nice to go away to college and not have *this* be the first thing people see about me. I want my own identity."

"Oh, June bug, you do have your own identity." She tucked a strand of hair behind her ear. "Honey, the store is a way to make a living. Our faith goes deeper than that. It's a part of us. Moving to a faraway campus won't remove that piece of you. You have to accept that the spirit is a part of you."

Her aunts would often disappear during full moons and come back invigorated, but Juniper never actually saw them do anything cool. Their faith had about as much glue as the binding of any bible. It was all just bottled bullshit, folklore, fairytales, and coincidence. She didn't have the strength for this debate tonight.

"I guess." It was a lame and unconvincing surrender flag, but her aunt accepted it.

"One day you'll come into your power and understand exactly how blessed you are. You'll see. But until that day comes, you need to master other skills, like algebra."

She rolled her eyes and collapsed back on the bed, covering her face as she groaned into her hands. "Why?"

Aunt Bel collapsed next to her. "Because we all had to. Consider it a torturous rite of passage." She patted her knee and got off the bed, pausing by the light switch at the door. "And you're grounded until you get that grade up to at least a C." The lights went out. "Sweet dreams."

There was no arguing her way out of her punishment. Aunt Bel had voiced the threat long before the quiz and Juniper bombed it anyway. Maybe she did need a tutor.

After she changed into her pajamas, she went to the window to adjust the blinds and paused as she stared down at the street. The sidewalks were fairly empty and the restaurants had mostly closed. There was one hour until midnight.

She should have told her aunts about the guy in the woods, but she didn't see the point. Let him tell the town they were witches. It wasn't like they'd show up with pitchforks and torches. Hell, sometimes her aunts told fortunes for extremely prominent figures like senators and celebrities. No one would care what some Amish guy said.

She shut the blinds and crawled into bed. Tomorrow morning she'd speak to her guidance counselor about possibly getting a tutor and see if there was anyone she might recommend. Until then, she didn't want to think about algebra anymore.

Her dreams were chaotic, short stints of visions that made little sense. A salamander raced over her legs, but she couldn't catch it. She faced a door of an alchemist's shop and stared at the triangular symbol, much like the symbol for the element of fire. A fox was trapped in the display window and then she was the fox, sitting in an antique barber chair getting a tattoo of a flaming phoenix on her arm. The tattoo parlor was hot and loud, but she couldn't open her eyes. The singe of the needle buzzed in her ear—

"Juniper, wake up!"

She jerked awake, unsure what was happening. The room was engulfed in flames and the crackling hiss of the fire was deafening.

"Get up! We have to leave. Now, Juniper!"

"What's happening?" Juniper jumped out of bed, shocked by the heat of the floor making it impossible to stand in one place for more than a few seconds. "The house is on fire!"

"I know. We have to move! The firetrucks are on their way."

Juniper instinctively ran to the door only to bolt back when the heat of the knob scorched her palm. "What do we do?"

"Get away from the door! We have to go out the window!"

"The window?" There were no trees by her window. Nothing to hold onto. She could hear the sirens but they were still too far away to see the lights.

"Now, Juniper! We can't waste anymore time."

The house whined as if a freight train were stuck inside, and glass shattered below. It sounded like the fire had spread to her aunts' apothecary room.

"Where's Aunt Venus?"

"She's spending the night at a friend's." Aunt Bel ripped the sheets off her bed.

Another crash of glass shattered below. "The store."

"That's not important. You have to get outside. We can't wait any longer." She tied the sheets together in a long rope. "Put this around your waist."

Juniper did as instructed, but her hands shook terribly and she couldn't stand still due to the increasing heat burning the soles of her feet. The sudden reality that they might die tonight hit with paralyzing force.

"Keep moving. Let's go!"

Fear choked her and she hacked, coughing brutally and tasting the thick smoke sneaking through the rafters and under the door. When her aunt opened the window, the flames roared against the walls and the bedroom door blistered, the paint melting right off the wood.

"Go! I'll hold this end and lower you down."

Juniper stared down at the sidewalk, certain the sheets wouldn't reach. Flames whipped into the night, setting the first floor aglow. There had to be another way.

Aunt Bel grabbed her shoulders and stared into her eyes. *"Ad Deam voco te ad protegendum. Elementum aquae invoco ut te ab igne custodiat. Libera neptim meam incolumem in auroram et ab injuriis."*

Juniper jerked back as if injected by energy. "What was that?"

"A protection spell. Go." She helped her out the window, and Juniper's first thought was how cool the air felt on her hot skin. "Careful. The walls aren't secure."

Her foot slipped as she searched for a foothold, but the heat was unbearable. The lattice wasn't strong enough to support her and she feared her weight might rip it off the house and she'd plummet to her death.

"There's nothing to hold onto!"

"I've got you. Just let go. I won't let you fall."

The sirens blared and she caught the flash of lights at the end of the street, but they were still too far away. "The ground's too far!"

Her aunt turned toward the door, the reflection of flames casting bright shadows over her face. "Juniper, listen to me. You have to do this. A broken arm or leg is better than burning to death, do you understand me?"

Somewhere, in the delirium of the moment, the irony registered. Another generation of witches burned. Was it some cosmic cruelty, an inescapable destiny?

She couldn't relinquish control. Nothing inside of her had the courage to let go and dangle freely into the spitting flames below. "The firetrucks are almost here."

"There isn't time. You can do this."

"I can't!"

"You can. You're stronger than you realize. Now go." Mabel fed the sheet over the window sill, and Juniper scrambled to hang on.

The siding was too hot to touch. The windows on the first floor exploded, shooting glass onto the street and unleashing hell on earth. The trucks blared closer and the red lights flashed in a strobe. She heard yelling but couldn't make out a single word as the heat of the fire cooked her clothes and burned her skin.

Aunt Mabel's face peeked down and then

disappeared. It was a moment locked in time, one where Juniper read everything with that single glimpse of panic in her eyes. Then the sheet gave out and pain exploded in her back and arms.

Flames engulfed the second floor, lashing into the sky and swallowing her bedroom window. "Aunt Bel!"

Throbbing splintered up her arm as she struggled to get up. Suited bodies rushed at the house, holding thick hoses and barking out orders. EMTs lifted her onto a gurney, and she fought as they hauled her away.

"My aunt's in there! We have to go back!" An oxygen mask was forced over her mouth and she shouted and coughed, shoving it away. "Get off me!"

"She's in shock."

"I'm not in shock! I need to get to my aunt!"

The hoses unleashed with a roar and the stench of singed wood and ash stole through the night like a noxious fume. People rushed around her, helping and hindering her. Stealing her choices and forcing her down when she needed to get up.

Chaos unfurled as she watched in horror. The house was gone in a matter of minutes.

Damaged beyond repair. Moldings singed to black, a scorched wooden skeleton where their sanctuary once stood. No sign of Mabel anywhere.

Juniper shivered in shock.

"Does this hurt."

"My aunt…" Nothing hurt. She was numb. Vacant emptiness filled her.

The sirens had stopped and a crowd of people gathered at a distance. Only ashes remained.

Officers managed the mob as firefighters drudged through the house, breaking apart fallen rafters and spraying down stubborn flames. The crunch of glass and stench of wet, singed wood was inescapable.

Among the strangers watching from the street, she spotted the familiar hat of an Amish man. Her heart plummeted as their eyes met. He was holding a pocket watch and looking right at her as he snapped it close.

"What time is it?" she wheezed.

The EMT treating her burns glanced at his watch. "A little after one."

She'd missed his deadline. An hour after midnight and this is what her silence had wrought. Was it a coincidence that he was there or could he have actually done something so destructive? They needed to find Aunt Bel so Juniper could tell her.

"We've got something," someone yelled and Juniper's head turned, her stomach locking with dread as her eyes blurred under the force of tears.

A gurney went in. Several minutes later, a body bag came out.

Her world collapsed as she screamed in denial that it was not her aunt. They had to restrain her, and when she lashed out, injuring one of the officers, she was strapped to the gurney and hauled inside the ambulance.

"No! I'm not leaving her!" Again, the oxygen mask was forced over her face and she was shoved down. A needle was pressed into her arm and the world wavered as the doors shut. The last she remembered was the support bars of the ambulance ceiling overhead.

CHAPTER 21

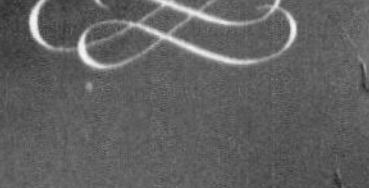

*D*estiny stared at the man beside her, searching for a single flaw and finding none.

"Do you always stare at your lovers in their sleep?"

Like she had lovers as in plural. "Where's Vito?"

Cain's eyes opened, reminding her of just how beautiful the irises were, and he stretched. "Ah, I can see you're back to your old investigative journalist ways. There are a hundred other ways I'd rather start my morning than discussing the rather large man sleeping in our den."

When he reached for her, she drew back. "Seriously, where's my brother?"

Cain sighed and paused as if listening for sounds in the house. "Your brother's in the next room. My sister is caring for him."

"Your sister?" She literally knew nothing about this man. Yet she had sex with him. What was wrong with her? She needed her head examined, a shower, and a drug store.

"Relax, Destiny. You're safer here than in your own home."

"I doubt that." She stood and collected her clothing scattered about the room.

Cain sat up, the sheets falling off his bare chest and rigid stomach in a show of sheer masculinity.

How the hell did she manage to land a guy like that?

He held out his arms in a show of innocence and grinned. "I'm Amish. Can't get much safer than that."

Her eyes narrowed. He might be living on an Amish farm, but nothing about this man struck her as safe or biblical-hillside-country boy-Dutch. "Where's your beard?"

"Our sect doesn't require beards."

"What were you doing in the woods and at the Foster woman's funeral? How come I can't remember you?"

"But you did remember me a little. And you said yourself that you had a nasty fall."

She only remembered the idea of him. Up until yesterday, she couldn't recall his face or name. Something wasn't adding up. It was like she'd been drugged. She wondered if there was a screening to test her blood for such a possibility.

She wasn't being herself. The connection she felt to this man last night made no logical sense in the light of day. "I need to talk to my brother."

"Fine." He rose and the blankets fell away, revealing his body in all its naked glory.

Destiny pivoted and shaded her eyes, un-used to seeing a man so unapologetically… manly.

"What's wrong?" She jumped as his hands rode slowly up her arms and his mouth whis-pered close to her ear. "You weren't this shy last night."

"Y-your pants are over there. I'll get them." She rushed out of his grip and grabbed the slacks, handing them back to him while still averting her gaze.

He chuckled. "Interesting."

There wasn't a mirror for her to fix her

appearance so she did her best by fluffing her curls and tucking them behind her ears.

"You're on edge. Perhaps after I show you that your brother is alive and well, I can give you a tour of the farm. Put your mind at ease."

She stuffed her feet into her UGGs and kept her mouth shut. It would take a lot more than a few goats and cows to build her trust.

He stepped into his pants and an open shirt, slinging everything loosely into place with a pair of leather suspenders. How was that doing something to her? This wasn't sexy-cowboy-farmhand appeal. This was something totally new and different, something that should have never attracted her but made her insides melt. It had to be the definition of his abs peeking through his gaping shirt. That, and the fact that she could still feel him inside of her this morning. No one had ever had sex so thoroughly with her body before. Her muscles, insides, and even her skin ached in the best possible way.

"Shall we?" He held the door. "Your brother's having breakfast. I can hear him."

She paused, listening for any sound, but heard nothing. Following Cain down the hall, she took in every detail of the house. Everything appeared quite…well, Amish, which had the strange effect of filling her with shame, as if she'd vandalized a church or something sacred.

The planked wood floors were worn and ancient and the walls were mostly bare, aside from calendars and tapestries made useful with pockets and such. Much of the hand-crafted wood showed details common stores couldn't replicate. Obvious time and effort went into every item, from the quilts upon the beds to the braided rugs in the halls. The house smelled of burning wood, as every room had either a wood stove or working fireplace. But there was also something sweet and comforting in the air—like cinnamon and apples.

They passed a stairway leading to the second floor of the house and then entered a large kitchen. She let out a sigh of relief when she spotted her brother sitting at the table eating a slice of crumble coffee cake.

"Hey, D, there you are. Isn't this great?" he said over a mouthful of crumbs. "Here, taste this. Best cake I've ever had. It's not dry or nothin'. Gracie made it. Did you meet Gracie yet?"

Destiny shook her head, and a small young woman wearing a bonnet, black gown, and an apron sprinkled in flour smiled at her. Definitely Amish. "Good morning, Destiny. Would you like some breakfast cake?"

Cake for breakfast? Was this heaven? "Um…no, thank you."

A little overwhelmed, she looked at her brother.

"Seriously, D, try the cake." He shoveled another bite into his mouth. "I asked little Gracie here to marry me after the first taste, but apparently they're not allowed to date outside of their order."

Once again, Destiny wondered what the hell might have possessed her to have sex with an Amish man. She glanced back at Cain and instantly remembered. *Oh yeah, he's hot.* She was going to hell.

Gracie laughed and placed a tall glass of milk in front of Vito, patting his shoulder. "Are you sure you wouldn't like a piece, Destiny? Cain?"

"No, thank you," they answered in unison.

Just then the front door opened and an older teenage boy, still in that awkward stage of growing where his weight hadn't quite caught up with his height, came in, holding a young girl's hand. Destiny couldn't help but smirk at the adorable picture the two of them made in their Amish garb.

The boy immediately looked to where Gracie's hand rested on Vito's shoulder and scowled. The little girl looked at Destiny, and also scowled. Okay, maybe they were touchy Amish children.

"Who's this?" the boy demanded, his accent different from Cain's and more modern.

Gracie's eyes narrowed at the boy as if they shared some unspoken secret. "This is Vito and his sister, Destiny." She turned to face her. "Destiny, Vito, this is Dane and his younger sister, Cybil. You'll have to forgive Dane as he's forgotten his manner."

Dane and Cybil... Why did she recognize those names?

The little girl released her brother's hand and walked to Cain's side, wedging herself between him and Destiny. She hadn't realized he'd moved so close.

The boy's lips firmed as a dash of red touched his cheeks, his disapproval sucking the welcome right out of the room. "They stayed here while Jonas and Abilene are away?"

Grace scoffed. "I believe we are well past the ages of needing a chaperone, Dane."

The boy's nostrils flared. Without another word, he pivoted and left the house, letting the front door slam behind him.

"I'm giving Destiny a tour of the farm," Cain announced and the little girl began rapidly signing something with her hands as she scowled up at Cain. Only then did Destiny realize she must be deaf. "We won't be long," he told the child, signing his words much slower."

Destiny tugged his shirt and quietly whispered, "I have to, um… Can I use your restroom?"

"Right. I forgot. It's out back."

Out back? She frowned, but he was back to signing with the little girl so she figured her way on her own. Sure enough, there was a wooden shed out back.

"What in the name of *Deliverance…*" she mumbled as she peered inside the small shed.

A sink, shower stall, and toilet occupied the small room. Thankfully, there was also a wood stove so it wasn't freezing. But the water was.

Destiny shivered as she washed up. She kept a small makeup bag in her purse that also contained a travel sized toothpaste and toothbrush. The mirror was more along the lines of marbled metal that only gave a minor reflection, which was probably for the best.

Once freshened up and invigorated by the icy water, Destiny headed back to the house but paused as she overheard people arguing.

"How could you let two total strangers stay at your house?" a male voice carried.

"Oh, please." The girl sounded like Cain's sister. "I'm perfectly capable of taking care of myself, Dane."

"That man is twice your size, Grace."

"Size isn't everything."

Destiny hid behind the outhouse door, trying to determine which direction their voices were coming from. With everything so open, their words echoed off the house.

"They shouldn't be here," the boy, Dane, snapped.

"And why not? They have as much right to be here as you and Cybil do!"

"We live here."

"Not in this house, you don't. And even so, you're as temporary as the ducks at the pond. Eventually you'll migrate somewhere else."

Dane and Cybil weren't Amish? Destiny thought there were rules forbidding such things. Maybe she misunderstood and there was hope for her and Cain after all.

Realizing how quickly her mind had spun into the unlikely, she reeled her emotions in. That guy was a cart and buggy booty call. Nothing more.

"As long as my sister is here, I'm staying. She's all I have left."

Destiny sucked in a sharp breath, making the connection. Dane and Cybil. They were the Foster children.

What the heck were they doing here? Maybe that was why she'd run into Cain at their mother's funeral. Maybe they were somehow related or old family friends.

"That doesn't make you one of us," Grace snapped.

"Well, it makes this my home, so you best accept me being around."

"As long as you accept that you and I are *nothing,* and you have no right to dictate how I live my life."

"Nothing?" he sneered.

"Yes, nothing, Dane. Friends. That is all."

They were silent for a beat and Destiny wondered if they walked off, then Dane said, "Keep lying to yourself, Gracie. I know what you're thinking. I know more than you realize."

"You don't know everything. And stay out

of my head! Regardless of what I think, I'm saving myself for the male whom God chooses for me. I know for a fact that isn't you."

"Fine," he said quietly. "But that guy in there is even less of your type so keep your distance."

"As if I would do anything of that nature with Cain in the house."

"Cain's never around long."

His final words resonated through Destiny. The reasons why Cain was meaningless kept compiling.

First, Cain was Amish, something she was pretty certain a person had to be born into. Second, he apparently had the reputation of a flight risk. Leave it to her to fall for the one Amish player in all of Lancaster.

When it was clear the two arguing had stormed off, Destiny returned to the house. Gracie was back in the kitchen, but not wearing her earlier smile.

Cain signed something to Cybil and whispered, "Be nice." Then he held up his hand in a sign that Destiny recognized as a universal symbol for I love you.

The little girl's cheeks tinted with pink and a dimple appeared at the endearment.

Then her stare narrowed on Destiny and she frowned.

Grace withdrew a book from the kitchen shelf. " It's time for your lesson, Cybil."

Surprisingly, the little girl responded to Gracie's spoken words without looking directly at her. Perhaps she wasn't deaf at all, but mute. Destiny recalled her interviews with the police and how they mentioned the victim's children had been quiet.

Had Cybil not spoken since the murder of her mother? Was this a result of trauma? Once again, Destiny registered how lucky she was that she only suffered a nasty fall in the woods. It had been completely foolish for her to go out there alone.

"We'll be back in time for supper," Cain announced, removing Destiny's coat from a peg on the wall. She frowned, not recalling how it got there.

Cain helped her bundle up and she savored the novelty of a man with actual manners—once more warning her head and heart to show some self-control.

"You okay?" he whispered.

She was concerned about the gaps in her memory but didn't want to sound crazy, so she forced a smile. "I'm great."

He frowned but accepted the lie. He held the door.

The tension in the house had grown uncomfortable and she was glad to escape outside. The sky was clear and there wasn't much wind, so the temperature was bearable for a change.

"How is it the Foster children have come to live here?"

Cain stiffened as if not expecting her to make the connection. "You remember them?"

"Of course. I covered the story of their mother's death."

"Then you'll recall their grandmother was ill."

"Was?"

"Yes, she passed several weeks back." He opened the gate at the end of their property and waved her toward a cluster of barns and stables in the distance.

"That doesn't answer my question about how they came to live here. They're not Amish."

His mouth firmed as he stuffed his hands in the pockets of his jacket. "Their grandmother had a connection to my father. When she passed, she left the children in his care."

"Where's your father now?"

"He and my mother are on a trip. They needed some time together, away from The Order."

"So, who's the actual caregiver of the children?" The state would require a legal guardianship, but the Amish often skipped the red tape in legal situations. Was this like that?

"Dane's old enough to take care of himself and there are enough of us around to see that they have everything they need."

"Dane's a kid."

"He's seventeen. In a few months he'll be a legal adult. He will have every right to request guardianship of his sister and our full support, but why bother when they have a place to stay here. They're safe here. Their needs are met."

She supposed he was right. But she couldn't imagine being seventeen and losing her last surviving parent then being forced to move away from all of her friends. "What about school?"

"He goes to our school."

"And Cybil?"

"What about her?" An unmistakable air of protectiveness filled his voice.

"She seems very attached to you."

"As I am to her."

"Has she spoken since the attack?"

He glanced at her, his eyes suspicious. "Who's asking?"

She stopped walking, unsure what he was implying but certain he was making some sort of accusation. "What do you mean?"

"I mean, are you asking as a friend or are you digging up dirt for your next story? The children are fine. They are safe here and adjusting to their new life. They don't need anyone interfering—"

"Cain, that's not why I was asking. God, what do you think of me?" His low opinion actually stung.

"Sorry. I just want to protect them. I gave my word, and that means something to me."

Another big, fat check slid under the honorable traits column. But none of that mattered, because in the light of day, Cain was unmistakably Amish and this was not her life. "I want that, too. I would never interfere with the opportunity you've given them. It's incredible. They're lucky to have so many people in their support system."

His mouth softened and twitched. He reached for her hand and squeezed her fingers. "I'm sorry."

She accepted his apology but still wanted to clear up any negative perception of her he might harbor. "I'm not a bad person."

"It's television. We're not used to media and press. When I saw you at the funeral…"

"I know what you thought. You were right. I shouldn't have been there."

He paused, appearing surprised by her confession. It wasn't always easy for her to admit when she'd been wrong, but here the pressure and competition wasn't as influential. She could see right from wrong, and it mattered how he saw her.

His hand closed around hers and he smiled. "Do you want to see the horses?"

Glad for the distraction, she nodded and followed him into the stables. The stalls were impeccably clean and several horses peeked their heads out when they heard them enter.

"This is Sully," Cain introduced. "I've had him since he was born."

She stared up at the horse's dark eyes and felt an unexpected connection to the animal. She'd never been so close to a horse before and found it calming and mesmerizing. "He's beautiful."

"Do you want to feed him?"

She smiled and looked at him expectantly. "Can I?"

He handed her a broken carrot. "Flatten your palm and fingers and hold it out to him."

She did as he instructed, laughing when Sully's wet lips closed over the carrot and his big teeth crunched down on the stick. Cain handed her another and she fed him some more, spoiling the horse until the bag was empty.

After the stables, he showed her the chicken coop and made fun of her when she called a hen a rooster. "Hey, English is my second language. I do my best."

"Were you born in Portugal?"

She couldn't remember telling him about Portugal, but her memory wasn't very dependable these days. "Yes. I lived there until I was seven. Then my mom sent me and my brother here to live with our aunts. They're all back in Portugal now living on my family's farm."

"Your family has a farm and you confused a rooster for a hen?"

"We raise goats, not chickens."

"Do you miss them?"

"The goats?"

He laughed. "Your parents."

"I visit once a year." It was a line she repeated whenever asked about her parents, but the truth was she missed them terribly. Technology made it possible for her to see her mom and dad's faces every day and hear their voices, but it wasn't the same as living in their actual presence. "I miss them a lot, actually."

"When's the last time you visited?"

"About six months ago. They're getting older now. I worry more than I used to. Vito's going this spring, so at least he'll see them."

"You should go with him if you miss them."

"I can't. The flights are expensive and I can only take so much time off of work." She didn't want her longing to spoil an otherwise lovely day. "The houses here are beautiful. Do you build them yourselves?"

"Yes. And the barns. See that house there? That's my brother's home. He recently built it for his mate, Anna."

"Mate?"

"Wife," he corrected.

"Is that the brother you mentioned last night?"

He cleared his throat. "That house to the far left with the smaller porch, that is my grandparents' home. My Uncle Fisher also lives there."

Understanding that he preferred not to speak of his brother's marriage, she accepted the change of subject. "Do men usually live with their parents past adulthood?" She had lived with her parents and probably still would if they hadn't returned to Portugal.

"Only until they are mate—married. Females as well. It's just easier that way."

She nodded. "Practical." Her family's old-world views shared some similarities with the Amish culture. "It's that way for my family too."

"Is it?" He appeared surprised that they might not be so different. "What else?"

She thought for a moment. "Well, the men in my family are completely spoiled by the women. They never have to cook or clean and wouldn't know the first thing about doing laundry."

He glanced at her, the side of his mouth hooking into a smirk. "You don't agree with that?"

"I think it's fine if a woman wants to take care of her man—same as if a man wants to take care of his woman—but basing expectations on gender roles alone isn't fair. My brother didn't have to do half the crap I did growing up simply because he was a guy."

He pulled her arm, turning her so her back pressed into a stone wall. He crowded her with his body. "A male needs to feel powerful. It's his duty to protect the females under his care."

And just like that, her feminism melted in a gush of heat as he looked into her eyes and pressed his powerful body against hers. She swallowed and looked up at him, hungry for his touch and strangely appreciating the way he made her feel delicate and small. Safe inside his arms.

"A good woman protects her man just as much as he protects her," she finally said, mouth dry and her lungs full.

He tucked a curl behind her ear and smiled. "And how would you protect me, I wonder, if I were that man? What would that look like?"

She swallowed. Were they really doing this? It felt like emotional role playing, so she let him have the full fantasy. "I'd love him in word and deed. I'd take care of his needs and make myself available to him. I'd honor him as he honors me, with a loving home that is always warm and welcoming. We would laugh like friends, lust like lovers, and share like partners."

"And what if he wanted you home so your focus could be on the family?"

He really was describing a fantasy. "Well, then he better have a good job."

"That's all it would take? Money?"

"Not money. Security. Women throughout history have suffered due to a lack of opportunity. For us to go backwards and stay at home, it has to look different than it did a hundred years ago. A woman at home doesn't justify a man's absence."

"You mean a partnership."

"Right. An emotional and physical one. Never servitude. Always present."

"And if a man was emotionally and physically present, loved you in word and deed, took care of your needs, made himself available to you, honored you, laughed with you, loved you, and shared everything with you...?"

Her heart skipped a beat at the unlikely possibility. "Then I'd give him everything I could offer."

"All of you?"

She couldn't imagine anything so perfect,

so there was no harm in setting the terms. "All of me."

He stared into her eyes as if trying to read a hidden agenda, but there wasn't one. She supposed, when it came down to it, her tastes were more old-fashioned than she let on. In her mind, women had changed, becoming more self-reliant, but mostly because men stopped trying as hard.

The sort of dependability she fantasized about no longer existed. Independence was a power play for single women, a byproduct of circumstance and a lack of options. Deep down, Destiny truly wished she had someone deserving of her love, someone she could trust with her heart.

His hand curved around her hip, his arousal pressing noticeably into her stomach. "You paint a pretty picture. Such an offer makes a male want to try harder."

"It's just a fantasy," she whispered, slightly embarrassed after sharing so much.

He shook his head. "Perhaps it's a premonition."

His words teased her hope. There was no tempting her with the impossible. She laughed, breaking the spell and his grip loosened. When she tried to step around him, he pushed her back to the wall again, only this time he kissed her, deep and demanding, the kind of kiss that stole through a woman like a hurricane, touching everything and anything in its path.

His hands cupped her jaw, tipping her head back. Fingers sifted through her curls, soft with subtle tugs. His hard body ground into her, announcing his desire, and re-minding her of his strength and power. Her muscles softened and she sank into him, ac-cepting every drugging stroke of his tongue and existing solely for his touch.

When he broke away, she'd forgotten where they were and what she'd been saying. All she knew was the fact that this man kissed her better than anyone had ever kissed her before. He touched her like he worshiped her, and met her needs so com-pletely she forgot what it was to want for herself.

He took her hand, lacing her numb fingers through his, and chuckled. "I'll just hold on to you. You look a little unsteady."

They walked for a while. He showed her the orchards and honey combs and where they kept the cows.

"You must love living here."

He gave her a strange look. "Why do you say that?"

She shrugged. "What's not to love? It's beautiful, peaceful, and so much less stressful than…where I come from."

"We have stress here too."

She doubted it was anything like the outside world.

"You said you only have so much time off of work." He led her to a fence that overlooked a corral of sorts. "Is being here causing an issue?"

"No, I actually have some time off right now." She was still ashamed by the incident in the woods, so she glossed over the fact that she'd given her crew such a hard time they needed a break from her. "After my fall, my boss thought it best if I take a few days to recover."

"But you're healed now."

Touched by his concern, she reassured him. "I feel incredible, considering the spill I took. It was a nasty fall."

He studied her for a long moment and she suspected he wanted to tell her something. "You don't remember any of it, do you?"

She looked down, embarrassed. "No. It's the strangest thing. I remember my phone dying in the woods and skitzing out, then… nothing. I woke up at home in my bed."

"But you found your way back here."

"I thought I went to a convent. My memories are all jumbled. I remembered the woman Larissa, but I thought she was a nun. And there was a cave or something. I must have had some really vivid dreams when I got knocked out."

"My sister is Larissa."

Her jaw went slack. "Sister Larissa?"

"Yes. All of our females are addressed as such. You must have misunderstood when she was caring for you."

There was no sense of familiarity with his words, so she had to trust that he spoke the truth. "That makes me feel so much better. All this time I was looking for a convent. So you're saying you brought me here?"

"Yes. Then I took you home."

She frowned. "Wait… How did we get from—"

"Back up." He pulled her off the fence and pointed to an enormous bull wandering toward them.

Her heart rate spiked as the giant beast breathed tunnels of steam into the air like a dragon exhales fire. "Is this fence strong enough to hold him in?"

"He likes the fence as much as us. It keeps trespassers out. He only likes when we bring the cows to visit."

She laughed nervously. "I never realized how big bulls were."

"Clive's bigger than most. Let's give him his space."

They wandered away from the corral and Destiny glanced back over her shoulder, respectfully cowering from the intimidating animal. "I think I'm more of a horse person."

Cain chuckled. His hand slipped into hers once again. "Since you have time off from work, perhaps you should stay another day."

Was he really asking that? "Another day or another night?"

He glanced at her, a suggestive, unmistakable glint in his eyes.

They had to be breaking some sort of commandment. "What exactly are the rules with you people?"

He laughed. "What do you mean?"

"Aren't you supposed to be extra religious?"

His hand tightened around hers. "God created man to sew his seed. It has little to do with faith."

And sew his seed he had. If she did stay another night, she'd act more responsibly. "So you can't get in trouble for having a woman in your bed?"

He paused and looked at her with laugher in his eyes. "I'm a grown male, Destiny. Who is going to reprimand me?"

"I don't know. Your priest?"

"We don't have a priest. We have a bishop and he's well aware that you slept in my bed last night."

"*What?*"

He tugged her to keep walking. "He and I have an understanding. Your presence isn't a problem."

"Even though I'm not Amish."

"I prefer it that way."

When they returned to the house, the sun was setting. Vito was pleased to learn they were staying for dinner since Grace had prepared a feast. Despite all of Cain's reassurance, Destiny felt awkward eating with her brother and Cain's sister.

After supper, there wasn't television or anything else to distract them, so Destiny excused herself to freshen up. She needed a few moments to catch her breath and regroup.

Once alone in the outhouse, she considered her options. They could leave and return to reality, or she could stay as Cain asked. It was already dark and… Oh, who was she kidding. She already had her heart set on staying.

She knew she'd stay the moment he asked. So why, if he openly expressed his desire to have her one more night, did her insides feel so jittery in such an unsafe way? She was either falling for him or giving herself a stomach ache.

Pressing a hand under her ribs, she stared in the hazy mirror and exhaled. She shouldn't get ahead of herself. He was Amish for crying out loud. And she was not.

She didn't even belong to a church or own a dress with a high neckline. His bishop couldn't possibly be okay with what they were doing. If he was, what kind of Amish order was this?

The outhouse latch moved and Destiny tensed. "Someone's in here!"

The door opened and she gasped, grateful she'd only been using the sink when Cain stepped inside. His grin should have been illegal in at least thirty states.

"What are you doing?"

"I came to wash up." He stripped off his shirt and slung it on a peg, careless of the chill in the air.

"But… I'm in here."

"I'm aware." His suspenders drooped and his slacks sagged off his hips. Stealing a folded towel from the pile on the vanity, he traced a finger across her shoulders, sending chills racing down her spine.

He hung the towel on the hook by the shower and—

"Wait, I'll leave!"

He dropped his pants.

She stared, unsure if she'd ever seen such a finely chiseled work of art. "There isn't a single imperfection on you."

He chucked and snatched a rough bar of raw soap from the dish. "Trust me, I have flaws."

Yeah, right. Not from where she stood.

Moving under the shower spigot, he pulled the chain that released a spray overhead. Rivulets of cold water drenched his body as his heated skin steamed in the chilled air. Her gaze dropped. Not a single thick inch of him seemed affected by the cold.

Her mouth went dry and slack as she

stared unblinking at the stunning display. Suds chased down his chest, between his legs, and his hand followed. He stroked himself intentionally, as if to show her he didn't mind having an audience.

When her stare lifted to his, he grinned. "Join me?"

Why was she debating sleeping with him again? He was lightyears out of her league. The fact that he wanted her at all should be a massive red flag, sure, but maybe she should just stop psychoanalyzing every interaction and just enjoy the time they had.

"Are you married or betrothed to someone or something?"

Laughter barked out of him. "What?"

"Are you single?"

"Completely untethered."

How was that possible? "And when you asked me to stay, you meant…?"

"I want my cock pumping between those thick thighs." His fist squeezed his engorged flesh, blatantly stroking as he stared at her. "Do you regret last night?"

It had been the best sex she'd ever had, but mostly because she assumed she'd never see him again. Yet she was still here. Now there might be expectations or a twist. The mystic was gone and new consequences appeared. She was starting to feel things outside of the unspoken booty call bounds.

Before she formulated an answer, he stepped out of the stream of water and crowded her against the wall. "Let me make it easier on you, Destiny. I was there. I know you enjoyed it, over and over again." He wedged his hand down the front of her pants and raised a brow. "And I know when a woman is aroused." He withdrew his hand, holding her stare, as he sucked the tip of his finger into his mouth like a chef might lick the cream off a spatula. "Need I say more?"

Something inside of her snapped and she lunged at him, unable to deny herself a second night of pleasure. Gripping his face, she kissed him almost violently. He growled and wrenched open her legs, lifting her off the ground. Carrying her into the shower stall, he ripped open her shirt and dropped his mouth to her breasts.

Her legs wrapped tight around his hips, she arched back and gripped the chain on the wall. Cold water spilled over them and she gasped, but Cain was not deterred.

Wrenching down her pants, he tore every scrap of clothing off of her and buried himself in her heat. She cried out, gripping his shoulders as he plunged into her, pumping hard against her tender tissue that had not fully recovered from the night before.

She didn't care if people might hear them or how roughly he handled her body. All she cared about was pleasure, hers and his.

He ravaged her against the wall. Bruised her and left her aching. He demanded more from her than any man ever had. And she gave him more than she'd ever given anyone else. She wasn't sure what tomorrow would bring, but she made the decision then and there to make every last second of tonight count.

CHAPTER 22

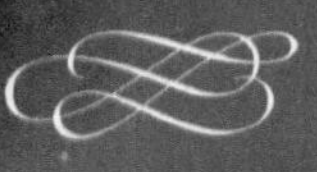

"*I* brought you some lavender tea with honey and moon water, June bug."

Juniper stared at the front door of her Aunt Venus's friend's apartment, as she lay plastered to the sofa, her face glued to the cushion with dried tears. "Thank you."

Venus had been burning hibiscus and lavender all day. There had been no sight of Wilder, the guy who owned the apartment, but his presence remained in the unfamiliar smells and furniture of the small loft.

Her aunt perched by Juniper's feet, her hands folded between her knees as her head hung in defeat. "I just…" She shook her head.

"Every time I try to process this, my first instinct is to call Mabel. I can't comprehend that she's gone."

A tear slipped from Juniper's eye as Venus softly wept. Her aunts had been three sisters, and now there was only one. First her mother, who passed postpartum, and now Mabel. She couldn't envision a world without Aunt Bel.

"It's my fault," Juniper whispered, sick with shame and regret.

"What? Oh, no, honey. This wasn't anyone's fault." Aunt V's compassion washed over her as she cleansed Juniper's aura. "The shop was old. It could have been the wiring or a candle left burning. Goddess knows Mabel loved her incense. This wasn't your fault."

Once they took her to the hospital, all of Juniper's focus had been on getting out, but she needed an adult guardian to sign the discharge papers since she arrived in an ambulance. As soon as Venus heard, she came to get her. Nothing would ever erase the gut-wrenching cry that left Venus when she learned that Juniper had come to the hospital alone, and Aunt Bel had been taken to the morgue.

It took three nurses and an orderly to calm her down, plus several pills she kept tucked inside her purse. All Juniper could think was this was her fault. If not for her stupidity, Aunt Bel would still be alive. But she was gone and they had nothing. No home, no belongings, nothing.

Beneath her heartache a cold rage slowly boiled. This wasn't just her fault. It was also that man's. She was certain she saw him at the fire, and sure he had done this to them. For what? Why did anyone deserve this?

"I have to tell you something."

Aunt V sat up and wiped her eyes. For once they weren't covered in black. The tears had washed away her makeup hours ago. "I'm listening."

"It's about the man who came into the store a few days ago."

"What man, honey?"

"The…" Even now, she felt foolish saying the word. "Vampire."

Venus tensed. "Mabel told me you were in the store when he visited. Don't worry. She sent him away and made it clear that we were not willing to work with him."

"I was there. I know what she said." Juniper forced herself to sit up. "I also saw him after that."

"What? When?"

"On the trail." Her throat constricted as shame choked her. "I should have said something, but I had a terrible day. So many weird things have been happening, and I was supposed to be in school, but I bailed when my teacher broke his arm."

"Slow down. What weird things? Juniper, you have to tell me everything. Did that man speak to you? Did he touch you?"

She was tired of lying, so she confessed everything, starting with how she stole Mabel's pot and got high in the woods, accidentally hurting Trent and hallucinating the fire moving at her command. Then she explained what happened to Mr. Weckle's arm in algebra class and how she ran into Jonas on the path.

"He said if I didn't get you and Aunt Bel to help him, he would tell your secret." She started to cry uncontrollably. "I'm so sorry, Aunt Venus. I really thought he was just some goth creep with an Amish fetish. Then he grabbed me and I got scared—"

"He grabbed you?" Venus's expression hardened and she sat up.

Juniper stopped talking. She'd never seen her aunt look so angry. "I got away."

"*Where* did he grab you?"

"We were on the trail—"

"No, Juniper, where on your body."

She closed her hand around her throat. "Here."

Venus looked away, her face pale and her eyes heavy with worry. "How long did he give you to talk to us?"

"Until midnight last night."

"And the fire started around one."

Her stomach hurt. She felt so responsible she feared her aunt would blame her. She deserved the blame. If not for her silence, this wouldn't have happened. "I saw him last night. He was standing in the crowd, looking right at me as he held a pocket watch. It was like he wanted me to know I was late."

Venus stood and locked the door. She paced the small living room and bit her nails. "Tell me everything you know about him. What he looked like. How he spoke. I need every detail."

"He looked Amish, but no beard. He had long black hair and plain clothes. He had a slight accent, but nothing too prominent. He was easy enough to understand."

"What was his name?"

"Jonas Hartzler."

She pulled out her phone and typed something in. For several minutes she said nothing then she sat down again. "The Hartzlers are a part of an order in Lancaster."

"You're going to help him?"

She looked at her like she was crazy. "No, sweetheart. I'm going to kill him."

Juniper jumped off the couch and followed her into the kitchen. "You're joking."

"I never joke about murder."

She grabbed her shoulders and pulled her back from the pantry. "Aunt Venus, stop. This isn't funny." When she faced her, her eyes were ravaged with tears. "That man is a psychopath. Let's go to the police and report him. They'll take care of it. He'll get arrested for arson and tried for manslaughter."

"Juniper, it doesn't work that way with vampires."

Her mouth gaped. "You can't be serious."

"Do I look like I'm joking?"

No, she looked terrifying. "Aunt V, we can't."

"Juniper, sit down. We need to talk." She ushered her to a chair at the kitchen table and gripped her hands. "When that man said he knew our secret, what did you think he meant?"

Juniper shrugged. "That we were witches."

Venus's face pinched with regret. "You really have no idea, do you?"

"What do you mean?"

She drew in a galvanizing breath. "Okay, sweetie. We had hoped this would come about naturally, under less worrisome circumstances, but we don't always get what we want, obviously. Your mother begged us not to tell you, so we tried to keep our word as long as possible, assuming one day we would have to break our vow."

"Tell me what?"

"Oh, honey, this isn't going to be easy—"

"Say it, Venus." Unlike Aunt Bel who always took the maternal role, Venus was younger and highly emotional at the worst times. They were only fifteen years apart, and sometimes it was hard to think of her as any sort of guardian even though she technically had been her guardian since her mom died.

"Your mom didn't suffer from postpartum depression."

"What do you mean? I thought that was—"

"I know what we told you. It was close to the truth, but also a lie. Your mother never suffered from depression, and she would have never hurt herself."

"Then what happened to her?"

Venus's eyes filled with tears. "She left."

Juniper scowled. "Left? What the hell does that mean, she left? She's still alive?"

Venus pinched her fingers together. "A little."

Juniper shot to her feet. "A little? What the fuck, Venus? Whose ashes are in the urn on the mantle?"

"Oden's."

"Oden? The Norse god?"

"No, Oden our old tabby." She rubbed her temples. "See, I feel like Mabel would have handled this way better."

"Well, Mabel's not here!" Her whole life was a lie. "Where's my mother?"

"You're yelling and I do much better with tranquil tones."

"Venus!"

"All right! All right! She's in Europe! Or she was last I heard."

Juniper's jaw trembled as she sank onto the floor. "She didn't want me."

"You were never unwanted, June bug. Mabel and I loved you like our own."

"I can't believe she abandoned me. All this

time I thought…" She lifted her watery gaze to her aunt. "Why didn't she want me?"

"Oh, sweetie." Venus dropped to the floor and wrapped her arms around her, holding her tight. "Your mother wanted you so much it nearly killed her to let you go."

"Then why did she leave me?"

Venus sniffled and brushed her hair away from her face, pushing their foreheads together. "Because your father was a selfish asshole who never wanted anything or anyone to tie him down. Your mom assumed he'd come around once he held you, but he didn't. And when he threatened to leave, she lost her mind. They had a very volatile, toxic love."

She wiped her eyes, unsure how anyone could cry as much as she had in one day. "What kind of mother leaves a helpless child behind for a man like that?"

"He wasn't an ordinary man, honey. And, like it or not, he's a part of you."

"No, he's not. I have no father."

"You do. His name is Niro and it's time you learned about him."

"I don't care about him. I hate him."

"Hate is not indifference. I know this, because your mother also hated him on some level, but she still loved him."

"I don't want to talk about this anymore."

"But we have to." Venus brushed a hand over her hair, soothing her the way she so easily did. "You see, when that man said he knew your secret, it wasn't that we are witches. It was that you're different. He must have recognized something in you, because he figured out what you were."

She drew back and frowned. "Huh?"

"Honey, your mother was a witch, just like our mother and her mother and so on. But Niro was from a different time and place. He lived in Rome and was born just around the year St. Peter's Basilica was built."

"What are you talking about?"

"Your father's old. Ancient, actually."

Juniper scowled. "Are you screwing with me? Is this some sort of twisted joke?"

"It's not a joke," Venus said defensively. "I'm trying to tell you, your father is immortal."

"There's no such thing as immortality, even Aunt Bel said so."

"Because everything alive must eventually die, duh, but what else are we supposed to call it? The guys been around for centuries."

"No."

"Yes."

"No," Juniper snapped, and shoved herself off the floor. "This is just more folklore. I'm sick of it! I don't need fairytales to get through my day. I need someone to tell me the goddamn truth!"

"You want the truth?" Venus jumped to her feet. "Your father is a vampire. Your mother fell in love with him and when he told her to choose, she chose him. She begged him to erase her memories of us and you, and off they went to live their life in Europe."

"You're lying." She turned and the candles throughout the room ignited, shooting flames high into the air before lowering to the wick. She spun back to Venus, staring wide-eyed. "Did you just…?"

"Lying is what we did when you were a little girl to help you fall asleep. You're not little anymore, Juniper. And it's time you realized what's inside of you. One drop of immortal blood has the power to save a life. There are no books or internet searches to tell us what happens when someone is half witch, half undead. There's a reason you don't scar, but you also have vulnerabilities."

She pointed to the candles with a shaky finger. "How did you do that?"

Venus's lips twisted and she shrugged.

"Did you honestly think we made a living off of crystals and tarot cards alone?"

Still in shock, she looked back at the candles, wondering if her mind exaggerated what she actually saw. "Do something else?"

"Are you listening to a word I'm saying?"

"Yes, but it's a lot. One thing at a time. I can handle the witchcraft. Show me something else." The kitchen window flung open and the curtains went wild. "Jesus!"

"You weren't high and hallucinating in the woods, June bug. You were coming into your power. It happens around this age for all of us, but you have to know how to harness it or the blessing will turn into a burden. I can help you."

Her chin trembled. "Do you think I hurt my teacher? Did I hurt Trent?"

"Energy moves like dominos. Sometimes one little push can make a big mess. Whatever happened, you didn't do it on purpose, so don't beat yourself up over it too much. We've all made mistakes. What matters is that you learn self-control. Once you have that, no one can take your power away."

"What about my dad, Niro, or whatever?" She'd always wanted a father, but learning hers was the reason her mom abandoned her changed that. "Is he dead?"

"No. That's another growing pain you'll experience, I'm afraid. They say it happens around adulthood."

"What happens?"

"The, um, appetite."

She drew back in revulsion. "No."

Venus waved off her concern. "It won't be that bad. By the time it happens, you'll want it. Sort of like sex. Boys used to be gross, but then—*poof!*—we can't resist them. You'll get there."

Juniper dropped into a kitchen chair and rubbed her head. "This is too much to process in a day." She wished Aunt Bel were around to guide her.

"Hey, it's gonna be okay."

She looked at her aunt and wondered how she could even joke that any of this would be okay. "No, it's not. I just wanted to go away to college and be normal."

"Normal's overrated. You're growing into an extraordinary young woman, June bug. Give yourself time to get there. You'll see."

She sniffled. "I have to tell you one more thing."

"What's that?"

"That guy, Jonas, he said he could track me."

Aunt V frowned. "He could only do that if he had your blood. We won't let him get that —Oh."

"I'm sorry," Juniper apologized. "I didn't know any of this would happen. I didn't mean to—"

"Hush." Venus pulled her into a hug. "I know you didn't. Vampires can be terribly manipulative. They cannot be trusted."

She sniffled, at odds with her own identity and feeling somewhat removed from her lineage since learning the truth. "You hate them. And I'm one of them." She always thought she despised being a witch, but now she understood there was something much worse.

"You're different. You're nothing like Niro or the others. That part of you will never take over the rest. That's why your roots as a witch are so important and why we must start practicing control right away. It's the greatest protection you'll have against other natural urges."

"What about the Amish guy, Jonas?"

"He's after a cure, but there isn't one. Not the way he envisions it. The laws of nature require balance. Everything living must eventually die, and once the rot sets in, there is no unsetting it." Her mouth curved with a maniacal grin. "Now there is a debt to be paid, and I will demand full compensation for the life he stole from us. He may get exactly what he asked for after all."

CHAPTER 23

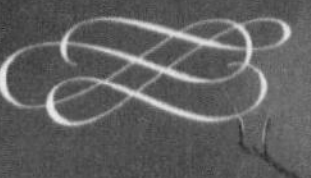

*H*e was there. Close. Cybil sensed him in the darkness. Fear gripped her tight. Why? Why was he doing this? He was always there in her dreams, seemingly as blind as she was rendered mute with fear.

He should have known her, but he didn't. She hated when he lost track of who she was. That was when he crept in on her, surrounding her. Too close!

Her hands sliced through the air as she frantically pleaded for him to stop. The moment she signed the word, stop, he did. He never touched her —only watched her with those seemingly unseeing eyes. There was a precarious thread on his control, and she sensed how dearly he fought not to lose himself to some greater power.

Why couldn't he see her for who she was? He should recognize her. She knew he should.

"Do you not know me?" she signed with trembling fingers.

Cold hands closed over hers, and her body shuddered. Never before had he touched her. She was on the brink of tears. She could see him when he kept his distance, but the moment he drew close to her, she lost sight of him. Nothing but blackness surrounded her, anchoring her there in this dark place with the gentle, but powerful hold of some phantom hand.

"Call my name, Cybil. Say it before it is too late, before I've gone too far."

It was not her name on his lips that filled her with revulsion. It was the closeness of his warm breath upon her cheek that provoked her. She tried to tug her hands away to sign for him to let go, but his hold tightened.

"Say it. You know it. Let me hear you speak it. I cannot come to you until you allow it. Speak my name. End this anguish that holds me apart from you. My soul is tortured by the infinite time you will let pass before I can truly know you. There is no call until it forms upon your lips. Say it. Call me to you, and when I hear your voice speak my name, our paths and my mind will be clear. Save me, Cybil, before I am truly lost."

Tears trickled past her lashes. She couldn't utter a sound for fear of permitting his wish. Part of her recognized him, but here, in her dreams, she was different.

"You're afraid, because you're young. But soon enough you will be grown. My soul has waded through what feels like an eternity of lies, but you are my truth. My salvation relies on you. Every day you do not speak my name I go unanswered. Every passing moon I am closer to my final death. My dreams are lost until you speak. Your voice will remind me. Show me, Cybil. Say my name. Tell me all is not lost before I give up and lose my soul to an eternal hell far worse than the one I've been living. Help me."

He released her hands, and she pulled away. For what was a sanctuary for him was a prison for her.

She hated the dark and that was where he found her, deep in the shadows of her mind, buried under hours of sleep where the light of day could not reach them and she could not fully see him. But part of her unwillingly recognized him. Different from how he appeared when she'd been awake. And she struggled to comprehend that he was, in fact, the same man.

"You already know me. Trust me when I say your fear will ease with time."

Such darkness surrounded him as it followed her. She could count more losses upon her fingers than gains. Life had been cruel and time had been slipping away since her mother died.

"The darkness overtakes those without light. You are my light, Cybil. I need you. Say my name so that I see the only path to salvation left for me."

Years of dreams, and he always delivered the same message. She was his and he was hers.

Why, then, had she always recognized his evilness before witnessing any good? Why did he come to her in nightmares when she was alone and afraid, always cloaked in shadows, speaking only half-truths and lies? She might know him here, but she knew him out there too. He was not the same and she would not speak his name, She would not give him such power.

"Cybil! I need you!"

She cowered in the corner, folding her arms around her knees and tucking her face into the hollows of her arms. There were only small pockets of peace in this world where she could hide. Safe places to run. Playing with Dane was safe. Tending to the baby kittens with Gracie was safe. He claimed he was safe, but her dreams were not, so who could she trust, knowing full well there was sometimes a darkness that consumed him?

She was so alone, screaming in the silence for

someone to notice her, to see her as something more than the sad orphan waiting for someone to claim her.

"I will claim you. You are mine. You need only to speak my name and I will hear God's call and know his plan. Without you, I am blind. Your silence ensures I stay that way."

His insistence weighed like a physical touch in the dark, and she cowered deeper in the shadows, hating when he read her mind and forced her to confront her fears.

"Say it, Cybil. Speak my name. Your silence is destroying me."

Her head shook as she pulled back, avoiding his grasp, whimpering for an escape. He would never hurt her, but his desperation formed an ache in her heart. She was his relief, but she wasn't ready. Not yet. And the longer she made him wait, the worse his fate would become.

"I need you, Cybil. Save me."

Her body jerked back and landed hard on the floor. Moonlight doused the shadows in a silver-blue glow and she recognized her bed and toys. Her heart raced as she searched the room, but he was gone. It was only a dream.

Slipping into the hall, she quietly padded into the kitchen and wrapped herself in a cloak. At the door, she found her boots and carried them outside. Sneaking past the front gate, she ran as fast as her legs would carry her.

The cold air held the dampness of morning dew and a hint of spring. Her heart was pumping when she reached his gate and her cheeks flushed. The hinge creaked as she locked the latch. The front door was open as usual.

The kitchen was warm from the fire that had burned all night in the wood stove. As soon as she saw his door, her inner panic soothed and tension gave way to relief. She turned the knob and stilled.

Cain lay sound asleep, but he was not alone. The woman she'd met earlier filled his arms. They slept close, like puppies, entwined without a hint of light able to sneak between them.

Cybil drew in a slow breath and glared at the two of them. Who was she? Why was she still there? Why was he holding her like that?

Fury burned through her chest as she narrowed her stare on the woman. She didn't belong here. And Cybil wanted her gone.

Her anger quickly turned to sadness as she backed out of the room, afraid and unwilling to return to her own. She wouldn't sleep. She didn't want to chance another dream.

Sliding down the wall, she lowered her body to the floor. Let him find her there and know that she saw him with that woman. She wanted him to feel what she felt now.

Cain was hers. Since moving to the farm, Dane had been different, preoccupied with other interests and acting silly whenever Gracie came around. He no longer took time to play with her or read to her or do any of the other things they used to do as brother and sister. She was angry with him. But Cain was different.

Cain played and made her laugh. He always took interest in what she liked. He cared about her, was good to her, and would never hurt her. But he might abandon her. That woman in his bed might take him away and then Cybil would have no one.

Her brow pinched as she stared hard at the floor and softly mouthed his name, *Cain.*

She wanted that woman gone.

CHAPTER 24

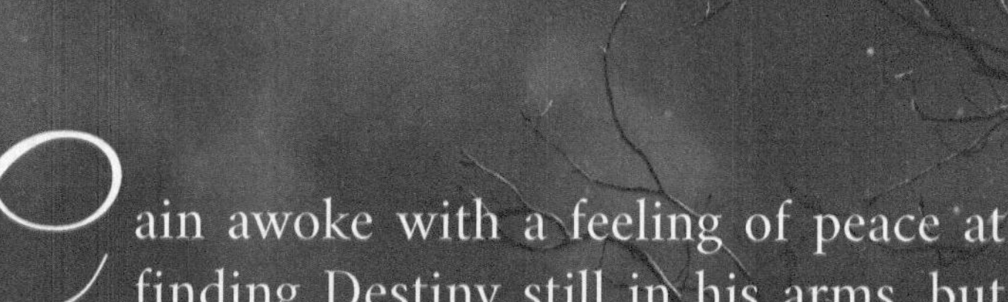

Cain awoke with a feeling of peace at finding Destiny still in his arms, but that peace quickly transformed to dread. She'd stayed longer than permitted and today would be her last day on the farm.

Where had this attachment come from? He found an ease with Destiny he'd not experienced with other females. Perhaps this was another attempt at self-sabotage. She was a mortal. He couldn't keep her. Once the bishop dealt with her, she would have no lingering memory of him and their time would be over. Forever.

He drew her closer, as if his hold could somehow prolong the inevitable. The sheets left imprints on her skin and a trail from his rough kisses left her flesh rosy and her lips swollen—all tells of mortal vulnerability. He nibbled her shoulder and snuggled closer to her warm, plush curves.

His mind replayed images of the previous night. He grinned at the memory of her shyness and loved how impulsive she grew the moment he convinced her of his attraction. He didn't understand her insecurity or doubt but respected her reluctance to trust as he, too, trusted no one.

The blended scent of her arousal and his lingered in the air. Tightening his arm around her and drawing her near, he shut his eyes and savored the feel of her in his arms. Her breasts spilled over his hands as his touch drifted lower, caressing the smooth, inviting heat between her thighs.

His body stiffened at the memory of her taste and a different hunger awakened. It had been some time since he last fed and he needed to see to his needs, but he was reluctant to leave the warmth of her body, hoping to have her once more before she left his bed. Left his life.

His hand curled over the curve of her hip and glided upward, teasing her supple breasts. The nipple rested in his palm, soft and flat, as he slowly teased her skin to life. Her back arched as she moaned, eyes still closed but her mind and body coming awake.

His nose nuzzled her throat, burrowing beneath all that wild hair until his lips found her pulse. He kissed softly, teasing her with a delicate nip of his teeth. "There is nothing as sweet as finding you here, still in my arms, still welcoming to my touch," he whispered, nudging his cock against the tight crevice of her thighs. "Show me how sweet you can be, Destiny. I want inside of you."

Her legs parted, and he found heaven. The slick heat of her arousal guided his hard flesh as he sank his length into her. The tight fit of her body awakened true satisfaction inside of him, and he took a moment to savor her hold as he seated himself to the hilt.

He liked to be in control. Destiny understood that and didn't challenge him. Her surrender ignited his passion and drove him mad with lust.

"You give yourself over so prettily to my command, yet you do so with your own free will. It's such a show of strength and beauty, surrender and confidence." He thrust harder, turning his body to cover hers in a show of total domination.

She arched, hitching her hips and bending so he could fully take her. Gripping her wrists, he stretched her arms overhead, and pressed his cock deeper, making sure she took every inch of him. Her full lips parted as she gasped, her eyes still closed, and her face a picture of pure tranquility.

If someone would have told him this mouthy, stubborn reporter could become so docile, he would have taken her to bed weeks ago. Her independence hid this submissive side of her well. She could be serene then frantic in her lust. When she wasn't hiding beneath an insecure façade, she was more open and honest than any lover he'd known. When she found her confidence, she took what she wanted, and he enjoyed meeting her needs.

His mouth closed over her shoulder, the sharp edge of his fang teasing down her back as his hunger roared for a taste of her. She was a temptation he hated to resist, an obsession he wanted to savor with every deadly sin.

His gluttonous desires filled him with impatience. It was only a matter of time before another pleasure would be taken away from him. His insatiable lust to possess her drove him wild with intense need.

Flipping her to her back, he drove into her. Big brown eyes looked up at him, glazed with lust and full of intimate secrets he hadn't meant to permit. A heady, powerful sense of rightness filled him. Holding such command over a woman could intoxicate even the most fortified male. She was a drug, a drink, the most poisonous poetry with a mouth made of sin and wine, and he was quickly growing addicted to her.

"You're insatiable." Her hand cupped his jaw as she leaned up and kissed him. "You must have slept well."

"I slept sounder than I have in months." His transparency surprised him as much as his preference for her kisses. She was breaking down his guards, stealing little touches when he was the one meant to be in control.

His hand closed around her throat, anchoring her to the bed. She didn't startle or even gasp. She simply submitted, her compliance driving him mad with wanting.

This was a Destiny he could manage. He would much rather pass his hours between a gorgeous woman's thighs than out in the cold woods chasing his hairy uncle. Let the others have their true called mates. Cain would take his pleasure elsewhere. He'd have his freedom and independence, while the others spent an eternity tied down.

But he didn't want just anyone. He wanted her. It was her beauty that attracted him, her strength and her devotion to his pleasure. She wasn't like other females, and his chest ached at the thought of letting her go.

He wanted another day with her. "If I told you to stay, would you?"

Her lips parted on a gasp. "I'm not a dog who obeys."

"Not obey. Honor."

"Are you asking or ordering?"

So used to getting his way with compulsion, he naturally phrased the question as a command. "Would you deny me if I asked?"

Her body stretched and she moaned, her legs wrapping around him. "I think you could ask me just about anything right now and I'd give you what you want."

His nostrils flared as he thought of all the things he wanted from her. His hand cupped her breast tightly, his aggressive need for her doubling in strength as he shoved his cock deep.

He kissed her roughly, driving his body into hers and showing her how much he appreciated her presence. When he broke the kiss, her cheeks tinged a shade darker and her pupils dilated, changing the warm caramel pools to crystal onyx.

She claimed not to trust anyone, yet the more time they spent together the more vulnerability and trust she displayed. He wondered if she was like this with all men, but found the thought of her with someone else immediately repugnant and pushed it away. Some male part of him demanded he be better than any male who came before. That need alone ensured he would protect her and never betray her.

She gripped a spindle on the headboard and his hand closed over hers. Her heartbeat played like a drum, only evident to his perceptive ears. Her breath came faster as his mouth closed over her pebbled nipple. She screamed out in pleasure as he sucked hard at her puckered flesh. The tight channel of her sex milked his seed, and he bucked wildly, driving them both to an unstoppable finish.

She stole his breath away, his release tingling from his scalp, down his spine, until he felt it in the tips of his toes. Never had he experienced anything so completely satisfying.

He collapsed at her side, thunderstruck

that a mortal woman could have such a potent effect on him.

He should have been gentler with her. Her skin would be bruised and tender from the night before. Yet, even now, he couldn't pull himself away.

He suckled gently at her breasts, letting his healing saliva nourish her sensitive skin. She held him protectively, delicately combing her nails through his hair. Kissing lower, he pressed his mouth to her swollen folds. He'd been rough and demanding, but he could at least take some of her pain away.

Placing gentle kisses upon her sex, she opened for him and he licked softly into her heat. Her moans lazed into raspy cries as he gradually drove her to a somewhat tamer release.

She trembled like an autumn leaf under his care, so fragile and temporary. He sighed and rested his head on her thigh, surrounded by her softness and comforted beyond measure. Sated.

Her surrender and final climax had wrung her out. Spasms and aftershocks trembled through overworked muscle leaving chills upon her skin. She held him as he rested, and he allowed it. Never before had he felt comfortable enough to lay so exposed in the presence of another.

As his thoughts returned, he acknowledged that he truly wasn't ready to let her leave, and he didn't trust his luck enough to believe she would stay. Even if she agreed, he sensed some greater authority would steal her away.

He needed to sneak out and feed, but before he fed, he would visit her car and buy them a little more time.

Destiny stared down at the damp, tattered rags that were all that was left of her clothing. She'd heard of men ripping off women's panties, but this was nuts. How had he torn her clothes into so many shreds? She barely recalled him tugging the fabric.

With a huff, she tossed the ruined rags into the corner and scrunched her nose at the black material folded on the dresser. He'd said he'd left something for her when he left at dawn to go check on the animals. Now, she wasn't so sure she wanted his gift.

Unfolding the stiff cotton, she frowned. "I can't wear this."

She held the dress up to her chest and

sighed. Her only other option was walking around naked. Dropping the sheet, she pulled the dress over her head, surprised by the roomy fit. Several pins, a bonnet, and an apron also sat on the dresser. She lifted the oppressive white cap that looked like a prop from *The Handmaid's Tale.*

"No way I'm wearing this."

Tossing the offensive accessory aside, she used the pitcher of clean water to freshen up. It wasn't cutting it.

She peeked out the bedroom door, hoping not to run into anyone until she was somewhat clean and decent. When the coast was clear, she walked quickly down the hall and out the back door to the outhouse. Thankfully, no one saw her.

She was grateful to find the basket of primitive soaps and toiletries on the vanity had been replenished. Recalling how cold the shower water had been the day before, she felt no desire to bathe.

Frowning at the rustic shower, she sniffed her armpit and sighed. She needed a shower. Desperately. Every inch of her reeked of sex, which made her both embarrassed and proud.

Stripping off the dress, she carefully hung it from a peg on the wall, then doubled back to make sure the latch lock on the door was secure. Gathering soap and a washcloth, she glared at the pull chain, thinking of the fastest way to clean her body without catching hypothermia under the frigid water. Head to toe, and it was probably best to hold her breath.

She took a deep inhale and pulled the chain. *"Jesus Fucking Christ!"* she screeched, as the icy water pelted her skin.

Her teeth chattered as she quickly soaped up the cloth. She stood outside of the cold water as she lathered her skin and only stepped under the stream to rinse as quickly as possible. Using the soap, she flipped her head and washed out her curls. The moment she was clean, she wrapped herself in a towel and shivered by the wood stove.

Was a hot water heater too much to request? No wonder why Cain didn't mind the cold. He probably had nerve damage from years of ice cold showers.

With no hair products her hair would grow three times its regular size, so she tamed it into a braided bun and used a pin to hold it in place. Fresh, and frozen to the bone, she returned to the house, grateful to at least have her fur lined UGGs to keep her feet warm.

She followed the sound of chatter to the kitchen and, once again, found her brother stuffing his face.

He snorted with laughter the moment he saw her. "Well, hello Sister Destiny!"

She scowled at his jeans and a Philadelphia Flyers sweatshirt. "Where did you get extra clothes?"

"I always keep spare clothes in my car. Never know when you'll end up stranded or on an Amish farm. By the way, my car's dead. Probably just the battery. After breakfast I'll call Triple A."

"You need Triple A to jump a battery for you? Don't you have cables?"

"What am I going to hook them to, a horse? We're in God's country now."

How could she forget? Her nipples were permanently frost bitten into points, chafing uncomfortably against a dress that felt stiffer than burlap. Still, she was glad to hear they couldn't leave and hopeful she might get another day with Cain.

Her body thrummed with anticipation and ached in the most delicious way. If she shut her eyes, she could still picture Cain's hands holding her, and his mouth teasing. She loved how he woke her up this morning. His—

"Look at the size of their sausage," Vito blurted, forking a fat link on his fork.

"That's what she said."

Grace turned and frowned. "Who said something?"

Destiny blushed. "Nothing. It's a joke."

"I don't get it."

She waved away her confusion. "It wasn't that funny. Can I help with anything?"

"No, no. You're our guest." Grace shuffled her back to the table, and Destiny lowered into a chair. A plate full of breakfast meats and eggs pushed in front of her.

Her mother would die if she saw her eating this way. Everything was smothered in butter and fried in fat. Apparently, cholesterol wasn't a concern to these folks. How were they all so trim? As a matter of fact, everyone Destiny had seen on the farm appeared in great shape.

"Our lifestyle keeps us fit," Grace said, as if reading her mind.

Destiny imagined what it would be like to live on a farm without television, music, computers, or cars. No blow dryers either. No wonder they all wore bonnets. Her family's farm in Portugal had been recently renovated, but even in its most rustic state, they still had a generator and basic technologies.

Cain's farm was beyond primitive. She couldn't imagine going without so many amenities. Yet some part of her still saw the charm and lure of such a simplistic way of life. Eventually, Cain would have a wife who baked him bread and washed his clothes in some old-fashioned way. Destiny instantly wanted to punch the girl, whoever she might be.

Grace giggled. "Cain should be back any minute. He needed to visit the animals in the barn."

She was an intuitive little thing.

Just then, Cain came through the front door, whistling and smiling with the morning sun bright at his back.

"Good morning." His color looked better, and he appeared especially chipper. He must have had coffee, because he didn't usually carry himself with such a pep in his step. "Vito, are you handy with an ax?"

Her brother looked up from his plate, his expression comical.

Destiny laughed. "The only ax Vito's ever used is sold in the drug store cologne section."

Vito narrowed his eyes. "I can use an ax."

Cain clapped a strong hand on his shoulder. "Good. I'm taking out a tree stump on the other end of the property. I could use some company."

Disappointed that he wouldn't be spending the day with her, she focused on her plate and tried to hide her displeasure.

"Destiny, would you like to learn how to milk a cow and bottle feed a calf?"

Excitement bloomed in her chest at Gracie's invitation. "I'd love that."

"Great. I just need to check on Anna, then I'll take you to the barn."

"What's wrong with Anna that you need to check on her?" Cain asked, concern overtaking his jovial mood.

Grace wiped down the countertops. "Annalise is fine. Her back's been aching, and the babe has dropped. It's getting close to her time. I'm just stopping by to bring her some muffins and calm her nerves."

"There are muffins?" Vito asked.

"You're a pig." Destiny carried her plate to the sink.

"It's too early," Cain said, his brow tight with worry. "She's not due for another two months."

"The baby will come when he's ready."

Destiny frowned. "She's having a boy? Do the Amish have ultrasounds?"

"Gracie just thinks it's a boy," Cain said. "Tell Anna I was asking about her."

"Cain, I don't want to add stress—"

"Just tell her." Appearing irritated, he grabbed his hat from the peg by the door. "Ready, Vito?"

"Ready."

He left without a glance in her direction. It was a painful reminder of her position but a healthy reality check. Whoever this Anna was, Cain still cared for her very much.

"Do you mind if I go with you to deliver the muffins?"

"Not at all."

She helped Gracie tidy the kitchen and pack a picture-perfect basket of muffins to take to their pregnant sister-by-law. "I feel like *Little Red Riding Hood* on her way to Grandmother's house," she said, swinging the wicker basket at her side.

"Is that a friend of yours?"

"No, it's a fable about a little girl who's tricked and eaten by a wolf."

"Oh," Gracie said, a touch scandalized.

"You English have such a tolerance for violent entertainment."

Destiny frowned. *Little Red Riding Hood* was just a children's story. But Gracie was right. No wonder they were so jaded and cold by the time they reached adulthood.

As Destiny imagined, Annalise was gorgeous. She was also *very* pregnant. It was difficult to believe she was only seven months pregnant.

When Destiny and Grace were alone, she quietly asked, "Did Anna and Cain date?"

Grace's eyes widened and she whispered, "You must not ask such things, Destiny. My brother Adam is a very possessive man, and he will hear you."

Destiny frowned. There was no one close by to overhear her, and that didn't answer her question.

"The baby is Adam's," Gracie quickly whispered. "Now speak no more of it. We must keep Adam calm, for Anna and the baby's sake."

She supposed there was quite the story there, but it wasn't Gracie's to tell. Maybe one day Cain would share—except there wouldn't be a "one day". This was likely their last day, and after this, they really had no future together. It would do her well to remember that.

Anna returned with a glass of water. "Adam says I have to keep drinking fluids. I feel like it's all going to my ankles."

The more Anna spoke, the stranger Destiny found her voice. It wasn't accented like the others' and sometimes she used slang. Her hair was also uncovered. Perhaps it was a pregnancy thing for comfort.

But there were other oddities as well. The lobes of Anna's ears bore tiny holes as if they had once been pierced. Most peculiar of all, as Anna poured drinks, she hummed the tune of what Destiny swore was the old Beatles song, *Lucy in the Sky with Diamonds.*

The song stuck in her head all morning. When they made it to the barn, Gracie asked, "What's that you're singing?"

Destiny hadn't realized she'd been singing out loud. "It's just an old song."

Gracie smiled. "Will you teach it to me?"

"Um, sure." She started awkwardly and off key, *"Picture yourself in a boat on a river with tangerine trees and marmalade skies..."*

Gracie's face knit with confusion as she went on. "That song makes no sense."

"Well, I didn't write it."

She laughed. "Anna loves music, too."

"Does she?" Did she also love Cain?

Ugh, Destiny had to stop thinking of him with any sort of entitlement.

The barn wasn't quite what she imagined. She'd pictured something more along the lines of *Charlotte's Web* with less of a manure odor. The animals were louder than expected and she never saw so many flies in winter. The reality was redeemed, however, by Grace's "eight maids a-milking" presence. Then Destiny remembered that she was dressed the same.

"The first thing we do," Gracie said after she led a cow to a trough filled with feed and sat on a stool, "is wash the udders. This is just gentle baby soap." She cleaned the underbelly of the cow and Destiny hunched her back, protectively supporting her own breasts and empathizing with the animal.

Once the cow's udders were clean, Gracie moved the bucket of soapy water away and replaced it with an empty metal pail. "Then you just pull."

She demonstrated, and milk whizzed into the pail, echoing against the metal walls of the canister. With each tug, another steaming stream shot into the bucket and soon it was full.

"Want to try?"

Destiny hesitated. Cows were much larger in person and she found them intimidating. "I don't know if I'm ready for that."

"I have another job that's less daunting." She filled a quart-sized container with cream and screwed a lid with a big red nipple on tight. "Follow me."

Inside a small pen sat a sweet baby calf, and Destiny fell in love at first sight. "Oh, my goodness! What's her name?"

"I call her Maribel. She's been milking from the bottle for almost two weeks now, so when she sees it, she knows it's time for food. Would you like to feed her?"

"Really? I'd love to!"

Gracie passed her the bottle. "Hold on tight. She's strong."

The calf knew exactly what to do and made the most adorable sounds while drinking. She tugged for all of three minutes, and then the bottle was empty.

"You're a little piggy," Destiny teased.

"They all are at that age." Gracie laughed and corralled the calf back into the pen. "We'll collect some eggs from the coop, then I'll show you how to make Shoo Fly Pie."

ain enjoyed laboring in the sun more than he had in quite some time. Vito proved to be good company and a hard worker, even as he continuously mentioned that modern tools required less effort and could get the job done twice as fast.

"You know you can get a gas-powered saw. You guys can use gasoline, right?"

"We even ride in gasoline vehicles from time to time," Cain teased.

Vito mopped the sweat from his brow. "So why not invest in a chain saw or a chipper?"

"Because modern technology comes with complications and it's a distraction we do not need."

"Yeah, it's a real waste of time. Nothing

like chipping away at a stump with a primi-tive ax."

"If it's too much work for you—"

"Yeah, yeah, yeah. I've got it. Just trying to make a point."

Cain rubbed his back, a strange twinge of pain shooting up his spine. He waited a second for his body to correct whatever issue he was having.

"You okay?" Vito asked, noticing that he'd stopped working.

"Fine." Cain massaged away the discom-fort in his back. Perhaps he fed from an ill animal this morning and his body was fighting off some sort of parasite. It was rare, but it happened on occasion.

The pain eventually subsided and they fin-ished grinding out the stump by late after-noon. The weather had been gorgeous, no doubt Cain's cheery mood had helped in that department.

He hoped the situation with Vito's car would cause Destiny to stay another night. Sooner or later, she'd have to get back to her life so he wanted to make the most of their time.

They walked back to the house at a leisurely pace. Vito appeared rather enthralled by the size of the farm and asked questions about their operation. Farming was all Cain knew, so much of his knowledge seemed like common sense. It was odd to think of a man making a living in other ways.

"Destiny said your family owns a farm."

"In Portugal, yeah, but it's nothing like this. We've got vineyards and goats."

"So you must understand some of the upkeep."

Vito chuckled. "We also understand the value of power tools and a good tractor."

Cain respected how attached the English could be to their modern technologies, but Destiny didn't seem as bothered by their primitive ways as Vito. He liked that she hid a curiously ambitious side to her and was willing to learn new things.

That morning, he enjoyed seeing her in a traditional dress, enjoyed knowing exactly what she hid underneath as she set out for the day to deliver care packages and tend to the calves. Even if it was a temporary fantasy, he enjoyed the glimpse of what their life could be.

Startled by his thoughts, he stilled. Where had that come from? They didn't have a life together, or any prospects beyond the end of the week, so he needed to reel in his imagination and ground himself back in reality.

She was a modern woman with modern comforts. Her kind didn't do the rustic thing. And his kind didn't do the mortal modern thing.

"You cool?"

Realizing he'd stopped walking, Cain took a step and grunted. Doubling over in distress.

"Cain?"

Perspiration beaded on his brow as shooting pain punched into his back. For a moment, he feared he might hurl. Something was definitely wrong, because immortals rarely sweat and almost never got sick.

The pain disappeared as fast as it arrived. Rising to his full height, he continued walking. "Hot today." He blew out a breath, his back throbbing with the echoes of a steady ache.

Vito shrugged. "It's a little chilly if you ask me."

Cain paused and grunted uncomfortably, another sharp pain knifing through him. "Did that breakfast sit well with you?"

Leave it to Gracie to try to poison him for the day. He groaned and slightly stumbled, his stomach cramping tightly.

"Whoa, you okay, man? You want some of this water? Maybe you overdid it." Vito held out the canteen, but Cain ignored him.

His vision blurred, and his heart raced. Was he having another heart attack? This felt different. Lower. His back ached and his—

"*Zum mordsackerment!*" He doubled over, bracing his hands on his knees and laboring for breath.

"Shit. What's wrong with you?"

Cain shook his head and licked his dry lips as incredible pressure pushed on his spine and abdomen. He would make Gracie pay if she did this to him. "I just need a moment."

Rivulets of salty sweat trickled into his vision, burning his eyes. He never felt like this before. Terrible pressure built in his groin, and his legs trembled as if he'd run a hundred miles. He squinted over the fields. They were almost home. If he could just run there and rest for a moment...

But Vito was mortal and that meant Cain had to keep a mortal pace. "Damnit," he cursed, stumbling off balance.

"Dude...?"

Cain held up an unsteady hand, determined to beat whatever this was. "Let's walk," he rasped, blocking out the pressure.

A sharp jolt of pain shot up his spine and he faltered. Another pinch and then something excruciating happened to his insides. He screamed as he never screamed before.

Legs buckling, he fell to his knees.

"Holy fuck! What should I do?" Vito held his phone then cursed, realizing there was no one to call. "Help! Somebody!"

"Don't—" Cain's fingers dug into the dry earth, claws distending as his pupils dilated and saliva filled his mouth. He couldn't transition in front of Vito, but he was in so much pain he couldn't find the strength to fight back his instinct. His body was under attack.

His fangs punched through his gums as another wave of agony stabbed from the inside out. He panted, keeping his head down, as he snarled through the pain.

Vito placed a hand on his back. "Dude, should I get—"

"*Don't touch me!*"

The man scrambled back and fell onto the grass. "What the fuck?"

Breath bellowed in and out of Cain's lungs as he panted through his clenched teeth. Was he dying? No ill blood or tainted meat could cause this much pain.

He tried to stand but collapsed to the ground. Sweat drenched his clothing.

"Yo, man, something fucked up is happening to your face. I think you need a doctor!"

Self-preservation disappeared as Cain tried to escape the onslaught of pain. He curled into a ball, gripping his stomach, but there was no relief. He needed to get inside so he could suffer in private.

Attempting to crawl toward his house, he roared as sheer agony, greater than anything he had felt thus far, took hold of him. A blood-curdling scream ripped from his lungs. Surely someone would hear him and come to his aid. Even Grace couldn't be that cold.

"That's it, man, just breathe through the pain," Vito coached from a safe distance as he paced and frantically searched for help.

Cain grit his teeth and roared. It was getting worse. "Make it stop!"

Vito nervously extended an arm and patted Cain's head, awkwardly. "You're doing great."

His body bowed as a wave of pressure rolled through him, pushing and pulling on his insides until he was certain he would die. Whatever was inside of him, needed to get the hell out. Bearing down, he breathed hard and pushed, clenching against the pain and screaming through his teeth.

The pain subsided for a few moments, and Cain collapsed to his back, panting and staring up at the clouds. Death seemed like a glorious option. He was too exhausted to do anything more than breathe.

"Do you want me to carry you back to the house?"

There was no way in hell Cain was letting another man carry him because of a stomachache. He shook his head. "I just need...a minute."

"Has anything like this ever happened before?"

Why was he asking so many questions? "Stop. Talking." The pressure inside of him built once again and he clenched his teeth. "No," he whimpered, turning his face toward the earth and bracing himself, but this time, once the pain started, it didn't stop.

Sharp pressure stabbed through him, building like a hurricane. Wind whistled through the trees as clouds rolled overhead and thunder crashed. Cain bore down, growling as waves of pain ripped through him, relentlessly jerking his body to the ground and whipping him about.

Rain released from the sky and pelted the earth.

"Breathe, man, breathe!" Vito encouraged. "It has to be over soon. Just breathe through it."

The wind kicked up and black shadows covered the wet land as the sun disappeared. Every sharp lash of pain that ripped through him sent a tear of lightning webbing through the sky. Cain became the pain, heavy and hot, all-consuming, shredding through the trees and blowing wildly over the land.

The heavens opened, and rain poured down. Vito shouted through the storm, but Cain couldn't make out his words over his screams and the howling wind. His blood churned wildly as the storm raged. Squalls ripped over the hills, tearing laundry from lines. An all-consuming pressure expanded in his gut, and he snarled through the pain, certain it would tear him in two.

"Shit, man, do you guys get tornadoes out this far?"

Cain couldn't answer. Ungodly heaviness crushed him down. He flattened his back to the earth and dug his heels into the mud. His hands fisted at his sides and his eyes screwed shut as he shouted through the pain. No man, immortal or not, could live through such agony.

Then, in the span of a breath, the pain and pressure were gone.

The wind eased, and the downpour shifted to a lazy drizzle. The cool, calm stillness felt otherworldly, as if a war had come through and he was a part of the ruins.

Pools of mud puddles freckled the fields, and the sun broke through the clouds. Panting, he took inventory of his body, but found nothing amiss. He was alive.

The shock of what he just suffered slammed into him, and for the first time in his adult life, he let out a sob and broke down in tears.

"Dude?"

What the hell was wrong with him? His body shook, and he couldn't stop crying. He'd been through hell and back, and he didn't trust it was over.

Vito patted his back. "See, man, whatever it was, hopefully it's over now. Probably just some gas."

Cain looked up at him, unsure if the last of

the pain had subsided or if there would be more. "Not even close."

"I never heard a man scream like that before. I don't want to see anything like that ever again. We have to get inside and change into dry clothes. Who knows if the storm's over or if this is just some fucked up calm before a tornado throws a house on us."

Cain wasn't sure, but he wasn't strong enough to stand just yet. "Give me a moment." He panted.

They sat in silence on the saturated ground, Vito rubbing his back with comforting strokes and Cain blinking cluelessly at the sky. No one would ever believe the pain he'd been through. Maybe that was a good thing, because nothing had ever made him feel so breakable in his life.

CHAPTER 27

"The skies have turned," Grace said, returning inside with a basket of linen. "The laundry will have to wait."

Destiny glanced out the window at the hillside where thick, gray clouds rolled in. "Look at that sky. Do you guys usually get bad storms here?" It wasn't like they had to worry about the power going out.

Gracie tilted her head and frowned. "Something's happening."

"What do you mean?"

The woman wrung her hands and paced by the door. "I should gather supplies."

"Supplies?"

Just then, Dane burst into the house and the wind cut through the room, lifting the curtains and howling against the glass. "Gracie, come quick! Anna's having the baby!"

"Already?"

"Her water broke and she's gone to bed. She told me to fetch you and Adam."

Grace shut her eyes as if praying, then sprang into action. "Her contractions are coming quickly. Dane, meet me at the house. Destiny, you go find Adam."

Destiny sprung to her feet. "I don't know what Adam looks like."

"He looks exactly like Cain, but smarter. He'll be in the barn. Go and find him."

"I'll just get my—" The kitchen was empty. Grace was gone and Dane was running through the rain.

Destiny shoved her feet into her UGGs and bolted into the storm, racing as fast as she could toward the barn. The wind was crazy, whipping through trees and pulling laundry off people's lines. Gates and shutters swung open, loosening latches and clattering as they slammed shut.

"Adam, Adam, Adam, Adam," she muttered with each panted breath as she jogged into the shelter of the barn. "Adam?" The sole of her boot slid over the wet hay and she caught her balance awkwardly before busting her ass on the ground.

"Yes?"

Holy shit, he did look like Cain, but not as sexy. "Anna's having the baby!" She caught her breath and pushed her fist into a cramp in her side. "You—Hello?" The barn was empty. "Adam?" He was gone.

She stared out at the storm. The clouds were so black and ominous, she could see where the rain poured. A windmill spun wildly and the cows cried as they gathered together. Lightning stretched to the earth and thunder shook the heavens.

Maybe she should just stay in the barn. The house was a good distance away and she didn't want to get struck by lightning. In the distance, men rushed horses into the stables. The roof of the barn shook under the thrust of the wind and she feared it might come loose. Did they get tornadoes in Lancaster?

Just then, a squall formed over the western field, rising high and tunneling toward her. The various metal saws and rustic tools rattled on the wall above her. She was going to die if she stayed there.

Gathering her skirts, she ran as fast as her legs would carry her toward Anna's house.

Wind howled and whipped at her clothing, slowing her steps as she leaned into the gusts. Icy squalls mixed with bursts of heat and it began to hail.

The rattle of ice pelting the tin roof of Adam and Anna's house assured her she was near. She could barely see more than a few feet in front of her as the world washed out in shades of gray.

As soon as she opened the door, it whipped out of her grip and slammed into the wall. A woman screamed and voices carried from above.

Dane grabbed the door and pushed it shut, and the howling wind whistled through every passable crevice. "They're upstairs. You can go up."

Soaked to the bone and shivering, she sloshed up the steps, unsure if she would be useful or in the way.

"Adam!" Anna cried, her labored breathing soughing through the agitated air.

"Breathe, *ainsicht,* breathe."

"He's almost here," Gracie said.

Destiny slipped into the room, never entering more than a foot past the door. Anna lay on the bed, panting and sweating, while Grace stood at the foot, guiding her.

Adam spoke encouraging words into his wife's ear. "Push, Annalise, you're almost there."

"Son of a bitch!" Anna's face twisted as a contraction took hold.

"Language. Our son doesn't need to enter this world hearing such things."

"Shut the fuck up, Adam! Until you have a human being coming out of your dick, you can keep your opinions to yourself."

Destiny's eyes widened at such unexpected vulgarity, and Grace chuckled.

"Push, now, Anna. You're fully dilated and the baby's crowning."

Anna bore down and pushed. When her strength gave out, she collapsed into the bed and moaned. "God damnit. I can't do this." Her eyes turned demonic as she pointed a finger at Adam. "If I can't have an epidural or drugs, I'm allowed to say whatever the hell I want."

Adam appeared too panicked over his wife's wellbeing to care about her language anymore. "She's in pain, Grace. The baby has to come out."

"A little more, Anna. I know you have it in you. Just a few more pushes and he'll be out."

Destiny held her breath as Annalise bore

down. Her face darkened as the veins in her forehead protruded and her scream rattled the rafters.

"I can see his head!"

A symphony of motion and sounds overtook the room and then the first squawk of a newborn cry pierced the air. The squawks grew louder, hearty and healthy as a wash of sobs and laughter replaced the pained cries of labor. Relief came in a wave of joyful tears the moment Gracie announced that both baby and mother were fine.

Destiny admired Annalise's strength and felt privileged to witness such a miracle. The room was dark from the storm, so Dane carried in a few extra oil lamps and candles. Shivers of joy skated up Destiny's spine as her teeth chattered and her skin chilled under her drenched clothes.

Some days took so much energy, they felt a hundred nights long. Once the baby was cleaned up and bundled in a soft blanket, the rain subsided. The skies remained an angry shade of gray, but inside that room, everything felt warm.

Soft drizzle tapped on the windows, and she wondered where Cain was. Would he be happy to learn Adam's wife had the baby? Relieved? She wanted to be there to see his reaction.

The sun fought to peek past the clouds, and Destiny sighed. Even the weather seemed different here.

"Isn't he perfect?" Grace whispered, flashing her a glimpse of the precious bundle. Never in her life had she seen anything so miraculous.

"You were right. It's a boy."

Gracie grinned. "I have a gift for knowing such things."

Despite her exhaustion, Anna held out her arms to hold her baby boy. Adam cradled her close and stared, mesmerized at their new son.

The couple smiled into the face of the swaddled child, a perfect picture of love and family, and Destiny felt a pinch of envy for their happiness. Although the baby was premature, he appeared a healthy size for a newborn.

"Here." Dane held out a quilt to her. "You're shivering."

"Thank you." Destiny accepted the blanket and wrapped it around her shoulders.

She and Dane left the room to give the family some privacy. Happy to wait by the wood stove in the kitchen, she silently imagined the precious moments unfolding upstairs.

Destiny had always assumed she'd have kids, but as the years went on and her love life fizzled, she wasn't sure a family was in her cards. She and Cain had been incredibly irresponsible these last few days, and she selfishly wondered if she might take home a souvenir. Not that she was one for entrapment, but seeing Anna and Adam's baby filled her with all sorts of longing.

A floorboard creaked and she looked up from the fire. Grace carried a basket of soiled linens down the stairs and set them by the front door. "Someone has to notify the bishop and give him a name for the records. Dane, would you mind?"

Dane stood. "Did they name him?"

Grace seemed to purposefully keep her expression blank. "Cain Paul Hartzler."

Dane's shock matched Destiny's. They were naming the baby after Cain?

"I know what you're thinking, but Anna insisted."

Once again, Destiny worried the baby might be Cain's. If it was, it would still look like Adam's. She was so confused.

Dane frowned. "Who's Paul?"

Grace shrugged. "Some McCartney fellow Anna admired."

Destiny did a double take. "McCartney, as in The Beatles?" How the hell did an Amish chick know who The Beatles were?

"I'll deliver the message to the safe house. I need to see the bishop anyway."

"What for?" Gracie's curiosity shifted into concern and her mouth pinched shut.

"I was going to talk to you about it later," Dane said, his eyes regretful.

"Well…" Grace gathered the basket of linens, her demeanor falsely pleasant when something had obviously upset her. "I should get back to Anna and the baby."

They went their separate ways and Destiny was left alone. The sky had cleared and it looked like a safe time to go back to the house. She wanted to find Cain and tell him about the baby, since no one seemed worried about informing him.

She hung the quilt over the back of a wooden chair near the fire to dry and quietly let herself out the front door. The ground was saturated from the rain and the air smelled of damp earth. Torn leaves clung to siding and puddles formed gullies on the ground, and she came up short when Vito snapped, "*Where the hell have you been?*"

Destiny flinched and paused from stripping off her muddied boots. Vito stood in the hallway on the other side of the kitchen, clothes drenched and hair ragged.

"What happened to you?"

"I was in a fucking hurricane and almost died, and we're on an Amish farm so there's nothing stronger than cider here for me to drink. My nerves are shot."

"Why are you shouting?"

"Because it's been a day. Where's Gracie? Cain's sick and I don't know what to do for him."

Destiny's joy slipped away. "What do you mean sick? Where is he?"

"I mean sick. Really sick. I thought he was having a seizure or some kind of heart attack. I never saw a man in so much pain. What the hell do these people do for doctors around here? Because I'm pretty sure he needs one."

"She's at Anna and Adam's. They had the baby." She rushed to Cain's room, worry making it difficult to breathe. She quietly entered and her concern doubled.

Looking nothing like his usual herculean self, he lay curled on his side, eyes staring off in defeated shock. "Cain?" she rushed to his side and gently sat on the edge of the bed, her fingers stroking gently through his knotted hair.

The curtains had been drawn, and his brow pinched with tension. The air held the musty scent of damp fabric. She touched his forehead. No fever.

He groaned and his brow smoothed under the delicate weight of her fingers, his eyes closing. "I wasn't sure I'd ever see you again?"

"I'm here. What happened? Vito said you're sick."

"I don't get sick. I think I'm dying."

That was a little dramatic. "You don't have a fever. Where do you hurt?"

"Everywhere. There was so much pain. I think I exorcised a demon."

She tsked. "Do you feel okay now?"

"Tired."

She pressed her lips to his head. "Well, try to sleep. I can make you some tea."

He caught her hand and squeezed. "Where were you?"

"Anna had the baby."

His eye's opened and, for a moment, she saw through him, glimpsing some sort of trauma he usually kept hidden. "Is she…well?"

"She did great. The baby's healthy and perfect in every way."

He sighed, relaxing and shutting his eyes as if this news brought him great relief. "That explains a lot."

"She, um…" Should she tell him? "She named him after you."

The relief in his eyes disappeared, replaced with obvious surprise then he frowned. "Why?"

"I…I don't know." She hoped he would tell her.

"Adam will hate that."

"It's his son. I doubt he could ever hate anything having to do with him." She didn't know Adam by any means, but she assumed that wasn't the case. "Cain, is there any chance the baby's yours?"

He scowled at her. "No. Anna and I never… We have a past and she's my…" He searched for the right words. "She's like a sister to me now. That's all. I don't know why she'd do something so foolish as to name her first born son after me. It's not like I'm any sort of role model. She should have named him after his father."

Destiny frowned. "It's a great honor. You're going to be an incredible uncle."

"Uncle." He let the title sink in for a moment. "Uncles are either fun, terrifying, or invisible."

"Some uncles are brave and wonderful teachers. You can be whatever kind of uncle you choose. Little Cain will love you, I'm sure."

He gave her a strange look she couldn't read. "Was he scrawny? Anna's early."

"Not at all. He's pudgy and handsome and a healthy shade of pink. "When you're feeling better, you should go meet him."

He looked away, his eyes clouding with worry. "In time."

Whatever he felt for Adam's wife was more than mere brotherly love. Destiny had no right to feel jealous of their attachment, but she was only human and his affection for the other woman awakened her insecurities. She didn't understand how Anna was so tied to Cain's past or why he always looked sad when anyone mentioned her marriage to Adam. If everything was platonic and on the up and up, wouldn't he hang out with them more often?

"Get some sleep." She rose from the bed and gathered his wet clothes off the floor.

"Destiny?"

"Yes?"

"Promise you'll be here when I wake up."

Surprised by his sweet request, she smiled. "I promise."

Destiny quietly shut the door and laughed at the rumble of her brother's snores filling the house. He was passed out on the small settee in the den, his belly rising and falling with each heavy snore.

She went to the kitchen and paused when she found Gracie weeping at the table. "Grace?"

The woman looked up, a startled expression on her face, and quickly blotted her eyes. "I didn't hear you come in."

"What's wrong?" Destiny set the damp clothes on a chair and went to her side.

"Nothing's the matter. I'm being ridiculous and over emotional."

She shifted into a seat beside her. "You're upset. There's nothing to be ashamed of."

Gracie sniffled and wiped her eyes. "I'm upset with myself. I'm acting foolish when I know better."

"Do you want to talk about it?"

"No." Her face screwed into a stubborn scowl. "It's all Dane's fault. He's angry with me because I..."

"You what?"

"He doesn't' understand how it is for us. We can't choose who we end up with."

Destiny frowned, disliking the sound of that. "Because you're a woman?"

"Because I'm…Amish. There are rules."

"And Dane is not Amish."

"Correct. He's also much younger than me."

There couldn't be that much of an age difference. Gracie barely looked old enough to drink. "Are you attracted to him?"

"No," she scoffed. "He's incredibly annoying and always filling my head with rubbish. He's pushy and bullheaded and nothing like the males I'm used to."

"Maybe that's a good thing."

"It's not. And my feelings are irrelevant. I'm saving myself for my true mate."

Destiny's brows drew together at her strange terminology. "Do you know who he is?"

"I'll know when God tells me."

Oh, boy. She masked any judgement and respected that Gracie had a very strong faith. "Well, you could always save yourself and date other people in the meantime. Just don't…go all the way."

Gracie's eyes met hers. "Like you and Cain?"

Destiny flushed. "Well, I...We...I don't think your brother's saving himself."

She chuckled. "No. He's rather a spendthrift in that department."

Destiny assumed as much. "We're just having fun."

"But he likes you."

Something giddy and juvenile awoke inside of her. She wanted to fish for more assurance and ask what she heard.

"He hasn't said anything to me," Gracie continued. "But I know how he thinks. You're different from the other females he sees."

"How many are there?" she asked dryly. Gracie spoke as if there were hordes.

"Oh, not that many. Cain has always been a bit of a hedonist." She smirked and covered her lips. "My father calls him the sinner and Adam the saint."

Cain wasn't a bad person. Yet Destiny got the impression he didn't have the best reputation among family. "Well, I think he's kind and thoughtful. Whoever steals his heart in the end will be a lucky girl."

"How so?"

Destiny shrugged. "I don't know if Cain

knows how to do anything halfway, so whoever he loves, I'm sure he'll love her as much as any man can."

Gracie looked at her and drew back. "*You* love him."

"What? No. I don't. We just met and barely know each other."

"Love has nothing to do with time. It's how two souls complement each other. And I think you and Cain complement each other very well. Do you ever dream of him, Destiny?"

"Um, not that I remember." Sometimes Gracie gave the impression that she was some sort of a mystic and it freaked her out. Uncomfortable with the conversation, she turned the topic back to Dane. "Have you thought about telling Dane how you feel?"

"He knows. He calls me stubborn. He's so full of emotion and anger sometimes, I want to make things easier on him, but I can't sacrifice my beliefs."

"He's a teenager. Give him time."

"He will be an adult in a few weeks. When I mentioned making him a gift, he said..." Her cheeks flushed and she looked away. "He told me exactly what he wanted from me."

Destiny grinned and leaned closer. "What did he say?"

Gracie looked back at the empty hall and whispered, "He has very adult thoughts about us, and he makes no effort to hide his feelings from me. It's embarrassing and it makes it impossible to be in his presence sometimes."

"Really? I love when a man's direct about his feelings. Most aren't."

"He's a little too direct."

"What does he say?"

"It's not what he says so much as… He has a lot of fantasies."

Destiny chuckled. Now they were getting to the juicy stuff. "And what about you? Do you ever fantasize about him?"

"I…" She looked away. "I've caught my mind wandering where it shouldn't. He has nice eyes and I don't mind the way he smells."

"Two important qualities. What about how he makes you feel?"

Her gaze lifted and she drew in a slow breath. "When he's around, I feel lighter. We bicker constantly, and he infuriates me most days, then I'm so frustrated I can't stop thinking about him. But then there are days when he brings me things."

"What sort of things?"

"He brought me a feather he found, and he carved my name into a piece of wood shaped like a heart. No one has ever given me gifts like that."

"He likes you, Gracie. He's trying to show you."

"Well, I wish he'd stop."

"Are you sure that's what you want?"

She stood and collected the damp clothes that Destiny had placed on the chair. "Yes. I don't have time for childish games, and I'm offended by his filthy mind."

So she planned to lie to herself.

"I'm not lying," Gracie snapped then quickly said. "If that's what you were thinking." She moved out of the kitchen, obviously through with their conversation and annoyed at feeling so exposed.

Destiny sighed and let her head drop back for a moment. There was a sadness to knowing she would never know Gracie and Dane's ending or watch little Cain grow up. How was she becoming so attached to this place and these people?

Preferring to keep her mind busy, she filled the kettle and set it over the iron burner like she'd watched Gracie do that morning. The tea wasn't in little bags like they sold it at the grocery stores, but rather kept loose in jars. She did her best not to make a mess but had no idea how to make tea from loose herbs. Twigs and petals floated to the top in a swirl of debris and she frowned.

"This should destroy any fantasies he had about being domestic." When she returned to Cain's bedroom he stirred from sleep. "I brought you tea. Fair warning, it's a little gritty."

He lifted the covers, inviting her into the bed. Smiling at the sweet invitation, she set the tea aside and slipped off her dress, crawling in beside him. His body was warm and welcoming.

He spooned her and she sank into his hold, savoring the novelty of resting in a man's arms. "Tell me about your day."

"Gracie took me with her to do her chores, and I fed a baby calf."

His lips pressed against her hair and he grinned. "I like the image of you holding a bottle to a calf's mouth better than the thought of you poking out your microphone."

She playfully elbowed him. "You act like I'm the paparazzi."

He chuckled. "Did she show you the kittens?"

She turned in his arms so their faces were nose to nose. "No. How old are they?"

"Only about two weeks."

"Will you show me tomorrow?"

"If you'll stay. Will you?"

She smiled softly, appreciating that he asked. "I'll stay."

He leaned forward and kissed her tenderly. She went to him willingly when he pulled her close. They kissed for several long moments, languid and comfortable with each other's closeness.

The sun set and they hadn't lit the lamps. Dark shadows chased away the light and her eyes adjusted. "Cain, can I ask you something?"

"You just did."

She smirked. "It's personal."

"Go on."

"Did you love Adam's wife?"

He drew in a slow breath and used the motion to put some distance between them. "I loved the idea of her. Anna's beautiful and she's a good partner, but she wasn't meant to be my partner. I do better on my own."

"You don't want a wife and family someday?"

"A wife, sure. But it's different."

"How?"

He held her hands under the covers, softly tracing her fingers with his. "Sometimes you just know what your destiny is going to be."

Maybe she could be his destiny. "Would you ever consider leaving the farm?"

"I have, but I always come back. My family's here. We don't always see eye to eye, but I need to be close to watch over them."

He was such a loyal brother and son.

She turned to face the wall and he played with her hair, twisting it into loose braids and lifting it into a bun. She'd never been with anyone who enjoyed touching her so much or did so so freely.

"How did you get this mark on the back of your neck?"

"It's a stork bite."

"A bird bit you?"

She laughed. "No. That's just what people call it. I was born with it. It's a birthmark."

"Oh."

"They usually fade by adulthood, but mine never did."

He kissed the mark. "It makes you unique."

"You really don't get hung up about a girl's flaws, do you?"

"What flaws?" he joked.

"Extra weight, looks, style, all of it."

"Those things aren't flaws." He unraveled her hair and spread it over her shoulders. She shut her eyes, loving the feeling of his fingers touching her. "Do you ever think of moving to Portugal with your family?"

"Sometimes."

"Why don't you?"

She shrugged. "My job and my brother are here. If I go back to Portugal, my mother will marry me off to some family friend, and I don't want that."

His hands curved possessively around her hips, drawing her closer to his front. "What is it you want, Destiny?"

She shivered whenever he said her name. "Passion. Love." She glanced over her shoulder. "Loyalty."

His hand slipped over her stomach and cupped her breast. "The one who betrayed you, did you have passion with him?"

"Some, but it wasn't worth the lack of loyalty."

"And you still loved him?"

"Sometimes love is just an easy convenience that helps you escape the loneliness."

"That's not love, Destiny."

"Then what is?"

He flattened his hand over her stomach, pressing her back firmly into his front. He was aroused, but comfortable simply lying close to one another.

"Love is a void you feel when it's missing. It takes up space inside of us and drives us to do unpredictable things. Love challenges us and makes us experience emotion so acutely even the good feelings can feel excruciating. It's feeling so fulfilled, you have no choice but to live in terror that one day it might all disappear. So you live through the fear, and live as if time were endless and every challenge were somehow an intentional gift moving you exactly to where you're meant to be."

"Live like you'll live forever, and you'll only be wrong once." She knew nothing of the sort of love he described.

"Or misguided for an eternity." His palm flattened and his fingers pressed between her thighs. "Why am I so addicted to touching you?"

Sliding her knees apart, she leaned back. "I'm just as addicted to your touch."

His hands stroked over her, teasing and arousing, and soon he had her on her back, his hard length filling her. "Kiss me as if this were our last day, Destiny."

Her heart pinched. It very well may be.

Her fingers raked through his hair and she pulled his mouth to hers, releasing her pent-up passion until the poignant sting of her intense emotions scared her. He thrust deep into her sex and she hooked her legs over him, scraping her nails down his chest and staring into his eyes.

His hand rode up her front, loosely cupping her jaw. "You make me hunger for things I cannot have."

"Can't we just pretend for a night that you can have whatever you want?" He groaned and pressed his face into the crook of her shoulder.

"Such a sweet temptation." His lips teased at her jawline, close to her ear and he tenderly nipped at her soft skin with his teeth. "If I had my way, I'd devour you."

"Have your way. I'm not saying no."

He groaned and dropped his head to her shoulder. "No matter how many times I have you, I'm always starved for more."

He thrust hard, pinning her beneath him and showing her how much he didn't want to let her go. She didn't know men could be so passionate or how any future lover would ever measure up. "I think you've ruined me."

He growled. "I wouldn't dare."

His mouth lowered to her breasts as he cupped and pulled at her sensitive flesh. Sometimes he'd bite her nipples, but then soothe the sting away with a soft kiss.

"I want you."

She lifted as he gripped her ass and surged forward, his pelvis pressing to hers. She gasped at the incredible sense of fullness. "You have me."

"I don't. Soon you'll be gone and this will be another lost memory."

She frowned. "It doesn't have to be. We could still see each other. I don't mind coming here."

"Shh." He kissed her. "Let's not worry about such things until we absolutely must. For tonight, let's hide from time. We can face tomorrow's cruel reality in the morning."

His touch varied from greedy to gentle as if using his body to say goodbye. Grasping the finality and understanding that this might be their last chance to be together, she had the urge to cry.

She poured everything she felt for him into their kisses. They moved together as if they were one and found a rhythm as natural as the tides. His body pushed into hers like the ocean waves glide into the sand, stroking and reshaping her with every press of his hips, lick of his tongue, and caress of his hands.

Why had she allowed herself to get so attached? There could be no future for them. The thought of Cain settling down with some innocent Amish girl created a crushing pain in her chest that threatened to escape in a sob.

Who was she to interfere with his life? It was unrealistic to ask an Amish man to give up everything he knew, his family, his home, for a woman he'd just met. Yes, they shared incredible chemistry and off-the-charts passion, but they were too different. And so what if he was one of the most loyal men she'd ever met? His loyalty was to his family and loved ones, not her.

When an Amish person left their order, they left permanently in exile. She couldn't ask that of him. *Wouldn't* ask that of him. But some foolish part of her wished he'd offer it all the same. And for that, she was a fool.

CHAPTER 28

Cain slipped out of the house at dawn to feed. On his way back, he passed Dane sitting on his grandparents' porch reading a book with a bright red cover.

"What do you have there?"

Dane startled and closed the book, quickly stuffing it under his leg. "Nothing."

"Nothing?" Cain approached the porch. "You don't hide *nothing*."

Dane sighed and removed the book. "It's a journal. I found it in a box with some of my mom's stuff."

"So you decided to read it? Isn't a journal private?"

"She's dead, Cain. Does it matter?"

He sensed the polite response would be to

say something comforting, but Dane didn't need coddling. He needed answers none of them had permission to give. "Did you find anything interesting?"

He shrugged. "Sure, I guess. It would be a lot more interesting if I could make sense of it."

"What do you mean?"

"She keeps talking about me like I don't live with them. She writes a lot about this woman named Daphne, and I think I was staying with her or something."

"You don't know who Daphne is?"

"I've never heard of her. Mom had a lot of friends, but never anyone by that name that I remember." He flipped through the pages of the book. "That's not all. She talks about my dad, but they're not married yet. He lives in a dorm, and she lives with my grandmother. How could that be?"

"Sometimes couples have children out of wedlock."

"They didn't, at least not according to what they told me. Either this book is a lie or my life is a lie."

Cain sighed. "Does it matter, Dane? Why not just let this stuff rest and remember the memories you had with your parents?

There's no point to getting angry with ghosts."

"I guess." He shut the book, but Cain suspected he'd keep reading it.

An awkward silence passed between them. "Where's Cybil? I didn't see her yesterday."

Dane looked at the big house then back to the front door of Cain's grandparents'. "Are those people still here?"

"They're leaving today." He was anxious to get back.

"Good," Dane said with notable disapproval. "I can't believe you let that guy stay there with your sister."

Cain shot him a questioning glare. "Gracie can handle herself."

Dane rolled his eyes. "That's everyone's answer. My mom was tough too. She's dead now."

Feeling sorry for the kid, Cain clapped a hand on his shoulder. "Try not to be so angry at the world. I speak from experience when I say it doesn't make the difficult emotions any easier to bear."

He left him to finish reading his journal and headed back to the house. When he returned, Gracie was cooking breakfast.

Destiny paused in the doorway and met

his stare, a thousand unspoken sentiments passing between them and his mind fighting back the urge to ask her to stay. No longer outfitted in the dress he'd given her, she wore one of his shirts and the pants she'd arrived in. Her appearance destroyed him, as he loved the sight of her in his shirt but hated the impression that she was ready to go. His sister must have mended her clothes.

Gracie turned from the cookstove, her gaze all too perceptive. He quickly blocked his thoughts and scowled at her for eavesdropping.

The front door opened and Vito came in. "We're all set. Hey, Cain. You feeling better?" Vito spun a metal set of keys around his finger and checked his pockets. "Don't forget your phone, D. Mine's charging in the car."

Cain's scowl turned toward the window. The car noisily idled like a kettle ready to burst. "You fixed the vehicle?"

Vito grinned. "Triple A. Turns out, it was just a loose plug. Nothing major."

Cain turned back to Destiny. "You're leaving now."

Her brows pinched over glassy, apologetic eyes. "Vito has work."

"You two can at least stay for breakfast,"

Gracie insisted, pulling Vito away from the door and seating him at the table. She looked back at Cain and winked.

He rushed across the kitchen and took Destiny's hand. "Come with me."

"O-okay."

Towing her out the door, he walked briskly toward the barn.

"Where are you taking me?"

"Someplace private. I thought we would have more time." He didn't want her to leave. Not yet.

"Cain, wait."

"I haven't had a chance to show you the kittens." He pulled her into the barn and couldn't catch his breath. "They're usually hiding by the wood pile where the mother chases mice."

She spotted the woodpile and only caught a glimpse of the kittens when he pulled her to a halt and pressed her body into the wall. Rather than find the right words to explain his frustration, he kissed her. Once again, God had tormented him with a woman he could not keep. He bit back his anger and tugged at her clothes.

"But the kittens—"

His greedy mouth bit at her full lips. "There isn't time. I need to be inside of you."

"Oh!" She gasped as he pulled at her clothing, doing his best not to tear the cotton. "Anyone could see us—"

"Let them see." With hurried hands, he shoved her clothing out of the way and took her against the wall.

It wasn't like last night when they made love or the moments she gave him control. This was pure desperation. His displeasure at letting her go threw his agility and he fumbled to get closer. It felt like she was already out the door and out of his life.

"Hold onto me, Destiny. I need to feel you holding me."

She dug her nails into his back and something snapped inside of him. She was so damn beautiful, so unlike any woman he had ever known. He needed her one last time.

She looked at him with such adoration and trust, and he hated knowing that he deserved neither. The bishop was likely already on his way, coming to take her memories of him and their time together. He never wanted her to stop looking at him the way she did now, but come tonight, she'd only ever see him as a stranger if their paths ever crossed again.

Why had God damned him with such lonesome misfortune? He forcefully shoved his length into her, punishing her for his own ill luck and she cried out but voiced no complaint. Damn her for enjoying his pain!

He wanted to hate her, believing it was easier to forget her when he didn't like her. If she yelled at him, cursed him, he would feel better about letting her go.

He pulled her hair and pushed her roughly into the wall. He was too crude, too aggressive. Females craved gentleness. None of them could truly accept what he wanted.

He unleashed his baser instincts and fucked her like an animal, giving no quarter and demanding too much. But she took every part of him and gave only a smile in return. And when her eyes glistened with tears, he sensed they weren't tears of pain, but tears of frustration, because she, too, did not want to say goodbye.

She matched his passion with her own. She clenched her thighs around him and held his shoulders in a white-knuckled grip as he took her in an absolute fury.

His body clenched and he fervently

pushed deeper, wanting her to take all of him, including his seed. She was his. The thought of another male—some meek, powerless mortal man—putting his hands on her enraged him. If she must forget him, he hoped she would at least remember this.

"You're my Destiny," he hissed, filling her and groaning through the jagged release. His spent body slowly retracted and he withdrew from her welcoming heat.

Dark curls fell around her face and she sank limply against the wall, his seed seeping down her thighs. He cupped her there, rubbing his palm over her until she gasped in pleasure.

"Never forget how good my hands felt on you, Destiny. How much you enjoyed this."

"Never," she promised, but the truth she spoke was only another lie.

Her body tightened as he worked her release. She trembled in his arms, as delicate and powerful as a flame. He needed to let her go, needed to say goodbye.

The sound of an approaching horse and buggy told him his sister and the bishop had arrived. Once they left this barn, Destiny's memories of this place and him would be taken from her. She and Vito would leave and everything he shared with her would be gone.

"I love you." The words whispered past his lips without thought. He only knew there would be a void in his heart when she was gone. He was acting impetuous and not thinking, but what did it matter? Cupping her face, he looked into her eyes. "No matter what happens, I'll never forget you."

She blinked up at him through glistening eyes. "I'll come back. I can be here tonight and the next day. It doesn't have to end like this."

That couldn't happen. The Elders would not allow it. "I would love that." His heart broke. Come tonight, she wouldn't remember the farm existed and she would have absolutely no recollection of him. "I'll wait for you."

She smiled and kissed him.

There was a sharp gasp, and he stilled. Destiny tensed, having heard the sound as well. Together, they looked at the barn door.

"Cybil—"

The child's mouth thinned to a tight line as she breathed hard, her eyes narrowing on Destiny. Her blonde curls trembled, denying what she saw, and then she bolted.

"Damn it!" Cain growled, yanking his

clothes back into place. Torn between going after her and waiting with Destiny, he looked at her.

"It's all right. Go after her. I'll see you tonight."

He hesitated and squeezed her hand. "Don't leave just yet. I just need a minute to make sure she's all right."

"Go."

He ran after Cybil but she was already gone. "Cybil?"

Dane came out of the woodshed carrying a stack of logs. "What's going on?"

"Cybil walked in on me with Destiny."

Dane scowled. "What do you mean, *walked in on?*"

"I mean we were fooling around, and she walked in without knocking. She's upset. I have to find her." He cupped his hands around his mouth and yelled, "Cybil!"

"There she is." Dane set down the wood and pointed toward the southern end of the farm. Cybil's red cloak waved behind her like a cape as she raced away from them.

"Cybil, stop running! I want to talk to you," Cain yelled, chasing after her.

A cloud of dust kicked up at the horizon. She was heading toward the bullpen.

"Cybil, stop!" Cain doubled his speed, careless of Dane's pace. "Stay away from that fence!"

She reached the gate and defiantly climbed the first rung.

"Cybil, *no!*" Clive was at the far side of the pen, but noticed the trespasser immediately. Cain bolted toward the gate. "*Cybil! Get out of there!*"

The bull huffed, steam billowing out of his nostrils as he stomped his front hoof just as Cybil's feet landed on the inside of the pen. Two thousand pounds of muscle and flesh barreled toward her.

"*Cybil!*" Clive charged, horns down, hide sweating. "*Run, Cybil, Run!*"

Dane shouted and the world went silent as her tiny body was flung into the air.

"*No!*"

Cain collided with the bull, plowing into its flank and knocking it onto its side. The ground rippled under the sliding impact, the beast's heft seemed to shake the trees. Cybil's body soared limply and Cain caught her slight weight in his arms. "Open your eyes, baby girl."

Limp and pale, her slight form disappeared in a crumple of wool and skirts.

Dane's screams of panic penetrated Cain's fear as he examined her. "Cybil, can you hear me?" He tapped her pale cheek with a trembling hand. "Cybil, wake up! Open your eyes. *Cybil!*"

"Is she okay?" Dane leapt the fence and crashed onto his knees at Cain's side.

"Get back!" Cain yelled as the bull clamored to its feet, already coming back for more.

Rage pumped through his veins as he cradled Cybil's slack body to his chest.

"Take her!" He draped Cybil in her brother's arms and growled at the bull, prepared to slaughter. The beast barreled towards them, head down and kicking up dust. Curving his body protectively in front of the children, he lengthened his claws and swiped at the bull the moment it was within reach.

The animal bleated in pain and Cain grabbed hold of the horns, snapping its neck with one sharp twist. The beast dropped in a heap of muscle and steaming flesh, as Cain panted and bared his fangs. Clive's black eyes went flat as he exhaled his last breath.

Dane held Cybil in his arms, lowering her to the dirt. "Why isn't she breathing?" His hand shook as he gently touched her pale cheek.

Cain crashed to his knees and caught his breath.

Dane's voice broke as he felt for a pulse. "She's okay, she's okay, she's okay."

Cain knew without touching her that her heart had stopped.

When Dane found no pulse, his panic doubled. He looked up at Cain with stark accusation.

"Tell me she's okay!" Dane shoved him angrily.

Cain's jaw trembled as he failed to find the words. Mortals were temporary. Fragile. And she was only a child. He could only shake his head, unable to speak the words.

"*No! No! Do you hear me?*" Dane shoved him again. "You fix this! You bring her back!"

Cain took pity on him, wishing he could undo what had been done, but it was too late. A boulder of regret formed in his throat, making it hard to breathe. "Dane, I'm sorry—"

"*No!* Don't you apologize to me! You fucking fix this!"

"I can't," the truth escaped in a brutal sob. What had he done? Cybil was gone. Crushing pain constricted his heart. Sweet, innocent Cybil…

The punch snapped his head back, but did nothing to slow his tears. Dane shook his shoulders, grabbing him by the shirt and forcing him to look him in the eye. "I know what you are! I know you can bring her back! *Why won't you save her?*"

"I can't. That's not how it works—"

"Bullshit! She's dead because of you! They're all dead! Fix her before it's too late!"

He looked down at her pale, lifeless face. "It only works if she's my mate."

"That's not true!" He cried. "I heard the other men talking. They said it can be done."

"I can't. It's not the same," Cain pleaded with him, but he was too distraught to listen to reason. "It'll change her."

"*You have to!*" the boy sobbed.

Cain's heart broke, wishing there was more he could do.

"Please, Cain. She's all I have left." He dragged the heel of his palm over his eyes. "I can't lose her too."

He looked from Dane to Cybil, and wondered how the world could be so brutal.

"God, forgive me." He pulled the child onto his lap and sank his fangs into the child's tender neck, he pulled greedily at her vein. The inborn predator hidden inside of him could taste the youth of her blood, and he reflexively began to purr. Why was nature so cruel?

Her rosy cheeks bleached of color as he reluctantly drained her. Puncturing the vein at his wrist, he turned her head and pressed his wrist to her lips, the crimson contrast of his blood spilling on her bone-white flesh was a vision that would haunt him forever. This was never what he wanted for her.

"She isn't swallowing it," Dane cried.

Cain tipped her head back, making a mess of her face and hair. His wound healed and he had to reopen the vein several times. God help him if he couldn't save her. He couldn't live with the additional memory of knowing he drained her dry.

Her bonnet fell to the ground as straggly white waves spilled over his legs. "Rub your hand over her throat. She has to swallow my blood for the transition to work."

Dane massaged her throat, crying and sniffling. It didn't look good. Her body was cold and it had been several minutes without oxygen to her brain or any sign of life.

"It's not working."

"Keep rubbing." Cain bit his wrist again, opening the vein more so his blood would spill more freely. "She only needs to swallow a drop to survive."

Her mouth gaped. Her tongue dark with blood and her face pale and lifeless. He couldn't do anymore for her. Shakily, he lay her on the ground.

"No!" Dane shoved him back and pressed on her chest. "Breathe, Cybil. You hear me. You have to breathe."

"Dane, don't." Cain tried to pull him off of her, but he lashed out and continued to pump his hands over her small chest.

"Don't you fucking leave me!"

The soft kick of her heartbeat met his ears like a puff of air. "It's working!" Cain shoved him out of the way, and pressed his wrist to her mouth. "Drink, Cybil!"

He flexed his fist, forcing the blood to flow faster into her mouth. She wasn't breathing, but every few seconds he heard the soft murmur of a heartbeat. When his wound closed again, he left it closed.

"Why are you stopping?"

"I've done everything I can do."

"What does that mean?"

"It means we wait." Words were useless at this point.

Minutes passed like eons as they silently watched her, ignoring the fact that they both were in tears. Perhaps he'd done it wrong. He should have given her some of his blood first. Mating was different. With mates, the blood exchange happened simultaneously.

"Did you see that?" Dane gasped. "Her finger twitched."

Cain watched her hand, but it didn't move. Another soft beat of her heart. He stood and pulled Dane to his feet. "Give her room." Her finger twitched again and Dane tried to go to her, but Cain placed a restraining hand on his shoulder, unsure how disoriented she might be. "Stay back."

Cain watched her chest, his eyes unblinking, as a red blush bloomed in her cheeks.

"It's working!"

Cain apprehensively watched as color rose in her neck, putting life back into her lips, and removing the gaunt appearance of her sunken skin. The cuticles filling the beds of her nails receded, and the chapped skin around her knuckles rejuvenated. Her hair thickened from baby fine to a weighty mass of healthy golden waves. Her lips plumped and pinkened, and her silver lashes doubled in length.

Breath wheezed into her lungs, expanding her chest and her mouth opened, exposing sharp, twin fangs. Then her lashes lifted, blue irises drowned by red pools that seeped into the whites of her eyes.

"Cybil, you're alive!"

Cain yanked the boy behind him. "That's not Cybil."

"What are you talking about? Move!"

Cain grabbed him by the collar and jerked him hard. "Don't you get it? She's alive, but it's not her anymore. I never should have let you convince me to—"

"Cain?" Destiny's voice crested the hill and he let Dane go.

"Destiny, go back to the house," he shouted, trying to keep his voice calm and praying she didn't come any closer. He looked back at Cybil who was breathing faster, her blood-red eyes wild and agitated. The bull and blood adding to the horrific scene.

"It's getting late and Vito wants to go."

"Go back to the house," he snapped. "Don't come any closer."

"But we're leaving."

Cybil sat up.

"Get back to the house, Destiny!"

Destiny came into view and Cybil shot off the ground with inhuman speed. Her body launched through the air and Destiny screamed, her cry cut short with a gurgle as the newborn vampire latched onto her neck.

"Cybil, no!" Cain ripped the child back and Destiny gasped and coughed, her hand pulling away from her neck as her eyes widened in horror at the sight of so much blood. She struggled to breathe. Cain tried to calm her, but every time he neared her, Cybil went ballistic biting and hissing, clawing at his eyes.

"Enough!" He snapped her neck.

"No!" Dane screamed, not realizing she would only rise again in a minute or two.

Destiny looked up at him, her mouth gaping in panic, her eyes wild with fear.

"I've got you." He caught her in his arms as she stumbled to the ground. Her panic was not with the blood, but with him. "I won't hurt you."

Blood spilled down her chest. They were losing time. She needed attention and he couldn't calm her. Cybil rose from the dirt and snarled.

"Dane! Take Destiny to the house. Tell the

bishop what happened. Tell him to help Destiny. I'll deal with Cybil."

Destiny scrambled back, hysteria taking over.

"Get her out of here!" he snapped, jolting the boy into action.

Cybil launched again, and this time Cain was prepared. He caught her midair and wrestled her to the ground. She hissed, scratched, and snapped at him, but he was stronger.

Possessed with rage, she gouged deep cuts in his neck as she tried to claw her way free, but he would not let her harm Destiny. Blood seeped from his skin as she fought him, and he held her down, taking his penance for all the wrongs he'd done and waiting for any sort of absolution to come.

He should have never brought them here. Not Cybil and Dane and not Destiny. Lives were ruined. And he had no one to blame but himself.

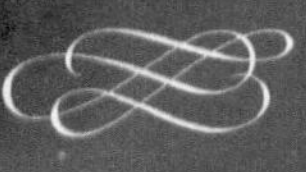

Destiny's phone rang and she muted it, not having time to take the call. Par for the course, Maria called her again. The woman would hammer dial her until she answered when she wanted something.

She answered. "Mom, I'm on my way out the door. I have work."

Her aunts' voices filled the speaker as they laughed and spoke in Portuguese. The time difference meant they were most likely several bottles of wine deep.

"Mom!"

"*Oi, tudo bom*, Destiny. Why aren't you answering the phone when I call?"

"Because I'm busy." Through the chaos on the other line and their general dysfunctionality with technology, her mother must have missed the part about her having to get to work. "I'm on my way out the door. Did you need something?"

"I haven't talked to you in some time. What have you been up to?"

"Nothing. My life is boring as usual." She didn't see the point of telling her about her nasty fall in the woods. The doctor said she was fine and after a few days off from work she was well rested and back to her regular routine.

"Is it getting warmer there?"

The weather had actually been miserable for the last few days. "It's cold and rainy." It had been sort of depressing and she hoped spring would break soon.

She grabbed her car keys. "Mom, I have to go. I'm literally running out the door."

"You call me later."

"I will."

"Kisses."

"Kisses." She hung up and raced out the door.

CHAPTER 30

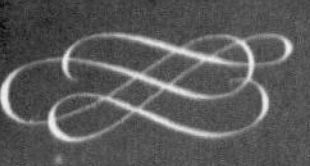

Rain soaked the fields and black clouds darkened the sky. Destiny was gone. The bishop had addressed her memories, and Cain struggled to accept the finality of their parting.

Once Cain situated Cybil in a cell at the safe house, he grappled to face all that he'd done. He forced himself to visit the changed mortal every day, a sense of responsibility and betrayal eating at him like a cancer the longer he silently observed what innocent little Cybil had become.

Cain's disgraceful actions once again tarnished their family's good name. No matter how he prayed for redemption, he left a blemish no amount of time could clean. A stain that everyone pitied and wished removed.

He longed for his mother and father's return, desperate for their love and guidance. Despite how he was shattering on the inside, his foolish pride would not let him shed one tear.

His eyes closed, remembering those last frantic moments with Destiny after the bull attack. He once more suffered the finality of his choices. Eternity was a cruel life sentence to live with mistakes he could not correct and regrets that would haunt him always.

Perhaps Destiny was the lucky one. Her memories were now gone. For him, those last agonizing moments with her would live forever like a scalding brand on his soul.

Cybil sat on the floor of her cell, her stare drifting over the wall as she traced a dirty finger down the mortar line of the cemented stone. The corridor was quiet, but Cain's mind never stopped screaming. He wondered what Cybil heard, if anything, in her mind.

Cain questioned what he'd done to deserve such a cruel outcome. In one fell swoop, he'd lost two people he adored. God saw to his loneliness, assured his regret, and taught a memorable lesson.

First Anna, then Cybil, and now Destiny. He understood loud and clear, he was meant to be alone. Destiny's words that morning had reminded him of such in a way that he would never forget.

"What is she?" Destiny shrieked. Accusation lighting her wide eyes as she kept her distance from him after he returned to the house, covered in blood.

Dane had been a mess, and Grace was torn between protecting the young man and calming Destiny. His sister trespassed into Destiny's thoughts and instantly read her disapproval and blame.

"Cain, you can't wait any longer. She's witnessed too much. She knows what we are and realizes what you did."

"We?" Destiny asked, eyes brimming with tears as she cupped a hand over her ravaged neck. "You're all like that?"

He moved to comfort her, but she cowered in horror, breaking his already shattered heart. "Please don't fear me, Destiny."

The wound at her neck was raw and gushing. She refused to let anyone close enough to examine the damage and her thoughts were too foreign and chaotic to control. He insisted the others give him space. He needed to calm her down so she might listen to reason.

"Stay back!" She snapped, holding up an unsteady hand. "Wh-what are you?"

Gracie lingered. "She needs blood, Cain. Her injuries are bad."

Destiny backed into the corner, her body shaking in fear. Humans were so damn fragile and by the amount of blood pouring down her chest, it looked as though Cybil nicked an artery.

"If you don't feed her your blood, she could bleed out."

Cain glared at his sister. "You're not helping, Grace!"

Destiny stumbled into the wall, her face pale and her eyes untrusting. Blood loss weakened her. And the snippets of conversation she'd picked up in the last hour likely horrified her.

"Fine. Fix this yourself." His sister stormed off, and Destiny sank deeper into the corner, her heart beating like a tribal drum before war.

"I won't hurt you. You have my word."

"That girl attacked me like an animal."

"She's not like us. She suffered a trauma and —" He still couldn't comprehend the loss of Cybil. "It doesn't matter. You're safe with me."

He knew what she thought of him. It was the

only title legend had upheld. But he was not vampire. Vampires lacked humanity and reason.

"All of you?" she asked. "Is it the entire order?"

There was no point in lying to her anymore. "Dane's the only one left on the farm who is mortal."

She shook her head and gave a humorless laugh. "Mortal. I suppose you aren't really thirty-eight."

"I am thirty-eight.

Twin tears fell from her eyes and her chin quivered. "Why?" she sobbed, showing him in one word how much she hoped they might work. Then she stiffened her lips and lifted her chin as if somehow forbidding herself to feel anything else in that moment.

He wondered what it said about her affection for him, if self-preservation could somehow turn her feelings off. Voice stern, she met his stare and asked, "What happens now, Cain? I know your secret. Am I in danger?"

"No. I won't let anyone hurt you." He'd even refused to let Eleazar near her until he was ready. His stomach sickened at the inevitable.

Destiny's face crumbled and she softly wept. Wiping back her tears, she scowled at him. "Don't do that. Don't try to act honorable and protective when you've been lying to me all this time."

"*Only about this. Everything else I told you was the truth, Destiny.*" His chest ached and he wanted to hold her. "*It's breaking my heart to see you so upset.*"

She shook her head, her tears smearing with blood as she wiped her eyes. "*You're not who I thought you were.*"

"*What I am is not evil, I swear it. I'm just different from what you know.*"

She scoffed. "*Do you... Oh, God.*" She swallowed and gripped her stomach. "*Do you drink... blood?*"

"*Animal blood. Our order frowns on human consumption.*"

She massaged her temples. "*How did I get here?*"

"*Humans breed and survive by consuming animal flesh. What we do is not so savage when you actually consider the difference. An animal doesn't have to die in order to sustain us. You only see it contrarily because your society neatly packages animal products in a market. The reality is, we're the less savage species.*"

His words seemed to calm her slightly, but then she lifted her gaze and narrowed her eyes. "*Have you...d-drunk m-my blood?*"

He looked away in shame. "*I was dying. You*"

shot me. It was the only way. I needed strength to get us out of the woods—"

"I'm going to be sick." She pressed her face into her hands and paced. "You violated me."

"I healed you."

Her glare snapped to him. "How? Oh, my God, don't say it—"

"We have a natural antiseptic in our saliva. The minerals in our glands promote rapid healing. That's why you have no scars on your back. You didn't fall, you were attacked in the woods."

"Stop. Just stop." She looked at him with ravaged eyes, her lashes wet with tears and her cheeks pink with hives and blotches of blood. "What happens now? I know you aren't going to let me and my brother just walk out the door."

His sister had Vito detained in the other room, but eventually a choice would be made and this madness would end. Voice strained, he told her, "We will heal your injuries and take your memories."

A quiet sob escaped her. "You've done this before, haven't you?"

"I cannot alter your thinking. You think in Portuguese."

She shot him a withering look. "You've tried though."

"This isn't the first time you were exposed to

our kind. Like I said, you were attacked, in the woods, by my uncle. I saved you, and you shot me with an arrow. It would have taken years to process such a trauma, and your exposure to our kind could have endangered those I love."

"What about me? You said you loved me."

Pressure built in his chest. He did love her. The thought of losing her again was an all-consuming agony he feared might finish him. He'd suffer a thousand more heart attacks and a million arrows rather than feel the anguish of hurting her. "I wish you no harm, Destiny."

Her eyes moved as she tried to rationalize the situation. "If you can't change my memories, how come I don't remember anything from the attack you speak of?"

"Bishop King speaks your language. He removed the memories of what happened in the woods. He overlooked some impressions of the farm, and that's how you found your way back. It was purely coincidence that you happened to drive to Lancaster the day after I took you home. Over time, those memories would have naturally faded, like a dream, and felt more like a fleeting sense of deja vu."

"Will I ever have those memories back?"

He looked away in shame. "Do you want them back?"

"I'll never know, will I?"

He betrayed her. That had never been his intention. "Destiny—"

"Just tell me what happens now, Cain. Will you call the bishop and have him take my memories again? Will he erase everything I saw today? All of my time here at the farm? My memories of you?"

"There's no other way. This was never meant to be permanent."

She snatched a book off his dresser and hurled it at him. "You knew this all along! In the barn when you told me to come back tonight, that was never going to happen!"

"I'm so sorry." Her sorrow gutted him. "If there were a way..." He lowered his stare. "I wanted it to be true. I wanted to keep you."

"God, I'm such an idiot. I honestly thought that we might..."

He reached for her and she shoved him away. "Don't touch me!"

"You're upset because it feels like I betrayed you—"

"You did betray me! You lied! About everything." She swiped away more tears. "I fell for you! I fell for all of it. I actually considered what it might be like to..." She sniffled. "I'm an idiot." Her

head shook as her face crumpled in disbelief. "Here I thought being Amish was the compromise."

Would she have stayed? It was a cruel realization to learn she might have cared that much. But her intentions were irrelevant. "Even if you wanted to stay, it doesn't work that way."

Time passed differently for mortals, as their time was precious and non-renewable. Even if staying had been an option, he would outlive her, and eventually say goodbye. Cybil was but a cruel reminder of what happened when immortals tampered with God's law.

"Only true mates can transition. If they're not chosen by God, then it doesn't work."

She sniffled and looked up at him. The flash of hope in her eyes gutted him. "Well, maybe we are—"

"Every male only has one mate." He shook his head. "You're not mine."

"How can you be so sure?"

To think her affection was not fully lost—but he would not be able to leave her until every bit was destroyed. For her own protection and his, he needed to see her hope irrevocably ruined until no sense of fondness stood the chance of redemption.

"Because Annalise is my mate."

"But she's married to your brother." The truth

struck like a bullet as always. She scoffed and shook her head in disbelief. "The baby..."

"The child is Adam's. Our situation is complicated, but my life is tied to hers. It's why I can't leave the farm and why I needed your blood to heal. The other day, when I was ill, it was her labor pains that struck me down. Just as the arrow you aimed at my heart punctured Anna's as well. Our souls are linked in agony, while Adam's soul is tied to her joy. She and I share suffering, I hers and she mine. One of God's cruel tricks."

After that confession, she completely detached. He tried to console her, but she screamed at him to leave her alone in her misery. "Just stop! I don't want to know this or you, anymore. I want to go home. Just stay away! Get away from me!" she screamed.

She wanted Vito and only to leave. Sobbing at the injustice of love, she cursed her tender heart and blamed him for her pain. His deceit was a betrayal she could not process.

The bishop arrived and took over her mind. Destiny settled into a subdued trance, as Gracie fed her enough blood to heal her wounds. Then Cain had to walk away.

He didn't have the strength to watch her memories disappear.

The bishop took pity on him. "It's better this way, Cain."

He placed a gentle hand on his back and Cain scowled. "Nothing about this is better."

"In time—"

"Don't talk to me about things you can't understand, Eleazar." Despite the bishop's recent mating to Larissa, Cain had lost too much for any ordinary immortal to comprehend. Fate had taken so much of his soul, only a hollow void remained where his heart once was.

"You should go." A sense of duty replaced the bishop's compassion. "Any sight of you could trigger the return of memories, and this goodbye must be final."

Cain looked back at Destiny one last time, but her gaze was unfocused and her expression flat. Head down, he turned his back on her and walked away. When he returned to the house that evening, all traces of her and her brother were gone. It was for the best.

The days that followed were wrought with accusation and grief. Dane blamed him and had every right to. Cain blamed himself most of all.

Looking at Cybil now, he wondered how he could have been so ignorant. The innocent girl was gone. In her place, a twisted mind and a vacant soul.

The crunch of sand and gravel underfoot had him scanning the long corridor. Oil lamps cast shadows along the stone walls, making it difficult to see. He sniffed the air. Male. Shutting his eyes, his senses identified David, the bishop's right hand, approaching.

Aged iron bars reinforced with steel bulkheads, sank into the solid earth, buried several feet below the surface. Solid stone and concrete lined the cells to ensure no prisoner could escape.

Cybil's hearing and sensory had increased to that of an immortal's and she now snapped to attention when even an insect skittered past. She gained speed and perception, and retained some measure of life, but her humanity was lost.

She shifted to her knees, her eyes alert and agitated and her neck stretched to see down the hall. Each cell contained a straw mattress. Other items were brought in daily for washing, but Cybil didn't care for such things and had a habit of smashing anything breakable or using it as a projectile weapon.

She despised captivity and showed little more than rage since they locked her away, attacking several powerful immortals when they transported her. Transitioned as she was, she had the strength of a newborn but the explosiveness of gunpowder. Her innocence was gone, replaced with something mercurial and dangerous.

While The Elders disapproved of what Cain had done, they found it a good opportunity to study such a biological change. Cybil had transitioned like *the others,* and The Elders wanted to understand what her limits were, her strengths, and her weaknesses.

He sentenced her to a life of captivity with the autonomy of a lab rat. Several times, while watching her pace in agitation and growl like a caged predator, Cain had questioned if it would be more merciful to put her down.

So long as Cybil served a purpose, The Elders would only reprimand him for violating the laws. As it were, they saw value in her circumstances. She was a vessel of information they planned to observe and dissect over time. If he went against them, however, his punishment would carry the weight of all his crimes. He could face possible exile and lose his family, lose Anna and any chance of seeing Cybil again. In order to protect her, he bided his time and watched over her closely, making sure no one overstepped. His presence ensured Cybil received kind treatment, regardless of how she treated others.

He was powerless among The Elders. His tolerance for their decisions and reliance on their mercy once again reminded him how ineffectual matters of the heart were. Love had been the root cause of all his sorrow and he only wanted the pain to go away.

Cybil would never see the light of day so long as she posed a risk to others. If she had the strength to injure a full-grown male of their kind, she was not safe to be around the females or young. Then there was the extreme risk of her escaping and reaching the human population. Cain's gut hollowed. As her sire, he was responsible for her actions and crimes.

The bars jostled as Cybil threw her body against the iron and snarled. Her flat eyes pooled with red and reflected the flickering light. She still did not speak, but vocalized in other ways, expressing her desires in throaty growls and snarled hisses.

When she slept, it was a restless slumber. She'd toss and turn and caterwaul like a feline in heat. Sometimes she'd whimper as if frightened, but she was safe in her prison cell. He had to keep telling himself that.

As she glared at him now, he felt her dislike for this infernal place and saw the accusation in her eyes. She was calmer with him than the others, so maybe part of her still recognized him as a friend, but there was nothing friendly about the way she bared her teeth or hissed at him.

The bars rattled again and the stench of negligence teased his nose. She'd been too volatile to bathe and showed no willingness in conducting the act alone. Not incapable, but disinterested. As it were, grime crusted her nail beds and caked in the fine creases of her knuckles. Sometimes she'd lick her fingers and purr at the traces of dried blood.

Feeding her was a challenge, on account of her heaving any offerings at the wall and using the dishes as weapons. She preferred blood to all other nutrition. Her hunger existed, but her tastes had changed and she had no interest in other food sources at this time.

Her already small body slimmed down to lean muscle, gaunt, angular cheeks, and sunken in eyes. Her flesh clung to the bone and the tattered remains of her clothing only partially covered her from view.

Cybil's head cocked and she stilled, her focus on some sort of intruder. She sprung from the bars, her speed incredible and her impact into the stone wall enough to shake free the dust that filled the tiny pores. She'd caught something. A cricket or spider perhaps. Her body was running on instinct now and she was hungry. The trespassing insect was gone before Cain could fully see what it was.

"If you stopped hurling your cups, you could have something a little more substantial in your belly."

She growled and kicked her feet over the dirt floor. The memory of her sweetness faded every day she watched him with such disapproval and blame, such endless accusation. And he deserved every second of it.

Footsteps drew closer and he forcefully blanked his face and mind of all emotion. Cybil stood and prowled toward the bars, curious and guarded. She paced like a caged animal, making frenzied gesticulations as she watched the shadowed corridor with a blaming, demonic stare.

Cain wanted to make promises he couldn't keep. He wanted to vow to see her healed by some unknown miracle. He wanted to get her out of that cavity of a cell, but he didn't have the authority. And any false promise could be viewed as intent to disobey his elders and result in punishment.

Too many powerful immortal males lingered at the safe house and he never knew who was listening. Even emotions put him at risk for questioning. He had to protect his thoughts at all times.

David finally appeared with a tray. Dispassionately, Cain noted the cup of blood and the syringe. They were going to attempt to tranquilize her again.

The Elders wanted samples of her blood, and the last time they tried, she hadn't allowed the intrusion, clawing and biting with feral self-preservation that left a male with a detached retina and another in need of a transfusion. Despite the incredible power of The Elders, Cybil's mind was too broken to penetrate. Compulsion could not work on her at this point.

"Brother Hartzler."

"Good evening, David."

More footsteps followed and Cain took that as his cue to leave but hesitated. He glanced at the cell, his chest aching for any lingering sense of innocence. Several strong-bodied males appeared.

Cybil watched the newcomers with uncertainty. Her eyes dilated, and she panted as the group of males crowded the bars of her cell. Cain sensed her fear and wished he could offer words of comfort, but he wasn't sure how much she would comprehend at this point. Shame on him for not having the stomach to watch.

David withdrew a key and a small vial. Cain hesitated. He couldn't leave her.

The metal key clicked into the ancient lock. She shuffled backwards, her shoulders pressing into the wall. Her hair twisted in un-combed snarls around her pale face as she growled, low and threatening.

The men entered, and she went ballistic, hissing and clawing, screeching and wailing. They moved quickly, overpowering her and pinning her to the tattered mattress on the floor. She bared her teeth and screeched, clawing and hissing like a feral animal trapped and suffering.

Her shredded clothing provided no modesty in the tussle. The knot of blonde hair worked as a handle to subdue her, and the moment David grabbed it, her fangs flashed like ivory tusks and she clawed his face like a cornered animal.

Inhuman hissing tore through the air. They moved in a blur of color and sound until everything silenced and Cybil stilled, her arms wrenched behind her back as David pinned her small form to the shredded mattress on the floor. He plucked a syringe from where he held it clenched between his sharp teeth and plunged it into her arm.

Cybil jerked and panted, her fangs streaked with blood. Unable to witness anymore, Cain forced himself to walk away. As he neared the end of the corridor, the frantic banging from her cell started again. She was constantly fighting, constantly angry. He shut the door and shut away his sadness at what poor little Cybil had become.

Rain pelted his chest on the walk home. His mood had soaked the fields, leaving the ground saturated and soft, and the buggies limited to only a few higher roads.

When he reached the house, he found Gracie sitting at the table with Dane by her side. The boy hid his face in his arms resting upon the surface as if sleeping, while Gracie's hand coasted over his hair in an act of comfort.

"How is he?"

"How would you be?"

Like everyone else, she blamed him. Because of Cain, Gracie had lost her young companion. It didn't matter that he'd acted on Dane's persistence. Cain was immortal and aware of God's law. He should have known better.

Cybil added purpose to Gracie's days and their lessons gave his sister a sense of value that was now gone. So much had been lost and there was no readily available solution to quicken this time of grief for any of them.

CHAPTER 31

Destiny waited at the same Tuscan restaurant she always patronized on first dates. This would be the eleventh blind date since last winter and there had been no thaw in her cynicism. Life could have been so much easier had she only been born a lesbian. Instead, she was chugging along on her hetero way, through a murky swamp of boys playing at being men.

The bartender placed a tall glass of pinot on a cocktail napkin and she slid him a twenty. "Enjoy." He was cute.

Her gaze went to his ring finger. Married. "Thanks." She sighed and took a long sip.

They probably thought she was a call girl, coming here every few weeks dressed up to meet a different man. If only her life were that interesting. At least call girls had sex. Destiny lost count of how long it had been.

Tonight she was meeting Eric. Five foot eleven, nice physique, and glasses. He seemed like a decent guy, according to his dating profile, but experience taught her that in terms of literature, dating profiles usually qualified as fiction.

Deciphering the facts from falsehoods required a certain level of skill and determination. It was no longer about swiping left or right on looks alone. She was mining for truth and weeding out the lies as efficiently as possible. She preferred the bad news upfront so she'd be less disappointed in the end.

Eric filled a low level position at an IT firm, had a civil divorce under his belt that didn't involve an insane ex, and a six-year-old son. According to his profile, he wasn't interested in having more children but acknowledged that his feelings could change with the right woman.

Overall, his stats were decent. And he liked curvaceous women—a plus for him since she was a plus-sized beauty herself.

Taking another sip of wine, she searched

the restaurant for her date. This was always the awkward part.

Pedro, her last date, had been awful. He'd been sexy and funny when they spoke via text, but when they met in person, the vibe was gone. He spent the entire meal staring at her chest. After dinner he insisted on walking her to her car, where he proceeded to kiss her. Turned out, Pedro was an irredeemable chin licker. Slobber everywhere. She would have gotten away cleaner if she'd made out with a Saint Bernard.

After Pedro came Sal. He was great. Gorgeous, toned body, spoke with a lovely Italian accent. He was a carpenter and built beautiful furniture. When he mentioned living with his parents, she didn't judge him. If her parents weren't in Portugal, she'd still live with them. Fiscally, it just made more sense than having a big, empty house.

She thought they hit it off, until he postponed their next two dates. At first, she chalked it up to coincidence, because sometimes freak things happen. She admired his loyalty to family and respected how he was always there for them in a pinch. Also, she admired a man who took good care of his mother, assuming such behavior hinted at attentive husband traits—until he mentioned bathing his mother.

"Oh, is she physically limited?" Destiny had asked, assuming the woman might have an illness.

"No, Mother just prefers I help her. She has since I was young."

Recalling the moment she realized she'd been on a date with Norman Bates, she shivered. That was the end of Sal.

Searching the bar for her date again and seeing no sign of him, she debated ordering another drink. She always chose this restaurant for her first dates because she loved the food. That way, even if the date bombed, she still got to enjoy a good meal.

"Destiny?"

She turned and recognized Eric's handsome face. "Hi." She smiled, taking a quick scan of his appearance. Everything looked accurate with no signs of catfishing.

"Sorry I'm late. There was an accident right before the exit. Were you waiting long?"

Accidents happened, so she didn't deduct any points. "Not long at all." He smelled really nice.

He settled onto the stool next to her. "Let me get your next one."

Flagging down the bartender, he placed an order and left a generous tip. Point.

The hostess informed them their reservation was ready, and they carried their drinks to a small table by the back wall. Destiny had decided somewhere on the ride there that she would order the chicken and asparagus with that yummy sauce they made, but she glanced at the menu anyway, pretending like she didn't eat there almost every week. It was a shock the staff didn't know her by name yet.

Once they placed their order, they settled back into conversation. "So, what did you do today?" he asked, and Destiny bullet pointed the highlights of her day. Nothing outstanding to report.

"How about you?"

A waiter dropped off a basket of bread and they each took a piece. "I worked on my EP."

"EP? Is that a computer thing?"

He grinned. He had a sweet smile with a good set of dimples. "No, EP stands for Emergency Pack."

"Emergency Pack?"

"Yeah, you know, for the apocalypse."

Destiny stilled, her glass half tilted toward her mouth. "You're kidding."

"Oh, no. Prophets have been predicting

the end for years." Negative one point. "I plan to be completely prepared. Fallout shelter and everything." Negative two. "I have rooms filled with rations. Enough for two, actually." He winked. Negative three.

She chugged her wine and snagged the waitress walking by and asked for another. Eric went on. "I have an entire storage unit filled with water and first aid." Dear God, negative four.

The waitress delivered her wine and she chugged as Eric went on and on and on. Somewhere around negative eleven, she said, "You know what? I'm not feeling too great. Do you think we could do this another time?"

Eric looked terrified. "Do you think it's the water? It's probably tap and you drank a few sips. You know, they say that's how it might happen, through the water."

"They?"

He nodded, a severe look marring his once attractive face. "The spies."

She opened her mouth and shut it. Her cash went on the table. "Yeah. I gotta go."

And that was how she ended up at home on her couch involved in a very raunchy threesome with two men named Ben and Jerry.

CHAPTER 32

$\mathcal{A}$ dull haze pressed through the dreary rain pelting Cain's bedroom window. Despite the busy rhythm of spring on the farm, his days were mostly met with long hours of solitude, and his evenings were saved for sleepless hours of regret passed down at the safe house.

Hearing the movement throughout the house, he swallowed back his grief and shut his eyes. The sound of nearby laughter triggered images of Destiny laughing and smiling in his arms, then falling apart and growing deathly afraid of him in the blink of an eye.

It had been months since she left and the rain never ceased. He wasn't sure it ever would.

His attention snapped to the door as someone softly scratched. "Cain?"

Gracie. She'd gone from condemning him to being over the top concerned for him. "Go away."

"I brought you a tray of food. You need to eat."

He needed to be left the hell alone. "I said go away."

The rattle of dishes told him she'd left the tray by the door. She did so every night until she took it away the next morning.

Turning to his back, he stared at the ceiling, savoring the soft prattle of rain until his eyes drifted shut. He drifted off and the babble faded. The rain only stopped when he slept. Of course, it did. He couldn't dream, so he wouldn't think of her in his sleep.

He awoke many hours later, the house quiet and everyone abed. Stepping around the tray in the hall, he ignored the food and made his way to the barn. His appetite betrayed him and he had no choice but to feed. The sheer act of meeting his needs sickened him. Everything about his nocturnal existence of late reminded him why he would spend an eternity alone.

He fed the way a drunk takes to drink—

careless of the flavor and only meeting a shackling need. When he finished, he walked through the rain to the safe house.

Cybil, like *the others*, followed a natural vespertine clock and typically rose after dusk. The Elders used her body's natural rhythms to perform their tests and extract her blood, but they discovered no new information about her state. She was still as lost and gone as she'd been the day the bull killed her, the day he intercepted any chance of her soul ever finding peace.

"Cybil," he greeted and she eyed him from under a mess of blonde tangles through demonic, distrusting eyes. "You've made a mess."

Blood smeared on the corridor wall, just across from her cell bars where a large crack marked the plaster, matted with hair.

"I hope they deserved it," Cain joked.

She flashed her teeth, snarling, and prowled, overly agitated tonight.

He stayed with her for several hours, mostly blathering on about how pointless his life had become. "Jonas is back. You remember Jonas, right?"

Chin down, her glare followed his fingers as he used a pocket knife to slowly carve an apple into thin slices. She'd lost a lot of weight in addition to going through a growth spurt. He tried to slip her food whenever possible, but she wasn't always responsive to his offers. Sometimes she was downright dismissive, meaning she spit and hurled objects until he left her alone.

"My mother, Abilene, is as big as a house with child. I think this one's going to make it." Pinching a thin slice of apple between the blade and his thumb, he slipped it into his mouth. "She's miscarried more babes than I can count."

He cut another slice and paused, silently offering it to her by not saying a word. She edged closer to the bar and leaned her head into the iron. Pinching the slice between his fingers and thumb, he stretched closer and held out the piece of apple.

Cybil snatched the fruit and raced to the far corner of the cell and ate it. He hid a smile.

"Larissa's little one is expected any day. That should tie up the bishop for a while. I suppose that might be somewhat of a relief to you."

She returned to the bars and he offered another slice which she took. She was hungry, but it seemed her pride was of greater value and if she had to choose between the two, she'd starve for self-preservation. He didn't need a blood test to glean that bit of knowledge. At least he'd restored enough of her trust to ensure she could take food from him instead of hurling it like a weapon as she did with the other caregivers.

Once the apple was gone, Cain put the knife away. Cybil kept her distance, lurking mostly in the shadows deep within the hollow of her cell.

She no longer signed, and for as much as he'd initially opposed Grace teaching her such a skill, he now missed it. In a way, communicating with her through hand gestures was almost as satisfying as hearing her voice.

He recalled how *the others* spoke in the woods. Their banshee like cadence was by no means comforting, but it proved her kind could speak if the compulsion was there.

"Cybil?" She looked up the instant he called her name. "Do you miss talking?"

She watched him through narrow, ruby eyes.

"If you used your voice, they might eventually let you out of here." That was a stretch, but anything was possible. "You would have to show them that you can be civilized and control your impulses.

Speaking would help them understand your intentions."

She continued to glare, but he forced himself not to look away, meeting her challenging gaze with one of his own.

"Come on, Cybil, say something. One word. It could be anything."

Her jaw twitched and her nostrils flared. She didn't like this game.

"Please?" He signed. "The least you could do is say my name."

At that, her head lifted and something resembling fear flashed in her eyes. Her shoulders drew back, and she shuffled deeper into the shadows.

"What did I say?" he murmured, giving up.

Rising from the floor, he brushed the dust off his pants. Mud caked the soles of his boots. No point in kicking it off when it was going to be a soggy trek home.

"Same time tomorrow night?"

She looked back at him, her brow tight with confusion when she typically showed no concern over his departure. Maybe pushing her to speak had upset her in some way.

"I'll see you tomorrow." He wanted to say sleep well, but she slept about as well as he did these past few months.

On the way out he heard approaching footsteps and blocked his mind. With a sniff, he recognized Dane approaching. "You're here late."

Startled, Dane's downcast stare jerked up. "I…didn't realize anyone was down here. I couldn't sleep." He brushed a hand over his rain-soaked hair. "How is she?"

"Calmer than usual. A little anxious. I asked her to talk and that seemed to upset her. Maybe you can figure out if there's anything more to it."

He shook his head. "Yeah right. I gave up on hearing her voice long before the accident. I haven't been able to make any sense of her thoughts either. It's all very dark and confusing. Each day the impressions get harder and harder to see."

That meant she was losing her innocence. Dane had an incredible gift to see young people's thoughts. He couldn't hear them, like Gracie could, but he gleaned impressions from open minds, mostly from children.

He claimed, other than Gracie, he could rarely see into adult minds. The fact that he could penetrate his sister's mind at all proved incredibly impressive, since she was immortal and Dane was not.

"Her mind's different now."

Cain took pity on the boy who had become a man overnight. "We're all different now."

He never apologized, because Dane had insisted Cain intervene. They were both responsible. Chances were, Dane's guilt ate at him as relentlessly as Cain's ate at him. One didn't have to be telepathic to read the regret in his eyes.

Together, their interference sentenced Cybil to an eternity of hell. Cain would have to live with that truth a lot longer than Dane.

"Be careful," Cain warned, before leaving him to his visit.

That night, he tried to think of other things, but his mind loved to torture him. He played over his memories of Destiny and tried hard to recall her exact scent. If he shut his eyes and concentrated, he could still hear her laughter and visualize the sweet way she smiled when he told her she was beautiful.

He managed a few hours of sleep, but his mind never delved far under the surface of awake and he stirred the moment he heard Grace set the kettle to heat. The repetitive routine of his days was another cruel practice of time. Time was all he had. Endless gaping time, alone with only his thoughts and self-loathing.

It was nice hearing his mother's voice around the house again. His father had been preoccupied since their trip and Cain sensed he had something on his mind, but chalked it up to worry about the babe. He'd likely feel relieved when the child was born and any danger to Mother or the child would be laid to rest.

A gentle knock tapped on the door. "Cain?"

The rain was heavy this morning and he hadn't heard a carriage arrive, but that was definitely his sister Larissa. What was she doing there? She was days away from giving birth and should be resting.

"Cain, please let me in. I want to talk to you."

Hesitantly, he got up from the bed and opened the door. "Why are you out and about in this weather?"

She sent him a sardonic look. "This weather is your department. If it bothers you, perhaps you could let the clouds pass for a while."

"I'm not in a sunny mood."

"Obviously. All of my shoes are ruined and

my dresses have mud spatters everywhere. If you had any sympathy at all for my aching back, you'd stop creating so much extra laundry for the females."

He glanced down at her protruding stomach. "You're huge."

Wedging her hand into the arch of her back, she waddled past him and sat on the bed. "This room needs fresh air." She fluffed his pillows then grew bored with the chore. "Gracie says you aren't eating."

"I'm feeding. That's enough."

She sighed. "It might do you well to share a meal with others."

"Who? My sister who blames me for Cybil or my brother who still hasn't forgiven me for hurting his wife? Or perhaps my father who has barely said two words to me since returning home. Which one is it, Larissa?"

Her mouth pursed. "Well, I'm here today. You could at least eat with me."

Again, he glanced at her stomach. "I think you've eaten enough."

She threw a pillow at him. "Wretch." Shifting her weight, she rubbed her belly. "Then do it for Mother's sake."

His mother had been different toward him since the day of Adam's wedding. After that, she'd been so preoccupied with their father's calling, she hardly spoke to anyone. The moment Clara passed, their father collected their mother and some belongings from the farm, and absconded her away to work on their marriage.

"I'm sure Mother's fine."

"Cain."

"What do you want from me, Larissa?"

"You're upsetting others. I want you to stop being so selfish!"

"Ah, well, that's me. I'm the self-serving prodigal son who only thinks of himself. No point in changing now."

Larissa rolled her eyes. "Your stubbornness contributes to your lonesome state."

He narrowed his eyes, his patience at an end. "I'm alone because my brother stole my true mate."

"Cain," she said his name with whispered censor.

"Why should I lie. She was mine, and Adam has her. End of story."

"You were a part of that decision."

"Yes," he agreed snidely. "And I will spend an eternity outside of their happiness learning to square away any bitter regrets my choices have wrought."

"You don't love Annalise that way."

His molars pressed tight. "Regardless, I'm sentenced to stay close by and live my life without risk or autonomy, so not to chance endangering Anna or jeopardizing Adam's precious happiness."

"Cain, no one expects you to put your life on hold."

"Everyone expects that, Larissa. I've not even met my nephew yet, my own namesake. They ask every sacrifice of me and offer nothing in return."

He could tell by the compassion in her eyes that she had not considered his circumstances from his position alone.

Shaking his head, he paced to the window that faced his brother's home. "I'd never intentionally hurt Annalise. I can't. My protectiveness lends itself to Adam's happiness, because I've watched what losing him does to her." He glared out the window through the rain and bitterness transcended into sorrow. "I see the way Eleazar looks at you and the way Father looks at Mother." When he turned to face her, his voice strained around the ache building in his throat. "What did I do that was so wrong that God refuses to allow anyone to see me in such a way?"

"Oh, Cain," she whispered, unable to deny the truth. He didn't dare turn, certain he'd only find pity in her eyes.

He thought of Destiny and how, in those last hours, she'd been willing to come back to him—how much he wanted to believe that she could.

"They say I'm reckless and self-serving, but I've given up everything in order to protect them. And now, dear sister, I just want to be left the hell alone."

"Cain—"

"Please go, Larissa. At least leave me my dignity and let me face this misery alone."

She placed a comforting hand on his shoulder and silently left him with his thoughts. A tray was delivered to his door, and the whispers followed. His grief was an imposition in their happy world, but he was not a problem they needed to solve.

Their vicarious suffering was nothing compared to the endless ache eating at him, day in and day out. It only felt great because it contrasted so drastically from their typically joyous lives. He had no sympathy to spare.

Later that day he was awoken by another knock at the door.

"Go away," he grumbled, and then frowned at the distinct chortle of a baby coo.

"Cain, it's Anna. I'm not leaving until we see you."

Flinging himself out of bed, he went to the door and ripped it open, glaring at her. Then his gaze dropped to the pudgy little male in her arms and something loosened in his chest.

"I'm sorry it's taken us this long to visit."

He looked just like her, but also like him. Not him. Adam. He hadn't anticipated that the babe would resemble both of them. The realization stirred a sense of misdirected pride then pricked his ego with endless needling envy. "Well, he's handsome."

"He looks like his father," she agreed. "And his uncle."

"He has your eyes." He couldn't stop staring at the boy. Reaching out a finger, he hooked it through the babe's pudgy fist. "You hurt me, kid."

"Do you want to hold him?"

"I couldn't—" Anna put the child into his arms and a warm sensation filled his chest as the slight weight settled in.

She pushed into his room. "I assumed you would have visited."

"I've been...preoccupied."

She glanced at the unmade bed. "I can see that." Moving to the window, she opened it. "Let a little air in here."

He kept his stare mostly on the babe. His motions softened from steps to glides and he bounced ever so slightly and made soothing sounds with his mouth. The young male seemed to like that.

"I named him after you—"

"You shouldn't have done that," he interrupted.

She scowled. "I didn't ask for your opinion. I named him after you, because I want him to think of others before he thinks of himself."

Cain scoffed. "That's not really my *modus operandi*."

"And I want him to be so humble that he does the right thing even when there's a considerable cost to himself." She met his stare. "That's true honorability, Cain. It isn't boastful or motivated. Larissa told me what you said today." Her chin quivered. "How could you think we don't appreciate all that you've sacrificed for us?"

"It's not fair if you cry. And let's not assume my brother shares your sense of for-giveness."

"Adam's scared. Everything he values hangs in the balance of your choices. You think you're the one without freedom, but his happiness depends on your mercy."

"I didn't bow out because of mercy or pity. I did it for you."

"I know that."

"So should he."

"He does. On some level."

She strode back to the window and the baby watched her, already bonded and finding her the most appealing woman in any room. Cain could empathize. Anna was easy to watch.

"Pride has a way of purposely masking the truth, Cain" She glanced out the window as the fading sun fought to break through the clouds. "Adam feels he owes a debt to you he'll never be able to repay, and a sense of obligation can easily lend itself to fear."

"I would never delude or betray him like that."

"I know."

"He should know it, too."

"He does, on some level. Adam's followed all the rules all of his life. He's worked very hard to be an honorable male." She smirked. "Imagine how frustrating it must be to see you abandon tradition and mock so many of the laws then perform the most selfless act of all."

He narrowed his eyes. "No one sees it that way. They all saw you as Adam's first."

"Adam sees the truth. He knows what you did for him, and he will spend his entire life contending with that debt. That's a long time for an immortal."

And Cain would spend eternity coveting his brother's wife. "If you truly feel that way, why have you shut me out?"

"Shut you out?"

"I know you've been busy with the baby, but you never come to me in my dreams anymore. I haven't heard from you."

She frowned. "Cain, I dream every night. I go to our secret places and search for you, but you're never there. I thought it was *you* who was shutting *me* out."

"You're still dreaming?"

"Yes. All the time. Babies sleep a lot, and mothers need their rest, too."

He frowned. Perhaps they were sleeping at different times of the day. "I've tried…" It was one thing to assume she was punishing him, but to learn that wasn't the case and their connection might actually be lost… "What does this mean?"

"Gracie told me you felt my labor."

He shot her an unimpressed glare. "I might have suffered a cramp or two."

Her lips twitched, but she held back a laugh. "Anything since?"

"No. But would there be?"

She placed a hand on his arm. "Try to come to me in a dream tonight. I'll do the same. If our connection is lost, I'm sure there's a reason. I want to know why."

After Anna left, he contemplated her words. Adam was a prideful male, always in complete control of his emotions. He couldn't imagine him struggling with any sense of inadequacy or feeling intimidated or threatened, but also didn't know Anna to lie.

That night, he visited Cybil for only a short time. He wanted to attempt sleep and see if he could find Anna in his dreams. He managed a few hours, but woke with no memory of a vision or experience with Annalise, only the same jarring emptiness that followed his first waking thoughts every day —Destiny was gone.

His heart was a prison he wanted to escape. Rather than pass the hours pining away in his gloomy bedroom, he dressed and readied a horse and carriage.

"Where are you going?" Gracie asked from the front porch, her mind naturally reaching for his.

"Into town. And stay out of my head."

He didn't need an audience, so he ignored her and climbed onto the buggy. He rode through the early morning mist, the rhythmic clip clop a balm to his senses. Trees were in full bloom and he resented the cheery landscape. Drizzle started to fall.

When he reached town, he parked the buggy in an empty lot and walked down the main thoroughfare, staring inside each display window. When he found what he was looking for in a shop called Country Antiques, he sighed.

He tried the door, but it was locked. "No." Scowling through the glass, he banged on the trim. "Open up." But the store was empty and dark.

The sign claimed they would open in two hours. Irritated by the delay, he found a bench and waited. Stretched out on his back, he folded his hands over his chest and stared at the bright morning sky. The air smelled of spring blooms and the trees lining the road were lush with green leaves and bright buds, a likely result of the endless rain of late.

When the store opened, Cain went right to the clerk. The bell above the door hadn't stopped chiming before he asked, "The television set in the window, does it work?"

"Should." The clerk, a middle-aged, overweight man, made a sucking noise with his tongue through the space of his front teeth. "Thought you Godly types were forbidden to use electricity."

Cain ignored him and went to the display window. Lifting the small television set, he carried it to the counter. "Turn it on."

The man eyed him suspiciously but guided the long-pronged cord toward an outlet. Once the set was plugged in, he twisted a knob and the glass screen sizzled to life. Black and white specks danced across the display. Cain adjusted the volume dial and the static hissed like the surf of the ocean.

He glared at the clerk, prepared to break his neck for lying. "It's busted."

"Ain't gonna get a clear channel without a cable box. And I doubt they're compatible with an old set like this."

He glanced at the many clocks on the wall.

He'd wasted an entire morning there. His hand smacked the side of the set.

"Hey, you break it, you buy it."

"If it doesn't work, it's already broken."

"Says you. You lookin' for somethin' in particular?"

"*Channel Six*. I want to watch the news."

The man shot a thumb over his shoulder. "Well, you don't need a television for the news. You just need a phone."

Cain's gaze zeroed in on the man's digital device. "Show me."

"Now, hold on—"

He met his stare and took hold of the man's mind. "Pick up your phone and show me the *Channel Six* news."

The clerk reached for the device and quickly navigated the screen. "It's live streamin'."

Cain took the phone. "Take a nap."

The man fell asleep on the spot, standing awkwardly and snoring softly. Cain settled onto a small stool and stared at the screen. The clerk dropped to the dusty floor with a thud and the bell above the door chimed.

Without taking his eyes off the phone, Cain said, "Shop's closed. Come back in an hour."

"I don't think so, *bredder*."

Cain's stare jerked to Adam standing at the entrance. His brother arched his neck, taking note of the clerk snoring softly with his mouth open behind the counter. "Was that necessary?"

"I wanted to be alone. Take a hint." Ads played on the phone and he grew impatient. "Did you follow me here?"

"I was in town and saw you. What are you doing here?"

"It is none of your business. I'm not harming anyone or placing myself in any danger. Go away." He wondered if he and Anna could no longer share dreams, if they would still share pain. That would be a welcome loss.

Rather than leave, Adam leaned into the glass door and made himself comfortable. The news program started with a serious man sitting at a desk listing various topics of the hour, and then an upbeat song played as images flashed over the small screen with people smiling gaily while doing an odd selection of random activities.

When the music stopped, the man at the desk reported on crime in the Middle East, a shooting, a line of convenience store robberies, and the upcoming traffic report. The longer he droned on, the more impatient Cain grew. All the while Adam watched him.

Another string of advertisements, and then the man was back. Finally, he said her name. "And out in the field today, we have Destiny Santos."

Cain's breath held as Adam's scrutiny burned into him.

"Thanks, Mike. I'm here at the new local skate park where kids are enjoying this beautiful spring weather." His heart hammered at the sound of her voice. He desperately needed to see her face, but the camera only showed young English children zooming up and down hills.

His grip tightened on the phone and then she was there. "This is Logan." She gestured to a young boy with curly hair. "He's twelve and lives about twenty minutes from here. What do you think of the new skate park, Logan?"

The boy leaned into the microphone with a wide smile. "I think it's awesome."

"Did your parents bring you here today for the opening?"

"Yeah. My mom's right there." The boy looked right at him and waved. "Hi, Mom!"

Destiny laughed, her beautiful face once

more showing on the device. Cain shut his eyes, savoring the comforting melody of her voice. "As you can see, Mike, the new skate park is off to a great start. A donation was made for the park by town native and skate legend, Tanner Quick, who we interviewed last fall when they broke ground on this project." Grinning at the camera, she seemed to look right at him as she said, "Looks like Tanner Quick may not be the only skate champion this town produces. Back to you, Mike."

The screen switched back to the man at the desk, and Cain's shoulders sagged. It was over in a flash, but more than he'd imagined. Seeing her again, hearing her voice, it only confirmed his fears. He hadn't embellished her beauty or exaggerated his feelings. He was still in love with her.

Adam took the phone and set it on the counter. "Can we go now?"

Cain stared at the floor, his mood shifting from light to dark. A murderous rage crept through him, and his muscles tensed under his clothing. "Why did you come here?"

"I told you. I saw you and—"

Cain was on his feet with his brother's shirt locked in his fist. "You came here to mock me! You can't let me have one moment of happiness, can you?"

"Cain, that's not it at all—"

"Then what?" He shook him roughly. "What is it you want from me? Does it prove something to you to see me at my lowest? I'm stricken. Empty. All I have is this godforsaken void in my chest since she's gone and you have *everything*! Is that what you want to hear? *Is it?*"

"No." He gripped Cain's fists where they twisted his shirt.

"Then why are you here? Don't lie to me! I know you were not in town on business."

"Fine." Adam flung his hands off of him. "I'll tell you the truth. I was in the barn when you left and sensed the upheaval of your emotions. I wasn't sure what you had planned, but I saw you going into action and I wanted to make sure you didn't go too far."

"I told you I wouldn't risk hurting Anna."

"And I'm grateful for your loyalty in that promise, but I also fear you might hurt yourself, Cain. I want my son to know his uncle."

"Stop setting the bar so high. I'm exhausted by your expectations. The boy would do better knowing an idea of me."

"No, Cain. That's not good enough. I want

my son to know the real you. All of you. You're a part of our lives."

He was a paperweight holding things in place while the world moved around him. "Did she look happy to you?"

"Who?"

"Destiny."

Adam sighed. "What do you want me to tell you, Cain? She looked like an English news reporter doing her job."

Cain shook his head. No answer would have comforted him. Happy or sad, he couldn't go to her. Not unless he chose to relinquish his family and leave The Order.

"How long do you plan to go on like this? You chose to let her go."

"I made no such choice. Everything about my circumstances has been decided by others."

"If you're so unhappy, then stop being so damn accommodating."

"Is that how you see me?" He sneered. "Well, I sure hope I haven't overcomplicated things for you with all of my compliance."

"I know what you sacrificed for us—"

"Well, would it kill you to acknowledge it once in a while? You shunned me from your home and haven't spoken to me in months."

"She nearly died, Cain!"

"So did I!"

His words cracked through the air like a bullet and silence echoed. Emotion choked him as his eyes burned with the reawakened longing to simply have a place among his family. He only wanted to know where he belonged.

Voice strained, he explained "I lost my mate and helped father find his. I took those children for Father and saw to their safety. Do you think he's whispered one word of thanks for my help? And now look what has become of precious Cybil." Cain covered his eyes, unable to face more disapproval. "I have no place here. No future. Wanting only to provide some level of value, I tried to help The Order and wound up shot in the heart, surrounded by an army of deranged vampires. The only reason I survived was because of Destiny. Then I came home to everyone's condemnation. I give and I give until I have nothing left of myself, and all I get in return is judgement and scorn."

He shook his head, unsure why he was sharing so much, but relieved to get his feelings off his chest. "That thing in the woods is vicious. It's soulless." He thought of *the others,* his mind instantly leaping to Cybil. "I'm running out of hope."

"The Elders will handle Isaiah."

Cain met his stare. "They may, or they may not. But, Adam, if that's what happens to an unanswered immortal, what sort of destiny does that leave me?"

His jaw slackened. "You're different. Your blood completed Annalise's transition."

"But we never mated." His voice broke. "God help me, but when I held Cybil in my arms and fed her my blood, part of me prayed…" He shook his head, disgusted by his own admission. "I know she's young, but I wondered if there might be someone else. She saw something good in me."

"We all see something good in you, Cain."

"Not like this. Cybil loved me and I destroyed her. Everything I care about gets taken away."

"You hoped the mortal child was meant for you?"

"No. But I hoped there might be some purpose to all the injustice we suffer in this cruel world. I wanted to save her."

"Cain, she was just a mortal little girl. If she were anything else, she wouldn't have died that day."

A tear fell from his eye. "I loved her. I swore to take care of her." Looking up at his brother and seeing the worry in his eyes, Cain laughed without humor. "Don't think I'm so far gone as to lust after a child, Adam. The one I want is gone. Also mortal, but at least of age."

"Then why did you let her go?"

"Because it was for the best."

"That's not the way a male loves his mate."

He looked up at his brother. "Do you think I don't realize that?" There had been a brief moment in time when he thought God might gift him with another. He'd been sleeping and dreaming of Anna, only to have his dream disrupted by Destiny. But it was not a dream of Destiny, only the hotel television waking him from sleep. She merely stole his attention for a moment. God had given him one and only one. "I have one mate."

"Do you—"

"Stop," Cain snarled. "You cannot turn this into something about you. I've given you everything I have, but I will not mollycoddle your fragile ego. I've loved Annalise like a sister since the moment you took her as your wife. But she is my mate, Adam. And I am bonded to her in a way that forbids me to stray far from her side or intentionally cause her pain." He shook his head and scoffed. "I can say, with absolute certainty, that all love hurts in the end."

"Do you love the English reporter?"

He nodded. "That was a different love. Like Cybil, she's mortal. There's no relief and the greatest kindness I could show her was in letting her go."

"You could have a life with her for a time."

"A blink. And if I chose that life, I would not be permitted to live on the farm."

"But you understand you have a choice."

"What are you saying? That I should leave?"

"It would break our hearts to see you go, but it's crushing us to watch you wait around and wallow. You deserve to be happy, Cain."

"You're threatened—"

"I'm not. I'd prefer to have you here because this is where you belong, and I'm strong enough to admit your presence is important to my wife. But I also want to see you happy."

The last time he saw Destiny, she scorned him. "It doesn't matter. She won't remember me. The bishop made sure to take all of her memories."

"Memories are only ever misplaced.

They're never completely gone. If she truly loved you, she'll recognize the rightness of your presence. She'll remember the way you made her feel and her heart will cling to that familiar comfort."

Cain considered how much he would have to surrender in order to live a life off of the farm. There would be no privacy or security. No one like him to talk to. No Anna.

"Did Annalise tell you that I haven't dreamed?"

"She thinks your heart and mind are pre-occupied. She believes it's temporary."

Not having that connection would make leaving the farm that much more insufferable. He needed to keep in touch with Anna, but his heart was being pulled in a different direction.

He considered what his life off the farm might look like. The country was all he'd ever known. How long would he have?

Eventually, mortals died. If he and Destiny made a life together, he could heal her for a while, but time wore on mortals differently than it wore on his species. Losing her was inevitable, but so was loving her. He'd rather have a five second life with her than nothing at all. But he would be broken when their time ended, worse off than he was now.

"Do you think they'd let me come back?"

"A mortal lifetime passes in a flash. We would insist on it. This is your home."

It wasn't a calling, but it had the potential to cure him of this endless sorrow that had been drowning him. "What about Cybil?"

"Cybil can't be your excuse, Cain. The girl is gone. Whatever is left of her is not any reason to sacrifice your own chance at happiness. She'll stay in that cell for years. And, eventually, they'll do the merciful thing."

Cain's heart sank. "You mean kill her."

"She already died. The fact that she's breathing at all goes against the laws of nature."

"I can't let that happen. I swore to protect her. Even now, I see something human in her."

"No one is rushing to any conclusions. The girl is safe for now."

"If I leave, who will protect her?" He looked at Adam with absolute intention. "You owe me."

"Cain—"

"Anna said you feel indebted. Let this be the balance. You protect Cybil while I'm gone.

See that she reaches adulthood and is un-harmed, and we will be even."

Adam frowned. "I don't understand this connection you feel to the girl."

"She trusted me when no one else did. If I let her down, what good is my word? What good am I?"

"In truth, she's father's responsibility—"

"No, Adam. I'm asking you."

His brother hesitated. What Cain asked would require a commitment for less than a century. There was no comparison to the eternal sacrifice Cain had made for him. He couldn't say no.

"All right. You have my word. In your absence, I will watch over the mortal transition and see that no harm comes to her."

Cain shook his brother's hand, trusting his vow without reservation. Adam truly was one of the most honorable, dependable males he'd ever known.

"And when the debt is paid, we will be even."

Cain loosened his hand and Adam's grip tightened. "Make it worth it, Cain. Don't just love her, learn to love yourself. That's where a true sense of belonging begins."

ain followed Adam out of the store after compelling the clerk to forget their presence. His nose twitched at the scent of burning materials in the distance. "Do you smell that?"

Adam scowled. "It's not the incinerator."

"Too strong," Cain agreed.

They searched the sky, and Cain's heart punched through his chest at the black cloud of smoke rising over the direction of the farm.

"Fire!"

He ran toward the farm, leaving his buggy in town, and Adam followed. The closer they came to their land, the more certain they were that fire was on Order property. The acrid air was not the earthy scent of leaves burning. Black ash and flaming shingles fell from the sky, carried by the wind.

"Cain, they need water!" Adam yelled, seeing the rising flames gather angrily on the horizon.

Cain opened his mind and commanded the skies to unleash. Heavy drops fell from the heavens, soaking their clothing and saturating the ground. He held the wind, hoping to contain the fire, but all of his concentration made it difficult to run.

"You go ahead. I'll catch up."

Adam disappeared. The blaze attracted the neighboring fire companies and sirens blared. Although their kind could not be killed by fire alone, it left them vulnerable to injury and other risks. Fires attracted outsiders', and if one of theirs got burned, it would be difficult to avoid medical attention. Once healed, questions would follow and things could quickly get out of control.

When Cain reached the farm, the reckless blaze had run rampant, spreading to fields and igniting barns. Horses and livestock scurried outside as members gathered in horror, watching buildings burn.

Cain's eyes burned from the air as he

scanned for the source. Following the thick plume of black, billowing smoke, his heart plummeted. His family's house was ablaze.

He crossed the distance in a heartbeat. "Where is Mother?" Cain scowled at the sight of Larissa, her distended belly covered in soot as she held a cloth to her face. "You shouldn't be out here. Get back!"

"I can't find her!"

He flinched at the fear in her voice, and searched the chaos. He didn't see her. Nor did he see his father.

Adam raced out of the house, holding Gracie in his arms as she coughed and choked. "There's Adam."

"Go help him." He was gone before Larissa finished the command.

Inside, searing flames engulfed the walls. The tinder of the wood stoves combusted and crackled as the rafters whined and the house moaned. The heat was unbearable, burning his eyes and making it impossible to see.

"Adam!"

"I'm here!"

Cain rushed over to the stairs, choking on smoke as his mother's pregnant body lay limp in his arms. The staircase crashed into pieces, discharging a burst of flames.

"You have to jump."

Adam leapt down and landed on his knees. "Take her. Go!"

Cain cradled his mother in his arms and raced through the inferno. Flames licked at his clothing, scorching and burning his flesh.

Once outside, he crashed into the muddy earth and deposited his mother on the ground. "She needs help!"

Anna appeared. "I'm here. Go get Father." Biting into her wrist, she opened her vein and forced blood into their mother's mouth.

Cain returned to the house where the walls had started to collapse. Adam was still coughing and searching rooms.

"Adam, you have to get out of here. Go. I'll find Father."

Adam wheezed. "I feel his fear. He's here somewhere, but not answering me."

"Go. I'll find him." The house was collapsing and soon the fire companies and other witnesses would arrive. He needed to locate his father and heal any damage quickly.

"Father!"

Cain listened, but the roar of the flames overpowered his senses. *Grace!* He opened his mind to his sister. *Where is Father? I can't see through the smoke and flames. Help me find him.*

Unlike Gracie's telepathy and Adam's empathetic link, Cain had only his senses to guide him. Heat moved the air in waves, throwing him back as unbearable heat scorched his clothes. The flames destroyed any sense of familiarity and his skin began to blister.

He was lost in the seventh circle of hell. *"Father!"*

Burns bubbled on his arm, and he bared his teeth, suffering the excruciating pain.

"Cain?"

"Gracie?"

"I'm here!"

He coughed. "I can't see you. Stay back! It's too hot!"

"He's upstairs," she yelled. "He's not alone!"

Confused, Cain lunged through the flames and hurled himself up to the second-floor rafter. "Go back. I'll meet you out there."

Embers burned through the planked floors and rafters smoldered overhead. His clothing sat like hot irons against his skin and his flesh crisped and melted into his muscle and bone. *"Father!"*

The door to the master bedroom was closed, not even a chip of paint affected by the flames. "Father, are you in there?"

He tapped the knob, checking the temperature and found it cool. His fist closed over the metal but the door was locked. "Father, unlock the door."

A strange chanting met his ears as the flames roared behind him and the fire blasted his back. He slammed his palm into the door, needing to escape the flames. "Father!" Harder he hit the wood, but the door didn't budge.

The roar of the blaze rose to his ears, hissing and creaking, as the flames engulfed the walls and ceilings. His eyes burned and he coughed, unable to steal a breath of clean air.

"Fath—" A brutal hack ripped through his lungs. *"Father!"* The wood floor splintered and he careened into the door with all his weight, gasping at the clear air on the other side.

"Ignis ac noctes accende dolorem tuum, animam in sola culpa." Two women stood on either side of the bed where his father lay, still with his eyes open.

"Who are you?" He rushed forward, only to double over in pain as a woman with teal hair raised a hand at him. Brain splitting sharpness pierced his skull.

She turned back to his father, arms extended, palms down, and fingers spread over his body. *"Tempora subsidia immortalitas, ne plus mali ex viis tuis commodis venire possit."*

Jonas screamed and Cain struggled to stand. "What are you doing to him?" His father's back bowed off the bed, arching while some unseen force anchored his arms and legs. Cain's body flung into the wall, crashing hard enough to crack the plaster.

"Venus, no! You said you wouldn't hurt anyone else!" The younger girl cried, her worry bouncing between Cain and the woman chanting over his father.

"Furor in tuo delicto domum ardet, intus Satin ardet."

His father roared in pain, his body spasming as his fangs punched though his gums and his eyes flashed. He clawed at his clothing, ripping them into shreds and gouging long cuts into his skin.

"Stop this!" Cain begged. "You're hurting him!"

Her fingers widened over the bed as his father thrashed. She shut her eyes and chanted low, speaking in tongues and drawing energy from the fire below. *"Linguam tuam, et aerumnas tuas serva. Expergiscere mentem tuam, dum recedit cor tuum. Tua erit aeternitas, sed labatur pro certo sanitas."*

"You're killing him!" Cain barreled forward, fangs distended, prepared to destroy—

She pivoted and turned her splayed fingers at him. "*Cerebrum.*"

Cain dropped to his knees as pain exploded in his skull once more.

"Venus, no! That's enough! You're killing both of them!"

The screeching rush of blood ripping through the capillaries in his brain had Cain biting down and wrenching in agony. He lost control of his body as blood vessels burst in his brain and debilitating damage short-circuited his brain. His body twitched and spasmed on the floor as he watched in horror.

"*Carmine meo sanguine signabo, ne unquam iterum aliam laedat animam.*" She gripped the blade of an athame in her fist and yanked it free, spilling blood over his father's chest.

Glass exploded from the window, and the witch was hurled to the ground. Snarls ripped through the air as Grace tore open her throat and the chanting stopped. The younger witch screamed. The moment the teal haired witch was dead, the pain in Cain's head subsided and he gasped, muscles still too taut and ravaged to move.

He lay on the ground, panting, as his sister

went feral. Blood sprayed the walls and soaked her chin and chest. Their father lay silently on the bed, his eyes open and terrified, but his body still. Grace hissed at the young girl.

"Gracie, no!" Cain called, horrified by the murderous glint in his sister's diamond eyes.

She stilled and snarled, roaring at the girl so she understood she'd been saved. The girl covered her head and cowered on the floor, scrambling into the farthest corner.

Panting, Gracie looked at him on the floor. Cain weakly held up an arm. "She tried to stop her."

The witch's blood spread over the floor and the walls caught fire, the room no longer protected by a spell. The young girl cried hysterically, falling to the floor and flailing as she stared at the dead witch. "What have you done?"

In that moment, humanity returned to Gracie's eyes and she staggered back.

Cain rose to his feet, body weak and trembling. "We have to get out of here. Get Father."

An explosion blasted from the next room and the fire snuck under the door, crackling and burning the moldings. "Now, Grace. I'll get the girl."

Grace lifted their father and jumped from the window. The girl sobbed over the fallen witch. "You must come with me."

"I'm not leaving her!" She threw her body over the witch's, and Cain yanked her back.

"The house is burning. You don't have a choice!"

"I don't care—"

He seized her mind. "Do as I say." She instantly complied.

Flames buckled the floorboards and the dead witch fell through as the rafters gave way. Cain lifted the girl and jumped from the window, landing in a squat in the muddy earth below.

He threw the girl into the mud at the bishop's feet. "Take her. She's a witch. The other one's dead."

The blare of the fire trucks overwhelmed the land with their shiny lights and rushing hoses. The injured were taken to his grandparents' and the healthy stayed behind, making sure any questionable impressions were removed from the firefighter's minds.

Cain found Adam watching from his

grandfather's porch. The house was gone, along with everything in it.

"How is Father?"

Adam looked at him, his eyes creased with soot and his stare haunted. "He's not speaking."

Cain panted. "It was witches."

Adam nodded, banked fury in his eyes. "They're going to see if Grace can get into Father's head to find out why this happened."

Cain shook his head. "Have we been infested? We've made no offense."

Adam's jaw ticked. "Perhaps Father knows." He handed Cain the pewter cup he held. "Drink this. You look like you need it more than me."

Cain glanced down at the cup of blood, his hand still trembling from the stroke he'd suffered minutes ago.

Inside his grandparents' house, Gracie sobbed into her palms, rocking back and forth as she sat in a chair. Anna consoled her.

A crowd of males gathered in the hall as his mother's cries bellowed from a bedroom. The stench of burnt flesh and hair soiled the air.

Cain followed his mother's cries to where his father lay. Jonas's eyes widened as a tremor ran through his body. He looked to be in pain but did not whimper or whine. A tear rolled from his eyes, and Cain rushed to his side. "Father, who were they?"

His hand closed around his father's arm, squeezing tightly. The witch's blood stained his clothes, and his eyes moved frantically.

"We can't get him to speak," his mother cried. "I don't understand what's happening."

"The witch did something to him. A spell of sorts. She sealed it with her blood."

His mother gasped. "Take these clothes off of him!" She ripped at his shirt, stripping his father bare. "Jonas, talk to me."

A blood vessel burst in his father's eye as his gaze went wild. His claws cut into the bedding and he thrashed as if something inside of him were trying to escape.

"He's in pain."

They turned to find Gracie filling the door. Her bonnet had come off and her long black hair unraveled down her back. Blood stained her pale neck. She looked so tormented and small, Cain wanted to protect her from others' views.

"The witch put a binding spell on him. He's dying."

"What?" Their mother gasped.

Grace shook her head, her eye devoid of sentiment and her voice cold. "He's been dying for some time. He wanted the witches to return his immortality, but they refused, so he forced them."

"What do you mean?" their mother gasped. "Jonas, what have you done?"

"He can't talk," Gracie explained. "They took his voice as payment. His soul is still dying, but they made him immortal as he demanded. Only now, he'll exist like this forever. Or worse." She crossed the bedroom and took his hand as another burst of pain ripped through their father's body. "What have you done, father? Your actions were not that of an honorable man. May God take mercy on your soul." She released his hand and walked out of the room.

Cain knew, in that moment, Gracie would struggle to forgive their father. Whatever he'd done, she heartily disapproved. And his actions had led to hers. She took a life only to find out she was fighting for a dishonorable male.

Cain went after her. "Grace—"

She pivoted and faced him, tears streaming down her face. "He's been lying to everyone."

"What lie?"

She looked up at him, fear making her voice small with so many around. "He never finished the bonding. He's still suffering symptoms from the calling, only now his mate is dead. He wanted the witches to save him. When they refused, he burned their house to the ground, killing the girl's aunt in the process." Her face bleached of color. "I just killed her other one."

"You were trying to protect your father."

Her eyes brimmed with tears and she covered her mouth. "I've committed a mortal sin. God will punish me."

"Stop it." He shook her shoulders. "You're good and kind, and no one is going to punish you."

A sob racked her body and her face crumbled. "I killed someone."

"Hush." He pulled her into his arms. "You were protecting your family."

"No." She shook her head, shoving him away and folded her arms over her stomach. "I heard his screams. She was torturing him. Something took over me. I'm a monster!"

"They burnt our home to the ground, Grace. They're the monsters!"

"And why do you think that is, Cain? That

fire was retribution for the one that father started, the one that destroyed their home first and murdered that girl's aunt. Now her other aunt is dead and she has no one, because of me!"

"Fine, you killed a witch. So what? That does not make this your fault. If you want to blame anyone, blame father."

"How could he do the things he's done?"

Cain wished he had an answer. All this time, they believed their father was well and mending his relationship.

"Grace?" Dane stood at the end of the hall, his eyes distraught as he stared at her.

"Stay away, Dane. Please. I don't want you to see me this way."

He scowled and closed the distance. "Are you hurt?"

Ignoring the blood, he caught her arm and examined her . Gracie sobbed, her tears a mixture of trauma and humiliation. Cain took a step closer, only to pause when Dane pulled her into his arms and hugged her tight.

"It's okay. You're okay. That's all that matters."

His sister surrendered willingly, and Cain backed out of the hall, figuring Dane had everything under control.

Cain wanted answers, so he fled for the safe house only to halt at the sight of more vehicles on the farm. The fire had been extinguished yet the trucks remained. The hair on the back of his neck rose and he turned slowly, scanning the vehicles once more.

There in the mix was the *Channel Six* news van. His heart stuttered in his chest and a cold sweat broke over his skin. He searched the crowd.

Firefighters and English neighbors clustered around the smoldering ash that was his home. Before deciding what to do, his feet were moving. The cameras and crew set up a shot just in front of the north field where several of the horses were tied.

The moment he spotted her, he raced forward. "Destiny!"

"Right over here, Mark. Let's get the horses, but also the wreckage."

"Destiny!"

"Whoa, hey, buddy, how about some space." A member of her crew slapped a hand on his chest and Cain scowled at the breakable appendage. "After the report I'll get you an autograph."

Cain's jaw locked as a growl built in his chest.

"Ready when you are, Mark."

The man's hand lifted from Cain's chest. Cain glared as the other man ducked behind a large piece of equipment and angled the camera to face Destiny. Cain wanted to snap both their femurs on principle, just to show who went where on the food chain.

"And three, two..." the camera man pointed at Destiny.

"We have some breaking news coming in," she said, stealing Cain's attention and quieting his rage. "Crews from several towns in Lancaster County have been called to a fire at a nearby Amish farm. You can see that the flames have been extinguished but the smoke and damage are still pretty intense. The fire broke out just over an hour ago. The cause is under investigation and so far, no one has been harmed. We will be staying here at the scene as the police arrive and updating you with any additional news."

She was staying!

She held her ear and nodded. "That's a wrap."

"Let's pack it up," the security guy yelled.

Cain scowled. She had just said she was staying.

Destiny turned away and walked back to the van.

His heart beat wildly at the sense that he was losing her again. *"Wait!"*

She stilled and glanced at him. The man who stopped him leaned close to her ear and whispered, "He must be a fan. Give him an autograph and let's go."

She frowned. "The Amish don't have televisions." Her stare met Cain's and smiled, a thousand broken shards of his heart forming back into one as she looked at him with such familiarity.

"What's your name?"

His heart plummeted. It was all a lie. Her fake smiles and her news reporter façade. This wasn't his Destiny at all.

She withdrew a pen from the pocket of her dress. "Did you want an autograph?" She truly didn't know him.

Swallowing back his disappointment, he spoke without thinking. "That was my home that burnt down."

"Oh, I'm sorry." Her hand touched his arm and he stared at the familiar sight of her fingers then her touch was gone. "Thankfully, it looks like no one was hurt."

She was a terrible reporter. There was literally a dead witch buried under the destruction not fifty feet from where they stood.

"What's your name?" She uncapped the pen.

There had never been a more painful question. She spoke to him like a stranger. Somehow her indifference burned more than the fire.

"Cain," he said thickly, no longer wanting to speak to her.

"Is there something you'd like me to sign, Cain?"

He looked at her, trying to see past the makeup and flashy clothes. Even her eye lashes weren't real. Gone was the natural beauty he held through the night.

He resented the artificial woman in front of him. Blamed her for taking the real Destiny away. "Are you happy?"

"W-wh…" She laughed nervously, pressing another plastic smile into place. "Excuse me?"

"Are you happy? It's a simple question."

Her brows tightened but then something shifted and her smile reached her eyes. "I have no complaints. How about you? Are you happy?"

He wanted to tell her he wasn't. He wanted to confess how broken and miserable he'd been, but he only said, "If you're happy, then I'm happy."

She cocked her head and flinched when the camera man yelled, "Destiny, let's go! There's a backup on twenty-two. We gotta get movin'."

She glanced back at him and left without another word. Gone. Everything Adam said about her recognizing the feelings he stirred was a lie. He'd been erased and she didn't recognize him at all. Better to find out now than later.

CHAPTER 34

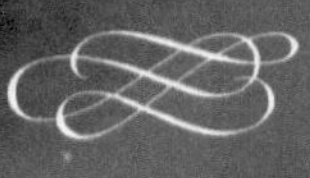

Moriah Abilene King was born in the heat of summer. With a thatch of black hair and diamond eyes, she was the spitting image of both her parents, Larissa and Eleazar King.

The Hartzlers were displaced since the fire, and scattered about the farm. Cain had the joy of staying in the private living quarters of the safe house with his sister and the bishop. It wasn't too terrible, being that parenthood preoccupied his hosts most hours of the day.

Grace had gone to stay with Adam and Anna, which provided Anna with extra help and Adam with edible food for a change. Abilene, however, had not left Ezekiel and Faith's home since the fire when they transported Jonas.

There had been no change in his father's condition. Each day, Jonas spent hours awake, apparently suffering from some unknown enemy, without speaking a single word. Sometimes his eyes would widen then squint as if he were in excruciating pain, but paralysis kept him silent.

When the witch cast the spell, the fire distracted everyone from listening to her words spoken in a foreign tongue. Grace had been the only one able to glean input based on their thought patterns, which was how she'd known the witches were attempting to kill their father in an act of retribution.

While Gracie didn't remember the spell, she gathered enough to recall three components. First, Jonas would not be able to speak. Second, he would get his request for immortality. And third, the witches would not slow his body from decomposing. He was dying on the inside while surviving on the outside, his body a prison cell for an eternal sentence.

The young witch, Juniper, was moved to a holding cell in the basement of the safe house.

At first, when her thoughts were chaotic and her hysteria at its worst, they had been able to compel her. But as her mind calmed and her resentment toward her keepers grew, she became more and more blocked.

The bishop referred to her as a plebe, a young, untrained witch, still in the infancy of her shadow work. Cain ignored her, as did Dane, whenever they visited Cybil.

Abilene's water broke late August and Jaden Hartzler was born. Their mother chose the name Jaden because it meant "thankful," but their mother did not mother this one as she had the rest of them.

Their father was absent for too many moments, emotionally trapped in a physical prison while life carried on. Despite his care and nutrition, his body was at odds, rejecting certain food sources and wasting away. Without proper blood nourishment, immortals would inevitably desiccate and mummify. It seemed that might have been the witches' goal all along.

Abilene was too distraught to do more than nurse the babe. Her mood had been so solemn, she rarely played or even cooed at the little one, but she also refused to let anyone else near him, claiming Jaden's presence comforted Jonas. Cain believed no such thing was true.

He and his siblings would speak of their father's fate in private, far away from their mother who had already suffered enough. It had become a habit for Cain and Dane to gather at Adam's for supper, since Gracie was the best cook and their mother would not leave their father's side. This also gave Larissa time alone with her family.

Gracie saw secondhand what their father had done to provoke the witches and still found his behavior disturbing and unforgivable. Her conscience was not clean and she'd likely struggle with that guilt for an eternity.

Adam questioned why their father wouldn't have told someone that he suffered lingering symptoms from the calling. Cain just assumed this was one more way for life, love, and loyalty to destroy any chance of peace in their family.

No good intention went unpunished.

"His intentions weren't good," Grace argued, overhearing his thoughts one night at supper.

"They could have just helped him."

"Witches do not work with immortals.

They have very specific laws that prevent them from defying nature."

"If you ask me, we're all cursed."

No one objected to Cain's theory because they all feared it might be true. For the time being, they would count their blessings and pray no other harm landed on their hearth.

The band of brothers was making headway in the woods. Being that Cain was staying at the safe house, he had access to firsthand information as it arrived. They had destroyed many of the ill-bred transitions but had yet to capture Isaiah.

The males took shifts policing the woods so that no other murders occurred. According to The Council, it wouldn't be long before they apprehended Isaiah, at which point he would most likely be executed.

When the fall harvest concluded and the green leaves changed to vibrant shades of gold, scarlet, and plum, construction started on the new house. There was much to do before the first snow, and they all seemed aware that a house would not return any sense of home.

Their family was suffering. Only the babies brought a sense of hope to the overall shroud that followed them. Adam complained of an overwhelming sense of pity emanating from others, and Gracie hated overhearing their simpering thoughts.

"They think they're better than us," she complained one night at supper.

"Who cares what they think," Anna argued. "They don't know what we've been through."

"They know enough." Gracie cleared the table. "Vicious gossips is what they are."

Time moved on, and The Council made no decision regarding Cybil's fate or the witch's. Cain visited the safe house cells every night when the witch slept. Dane, however, visited during the day and would occasionally converse with the young girl.

"You must be careful, Dane," Gracie warned the following week after finding out Dane spoke to the witch. "That witch is more powerful than she realizes and she lacks self-control."

"She's not evil. If The Elders would talk to her, they'd realize—"

"They have nothing to say to her and neither should you," Gracie interrupted. "She hurt my father and thereby hurt my mother and us."

"Your father threw the first stone."

Gracie stood, rattling the dishes with her abruptness, and scowled down at Dane with disapproval. "If not for my family, you would be homeless. Where do your loyalties lie, I wonder?" She stormed off before he could respond.

"I was just trying to make a point."

Cain chuckled. "If I were you, I'd stay away from the plebe and all other young females so long as Gracie's unattached."

Dane frowned. "What does that mean?"

Anna took pity on him and patted his arm. "It means Gracie likes you."

Dane gaped and Cain laughed. "Oh, come on. I know you're mortal, but your brain cannot be that slow. We all see it."

"We're friends."

"Of course, you are," Adam muttered. "Pass the biscuits."

Dane left the table, following Gracie outside.

"Ugh, this is painful to listen to," Anna said, taking a long sip of her water. "We need music."

Cain chuckled, his ears tuned to Dane's clumsy chatter outside.

"I'm embarrassed for him," Adam muttered, then the three of them flinched.

"That had to hurt." Cain bit into a biscuit and they all looked down when Dane returned, holding his cheek.

"She's not interested."

Adam slid him a glass of bourbon. Dane sniffed the cup and drew back. "That doesn't smell the least bit appealing."

"Tough it out," Cain said. "It'll put a little hair on your chest."

Dane slung it back and gasped. "Ugh, that tastes like paint thinner."

"Hold on," Anna said. "I thought you could read Gracie."

"She blocks me now." His fickle expression showed how hard up he was for a little female attention.

Even the unfeeling bishop took pity on Dane, implying that Cybil could stay safely and indefinitely in her cell, as long as it pleased the boy.

But the boy was now a man, and he didn't fit in with the adult males any easier than he had blended with the children on the farm. Cybil had been his one source of familiarity but no longer shared his familial affection.

Cain knew what it was to crave a sense of belonging and could empathize with Dane. Ironically, their differences formed a common ground. Having felt ostracized many times himself, Cain assumed a more brotherly role with the mortal, and from there a sort of bond was formed.

By the first snowfall, the framework of the new house had been built and the construction was mostly finished. Yet their mother showed no interest in moving their father out of his parents' home.

Cain also debated if he wanted to go back to a place that brought him nothing but pain over the last two years. His thoughts of Destiny lessened but his feelings never faded. He learned to stifle the longing and live for other joys. But when Annalise announced she was once again pregnant, he struggled with the return of bitterness and jealousy.

Unfortunately, no matter how much he silenced his heartache, agony still breathed inside of him, and his empathic twin brother suffered every bit of his sorrow whenever in Cain's company.

Adam pressed Cain to go to Destiny like they had decided the morning of the fire, but after seeing her, he lost his nerve. She moved on, and he saw no sense in disrupting her life if she was happy. He feared seeing her with someone else, feared he might selfishly interrupt her life to serve his own interests. As much as he wanted to claim her as his own, he also wanted to do the honorable thing.

Loving her meant letting her find happiness without him. Which, according to her, she had.

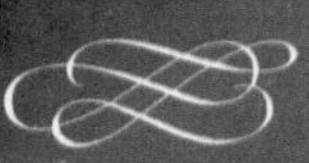

ain watched in awe as a toy rattle scooted across the floor into Moriah's pudgy hand. "She'll never need to crawl at this rate."

The child had a unique gift for telekinetically luring desired items into her possession. So far, she managed to pull toys, bottles, and pots and pans from shelves.

"At least it's something she's supposed to have. You have no idea how many times I catch her trying to take something dangerous she shouldn't have," Larissa said. "I'm going to have to nail down the furniture."

Just then, a bowl of pears went skidding from the table. Eleazar lifted a hand, his kinesis disciplines much more powerful than the child's, and the object slid back into place.

"At least Eleazar can intervene when he's here. But when it's just us, Moriah has me chasing down all kinds of objects. She's getting faster at it, too."

Cain chuckled. "Overpowered by a mere infant. What has become of you, sister?"

Larissa snatched his breakfast plate out from under him. "It's not funny. I'm exhausted."

"I wasn't finished eating."

"Then you shouldn't have teased me." She chucked the scraps in the compost and took the dish to the sink.

Cain went over to where his niece played on the floor and held out a finger. "Are you torturing your mother?"

Moriah gripped his finger in a chubby, pink fist and tried to put it in her mouth.

He laughed. "I'd feed you, but your mother took away my plate." He kissed her head and stood. "I'm going to say good morning to Cybil."

"Try to get her to eat something if you can. I'll bring a tray down for the other one in a bit."

He grabbed a pear from the bowl on the

way out of the kitchen. Council Hall was connected to the bishop's home, so Cain had been visiting the holding cells more often. The main floor was quiet this early in the morning, but he could scent Dane nearby.

The heavy door opened, and Dane spotted him. A bench had been brought into the lower corridor so they had a place to sit.

"Hey," the young man greeted, his voice so much deeper than it had been when he'd arrived on the farm.

"How is she?"

Cybil hissed and rattled the bars when she saw Cain, but they ignored her outburst.

Over the past several months, Dane finally accepted his sister would never be the same. At one point, Cain had found him crying and regretting that they hadn't let her die in peace. Another reason he decided to take a more active role in Dane's life. Now he actually enjoyed the boy—who had grown into a man.

"Her mind's full of nonsense this morning. She's been in a panic since she awoke, and she keeps trying to see the door. It's like she's waiting for someone."

Cain looked at her and held out his arms. "I'm here."

Cybil hissed and angled her neck to see down the long hall.

Cain frowned and followed her stare to the heavy door at the end of the hallway. "Think she's expecting company?" he joked.

"She's anticipating something." Dane studied her a while longer. "You know, when my mom used to be on her way home from work, Colby could tell when she was close. He'd always jump up and go to the window a few minutes before she pulled up."

"Dogs have good hearing and they know the sound of their owners approaching."

"Just dogs?"

Cain frowned. "What are you asking?"

He shrugged. "Maybe she hears something we don't."

Cain closed his eyes and listened. He heard the leaves rustling in the wind, the horses and hogs mucking about, chatter, babies, birds, beetles, even a power tool several miles away and the hum of distant vehicles passing on the interstate. "I hear nothing unusual."

The young witch pretended to sleep in the cell beside Cybil's. She did that a lot, no doubt hoping to overhear something she shouldn't. But Cain could always tell when she was awake by the pace of her heartbeat and pattern of her breathing.

He didn't care for the little witch. She'd been questioned and compelled to undo whatever spell they casted on his father, but the girl didn't know how. Her presence was only needed to harness more power to complete the spell, and when the other witch died, her wisdom went with her.

"The plebe's awake," he told Dane.

Dane nodded, as if he figured as much.

Cain's mother suffered the burden raising a new babe while caring for an invalid husband. She'd waited so long for another child and the blessing had transformed into a curse at the hands of a witch.

As immortals, they were not used to such exhaustive efforts, especially when there seemed no hope of recovery. His mother cried daily, her loyalty tested with each challenge. Cain wondered how mortals managed to care for their ill and elderly so selflessly.

Immortality left them inexperienced with sickness. Mortals accepted death much easier because it was an expected part of life. Cain assumed that was what the witches had tried to explain to his father before he threatened them. Now his father could not die, and his eyes silently begged for a merciful end every day. He feared that one of them might eventually grant his wish, but they could only offer such mercy if they were certain his father could be killed.

He scowled at the witch faking sleep in her cell. She sometimes cried, but at least she was comfortable. His father was aging and rotting from the inside out with no way to communicate and no relief in sight.

A book fell to the floor with a soft thud, drawing Cain's attention. "What's that?" The vibrant red cover struck him as vaguely familiar.

Dane bent to pick it up. "It's another one of my mom's journals."

"There were more than one?"

"I found seven books like this. They all fit inside a box, but there's room for eight. One's missing."

"Have you checked the storage?"

"It's not here. I've looked everywhere. I don't know if I want to even find it. Every time I read one of her journals, my life turns into more of a lie."

"Life is what we make of it, Dane. Who cares how your mom perceived it?"

"I do. According to this, she wasn't even

our real mother. I think it was that Daphne woman she keeps mentioning. I have no idea where she is or why she gave us up. I just know my mom and dad adopted us shortly after Cybil was born."

"You could have a family out there."

Dane's mouth pressed into a flat line. "They didn't want us. I'm not going to romanticize it into something it's not."

Cain's head cocked to the side, admiring the boy's fixed attitude, but wondering if his stubbornness might cost him a chance at a normal life. Sometimes he wondered if Dane would be better off starting over with a pocket full of money and no memory of this place.

The witch sniffled softly and Cain followed Dane's stare to where the girl lay on a straw pallet on the floor of her cell, her back facing them.

The tension in Dane's face loosened. "Do you hear that?"

The plebe was crying again. "Ignore her."

Dane frowned and narrowed his stare, then sat back with a huff.

"Can't read her?"

He shook his head. "She has me blocked."

Cain lifted a brow. So the little plebe

wasn't completely useless. She obviously had some skill. Cain pushed into her mind, getting a swirl of overwhelming images from what he assumed was her old home and seeing memories of a woman with dark curly hair smiling. "She misses her family."

Empathy flashed in Dane's eyes.

"Hey," Cain nudged him. "She's the reason Gracie cried that day."

The mention of his sister had Dane's expression hardening. Any sympathy for the witch disappeared.

Cybil snarled and shook the bars, stealing back their attention. Cain rose and pulled out a knife, slicing into the pear. "Easy now." He cut her a sliver and she snatched it from his hand, the moment he held it within her reach.

He looked back at Dane, but his nose was buried back in the journal. Cain carefully cut up the pear and fed it to Cybil. When nothing but the core remained, he stuffed it in his pocket with the knife.

The door at the end of the corridor opened, and Larissa entered carrying a tray of food for the witch.

"I have chores to handle." Cain paused, noticing Dane's scowl as he scanned the red journal. "Something amiss?"

"Good morning." Larissa greeted them with a smile then read the room. "What's wrong, Dane?" She lowered the tray to the bench.

Dane scoffed and shook his head. "You know, I honestly didn't think I had any interest in finding these people, but they still somehow managed to disappoint me all the same." He snapped the book shut.

"What do you mean?"

"What people?" Larissa asked.

"The woman in my mom's journals. That Daphne chick." He lifted the book and tossed it aside. "This just confirmed she's my birth mother. My parents adopted Cybil and I from another couple shortly after Cybil was born."

"Oh, Dane that's wonderf—"

"She's dead."

Cain sighed. He clasped Dane's shoulder. "I'm sorry."

Dane shook his head. "I'm not surprised." His sarcasm was clearly a disguise for his hurt.

Cain wished he never discovered those books if nothing good would come from them.

Larissa tsked and took a more nurturing approach. "What about your birth father?"

He shrugged. "I got a name, but she barely mentions him. My real mom didn't like him. She said he manipulated Daphne a lot. He sounds like a dick."

"So your parents knew your birth parents?"

"Daphne was a friend of my mom's. Or I guess I should say my mom was friends with my birth mom." He groaned and rubbed his temples. "Nothing's ever simple."

Larissa could be so caring and comforting when someone was upset. "What was your birth father's name?"

"Cerberus Maddox VI."

His sister noticeably stiffened and Cain frowned, eyeing her suspiciously. "A friend of yours?"

Larissa stood, her hands fidgeting as she unlocked the witch's cell and placed the tray of food inside. Distractedly, she said, "I think you should come with me."

Dane looked at Cain then back to Larissa. "Is something wrong?"

"Hopefully, I am. But we need to find out. Bring your mother's journal."

CHAPTER 36

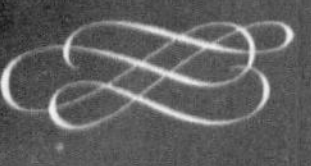

Cain and Dane followed Larissa back to the safe house where she insisted Eleazar call on his friend Adriel, one of the eldest females on the farm. Larissa wouldn't explain what was going on, until they were all inside the bishop's private office with the doors shut tight.

"Show him," she said to Dane the moment the door closed.

Dane glanced at Cain, unsure what she wanted. "Uh, what exactly am I showing him?"

"Show him where the journal mentions your birth father's name."

Adriel sat on the settee, her copper hair defiantly peeking from her bonnet as she curiously waited to discover why she'd been asked to join this private meeting. Dane opened the journal to the proper page and passed the book to the bishop.

Eleazar frowned and glanced at the page then stilled.

"Is it?" Larissa asked, chewing her lip.

"It appears so." The bishop turned several pages then frowned at Dane. "This doesn't make sense."

"What's going on?" Cain asked, losing patience with the whole cloak and dagger act. "Some of us have chores to attend."

"The boy's father is like us."

Cain straightened. "You mean…"

Eleazar rolled his eyes. " Yes, immortal. Let's not pretend ignorance and act like he doesn't know who we are. At least not for my benefit. I've been reading his thoughts for over a year. I've given immunity to him, so long as he and his sister remain on the farm. He won't betray us." His bored expression turned threatening when he glanced at Dane. "Will you?"

Dane drew back, rightfully intimidated. "No."

"Good." The bishop drew in a breath and

handed the journal to Adriel. "You'll want to read this."

The female reached for the book and frowned. The second she glanced at the page it fell out of her hands and she was on her feet. "No."

"Relax," Eleazar said in a calming voice. "These records were written years ago and nothing has happened."

"I don't get it. You know him? And he's like you? He's…?" Dane's frown deepened. "But I'm…" He shook his head. "Why do you all look like that? Who is he?" He turned to Cain. "Do you know him?"

"I'm as clueless as you are."

"Was he, like, a serial killer or something?"

"Or something," Adriel muttered. She turned to Eleazar and wrung her hands. "What does this mean? The boy is barely an adult. If Cer is his father…"

"He's been free for nearly two decades."

"How is that possible? We buried him."

"Humans are always excavating and building. Someone likely dug up his grave and paid for their mistake with their life."

"*Grave?*" Dane interrupted. "What the hell are you people talking about?"

Adriel rushed to the door. "I need to leave."

The bishop blocked her exit. "Adriel, if he intended to do you harm, he would have found you by now."

She paced the room with agitated steps. *"Where the bloody hell is my bonnet?"* Realizing it was still on her head, she uncharacteristically burst into tears. "I will not go back to that, Eleazar. Do you hear me? I will not! And no council of arrogant males will decide my fate for me!"

The bishop clasped her narrow shoulders and shook her. "Adriel, get ahold of yourself. Do you honestly believe any elder would send you back to such a cruel male? For God's sake, your son is on the bench. Christian loves you and will always protect you, as will I."

Her trembling fingers went to her bone-colored lips. "Dear Lord, Christian. He will find out. He will know. What if he blames me for denying him a father? I have to speak to him—"

"First, you must calm down."

"He is my mate, Eleazar!" The room silenced and Adriel dropped into a vacant chair, her voice trembling. "After what I did to escape

him…" Her quivering fingers went to her lips. "He will end me."

"*Somebody tell me what the hell is going on!*" Dane shouted, tired of being ignored.

"Well, Dane," Larissa said, taking his hand while the bishop comforted Adriel. "You may have lost two mothers, a father, and part of your sister, but I believe we've found your half-brother."

CHAPTER 37

Sex would be happening tonight. Destiny was meeting Louis at the swanky little bar down the street from her work. Louis, a station manager who had been asking her out for months, wasn't overly good-looking, but he had nice eyes, dressed okay, made a decent living, and had begged her for a date enough to convince her he wouldn't be a quitter in bed.

She could do it with Louis. Sure. She wasn't expecting fireworks, but sex with any-thing that didn't require batteries or a charge was a step in the right direction.

Who was she kidding? Louis was so not her type, but concerned that her body had gone into retrograde and her virginity had grown back, forced her to make a move. That and the fact that when her vibrator broke and she reacted as if a friend died, had been a reality check to say the least.

In the past year, she had slowly put on an additional fifteen pounds. She needed to join a gym and stop ending every social fiasco with a pint of double dunker ice cream. It didn't help that her friends were all married and now either had children or were expecting.

The moment she entered the bar, Louis spotted her and waved. He hustled to the door to greet her, and she realized Louis never walked anywhere. He always hustled.

"You made it." He greeted her with a kiss on the cheek. "Can I order you a drink? What do you like? Is the food any good here? I haven't eaten since lunch, so I already ordered a beer. The waitress should be back with it soon. Gotta keep my sugar up or I get the shakes." He hustled her back to the high-top table he'd snagged at the bar. "Aren't you glad it's Friday? Man, this was a long week."

He wasn't the kind of guy who required answers.

The waitress delivered his beer, and she ordered a glass of Moscato. For the next hour she simply nodded and sipped her wine as he prattled on.

"So, I'm on this zombie kick right now. I've read, like, five series in the past month. Totally hooked. I was doing the vampire thing for a while, but now I'm on zombies. You like sci-fi? Bet you were really into those *Twilight* books."

Literature was one thing they had in common which was how they started talking. He'd spotted her in a book store and discovered a common thread.

She shrugged. "I read them, but I'm not into paranormal anymore." It was easier to fantasize about characters that had the slight possibility of existing.

Louis moved the conversations onto Stephen King and rambled on about how much he disliked scary clowns. Destiny people-watched as happy hour ended and the evening crowd ambled in.

The more her date talked about any and every fleeting thought that crossed his mind, the more she realized why she preferred hanging out with introverts. Getting laid was going to require copious amounts of alcohol, so she ordered another drink and told the waitress to keep them coming.

By eight o' clock she was wasted. Louis had been listening to himself talk all night. The room spun and faces blurred. *Time to go.*

She leaned close to him and slurred, "What do you say we go back to my place?"

Louis paused as if it had never occurred to him that she might actually sleep with him. He looked around nervously. "Y-your place?"

"Yeah." She pressed her hand into his thigh and nearly fell off her stool. *Nice, Destiny. Real smooth.* She was definitely drunk.

"Uh, okay." He dug money out of his pocket. "I'll get an Uber."

"Before you do, let's order a shot." She waved her hand to flag down the waitress. When she arrived, Destiny ordered two Mind Fucks. "And could you make mine a double?"

SHE DIDN'T REMEMBER LEAVING the bar, and worst of all, she couldn't remember the sex. She was definitely home. Her face pressed into her pillow, and she peeked through her left eye at the familiar stack of books sitting on her nightstand. A hand curled over her bare shoulder, and she tensed.

"Good morning, beautiful." The hand traveled lower—

"Jesus Christ!" She sprung off the bed, yanking the sheet with her. "Adrian? *What the hell are you doing here?*"

His satisfied grin faded, and he frowned. "You invited me."

"When?"

"Last night. You called me and asked me to pick you up. Then you asked me to stay."

She found it ironic that when Adrian owed her something, he was unavailable, but when sex was on the table, he picked right up. Oh, God…"Did we…?"

"You don't remember?"

She searched for any memory after leaving the bar. She remembered getting a shot and Louis ordered an Uber. Then… nothing. Wait. Crap. "What happened to Louis?"

"The zombie dork? We left him at the bar."

Ashamed, she dropped her face into her hands. How was she going to face him at work on Monday?

Adrian stretched, folding his hands behind his head and smiled suggestively when his erection tented the sheets. "Come back to bed."

She stared at him, wondering how this man represented the most successful part of her dating history. Once a cheater always a cheater, she thought, disturbed by the slight temptation he still stirred.

They would have beautiful babies. He was good-looking, fit, and he still wanted her. God, what was she thinking? How pathetic was she to even consider forgiving him? He couldn't even make her come. Or could he? The details of last night were still sketchy. Maybe she should go one round with him while sober to see if his bedroom skills improved.

What the fuck happened to her standards? God, she hated how desperate she'd become.

Adrian *did* love her, though. On some level. Maybe that was safer than sleeping with a guy from work who really didn't turn her on.

She was pathetic. She was going to do it. Taking a step toward the bed, he smiled and then his cell rang. "Hold that thought, babe."

Destiny scowled as he held a finger up and reached for his phone. He was seriously going to take the call? Now?

"Hey," he answered the call and looked away, lowering his voice. "No, baby, it's not like that. We're just friends. She was on a date and needed a ride home. It was late, so I just crashed. You know I love you. Don't be mad…"

Destiny stood paralyzed, listening to the stream of lies pour out of her ex's mouth. When he clicked off his phone, he tossed it aside and smirked pointedly at her. As if nothing had interrupted them, he pulled back the sheet over his lap and said, "Come to papa."

She didn't think. Her hand just picked up the first object within her reach, which happened to be a five-hundred-page, hardback, Dean Koontz novel, and hurled it at him. *"Get the fuck out of my house!"*

Adrian protected his manhood and his face when the book hit him in the chest. "Yo!"

"Get out!" She hurled another hardback at him. He scrambled out of bed and ducked as a paperback whizzed past his ear. She landed a nice shot with a copy of a Western romance just as he started hopping in his pants.

"I'm so sick of your bullshit!" She fisted a handful of change from the jar on her dresser and lobbed it at him. "You're never going to change!" She threw another book. "I can't believe I slept with you!" She picked up a lamp.

"D, wait!" He held up his hands in surrender. "We didn't sleep together!"

She froze. "We didn't?"

Out of breath, he rushed to explain. "No. When I picked you up, you could barely walk. You puked on the ride home and passed out as soon as we got here."

"Are you lying?" Adrian was the biggest bullshit artist she ever met. Only an idiot would trust him.

"I swear, I never touched you!" She lowered the lamp. "See, I'm different now. You can trust me."

"You're dating someone and naked in *my* bed!"

"She's…" He shrugged. "We're not serious."

"I just heard you say you loved her!" She smashed her face into her hands and dropped onto the edge of the mattress. "God, just get out. Don't call me or text me or bother with a Christmas card. I just want you out of my life. For good this time."

She didn't look up from her hands until she heard the front door close behind him. Then she fell back and whimpered in disgust. Perhaps it was time to swear off men all together.

CHAPTER 38

Cain heard shouting and left the safe house, following the sound of the ruckus only to find Dane being forcibly dragged against his will by David toward Council Hall.

"What's the meaning of this?" Cain hopped off the porch and grabbed hold of Dane's other arm.

"I'm following the bishop's orders."

"He told me I had to come with him for testing," Dane snapped. "When I refused, he grabbed me."

Cain scowled at David. "You couldn't compel him?"

"Fuck you, Cain! That's no better."

"All right, relax." He held up his hands. "What kind of tests does the bishop want to run?"

"That's not your concern."

Irritated, Cain rolled his eyes. "Fine. But you're not taking him anywhere until I speak to Eleazar. Wait here."

He ran into the house and found the bishop lecturing Moriah about pulling books off the shelf.

"What's your intentions with Dane Foster?"

The bishop arched a brow. "I know you've been our house guest for some time, Cain, but that doesn't give you the right to question my authority. I'm still your bishop."

"That kid is my responsibility."

"He's not a kid. He's an adult male and possible half-breed immortal living among our order. I have a greater responsibility to our flock."

"Oh, come on, Eleazar, you know he's not a threat to us."

"I know no such thing. If his father is who the journal claims, he would be genetically linked to one of the cruelest immortals I've had the misfortune of meeting in my very long existence."

Cain shook his head and quietly said, "He's been through enough. Don't do this to him. If we scare him, he'll leave, and then he'll truly have no one."

"I only intend to take a blood sample. If he cooperates, there's nothing to fear."

Sighing, Cain left the house, returning to Dane and David in the yard. "They only want a blood sample. Quick and painless."

"Then what?"

"Then...I don't know. But opposing the bishop will only make things worse."

Dane jerked his arm but couldn't break free of David's grip. "I want to talk to Larissa."

"She can't help you, Dane. This is council business. The females aren't a part of such things, and she'll never oppose her mate for this. Just submit and it will be over quickly."

"This is bullshit."

"If you want, I'll go with you."

Furious, he tightly nodded.

Cane followed them to a room in the safe house he hadn't known existed. Cain wasn't fully convinced this Cerberus male was Dane's father. While he did have some psychic abilities, he showed no other signs of immortality. And if Cerberus was also Cybil's father, why had she not transitioned? He didn't understand half-breeds as they were incredibly rare and not openly accepted among their kind.

The door opened, and the bishop stepped in with a mortal male wearing a white lab coat. "Sit," he commanded, and the man dropped into a chair like a well-trained collie.

"Uh, is he all right?" Dane asked, eyes concerned.

"This is Dr. Hunter. He is going to help us run some tests." Cain wondered why their healer had not been brought in for this.

There was a light scratch at the door, and the bishop opened it, letting Adriel and her son, Elder Christian Schrock, inside the examination room. The doctor remained in a catatonic trance while Dane fidgeted.

Adriel cleared her throat. "Dane, this is my son, Christian. He is an elder on The Council." She uncharacteristically wrung her hands. "Christian, this is Dane Foster, your possible half-brother."

Christian nodded, greeting Dane with an unwelcoming stare that took his measure in one unimpressed swipe.

Empty vials sat in a case on a metal tray with two packaged syringes and a long rubber strap. These were not tools Cain was used to seeing on the farm.

Christian took a seat and rolled up his sleeve. Apparently, he understood what would happen there today.

"Dr. Hunter is going to take a sample of your blood," the bishop explained. "Dr. Hunter, please take a sample from both men."

Dane rolled up his sleeve as the doctor opened the syringes and wrapped the strap around Christian's arm. Cain inspected both males, searching for similar features. Unlike Adriel's copper hair, Christian's hair was dark, like Dane's. They were both tall and made similar expressions when irritated. Christian had always been a moody bastard, mostly because he was a bastard and others had tormented him about such things in the past.

The Elder's gaze slid to his and he shot Cain a look of pure disapproval. Cain quickly reinforced the guard he had on his thoughts. Damn elders were always sliding in and out of younger immortals' minds.

The test was over in a matter of minutes and then they waited in uncomfortable silence for the results. Christian appeared unaffected and bothered by the inconvenience this added to his day. Adriel watched her son with anxious eyes. Dane seemed pretty sure this was all a waste of time. Cain didn't know what to expect but found it interesting that modern medicine had the power to determine a genetic link.

"We have a match," Dr. Hunter announced, and they all turned expecting more of an explanation, but the doctor had been compelled only to reveal the results.

"That settles it then," the bishop said, his eyes watching Adriel. "Dane has our blood. He's one of us."

"He's a half breed," Christian corrected.

"H-how is this possible?" Dane asked, rolling down his sleeve.

Eleazar wore his shock with quiet tension behind a mask of composure. "You and Christian share a specific DNA. Cerberus is your sire."

"Then what the hell is wrong with my sister?"

"Cybil's blood is different," the bishop explained. "There are similarities, but there appears an unusual antigen that is causing a disease in her platelets. Our technology is limited, but so is the technology of the modern world. Without risking exposure, we can't investigate as deeply as we would like."

Dane frowned. "Was this from the transition or was her blood always like this? Maybe she's..." He glanced at the door, his confidence flagging as sadness stole across his face. "What if we aren't actually siblings or maybe she has a different father. There's still another journal I haven't found. We don't know—"

"We believe the mutation in her blood was caused by the transition."

Cain's body sank into the nearest chair. He did this to her. He knew better. This was why they weren't permitted to change mortals that were not chosen by God.

In that moment, he silently admitted that he'd been questioning if he could change Destiny. But he would never do anything to risk her safety or sanity. She was born a mortal and she would die a mortal. That meant he only had a short time left with her and he was wasting it here. Sooner or later, he would have to choose between her and his life on the farm.

"So that's it?" Dane snapped. "The parents I knew weren't actually my parents, and I get to lose another set all over again? My dad is some immortal psychopath, and I have a half-brother who looks at me like some sort of mutt. And my sister is gone to some disease we don't have the technology to figure out? That's what you're telling me?" He raked a hand through his hair and paced in the crowded examination room, his voice growing louder with every declaration. "I just want to be real fucking clear that I have all the details. I'm a goddamn human hybrid and the only family I have left is a bunch of crazy fucking Amish vampires!"

Cain sensed he should warn him to calm down, but what was the point? He was right. The kid had no one, and with their limited technology, they would never have the means to cure Cybil, even if a cure was possible.

"Might I make a suggestion?" Adriel asked, stepping around the catatonic doctor. "Why not speak to Vashti and Caleb's great-niece?" When everyone stared at her blankly, she huffed. "Does no one recall what happened to her twenty-some years ago?"

"Magdalene." The bishop nodded. "Excellent suggestion, Adriel."

Cain frowned. "What happened to Maggie?"

"It happened to Elizabeth, her mother,"

Adriel explained. "When her buggy broke down, she was attacked by an English mortal."

"How is that possible?" Dane asked. "You guys are insanely strong. I've seen what you can do. Even the women—"

"She was badly injured and in need of blood. When we're weak, we're at our most vulnerable. Had Elizabeth been mortal, she would have died that day. She only survived because of how our bodies can recover once we feed."

Dane's lips parted. "So, when you say she was attacked, you mean…"

"She was raped."

Cain had been a young boy and unaware of Elizabeth's story at the time. Maggie was younger than him and he knew of her, but they had never shared a regular friendship. He wasn't sure if that was Elizabeth's doing or because their kind maintained a closed-minded intolerance for anyone who lacked distinct bloodlines.

He studied Christian for a moment, wondering how he could cast aside any interest in a half-brother when he himself had been branded "The Bastard Schrock". He was only an elder on The Council because his mother had come over on The Charming Nancy and been forbidden a seat due to her gender.

"Was the man ever caught?" Dane asked.

"Amish do not involve themselves in English law," Christian coldly explained.

"They also don't do a damn thing when one of their females is brutalized." Adriel's expression hardened. "Elizabeth was an innocent. She knew nothing of the evils of the world. Someone should have been with her that day."

"She shouldn't have left without a chaperone," Christian argued. "We set laws to be followed, Mother. Capricious females who act impetuously reap their own misfortunes."

Adriel glared at her son. "Is that it, then? Karma? I raised you better than that, Christian. Don't you dare try to blame the brutality of a male on the female victim simply because your position gives you the right to pontificate, and this relic of a patriarchy permits an astounding amount of ignorance whenever the truth gets too complicated. You sound like a fool." She turned to the bishop. "Eleazar, if this boy is in our care, it's our responsibility to care for him properly. We should visit the Esch property."

Cain smirked, as Christian Schrock got semi-publicly spanked by his mommy.

The Elder glared at him, once more trespassing in Cain's thoughts.

Cain's grin widened. It was good to see some of The Council members taken down a peg. Lord knew they had enjoyed his humiliation in the past.

They readied a buggy and rode in silence. The Esch homes were similar to all the rest of the houses on the farms, each boasting a wraparound porch and shuttered windows. They parked outside the picket fences. Laundry rippled on the line and Magdalene appeared, holding a basket to her hip.

"Whoa," Dane rasped. "Is that Maggie?"

"That's her."

The wind tousled her tight blonde curls as she shaded her eyes and tried to identify who was paying them a visit. When she saw the bishop, she yanked a bonnet out of her apron and rushed to tug it on her head.

"She looks like Marilyn Monroe," Dane whispered.

Cain glanced at the female's round cheeks and youthful face. "Who?"

"Bishop King," Maggie greeted, rushing

over to unlatch the gate. "Were we expecting you?"

Eleazar assisted Adriel down from the buggy and Christian followed. Cain hopped off the back and looked at Dane. "You just going to stand there gawking?"

He shook his head and jumped down.

"You look well, Magdalene," Eleazar greeted. "We've come to visit with you and your mother. Is she about?"

Taken off guard, Maggie set the basket down and held open the gate. "Yes, of course. Come in."

The Schrocks followed the bishop, nodding in greeting.

Maggie grabbed Cain's arm the moment he passed. "Cain, what's going on?"

"Nothing is amiss. We came to introduce you to our friend, Dane."

She glanced behind him where Dane stood. "Oh." Instantly shy, she released Cain's sleeve and stepped out of their path."

Elizabeth appeared on the porch, as startled by their presence as her daughter. "Bishop King?"

"Hello, Elizabeth. We only came for discourse. There is nothing amiss."

Elizabeth nodded but looked at her daughter nervously. "Please come in."

The house was busier than what Cain was used to. While every decoration served a purpose, the colors and patterns of such objects were hectic and distracting. Art was considered wasteful among the Amish, but the Esch females took functionality to a new extreme.

Their timekeeping pieces hid birds and cooed on the hour. The embroidered birth records hung openly with vibrant needlepoint and colorful accents. Inspirational psalms showed in canvas work throughout the house. Greeting cards clustered along the wall.

The bishop didn't miss a stitch. His critical gaze scanned the house with tight-lipped disapproval.

Elizabeth wrung her hands. "Can I offer you something to drink?"

"Just water."

Cain hid a chuckle. Eleazar probably feared they'd serve some new-fangled punch too progressive for his tastebuds. They sat at the long table and waited as Elizabeth and Maggie filled everyone's glass.

Finally, Elizabeth sat and asked, "What did you want to discuss?"

"How is Magdalene different from us?"

Adriel noticeably flinched at the bishop's lack of tact.

"Wh—what do you mean, Bishop King?"

"I apologize for placing you in an awkward position, but we seek knowledge about half-breeds." When Elizabeth made an offended sound in the back of her throat, he quickly corrected, "My apologies. Half-immortals."

"Maggie is just like the rest of us," Elizabeth said. "She heals a little slower and is still aging, but her body doesn't scar."

"And what about her diet?"

"I couldn't nurse her if that's what you are asking. At least not the way our females typically do. Maggie didn't start ingesting…" She glanced at Dane. "I don't know you."

"This is Dane," Cain introduced. "He's like Maggie."

Elizabeth noticeably relaxed, her gaze taking Dane's measure with instant intrigue. Maggie smiled and Dane flushed.

"You may speak truthfully in front of Dane," the bishop assured.

"Fascinating." Elizabeth grinned. "To answer your question, Magdalene didn't start ingesting blood until sometime after her eighteenth birthday. She was getting lethargic, and her moods were…off. I figured there had to be some sort of an imbalance in her system, but proteins, vitamins and minerals weren't enough to alter her discomfort. The sun started to bother her. Her skin would blister terribly. And she suffered dizzy spells."

"Those are symptoms of a calling," Adriel said. "Perhaps she was being called. Have you ever dreamed, Magdalene?"

Magdalene smiled, two deep dimples beveling her ivory cheeks. "I dream almost every night. I always have. I don't think my kind has callings the way your kind does. We're free."

Cain liked the way she put a bright spin on her differences. He supposed it would be liberating to have the freedom to choose a mate. He instantly thought of Destiny and how quickly he would choose her.

Eleazar studied Dane. "Do you dream?"

He shrugged. "I guess. I had a lot of nightmares after my mom died. Other than that, I just dream normal stuff. Nothing special. Why? Don't you guys dream?"

"Only if and when we are called." Christian spoke with tedium. No wonder, since the male was several centuries old and Cain never once saw him with another female. The guy was way overdue to get laid.

Christian's gaze snapped to Cain.

"Problem?" The guy could have been nicer to Dane. Until Cain saw at least a minuscule effort on his part, he wasn't taking it easy on him.

"I imagine dreaming so often might make things difficult for you, Magdalene," the bishop remarked.

"Oh, I don't mind," the young female admitted, cheerfully. "I know I'm not like the rest of you. I can't do anything special. I don't have any disciplines, and the males on the farm look right past me." She shrugged. "But I can also go much longer without blood, so I can live a much less inhibited life if I choose."

"How long will you live?" Dane asked.

When Maggie met his stare, her smile softened. "I don't know. I've heard it said that cats have nine lives. Perhaps I'm like that. I've been injured, but I'm more resilient than a normal human. And, when I feed, my body returns to peak physical condition. Have you…?"

"No." Dane shook his head. "I just found out my father was—"

"Immortal," Adriel interrupted.

Cain suspected she wasn't ready to announce to The Order that her psychotic mate had returned from the dead and was siring bastards across the globe.

"That's enough!" Christian slammed his fist on the table, glaring at Cain. The room stilled and The Elder cleared his throat. "My apologies. Go on."

Cain snickered and Maggie asked Dane, "Do you have scars?"

He examined his palms. "Once I fell off my bike and slid across the blacktop. Gravel embedded in my skin for weeks. New, silver skin eventually covered the little black dots and I thought I'd have them for life. Then one day, my body sort of pushed them out. It hurt and the skin had to open back up, but after that my palms looked as though they had never been injured at all."

"That's how it is for me," Maggie said. "It used to take weeks, but once I started feeding, my body could heal in days, sometimes hours. Blood will help."

Dane paled and Cain covered a laugh. "You look a little green." Mortals were so sensitive.

"I think I need some air."

"I'll go with you," Maggie offered, rising from the table.

Cain waited, not wanting to miss any revelations the others might learn from Elizabeth, but he kept his ears honed on the younger two as they left the house.

"It's not that bad, you know," Maggie's voice carried from the porch. "I mean, the blood takes a while to get used to, but I've been around it all my life. Everyone's pretty polite about me being different, but they never forget it, you know?"

"Did you always know what you were?"

"Yes, but I also used to pray that God would make me like everyone else. See, I've never left the farm, so The Order is my world. I didn't learn about my father until I was thirteen. That's when my mother told me what happened to her."

"Something bad happened to my mom, too."

Her voice softened. "I'm sorry to hear that." After a moment of reflection, she asked, "Do you think you'll stay here?"

Cain hoped Dane would stay. He needed someone else to keep an eye on Cybil if he was called away for any reason. Although

Adam had offered, his brother didn't know or care for Cybil the same as he or Dane did.

"This must be overwhelming for you."

"It is," Dane agreed. "Not only is there always someone around, you never know who's in your head."

Cain found it interesting that Dane didn't confess his own gifts for telepathy, which made a lot more sense now that they understood his bloodlines.

"Where are you staying?"

"Right now I'm using a room in Ezekiel and Faith Hartzler's. But it's getting crowded over there."

"There's an old barn not far from here. It's been vacant for some time. It could make a nice house if someone put the work into it."

Cain instantly pictured the barn. It was small and isolated. Perfect for a young male who needed time to process. He cleared his throat. "I have a suggestion." The chatter at the table stopped. "The old barn, just west of here, why not let Dane renovate it into an apartment?"

"The boy has a home," Eleazar argued.

"The boy is a man. And my grandparents' plate is full with my mother and father and the baby now living there."

"That's temporary."

Sometimes the bishop could be so dense. "I think it would do Dane well to have his own private space."

"I'll consider it."

That evening, after they left the Esch property, Dane was quiet. He visited Cybil then returned home.

When Cain arrived at Anna's and Adam's for supper, Gracie instantly noticed his stress.

"What happened?" Before he could answer, she went rummaging through his memories and gasped. "Is that true? Dane's…" She gaped in shock. "He's like us?"

Cain blocked his thoughts. "There's a little more to it, but yes."

A burble of silent laughter escaped her lips and her fingers went to her mouth as if to hide her excitement. "This changes everything."

Cain's brow creased in confusion. "How so?"

"If he's immortal—"

"Half immortal."

She waved away the detail. "He can live like us."

"We aren't sure what limits he's going to

face, Gracie. Don't get ahead of yourself. We visited Maggie Esch today—"

"Magdalene Esch? Whatever for?"

"To find out anything we could about Dane's condition."

"Magdalene's a half-breed."

"So is Dane."

"It's different," she argued.

"It's not. They have a lot in common."

Gracie's lips pursed. "I see. Well, I'm sure the two of them will be great friends." She stomped off into the kitchen leaving Cain too confused to even guess what bee just flew into her bonnet.

CHAPTER 39

$\mathcal{D}$estiny sat in a hotel bar, sipping the last of her watered-down iced tea and vodka. Her hair was loose and clinging to her bare shoulders. She crossed her legs and admired her black dress. It had been a beautiful wedding, even if her date was a tool bag she would never be calling again. She should have left hours ago, but going home alone seemed the final nail in her coffin.

Constance, the bride, had been the last of her single friends. It was only Destiny now. Everyone else was having babies and buying homes and SUVs and contributing to the bigger picture in some way or another. Not Destiny, though.

The bartender replenished her cocktail.

When she reached for her clutch, the small purse slipped out of her hands and fell to the floor. She groaned.

"Let me get that for you." The deep voice sent chills racing down her spine, and her breath caught when she looked up. "Mind if I sit down?"

"Sh–sure."

The beautiful man sat down beside her, and she breathed in his clean scent, finding it calming with an edgy trace of outdoors. His skin was tanned as if he worked outside even in the winter months, and his sandy brown hair was tied back with a strip of leather.

The bartender asked what he wanted, but the man held up a hand. "Nothing, thank you."

"You don't drink?"

"Not tonight. You are Destiny Santos, the reporter from *Channel Six*, correct?"

Oh, God, he knew her. "The one and only."

"Are you seeing anyone?"

He was literally so beautiful if was difficult to look him in the eye. There was no way this guy picked her out in a crowded bar. He was Brad Pitt *Legends of the Fall* beautiful. Literally striking enough to make basic speech a challenge. She found his eyes comforting, but felt no familiarity or sense of connection that they might have met before. If they had, she couldn't place him.

"I, uh, I'm single."

"Good." That single syllable sent chills racing to all parts of her body that had gone dormant over her long, cold, sexual ice age.

She waited for him to say more, but he only stared at her. "Did you, uh… Are you sure I can't buy you a drink?"

"Oh, no thank you. I'm married. My wife wouldn't like that."

Her face numbed and her jaw fell open. What the hell was he doing talking to her then. "Right. So, did you want an autograph…?"

"Adam. And no. I have everything I came for."

She was officially freaked out. This guy went from celebrity-grade eye candy to possible kidnapper in the span of one minute.

She slid off the stool, ignoring her drink. "Well, I'm gonna go find my friends." Her friends had left hours ago, but he didn't need to know that.

She glanced over her shoulder to make sure the guy wasn't following her, and he was gone. Doing a three-sixty, she searched the bar. "What the fuck?"

Confused and distressed, she pulled out her phone and called Vito. As soon as he answered, she said, "Hey, I need you to come pick me up. I've had way too much to drink."

She substantially sobered by the time Vito arrived. "You seem fine to drive."

She didn't want to freak him out and tell him she was scared about some guy following her, or worse, that she hallucinated some guy, so she simply said, "I'm past the legal limit."

Once in the car, she was silent.

"You okay?"

"Just…sad. Constance was the last of my single friends. Now it's just me."

"Hey, I'm single."

"Guys are different. People just look at you and see a bachelor. For girls it's more of a blemish."

"You're being ridiculous. There's nothing wrong with being single. You're a strong, independent woman. Men are children. Why tie yourself down?"

"I guess." She crossed her arms and stared out the window. "You wanna know the strangest thing? I feel like I had it and I lost it."

"With Adrian?"

She gagged at the mere mention of her ex. "No, not with Adrian. With no one. I mean, there hasn't been anyone else, but I feel like I somehow know what love felt like. I can't explain it. I never used to feel this way. It's like I loved someone and they died but took all our memories with them. I just have this endless grief and longing inside of me for…I don't know what." She glanced at her brother. "I sound crazy, don't I?" She definitely had too much to drink.

"You sound sad. Maybe you need a trip home. Sometimes I feel empty when I miss Mom and Dad."

It was sweet of him to empathize, but she knew that wasn't it. Nothing filled this void. It was like a part of her was gone, but she couldn't remember which part, so any chance of finding it again was also gone.

For a brief moment tonight, she actually thought that man at the bar might save her. There was something so beautiful and familiar about him, but he was a stranger. A married stranger who hopefully wasn't following her home.

With a sigh, she glanced in the rearview

mirror. Another wedding. Another hangover. Another reminder that she was alone.

CHAPTER 40

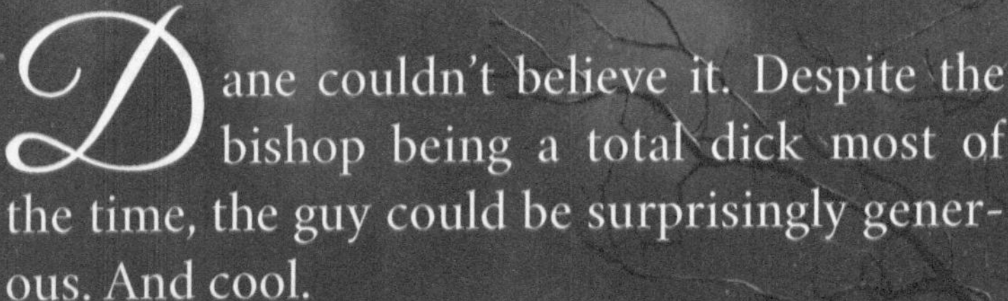

Dane couldn't believe it. Despite the bishop being a total dick most of the time, the guy could be surprisingly generous. And cool.

Learning that he'd been adopted was a tough pill to swallow, but then to find out his biological father was actually immortal and the worst sort, had been a total punch to the gut. Dane didn't have a problem with immortals, he just didn't want to be one. He liked Gracie and he liked Cain. The Hartzlers were all pretty nice. But everyone else left him on edge. And Christian, his older-than-dirt, asshole half-brother, didn't make matters any better with his half-breed comment.

Dane hoped the blood test might prove

there was still some hope for saving Cybil, but that didn't look likely. According to the bishop, Cybil's deranged mind was incurable.

In a moment of panic, he considered running away, leaving Cybil and disappearing without a word. But what would happen to him if he started getting cravings? He didn't want to drink blood, but if he needed to for survival, he wanted someone like Cain or Gracie to walk him through it.

He was a freak. Not fully human and not fully immortal. He missed the outside world but also started to fear it, having gone too long away from all the noise and motion. He didn't belong there, and he was certain he'd always be an outcast here—until he learned about Magdalene.

Beautiful, vibrant, bubbly Magdalene. She looked more like a Maggie. After speaking to her, he felt calmer and more optimistic about his fate. The thought of drinking blood still turned his stomach, but having super healing powers sounded kind of cool. He only regretted that there was no way of knowing if Cybil had such healing powers. Deep down, he knew they were different. If she had been like him, the bull might not have killed her.

After meeting Maggie, Dane needed time

to process. He wanted to talk to Gracie about everything, but she said she was busy and blew him off. She'd been acting strange lately, and he didn't know what her problem was.

He had visited the safe house and told Cybil, but she only looked at him and prowled about in her cell. But the witch, Juniper, had overheard everything.

"You're one of them."

Startled by the witch's sudden interest, he drew back. "You're awake."

"Just because I choose not to look at you people, doesn't mean I'm unconscious. I've been listening for months."

He scowled, blaming her for harming the Hartzlers. "I'm not one of them. And mind your own business."

"Your father was one, so what does that mean?"

He hardened his glare. "It means that I could probably kill you without breaking a sweat, so why don't you go back to your cot, little girl."

She laughed without moving her lips or eyes. "Careful, boy."

He scoffed. "You don't scare me. I heard all about you crying when Gracie ripped your aunt's throat out."

"Fuck off!"

"What? Not so tough now?"

Cybil sensed his hostility, getting some sort of charge out of it. She growled and purred, rattling the bars as she laughed maniacally.

"Oh, please," the witch said. "I have more power in my little pinkie than you have in your entire body."

"If you had any power you would have used it to avenge your aunt."

"Like you used your power to avenge your mom?"

His gaze snapped to hers. "Who told you about my mom?"

She shrugged and tsked. "Well, she wasn't actually your mom, was she?"

"Way to go. You can eavesdrop."

She chuckled. "One day, you and all your friends will see just how much power I have."

His eyes narrowed. "Yeah, that's why you're locked in a cell. What's wrong, did your escape broom burn in the fire? Your aunt might have been powerful, but you're not. You're just another orphan with a fucked up past, pissed off at the world and making up stories to get through the pain."

"Aunts."

"Huh?"

"I had *two* aunts. Because of him, they're both dead. And soon, he'll be dead, but he'll never fully die. His body will be his tomb and his rot will be insufferable."

Dane's skin chilled, certain the effects of such a spell had already begun.

"And then that little bitch who attacked my aunt will die too," she vowed, her eyes and promise lifting the hairs on his arms. She was talking about Gracie.

"You stay away from her."

She tsked and taunted, "Oh, did I hit a nerve? Does the wittle half-breed have a crush on the Amish bloodsucker?" She laughed. "Good. Maybe I'll let you watch when I kill her."

He left, hiding his panic, but reporting right to the bishop. "She threatened Gracie."

"She's a plebe, Dane. If she had any skill, she wouldn't be locked in a cell." The bishop placed a heavy hand on his shoulder and studied him for a moment. "I had a thought. Now that you're one of us, you should probably make yourself more at home. There's an old barn, not too far from here. I was thinking you might want to fix it up and make it your own."

His jaw dropped. Was it the same barn Maggie had mentioned? The bishop's offer shocked him, and Dane wondered if there was an ulterior motive to his kindness.

"Why?"

"Why what?"

"Why would you offer that to me?"

The bishop frowned. "Don't you want a place of your own? I assumed a man your age would appreciate the privacy."

"I would. I do. I just don't get it. Why are you suddenly being so nice to me?"

He clapped Dane on the shoulder. "Don't look so shocked. You're one of us now. We take care of our own."

Dane fell in love with the barn on the spot. He instantly envisioned how it would look as a home. But boy, did he underestimate how much work it would take to get it to that point.

After gathering several tools and hauling them back to the property, he started the long process of clearing out the space. Using a wooden rake, he shoveled and swept debris from the floor. He started in the loft, working from the rafters where years of cobwebs gathered, and pushing everything down and toward the door. His eyes and nose leaked from all the hay and dust, but every inch of progress filled him with pride. It was hard work, but it was his.

"Dane?" A voice called from below and he stilled.

"Up here." He stopped raking and watched where the rickety ladder poked through the loft floor. His mood instantly improved when Maggie appeared.

"I thought I saw you come in here." A piece of straw clung to a curl that escaped her bonnet. She surveyed the old barn. "Did the bishop say you could have it?"

"I didn't even ask. He just offered it."

Her smile widened. "So it's yours? You're staying?"

He wasn't sure when or how he would get furniture, but he planned to camp there tonight. "I'm staying."

"Oh, yay!" She pulled herself through the trap door and rushed to hug him.

It had been so long since anyone touched him with any sort of affection, he stiffened.

"Sorry," she apologized, sensing his discomfort. "I'm a hugger."

"It's cool. You just caught me off guard."

She looked around. "Can I help? Do you have another rake?"

"I only brought this one."

"Oh." She smiled at him. "Well, I could still keep you company if you don't mind." The green irises of her eyes darkened in the dim light of the barn.

He reached up and gently untangled the piece of hay from her hair. He showed it to her before tossing it to the ground. A soft shade of pink crested her cheeks.

"I'd love the company."

Her blush darkened. "You know, there's a—"

Maggie's words cut off as the loft floor creaked and snapped. The ground fell out from under them and he landed on his back with a hard thud followed by an awful clatter as the boards collapsed.

Dust rose high overhead and he coughed. The impact of the fall registered in his back and he groaned. "Shit. Maggie?"

"I'm fine." A board lifted off of his leg and her face came into view. "Are you okay?" Dust motes and sunlight filtered around her curls giving her a sort of halo. "Guess it's not in that good of shape after all."

Dane laughed, then groaned and coughed.

"Oh, Dane, you're bleeding."

"I am?" he searched his body.

"I can smell it."

He looked up at her. "You can?"

She bit her lip. "Is that weird for you?"

"No, it's just… Yeah. It's a little weird."

Wood particles, sand, and hay dust settled in the air. "You'll get used to it." She pointed to a tear in his pants. "There."

He ripped the fabric and found a large gash in his thigh. "Shit."

She laughed. "Don't let The Elders hear you using such words."

He looked up at her and smirked. "Fuck The Elders."

She sucked in a breath and covered her mouth. Crouching down at his side, her dress forming a cloud of mauve around her knees, she whispered, "I didn't know you were so rebellious."

It wasn't like he'd ever really been disobedient in his life, but to the Amish he probably appeared totally corrupt. The thought of her seeing him that way inflated his ego.

"I'm not from around here." Okay, he needed to reel it in. He was starting to sound like a corny western.

"That cut looks bad."

He examined the deep gouge as blood ran down his thigh. "It might need stitches."

"Stitches?" She giggled. "You know, you could just…"

"Just what?"

She shrugged. "I was going to say you could feed, but you're not there yet."

His stomach turned. "You mean drink blood?"

"It's not as bad as it sounds. Your body knows how to accept it. It'll make you heal faster."

Part of him wanted to try simply to prove he wasn't a pussy, but another part of him would rather drink battery acid. He should at least test the theory, but… Nope. The thought repulsed him.

"I bet you like it. I heard that when a male feeds from a female it's different."

"Different how?"

She shrugged and he noticed how close they were sitting. "Nice. Like kissing."

Kissing. He liked the sound of that. Since moving to the farm his body had massively changed. His voice wasn't cracking anymore and he often woke from a dead sleep…ready. But there was no one here for him. They weren't like him, and their differences had nothing to do with them being Amish. But the Amish thing wasn't helping him fit in.

He missed his school friends at home. Missed television and texting. He wasn't even sure what social media was trending anymore. When he vanished, his entire existence changed and he'd been alone ever since. Not alone, but utterly lonely.

He looked at Maggie, thinking of all the ways they were different from the others but somewhat the same. He liked the pert set of her pink lips and the way her laugh filled the air so easily. He felt warm whenever he saw her, and he often caught himself wondering what she hid under that Amish dress.

He cleared his throat and repeated her words. "Like kissing?"

"Yeah." She bit her lower lip and his insides heated.

"Are you offering?"

She glanced at the door and back to him. "I wouldn't mind." She leaned closer and he hesitated.

"Are we allowed to do this?"

She looked around. "Who's going to stop us?"

His body hardened. Maggie wasn't like the other Amish girls he met. And she was really pretty.

"M-maybe we should start with kissing."

She laughed. "Don't be a baby. You're older than I was when I started feeding. Your body is probably begging for it."

His body was begging for a lot of things these days.

She leaned closer and pulled the collar of her dress aside. Her tapered finger rose to her pulse and pointed seductively at her throat. "You'll want to bite right here." Her finger nail lengthened.

"Wait." He'd overheard others talking about Abilene feeding from Jonas, but Gracie supposedly only fed from the animals. Something didn't feel right. He thought about Cybil. "Will it change me?"

"It'll make you stronger."

"But will I … turn?"

She shook her head. "No, silly. You already have immortality in your bloodline, so your body will accept it. A mortal needs to be completely drained in order to transition. I'm only feeding you a small amount."

Should he? Shouldn't he? Maggie shifted to her knees and removed several pins from her gown.

"What are you doing?"

"Trust me, you'll like it." She exposed her

neck and the soft ivory curve of her shoulder. "Don't worry. Come a little closer."

The soft scent of her hair and skin lured him in. Her skirts billowed over the black of his pants.

"Ready?"

"I guess…"

Her nails sliced a crimson line down the side of her narrow throat. "Now, Dane."

Unsure what to do, he fastened his mouth over the cut and she sighed.

"You have to suck a little."

Warmth coated his tongue, but he didn't taste anything metallic or repugnant. It hit his stomach like something sweet and equally savory, like warm, homemade pie. He moved closer, angling his head to pull harder and she softly gasped, her fingers digging into his sleeve.

His body throbbed with awareness and the pain in his leg subsided. A new ache took form and he wanted her hands lower. He eased her onto the hay-covered ground, and she tipped her head back, her knees opening so he could easily lay over her.

Sharp nails scratched down his back as her gasps filled the air. "That's it, Dane."

He wanted more. He had the urge to bite her and rip her dress off. His hands rode up her hip and found her breast and he squeezed. His body rocked into hers. His muscles were on fire and his nerves were responding to every little pleasure. Then he had the sudden urge to come.

Jerking back, he dragged his arm over his mouth, shocked by the ravenous greed tunneling through his veins.

"You forgot to lick it shut," she rasped.

He frowned, afraid if he touched her again he might embarrass himself. But also afraid he might never have the chance to touch her this freely again.

No longer bothered by the idea of tasting her blood, he leaned over her and licked the slice on her neck. Was it just hers or all blood? "Whoa." The scratch healed before he sat up.

She smiled, her face framed by a tousled mess of curls. Her pupils elongated like slits. "You know, we don't have to stop." She bit her full lip, and his dick twitched.

He crushed his mouth to hers, tasting equal inexperience in kisses. She tugged at his clothing and he tugged at hers. Her breasts were warm as they filled his palms perfectly.

His hand drifted under her skirt and closed over hot cotton.

"Take them off," she panted, shifting her skirts higher.

He fumbled with the ties, so she brushed his hand out of the way, quickly undoing the strings. She lifted her body and shifted out of her underclothes, then pulled him back to her.

"Now yours." Her hand loosened his shirt and tugged his pants down. The moment his flesh touched hers, he feared he'd explode.

Aligning their bodies, he found her slick heat and shoved forward. She gasped and gripped his shoulders as he drew back and thrust again. Her body clenched around his throbbing cock and his eyes shut as he quivered. His head dropped to her shoulder and he caught his breath, praying he could last a little longer.

Her hand softly closed over his head. "Are you okay?"

He was better than okay. Panting, he rasped, "You feel incredible."

She pressed a kiss to his ear and whispered, "Do you know what would feel even better?"

He lifted his head and looked down at her. She smiled and dragged a sharp nail over her breast. Blood pulled on her ivory flesh and Dane stared in awe. "Oh, my God."

She blushed. "Drink it. I like when you do."

His mouth closed over her soft flesh and he lost control. Lifting her body closer, he dragged her over him as he rose onto his knees. His mouth pulled, swallowing down her blood as she moved over him, riding him, taking him into her heat, again and again.

He felt like a God. He felt like a man. He felt like an immortal. Until he was ready to come, then he felt like an idiot.

"Shit." He cursed, pulling her off of him before he finished. He cupped his length in his hands and threw his head back and moaned. Embarrassed, he shut his eyes. "Sorry."

When he looked through his lashes, she was watching him in awe. "I didn't know that would happen."

He frowned, his fingers wet with his release and his ego rapidly shrinking. "Well, yeah. That's how it works."

"Now, I'm embarrassed," she admitted. "If

I'd been experienced I might have known your body would react that way."

"Don't be." He rubbed the back of his neck with his clean hand. "That was my first time too."

Her smiled returned. "What's your full name?"

"Dane Foster."

"Well, now I'll always have something of yours, Dane Foster. And you'll always have something of mine."

He used a rag to clean his hand and they dressed in silence. Dane watched her slide back into her underclothes and spotted a small stain of blood on her shift. There was also blood on her collar from him feeding from her. He turned to step into his pants and hoped she would have a chance to change before anyone saw her.

"Hey, we have the same birthmark."

He looked over his shoulder. "Huh?"

"Look." She turned and lifted the curtain of blonde curls hanging over her shoulders where her bonnet usually covered. At the base of her hairline was a little raspberry mark.

"That's weird." He pulled his shirt over his head.

They finished dressing, and Dane watched

as Maggie walked back to her house. When she turned at the gate and waved, he smiled and lifted a hand.

Looking back at the mess of the barn, his grin disappeared. He needed help.

After sweeping the mess aside and gathering the broken boards to burn, he walked to Anna and Adam's. Adam was an incredible carpenter. He'd be able to tell Dane how to fix the loft. He might even offer to help.

When he knocked on the door Gracie opened it. "Dane, where have you been?" She smiled and plucked a piece of straw from his hair then scowled and drew back. "Oh!" She grabbed her temples and glared at him, her mouth gaping in repulsion.

He quickly blocked his thoughts. "Damn it, Gracie, I thought we agreed not to do that!"

"Don't blame me! You're broadcasting your filthy thoughts for the entire order to hear!" She shoved past him and stomped off the porch.

"Grace, wait! Is Adam home?"

"Is that all you care about?" She spun and shoved him hard. "I can't believe you! You don't even know her."

"We're friends, Gracie. It's not what you think,"

She slammed and pivoted to glare at him. "Oh, no, Dane Foster, it is definitely not what I thought." She shook her head. "I hope you enjoy your new *friend,* because *our* friendship is over."

"What? Why?"

"You know why!"

"I don't. It's been over a year since you figured out how I felt about you. You never showed any interest."

"So I guess it makes sense to just move on to the next warm and willing body."

"I tried to kiss you and you slapped me, Grace. You've told me in every way possible that you're not interested in me. You cannot seriously be mad that I was with someone else."

"I'm not mad."

"Then jealous."

She scoffed. "Over you? Doubtful!"

"Then why are you throwing away our entire friendship?"

Her lips pressed shut and her chin jutted out as she looked at him with scorn. "Because I can do better than some half-breed teenage boy who would share his body with any willing body!" With that, she slammed the gate and ran away.

"Oh, yeah? Well, we didn't just have sex! I had her blood. And it was the best thing I tasted in months!"

Gracie growled and disappeared, running off into the distance.

CHAPTER 41

The days were getting longer and warmer after what seemed like an endless winter. Cain leapt the porch steps of Adam and Anna's house and let himself inside. A loud bang clattered from the kitchen. "Adam?" Dishes crashed. "Anna?" Cabinets slammed as he entered the kitchen. "Gracie?"

His sister looked up at him with a tear-streaked face. "Go away, toad."

"What's the matter?" Gracie rarely cried, and the sight of her so upset made him want to do whatever it took to make it stop.

"I said go away!" she snapped, slamming a skillet onto the counter.

"Gracie, tell me what has happened."

She tossed the celery onto the skillet and

pressed her face into her palms, a muffled sob ripping out of her. "I don't want to talk about it."

He rounded the counter and rested a hand on her back. "Has someone hurt you?"

"Only because I was the fool who allowed it."

"You're not a fool, Gracie."

Her body shook as she drew in a jagged breath. "Oh yes I am, Cain, I am very, very foolish."

"Why do you say such things?"

She glanced up at him with watery eyes. "Why is this life so cruel?"

He hesitated to answer. He'd asked himself that question an infinite amount of times and found no comforting answer to exist. "Life was never promised to be fair. We set expectations as if we are entitled to…" His heart shuttered at all the things he once believed he deserved. "Maybe we just expect too much."

She sniffled. "Is it too much to expect decency and a little patience."

His brows lowered at the thought of anyone being impatient with his gentle sister. "I'm not sure I understand. Was someone indecent to you?"

She wiped her nose and sighed. "I'm tired

of waiting for a possibility that might leave me worse off in the end. What if I wait a lifetime for a partner and all I find is pain?"

"That won't happen."

He could somehow rationalize his own misfortune after years of questioning his faith and mocking their beliefs and traditions, but Gracie was good. Her moral compass was solid, and she had always believed that God would call her to the right mate at exactly the right time. He needed her hope and optimism to remain true or there would be no hope for the rest of them.

"You can't promise such things." She let out a jagged breath and wiped her eyes. "Why did God give Anna to you *and* Adam? Why did He allow mother and father to fall in love when they were not true mates? And why did He send the Fosters here only to ruin little Cybil's life and leave Dane with nothing?"

He hadn't expected her emotions to trigger his own. Voice tight, he whispered, "I don't know, Gracie. I wish I had the answers, but I don't."

It was a sad day when his usually cheerful sister was so distraught. He pulled her close and hugged her, wishing he could somehow offer more comfort. When her arms wrapped around him, he shut his eyes and rested his cheek on the top of her head. He forgot how good a hug could feel. Perhaps he needed this as much as she.

"You're lucky, Cain."

He scoffed. "Lucky's the last word I'd use to describe myself."

"You are." She released him to wipe at her tearing eyes. "The wait's over. You can love whoever you want now, without ever fearing you might get called away from them."

"If it was only that simple."

Her brow twitched. "Is it really that complicated? You love Destiny. Why haven't you gone to her?"

"She's moved on. Our lives are on different paths. I want her to be happy—"

"Then make her happy, Cain."

"This isn't the life I want for her. She's modern. Her life is out there—with the mortals. I don't want to disrupt that or take her away from something good, only to give her a primitive, plain life of simplicity. She'll miss too much."

She shoved him in the chest. "When are you going to see yourself the way we do? You are not a consolation. You're a male of honor and integrity. Any female would be lucky to have you. And when two people love each other, the setting doesn't matter. They simply do anything not to be apart."

He glanced away, preferring when she was short tempered with him and calling him toad. "I can't leave Anna. I know she only needs me to stay safe and I can do that any- where, but… I don't want to leave the farm. She *is* my mate and, as such, we share a bond that makes it difficult to be apart from her."

"So you choose to be away from the fe- male you truly love."

"I love them both."

"But one can give you a life the other can- not, Cain. You're not living here. You're only passing time."

His chest constricted as the truth of her words strangled him. "All my life, all I've dreamed of is finding that other half of my soul, but now…" He'd found her, but would only ever have half of her. That wasn't even true. Each time she and Adam had a child, his half would divide again until he only owned a sliver of her soul. But he couldn't walk away. "This is my home. Since the baby, Anna and I no longer share a dream link. Being away, without contact..." He shook his head. "It would kill me."

"You're stronger than that, Cain. It would be difficult at first, but over time you would adapt."

"Someone has to watch over Cybil."

"She has her brother." The mention of Cybil caused Grace to drop her gaze. "But I fear she is lost to us. You're too important to trade your life guarding someone else's."

He feared Gracie was right that Cybil was lost but forbade himself to say such things aloud.

She wiped her eyes and took a deep breath, as if forcing away her emotions. "I think there's something you should know."

"What's that?"

She swallowed and shook her head as if what she was about to say disturbed her. "I saw something I probably shouldn't have. A personal detail I accidentally gathered from someone's private thoughts."

"Whose?"

"That's not important. The point is, I've gleaned a similar vision from your thoughts, so I think you should know."

His brow creased. "You're going to have to be a little more clear."

"The birthmark on Destiny's neck…"

He stiffened at the mention of Destiny, his entire nervous system going on guard. "What about it?"

"Dane has a similar mark."

"So? Mortals have all kinds of markings."

"Not like this, Cain. This is a very specific mark at the base of his neck, just like Destiny's. It has the same shape and wine tone with the same detail."

"What are you saying?"

"Magdalene has one too."

The feeling in his legs vanished and he needed to sit down. His hand gripped the counter and he wobbled. "You think it's the marking of a half-breed?"

She nodded. "It's a hunch. But I've seen Dane's, and I've seen Magdalene's. Show me Destiny's."

He shut his eyes and opened his mind, his memory going back to the evening when he held her in his arms and played with her hair. He could smell the sweet jasmine in the air and taste the salt on her skin. His thumb traced over the scarlet patch.

"How did you get this mark on the back of your neck?"

"It's a stork bite."

"A bird bit you?"

She laughed and he remembered how much he loved the melody of her joy and the comfort of their ease together. "No. That's just what people call it. I was born with it. It's a birthmark."

"Oh."

"They usually fade by adulthood, but mine never did."

He kissed the mark, thinking how delicately she'd been designed and how completely beautiful she was. "It makes you unique."

Gracie clasped his hand and his eyes opened. "They're identical, Cain. All three of them. This could mean…"

He withdrew his hand and closed off his mind. "Don't make assumptions. Destiny is mortal."

"Then why couldn't you get into her mind?"

"Because her first language is Portuguese and I don't speak Portuguese. The bishop can, and that's why he was able to erase her memories."

"But he didn't erase them completely."

"The last time he did. I saw her, Grace. The day of the fire. She has no memory of me or this place. It's all gone."

"Our memories are never gone. They're

only covered. Anything covered can be un-covered, Cain."

"You said yourself it was only a hunch."

"Aren't you the least bit curious? You love her. Even when you block your thoughts, I can read it in your eyes. As an empath, Adam has been suffering your heartbreak since the day she left. Why would you deny yourself the chance to have a life with her?"

His jaw locked when it started to tremble. "Because the moment I dare to care about anything, it somehow gets taken away."

Before Gracie could respond Anna entered the kitchen and paused. "Am I interrupting?"

Cain blanked his expression and turned away. "I was just seeing why supper was taking so long."

Gracie picked up the celery and moved it to the cutting board. "We're eating late tonight. Adam's still on his way back to the farm."

Cain hadn't realized his brother was away. "Where did he go?"

Anna heaped baby Cain into his arms. "He had an errand to run. Let me help you, Grace."

The kid was getting heavier and squirmed

much more than he used to. Cain set him down on a quilt spread out in the corner of the kitchen with toys scattered about.

Dinner got underway and the table was set. They were just sitting down when the front door opened and Adam appeared. Both Gracie and Anna looked up at him expectantly, and Adam nodded, confirming some unspoken question. Cain frowned, feeling left out of whatever conspiracy the three of them had been hiding. Too hungry to play detective at the moment.

Gracie smiled. "Shall we eat then?"

Anna greeted her husband, pressing a kiss on Adam's cheek. "So it's a yes?"

"It's a yes," Adam said, and Anna tensed with excitement, then let out a squeak of joy.

"Where were you?" Cain reached for a dish and paused as his brother filled the seat at the head of the table. His curiosity dissolved the moment he caught a whiff of Adam's clothes.

The unmistakable scent of jasmine along with several other familiar notes, had his fangs punching through his gums. A snarl ripped from his throat and he was out of his seat, pegging his twin to the wall.

The females screamed as Cain threw his

body into Adam's and growled. *"Why?"* His fists and claws tore into Adam's shirt.

"Brother, you misunder—"

"Do not lie to me! I can smell her on you."

"Cain!" Anna yelled, but he ignored her.

Adam grunted as Cain's grip tightened. "Let me explain."

"Is it not enough that you already have my mate?"

Adam shoved him and Cain reacted on instinct, clawing open Adam's throat and lunging into a foray of snarls and bites. They slammed into the floor and rolled into the table, jostling the dishes and sending Gracie and Anna to their feet.

"Adam, don't!" Anna yelled and they stilled. Panting and feral, Cain looked up at Annalise. Adam's claws extended, prepared to swipe at Cain. "If you hurt him, you hurt me."

Adam shoved Cain away and they both seethed.

"Tell her where you were," Cain demanded.

"She knows, you fool." Adam stood and brushed off his clothing. His shirt was stained with blood, but his throat had already healed. "Do you honestly think I would ever betray her like that? Betray *you?*"

Cain didn't know what to think. "Then why? You have no business—"

"I went for you!" his brother snapped. "I was tired of watching you sulk and suffer. I wanted information."

Cain's anger shifted into fear and deep curiosity. "What kind of information?"

"Well first, she definitely has no recollection of us. But also, she's not in a relationship. She might have told you she's happy, but one night observing her with friends and I could see how lonely and wistful she truly is."

Cain's gut pinched with a sense of urgency. He didn't want to think of her out there living a solitary life without reverie. "She said she was happy."

"Content, perhaps, and very guarded. But a long way from what I'd consider happy."

"Did you talk to her?"

"I did. Briefly. I think you need to go to her, Cain. Being here, you're not just putting your life on hold, you're wasting hers. If you truly want to know she's happy, go make it so."

Cain glanced at the scattered dishes, ashamed by his jealousy and rage. His mind and heart not ready to process all his brother just dropped on his shoulders. "I've spoiled supper."

Gracie righted a toppled cup. "It's just one meal, toad. It could be worse."

"Yeah," Anna agreed. "You could spoil your entire life. Why are you still here?"

He looked at them, unsure what they expected of him. "I don't know what to do."

"You talk to Eleazar and get permission to go to her." Adam said. "I'll keep my promise and watch over Cybil."

"There's more," Gracie announced. "Cain, you might as well tell them."

He sighed, experience teaching him not to get his hopes up. "Grace thinks there's a chance Destiny might have immortal bloodlines."

"What? Is that possible?" Anna looked to Adam who nodded.

"Anything is possible." Adam faced their sister. "What makes you think that, Gracie?"

She explained about the stork bite birthmarks. Anna seemed the most encouraged by this information. "Cain, you have to go to her. Tell Eleazar about Gracie's theory. He has to let you go. If she's like us, she should be permitted to come back with you. Then you wouldn't have to leave."

"She has no memory of me. I can't just kidnap her."

Anna's lips twisted and she shrugged. "It happens. Your brother kidnapped me. I got over it."

"Or you could make her remember," Gracie suggested. "The memories are still there, like I said. You just have to figure out how to uncover them."

Cain dragged a hand over his hair and paced. "I need to speak to the bishop."

His siblings agreed and pushed him out the door. He walked to the safe house in a blur of confusing thoughts and various assumptions. His stomach rippled with possibility, turning over until he felt nauseous. He was afraid to hope. Terrified he might get hurt again.

Eleazar was already in his office when Cain arrived. "I need to speak to you."

He looked up from a ledger and eyed Cain with a suspicious gaze. "What now?"

He got right to it. "I love her."

Eleazar sat back and folded his arms at his chest. "Which one, Cain?"

His head jerked back. "What do you mean, which one?"

Quietly, without facetiousness, Eleazar asked, "Destiny or Cybil?"

Cain gawked at him. "Cybil is a child."

"I am aware, but she will not always be so. The two of you share a unique bond. Even now, with her mind unwell, she calms in your presence. Was it not the sight of you with another female that sent her off in a fright? If we are to speak with veracity, let us at least recognize the complete predicament with all the impediments on the table."

Cain's jaw tightened. "I do not feel that way about Cybil. I love her like a little sister. That is all."

"I've offended you. I forget how young you are. You see, Cain, at almost six centuries old, I've seen a lot. Immortals live a very long time, sometimes we have several lifetimes in one existence and other times, like in my case, we must wait half a millennia for the right female to come along. I watched your grandfather wait for your grandmother to come of age, just as your father awaited your mother. I was there the day your sister, my wife, was born. Immortality makes us timeless. As such, age only matters for a very short time. In six years, that child will be an adult. Unwell or not, she has a very long life ahead of her."

"If Cybil was my mate, her body would have accepted my blood without it affecting her mind. I don't expect to find another mate. Annalise was it. But that doesn't mean I can't love again."

"So it's to be the mortal gossip then?"

"She's a reporter, not a gossip."

"Is there really a difference? You understand I cannot permit her to live here. If you choose to be with her, you're choosing a life outside of The Order."

"What if she had immortal bloodlines?" When the bishop looked at him in confusion, he explained Gracie's theory. "If she's right, that changes everything."

"*If* she's right, Cain. A marking is not a scientific surety."

"But a blood test is. There has to be a unique quality that identifies immortal bloodlines even when the biological parent is unknown."

"We would have to run tests between Magdalene and Dane's blood to find similarities."

He suddenly realized what must have upset Gracie and had a disturbing thought. "Is there any way Magdalene could be related to Dane?"

"She is not. Her bloodline is Esch and mortal. Dane's immortal strain comes from a paternal gene, identical to Christian but not of the Schrock line."

Technically, the bastard Schrock should have gone by a different name, but Adriel refused to link her son's identity with Christian's father, so she raised him under her name alone. Bloodlines were a complicated business the Amish observed carefully. This was the first time his people have ever tried to understand something as complicated as DNA, but technology proved much faster than sifting through pages and pages of birth charts and genealogical records.

Happy for Dane, but more excited for his own possible good fortune, he met the bishop's stare. "I'm going to need that test."

They could test Destiny's blood, but without a sample from another, they would not have the means to link her paternity. While their order contained only immortals, there were many other immortals living lawlessly in the modern world among the English.

"How long do half-breeds live?" he asked, afraid to hope of inevitably feeling the effects of blind optimism returning to his heart.

"We're unsure. Without older representation, we can only approximate. We know they heal faster than full blooded mortals, more so once they reach adulthood and start consuming blood, but we're reluctant to test how much injury they can truly withstand. The Council will be investigating more cases in the future. I'm proposing that we search the globe for elder half-breeds so we can set a precedent."

In that moment he realized it didn't matter. He wanted to be with Destiny regardless of how much time she had left. One day or five hundred years, every moment was worth it.

"I want permission to go to her. If her bloodlines show any similarity to ours, I want to ask her to come back with me. Either way, if her DNA contains any strain of immortality, she should know what that means."

"And what if you're wrong? Will you stay with her, living out her mortal life?"

Now that his heart was open to the possibility and he believed he wouldn't be disrupting better opportunities for her, he could see no other option. "I will. If she'll have me." Convincing her to give him another chance might take some time.

The bishop glanced at the door. "Your sister will miss you."

"And I will miss her. I will miss all of them, but my time here has taught me that living without the female I love is not living at all. She consumes my waking thoughts, and I'm filled with a gaping void that pains me daily. My longing won't relent."

"I could compel you."

"I don't want to forget her. I know what it is to love her. I've felt it and I want to feel it forever. The memories of being with her feed my soul. They fill me with hope and drive me to be a better person. No matter how much loving her has cost me, it has also changed me for the better. After just a short time of knowing her, she's had an extreme impact on my life. Our time together humbled me in ways I never expected. My love for her has made me a better brother and son. Destiny motivates me to be a more honorable male, a selfless male, and I'm proud of who I've become."

"Then I suppose I have no choice but to let you go—under one condition of course."

"What's that?"

"You must keep us updated. It's best if you not return until your time with the mortal is…concluded. But until then, I will expect annual updates. I'll want to know where you are and how you are faring so that I can inform your family. But I will not share details from the farm in return. Secrecy and protecting The Order from exposure remains one of our highest priorities."

CHAPTER 42

"What's going on with the kids?" Destiny asked, shouting over the bass pounding from the speaker behind their table. They were getting too old for the Friday night bar scene.

Carmella lowered her willowy body into the booth and slipped her cell phone back into her purse. "Nothing, Jason just wanted to make sure we were okay to drive. I think he's trying to get out of the house and leave the kids with my mom."

"Isn't it amazing how quickly they get burnt out?" Rochelle swirled the straw in her Malibu Bay Breeze and adjusted her cardigan. "I mean, Matt goes to a hockey practice three nights a week and I don't bat an eye. I leave the house to get the mail and goes into a full blown panic, asking how long I'll be gone and what he should do with the girls. They're babies not bombs!"

Brenda hadn't said much so Destiny tossed a crumpled napkin at her. "How's work?"

Brenda shrugged. "It's a job. What happened on your date the other night?"

Ugh, Destiny didn't even want to think about that disaster. Another one for the record books. "My date referred to himself all night in the third person, and when I got home my heel broke on my favorite shoes."

"The black ruffle ones?"

"Yup."

All three of her friends cocked their heads in sympathy.

"That stinks."

"What's with your bad luck lately?"

"It's fine. I'm over the whole husband hunt." She wasn't, but convincing herself to give up might be healthier than dating every loser on the east coast.

"Let's talk about something else."

The topic turned to which children's store

was going to have a sale that week. She and her girlfriends didn't get together as often as they used to, but whenever they found the time, the vibe was always the same. They laughed, they joked, and their three wedding bands silently taunted Destiny with loads of self-destructive feelings of inadequacy.

More than her wish to find someone was her desire for this endless longing to go away. She used to be fine with being single until a little over a year ago. All of a sudden, she woke up one morning with this inconsolable yearning for something she couldn't name. The Germans had a word for such inexplicable yearning. They called it *sehnsucht*.

It consumed her in such a way, she questioned if people could actually exist on a time continuum, existing in two dimensions at once. The sense that something had been taken from her and was now missing was so inescapable, she believed another version of herself might exist on another plain.

"Destiny, are you okay? You got so quiet?"

She forced a smile. "I'm fine." As close as she and her friends were, she couldn't explain her thinking to them without them looking at her like she'd lost her mind. Then Brenda would feel the need to set her up on another blind date.

"How about I get the next round?" Destiny moved to scoot out of the booth and came up short when a tall body stood in her way.

"Pardon me," a deep voice rumbled.

Destiny's gaze lifted and her jaw dropped, excitement morphing into disappointment. "You."

The man frowned and her friends collectively gaped at her. Yes, the guy was incredibly gorgeous, but he was also creepy. And why wouldn't he be? Her loser magnet was so powerful, NASA should study it.

"Well, hello," Rochelle greeted.

Brenda kicked Destiny in the shin and she flinched and scowled, rubbing her leg. "What the hell was that for?"

"Talk to him," her friend mouthed, not so subtly pointing at the guy.

The fact that she was running into this guy again, at a different bar, a week after she'd met him the first time, only made his presence more suspicious. "He's married," Destiny hissed. She turned her scowl to the guy. "Are you following me?"

"I'm not married. I need to speak to you."

She folded her arms over her chest and narrowed her stare. "Last week you told me you had a wife."

"That wasn't me."

"Oh, okay." She rolled her eyes and dragged her drink closer, sipping out of the straw.

"I'd like to buy you a drink," the man said just as her straw reached the bottom of the ice and made an obnoxious slurp.

"She accepts," Rochelle blurted, shoving Destiny out of the booth.

She clumsily clattered to her feet and the man steadied her. Destiny jerked back, preferring not to let the weird ones touch her. Pivoting to face her friend who just ejected her from her seat, she hissed, "What's the matter with you?"

Rochelle threw her oversized purse on the bench. "In the words of *Mean Girls*, you can't sit here."

Appalled, she looked to Brenda and Carmella. Carmella wouldn't meet her gaze and Brenda shrugged. "Rules are rules." She arched her neck to look around Destiny at the guy. "She likes her martini *extra* dirty."

The man grinned and Destiny rolled her

eyes again. He was stupid pretty. "I have a seat at a table over there."

"Right. I'll meet you there." As soon as he left, she pivoted and snapped at her friends. "What is wrong with all of you? The guy is married."

"He said he's not."

"Well, the other day he said he was. He's a total creeper."

"I may be wrong," Carmella said, chasing her straw with her mouth. "But I'm pretty sure we've all fucked a creeper at some point or another. He looks harmless."

"And hot." Brenda sat back and sighed. "God, did our husbands ever look that good?"

"Did you see his arms?" Rochelle asked. "They were like ropes."

"Um, hello, this is how women get murdered. You all want me to have sex with this guy even though he could be a total psycho? Do you even see how he's dressed?"

Brenda and Rochelle glanced across the bar and Carmella said, "He's wearing clothes? I was picturing him naked this whole time."

Destiny scowled, tapping the table to get everyone to focus. It was like an attention deficit convention when they drank. "What the hell should I do?"

"Um…" Brenda pressed a finger to her lips. "I'm pretty sure you let him buy you drinks while we spy and try to lipread, then go home with him and ride his face until you come."

"Oooh, that's a great plan!" Carmella cheered.

"But don't just ride his face," Rochelle said. "Ride that dick."

She pinched the bridge of her nose. "You're all married. How could you possibly be *that* sex starved?"

"Honey, eating regular meals isn't the same as enjoying a decadent feast." Brenda pointed at the table where the man waited with Destiny's martini. "*That* man is a banquet for the senses, and we need you to go make a meal out of him."

Destiny reluctantly glanced back. They were right. He was easily the hottest guy she'd ever seen in person. "He offered to buy me a drink. It's not a marriage proposal."

"You don't need to marry him to fuck him," Carmella slurred and the girls laughed. She waved her away. "Go on now. Go."

"I hate all of you," Destiny hissed, then crossed the bar. She lowered onto the seat across from him. "Thanks for the martini."

"You're welcome, Destiny."

She paused, unsure if she'd told him her name the other night. "Thanks…"

"Cain."

Her gaze lifted and she frowned. "I thought it was Adam."

"I have a twin named Adam. You've met."

The resemblance was so uncanny she didn't believe him. "Right. Is that like a Dr. Drake Ramoray line you use when your first hookup attempt fails? Let me guess, Adam's your evil twin—the Hans Ramoray to your Drake."

"I don't know these men you speak of."

"They're not real," she murmured, sliding her martini closer. "It's from an episode of *Friends*." And yes, her social life had been so bleak lately that she was spending more time with fictional characters than real people. So what?

"Friends?" he repeated, then looked at the booth of drunk women ogling him. "Are they your friends?"

When she nodded he ducked his head and she swore his cheeks darkened. His shirt was plain with the cuffs rolled to the elbows, but there was something odd about his attire, something that told her he didn't shop at

Target or Marshalls. "Are you from around here?"

"No, but I don't live far."

She wiped her sweaty palms on her knees under the table. Crazy or not, the guy was hot enough to make her nervous. It was like some primitive part of her brain recognized the fact that he would be a good hunter and together they could have strong babies. "You're really not married?"

"I'm not married."

"Divorced?" She needed to figure out what was wrong with him. As always, it was her policy to get a guy's negative stats first.

"No."

"Children?"

"Not yet."

"Gay?"

"No."

"Homeless?"

"No."

There had to be a catch here. He was probably hung like a light switch. "Do you live with your mother?"

"I live with my sister—"

"Ahha!"

He paused, silently laughing at her response, then calmly said, "My house is being built and should be finished in the spring. It's temporary."

She frowned. He was well off enough to have a home custom built? That didn't make sense. Her typical guy usually had debt, and a backstory a million miles long, with a crazy ex, and at least one custody agreement. There had to be something.

"Let me help you." He leaned forward, resting his thickly muscled forearms on the table. "I'm Amish."

"Amish?" The clothes suddenly made sense, but he didn't have a beard or wear a hat. "Then why are you in a bar?"

"I came to find you."

Her shoulders tensed and she drew back. "Righhht." She slid away her martini. "Okay then. Well, it was nice talking to you, but I have to get back to my friends." She stood.

"Wait." He caught her hand and she stilled. "Please don't leave."

His speed startled her. Tugging her hand out of his grip, she took another step back. "Look, you're just not my type. You're Amish. I'm not. And you're putting off a real creeper vibe with that intense stare. I'm just gonna go back to my friends. As long as you leave us alone, I won't make a complaint to the manager."

She turned to walk away. Before she could take a step, his hands caught her upper arms and he spun her around to face him. She gasped, prepared to scream as he looked into her eyes.

"Lembre-se de mim." Remember me.

Destiny stumbled back as if the wind were knocked into her lungs rather than out. A thousand chaotic images flooded her mind with no real explanation or reason. The woods. A monster. Cain saving her. The cave. The farm. The bishop kissing the nun who wasn't a nun at all. Vito eating pie. Cain kissing her, making love to her, holding her, laughing with her. Feeding a calf. Falling in love. The moment she realized she couldn't stay. The joy of hearing him say *I love you.* Her euphoria when he asked her to come back. Then the horrific moment when she was attacked and she realized what he was. The pain of knowing he lied. That terrible moment when she told him goodbye. The bishop coming to take away her memories when she looked at Cain one last time. And then seeing a stranger for a split second before waking up the next day, alone in her bed with only the memory of having the flu.

She stumbled to the table and dropped onto a seat. "Wh-what… How…"

He slipped into the booth across from her and took her hand. "Tell me you remember me now."

Disoriented and terrified she was having some sort of reverse dementia, tears rushed to her eyes. "I don't understand." Her heart raced and she felt a little sick as if she'd just ridden a rollercoaster.

"When you left, we couldn't let you take certain memories with you. Our laws forbid it."

"Laws…" she repeated dumbly. "Because you're… I saw you. The blood. The Foster girl."

"It was a terrible, tragic accident."

The air seemed to thin and she couldn't catch her breath. Her hand lifted to the side of her throat. "She bit me."

"She's unwell."

Sucking in a hard breath, she leaned back. "Your sister, Grace, she fed me—" Her hand covered her mouth. "What's going to happen to me?"

His hand tightened around hers, lifting her fingers to his lips so he could kiss them. "Nothing. The blood healed you. That's all over now."

Her mind danced around images and forgotten sensations. Overwhelmed, she tried to decipher what was reality and what was a dream. She remembered Adam and Annalise. "He was your brother. Your twin. The one I met last week. I remember him now."

"Yes."

"Why was he here?"

"Because I didn't want to risk disrupting your life. Had I come, and found you with someone else, I couldn't trust myself not to intrude, or worse. Adam came to find out if you were in a relationship."

She scoffed then frowned. "You sent your twin to spy on me?"

"I did no such thing. Adam acted out of his own concern on my behalf." His thumb moved over her knuckles and she couldn't deny how incredible it was to feel his touch again. "Passing the last year without you, it's been…" He shook his head. "A hopeless hell."

Her breath hitched. "The fire. Oh my God. You were—That wasn't my first time on the farm. How did you… I had no memory of ever being there. And your house! That was *your* house."

"Yes."

"Why didn't you tell me then?"

"Because you said you were happy, and your happiness will always come before mine."

Her heart pinched, but then more memories flooded in. This was why she'd felt like something was missing. Vito must feel the same. "You erased my brother's memories too."

"The bishop did."

She didn't want him to tamper with her mind. Those were *her* memories. "Will it happen again?"

"No."

"Why? What's changed."

"This time I'm not leaving your side. We belong together, Destiny. I've spent months trying to forget you, but I can't. I've never cared about, wanted, or obsessed over anyone the way I do you. I want a life with you, for however long we have. I want to marry you."

A startled sound fell out of her mouth. "But... you're Amish." One hurdle at a time, she thought, purposely ignoring the fact that she had a real Edward Cullen situation on her hands. "Oh my God. The thing in the woods… Vito was right."

"We are nothing like what's in the woods. That's why we choose an Amish lifestyle."

Her head shook, too overwhelmed to process everything at once. "But your sister said you can only be with others like you."

"There are exceptions to the rule. I'm one of them. My life on the farm is all I've ever known, Destiny, but I'd give it all up if that's what it took to be with you."

"What about your family?"

His brow creased. "I will have time with them later."

"But you just said you would give up your Amish life."

"You understand what I am, don't you?"

"A…" She glanced around the bar and leaned closer, but struggled to get the word out. Feeling foolish, she whispered, "Vampire?"

"No."

Relief tunneled through her and she sank into the seat. She must be confusing the lost memories with dreams or something she saw on television. "Oh thank God. Here I was thinking you drank blood."

"I do."

She stiffened. "But you said you're not a vampire."

"A vampire is a soulless creature. I have a soul."

Her tension was back. This was getting a little too *strange Hollywood*. She had an open mind about kink, but this was next level weird. "Then what are you?"

"I'm immortal."

Immortal. Eternal. Timeless. Sort of like the Amish. It made sense until the entire food chain went out the window. "Do you eat people?"

"God, no. Think back. I've explained this to you. We feed from animals, but preserve their life."

Her heart raced. "You drank from me." She remembered him telling her, but the actual experience eluded her.

"Only for survival. It was our only chance of getting out of the woods alive."

"Why don't I remember that?"

"You were injured and very weak. You had a blood infection and the fever made you delirious. I healed you."

Her stomach swooshed. "With blood?"

He shook his head and she felt instant relief. "Our saliva carries a natural antiseptic that causes rapid healing. Without it, you might have died."

"I'm a walking biohazard."

"You would have died." His hand tightened around hers. "What I did, I only did it to protect you."

Her gaze lowered as vague memories of her fear in the cave returned. She could recall the pain and how sick she felt. "You saved me." Bits and pieces of memories fell back into place. She hadn't had a nasty fall. She'd been attacked. And he saved her. "That thing in the woods, it's what's been killing all the women, isn't it?"

Cain nodded. "*That* is what a vampire does when there is no humanity left in the soul."

"We keep reporting it as an animal attack." She massaged her temples. "Vito was right."

He sat back, releasing her hand and she immediately felt the loss of connection. "You can't tell him."

She looked at him with startled concern. "Why not? He was there. How come I can know what you are, but he can't?"

"Because you're different."

"Different how?"

He removed a small device from his

pocket and set it on his table. "Do you know what this is?"

It was long, twice as wide as a pen but only half the length. "It looks like the thing diabetics use to test their sugar."

"If you push this button, a tiny needle ejects. I need you to prick your finger."

"Excuse me?"

"I know this is overwhelming, but we have reason to suspect you might have immortal relatives in your bloodline. One way to tell is through a simple blood test. I think it's best if we find out sooner, rather than later."

"We?"

"The Order."

What if the sight of her blood sent him into a rage? She remembered the moment the little girl attacked her, her mind instantly re-fusing that she was anything like them. "I'm not immortal. I get pimples, and I'm not built like you. My hair's too thin, sometimes I have dandruff, my toes are so stubby I sometimes think I was skipped by evolution, and I can't run fast to save my life."

"A lot of that could be because your body isn't getting proper nutrition."

"You mean blood."

"Yes. I could help you, Destiny. There is so

much you could experience with me if—" He held up a hand, cutting himself off. "You should take the test. Our suspicions could be wrong."

"You have it here?"

He withdrew a small kit. "We had a doctor develop this. All you have to do is prick your finger and drop a dot of blood on the strip. If a mark appears, you have immortal blood-lines. If nothing happens after five minutes, you don't."

The clinical approach was a lot more comforting than trying to decipher folklore fiction from fact. "How accurate is the test?"

"It depends how strong your lineage is."

"And why do you suspect I might be like you?"

"You're difficult to compel, but also because you have a mark on your neck."

Her hand lifted to the birthmark at the base of her skull. "My stork bite?"

He nodded. "Others have similar marks. We're just now discovering a pattern and trying to understand if the mark links mortals to an immortal bloodline."

Setting her phone on the table, she picked up the device and paused. "Is this going to affect you?"

"Everything you do affects me. If you're asking if the sight or scent of your blood will send me into a fit, the answer's no. Make no mistake, I want you in every way—including fantasies where I drink from your vein while I pump my throbbing cock inside of you—but I have impeccable self-control. I'm also in love with you so hurting you is out of the question."

Her heart raced. She should be running for the door, but nothing inside of her wanted to leave. He loved her.

She pricked the tip of her finger, flinching when the small needle stuck her skin. "I don't trust many people, but I do trust science. What now?"

He lifted her finger and applied slight pressure. A pearl of crimson formed on her fingertip. He discretely opened the test kit and pressed the drop onto the strip. She checked the time then he sucked the injured fingertip into his mouth and the sting disappeared.

"Good as new."

She inspected her finger, finding no sign of the puncture. "Whoa." How would she ever explain this to her friends? She realized why secrecy was so important. If their saliva and blood could heal, they would be hunted to extinction just like every other species that had once proven valuable.

She shivered with understanding. If she was like him, she would be equally endangered.

A minute passed. She studied him while he stared at the test strip. Her belly tightened, her pulse fluttering wildly. Her mind may not have recognized him right away, but her body had a very long memory. Not only could she remember their time together, she could feel his hands on her and recall how perfectly he fit inside of her.

His gaze snapped to hers. "You're aroused."

She gaped at him. "What? How did you…?"

He grinned. "I know your scent. I can tell."

"You can *smell* me?"

His grin widened. "Don't look so terrified. Your pheromones are sweet, like jasmine. When you're aroused, the scent intensifies."

"Oh." Well, at least it was a nice scent. "Can you smell other women?"

"Yes, but their pheromones don't appeal to me. I like your scent best."

"Aw," she blushed. Proud of her sweat glands for the first time ever.

The memories became more precise and sharp. Fresh in her mind. "I feel like I just left you."

"I feel like an eternity has passed."

Shaking her head, she confessed. "All this time, I knew something was missing. It's the weirdest feeling, missing something so profoundly and not knowing what it is."

He once again took her hand and looked into her eyes. "I'm sorry you had to go through that. I was only trying to protect you."

"And now?"

"Protecting you is still my goal, but it was killing me to be apart. I want a life with you, Destiny. One where I can watch over you and wake up beside you for however long we have together."

His words were more than anyone had ever offered her, and she feared how much she wanted them to be true.

She didn't condone his deception but understood he didn't have another choice at the time. Now her memories came with perspective. The terrible ache in her heart was gone, and Cain was here. She didn't want to let him go, but she feared no man could love her so unconditionally.

She once again looked at the test, torn by what outcome she desired. Deep down, she believed his love was conditional, and he would only want her if she was like him. She didn't trust others, so assuming this incredibly beautiful, caring man—who belonged to some superhuman species—might actually choose a life with boring her over his entire superhuman family, well it just seemed unlikely.

She covered the test with her hand. "No matter what happens, promise you'll never lie to me again. I can't be with you if I don't trust you."

"When you're like us, you are taught to lie first and make exceptions later. It's how we managed to survive for so long."

"But there's a chance I'm just a normal person, Cain." She was certain that would be the case. "Even if I'm not like you, we have to be honest with each other."

He took her hand. "I promise. And for the record, I don't care what the results are. I just want to be with you. I want you exactly as you are."

A kaleidoscope of butterflies took flight in

her stomach, each one propelled by hope. The cynic inside of her stood as still as a sniper wondering if she should shoot each little flutter of hope to the ground.

She anxiously glanced at the text and then checked her phone. It had been four minutes. The waiting was torture.

Her heart wanted a life with him, but her mind had questions. She didn't want to live a life of seclusion without her family, but she wanted him. How selfish was she, being that he was basically offering to give up everyone he knew to be with her?

"Do I have to choose between you and my family?"

"Assuming we find a genetic link, no one can know you have immortality in your bloodline. But I see no reason for you to cut them out so long as you practice self-control."

He only spoke of an outcome where she was like him, which she interpreted as his preference. And why wouldn't he prefer her that way? If she was like him, he wouldn't need to make any sacrifices.

"When you say fed, you mean—right." Her brow tightened. "Would I have to do that?"

"If you're immortal, even slightly, your body will crave it."

"Well, being that I get squeamish around blood, I don't think self-control will be an issue for me. Although, I do like my steak rare."

He chuckled. "That's not quite the same."

She also liked when her grandmother used to make *arroz de cabidela,* a Portuguese blood rice dish. "How is it different?"

"Feeding from the vein can be erotic, which is why—should you need to feed— you'll only ever take my blood."

"I thought you said you only drank from animals."

"I did and I will. But I will drink enough to feed you. Our kind has very grounded beliefs when it comes to meeting the needs of our females. I would make sure you wanted for nothing, Destiny. Every hunger, I would feed."

She swallowed tightly. Why was all this talk of feeding and hunger now turning her on? She impatiently looked at the test and sank a little when it was unchanged. Cain did as well. Their five minutes were up.

She leaned back, pulling her hands onto her lap. "You don't have to stay. I know this changes things for you—"

"I told you the results didn't matter to me, Destiny. And I promised not to lie to you."

"But you made that promise after you said that."

"I was telling the truth. I don't care if you're mortal. I only wanted to know the truth. It was only a hunch and sometimes hunches are wrong."

For as afraid as she was only minutes ago, she now felt like something extraordinary had been irrevocably stolen from her. "I'm sorry."

"Why?"

"Because I know you're disappointed."

He lifted her chin and looked into her eyes. "Impossible. And it doesn't matter anyway."

Her vision blurred. "How could it not matter—"

"Because the doctor was wrong."

She frowned. "What do you mean?"

He smiled. "The results take six minutes."

Her stare jerked to the test strip and she gasped at the sight of a dark gray line. She jumped out of the booth and he was there beside her, pulling her into his arms as she bounced triumphantly. "I passed!"

His lips crashed over hers and her body stilled, her knees softening and her mind falling into a welcomed calm as everything in her heart aligned and the sense of imbalance she'd suffered over the past year disappeared. She was exactly where she was meant to be.

His lips curved against hers as a purr of satisfaction rumbled in his chest. "Say goodbye to your friends."

Her smile fell. "Forever goodbye?"

"No, but I plan to keep you occupied for a long while. We have a lot of lost time to make up for."

Anticipation slipped out in a breathy half laugh. "I'll get my purse."

CHAPTER 43

Cain's back slammed into the wall the moment they entered Destiny's home. Keys and shoes went flying as she pulled at his shirt and kissed him like a woman possessed. He hadn't known how the return of her memories might affect her, but he was glad to see her feelings for him hadn't changed. If anything, they intensified.

"You have too many clothes on!"

He ripped off her shirt and tugged at her jeans, fumbling with the complicated belt. "You and your damn male clothing. Dresses, Destiny, I want you in dresses." The belt whipped free and he threw it across the living room.

The moment her legs were bare, he lifted

her and slammed her into the adjacent wall, grinding his cock against her sex. He kissed her with wild, pent up passion and she met him stroke for stroke with her tongue.

When he broke the kiss, she gasped. "Your eyes. They're glowing."

He no longer had to hide who he was with her. "They do that when my emotions run high."

She clung to him, breathing heavily. "What else?"

He grinned, flashing her a glimpse of his fangs and her breath caught. "Don't be afraid. It won't hurt when I bite you. I'll make sure of it."

She stared up at him in awe. "I didn't know you could do that!"

He purred and dragged his nose up the tempting column of her throat, licking where her pulse tremored. "I've been dying to sink my fangs into you again."

"Oh my God, what's wrong with me that the thought of that is totally turning me on?"

He growled, dragging his lips and hips over her, marking her with his scent. "Because you're mine."

"There's no harm in sharing blood?"

"For us, no. Anyone else tries to touch a

drop of yours and I'll annihilate him." His mouth crashed over hers, his tongue driving deep as his fingers dug into her hips.

She broke the kiss. "Will your blood change me?"

"It will strengthen you. You're already strong due to your own bloodlines, but my blood will make you more so."

She gasped. "The attack in the woods, is that why I have no scars?"

"Typically, your body would take longer to heal, but I helped it along."

She laughed as if mesmerized. "I want you to do it, Cain. I want to feel what it's like. I want to experience everything with you. Will you show me?"

His nostrils flared. "I'd enjoy nothing more." He kissed her, their bodies wild with need as their hearts overflowed with love and their minds spiraled with lust.

She jerked her mouth away and bit at his shoulder. "Is it weird that the thought of you biting me turns me on?"

"There's nothing between us that should make you feel self-conscious. I want you to be yourself and share every thought with me. I want us to know each other better than we know ourselves."

She met his stare with nothing but open vulnerability reflecting in hers and she kissed him. This time the passion was there, but her motions were less frantic. When she looked in his eyes again, she smiled. "Make love to me, Cain."

He carried her to a bed and lowered her to the mattress, touching and exploring her with unveiled determination. His mouth nipped at her tender spots and she arched into every caress. Spreading her thighs, he lowered his mouth and kissed her sweetly, savoring the taste of her there and eating his fill.

She pulled his hair and arched as he licked every delectable part of her. By the time they were through, there wouldn't be a single inch of her body he hadn't touched. He planned to know every secret and every inch of her by heart.

As her body shook with release, he turned his mouth to her lush thigh and sank his teeth into her femoral artery. She gasped, moaning loudly as her back arched and her fists knotted in the sheets, her climax peaking higher with each pull from her vein. Her essence filled him, nourished him, fed him in ways he'd needed for far too long. He wanted all of her but knew he could not take too much.

Licking the small puncture closed, he grinned and crawled up her lush body. She was his now. For however long they had, she would be his purpose, his one true love.

She looked up at him with dazed eyes and a cockeyed smirk, a cloud of black curls framing her beautiful face. "*That* was incredible."

His chuckle was full of ego and pride. "I love you, Destiny."

Her eyes lit and she cupped his cheek. "I love you, too, Cain."

He filled her in one stroke, burying himself to the hilt. Her nails scraped down his back and she moaned. Somehow, his little half-mortal erased the memory of all the females who came before.

"There is nothing more satisfying than having you like this." He thrust hard and held her to him, not allowing an inch of space between them.

He made love to her but also took her fiercely as if his survival depended on it. His existence surely did.

He was not living any sort of life without Destiny. Holding her in his arms again reminded him what it truly felt like to be alive, to desire someone with such passion. Their connection meant everything to him, and he intended to cherish and protect their bond as long as they both shall live.

His hunger for her would act as a reminder of her temporariness, so that he never forget how precious a gift she was or take for granted a single breath they shared. She would eventually become his wife, but even then, he would not be able to feed from her, bond with her, the way true mates could. And for eternity, or however long he had her, every intimate boundary they pushed would be cherished. For he knew not how much time they had, but he knew every moment they shared would forever be written into his bones and he'd bear the scars of her love to the end of time. She was his salvation, his destiny.

When he climaxed, he took her over the precipice with him. Her cries of pleasure matched his. They collapsed in a twisted knot of limbs with his seed deep inside of her.

His body wanted her again, and her eyes widened as she felt him swell inside of her.

"Are you kidding?"

She could only blame herself for causing

such insatiable lust. "Turns out I'm a very self-centered male. I want to stay here, inside of you, for the rest of my life."

She laughed, and he pinched her nipple. When she tried to escape him, he yanked her close and calmed her with a devastating kiss. "I'm never letting you go," he whispered.

"Mmm, promise?"

He thought back to their time apart and his mood sobered, remembering how heartbroken he'd been without her. "I give you my word. I can sacrifice a lot, Destiny, but you're something I'm simply not willing to live without. If I can't hear your every heartbeat, we're too far apart."

She looked up at him, her eyes brimming with emotion and her heart pounding against his. "Thank you."

"For?"

"Returning to me. I've been waiting all this time, but I didn't realize how great—how right—it would feel when you actually found me." She nuzzled her nose along his. "I'm going to take good care of you, Cain. And you're going to take care of me."

"A marriage."

She stilled as if he shocked her.

He chuckled. "Did you not realize I'd want

to marry you? I'm selfish, but I'm also possessive." He grabbed her behind and yanked her closer. "You're mine, Destiny Santos. And I don't like to share."

"Is that your version of a marriage proposal?"

"Is there another way?"

She bit at his lips and whispered, "Modern girls like to be asked, not told."

He sighed. "Fine. Destiny, will you be mine for this lifetime and the next?"

She smiled then her stare drifted off. "Wait, how long can I live?"

He'd been dreading this conversation, unsure how much time they would truly have together and not willing to waste another second. "We're not sure. Until we find more mortals with similar bloodlines, we can only speculate. It depends how strong the bloodline and what sort of lifestyle you choose."

She frowned. "You'll live longer. You're, like, a pedigree and I'm just some mutt."

He hooked a finger under her chin and forced her to look at him. "Don't ever let me hear you degrade yourself like that again. You're an exceptional woman and incredibly special to me. Your bloodline means nothing, do you understand?"

She nodded. "But I'll age."

"And I'll love you at every stage." When he saw she was still worried, he sighed. "If aging is such a concern, I will just feed you more frequently. Immortal blood will keep you young and sharp."

"It will?"

"Yes. Why do you think we guard our privacy so completely. Our blood can do amazing things."

"And if I don't want to take your blood?"

He couldn't hide his disappointment, mostly at the thought of her not sharing such an intimate experience with him, but he would respect her choice. "Then we will value every precious second we have together."

She looked down and quietly nodded, a delicate smile curving her lips. "All right."

"All right?"

She met his stare. "I'll marry you."

CHAPTER 44

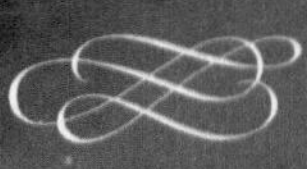

"If I'm immortal, why have I been touching up gray hair since I turned thirty?" Destiny had been questioning him since they got in the car. She was driving them back to Lancaster where they planned to inform the others of her lineage.

"I think it's because you don't feed. Magdalene said her hunger changed when she came of age. Without blood, lethargy sets in."

"I wonder if that's why I never have the energy to clean my house. I thought I had some sort of vitamin deficiency."

"Or an aversion to housework," he teased. "It'll do you good to feed. When we get situated at the farm, I'll show you—"

"I'm not ready."

He frowned. "Why would you wait?"

"Because I need to do this at my pace, Cain. My brain is on overload."

He decided it was best not to push her. The blood test proved she had immortal blood, and he trusted God's design. Over time, her base instincts would guide her and she'd come to it naturally.

She drove in silence for a stretch, then said, "If I have vampire blood in my DNA—"

"Immortal."

"Right. Immortal. If I have immortal blood in my DNA, wouldn't that mean Vito would also have it?"

"That depends."

"On?"

"If you two are actually siblings."

Her gaze jerked to him. "Are you suggesting I'm adopted?"

"Or maybe Vito is. You two look nothing alike."

"But we both look like my parents. Vito looks identical to my dad at his age and the older I get the more I resemble my mom."

"There are a lot of immortals in Europe, Destiny. Your bloodline could be old or new.

Once we're settled, we will run more tests and see if your blood matches anyone on the farms, but there are countless lines out there."

"You keep saying once we get settled. Where do you plan for us to live."

He glanced at her. "On the farm, of course. We have privacy there, and we can be ourselves."

"What about my job?"

He considered her question as well as her position as a modern thinking female. Without trying to offend her, he asked, "Why do you work?"

"To pay my bills and support myself."

"So, if you could achieve that without working, would you keep the job?"

"Well, I guess not. But I'd have to do something."

"There is plenty to do at the farm."

She laughed. "I'm not sure I can do any of the things you're picturing—at least not well."

"You'll learn."

"So while I'm living my best Amish life learning how to milk the chickens and ride the cows, what will we live off of?"

He looked at her in alarm then realized she was joking and instantly relaxed. "The land sustains us. We aren't dependent on technology and our lifestyle is a simple one, but our basic necessities will be met."

She blew out a long breath. "You're really asking me to be Amish? Like, the whole bonnet and apron thing?"

"I'm asking you to try."

"What if I can't do it?"

"Then we come up with another solution."

"But the religious aspects… I'm no saint."

"I prefer you a sinner."

"Oh my God." She looked at him. "Annalise was like me, wasn't she? That's why she never has a bonnet on and knows lyrics to Beatles songs. It's why the baby's middle name is Paul, after Paul McCartney."

"Anna was mortal. She transitioned." It was the first time he felt no envy in referencing her as Adam's mate.

"So she wasn't immortal but now she is? Completely?"

"Irrevocably."

"Can you do that to me?"

"No. We can marry, but we will never be fully mated."

"You don't want that?"

"It's not a matter of wanting. I don't have the power to choose and, although you have immortal bloodlines, there is too much risk involved with a blood exchange. I won't risk you that way."

"You mean it could kill me?"

He considered Cybil. "It could change you in terrible ways. It's not worth it."

"What about when I'm old and dying, would it be worth it then?"

He didn't want to think of a time when he might lose her. "We'll cross that bridge when we come to it."

"I don't understand, how come Annalise could transition and I can't?"

There was no sense in protecting her from the truth and best that she found out from him. "Annalise was called. Only a called mate can fully transition. It's a very specific blood exchange called a bonding only experienced by destined mates."

"And Adam is Anna's?" When he didn't immediately answer, she frowned. "Cain?"

"She was called to both of us. It was some genetic abnormality caused by our twin gene. It's why Annalise and I share pain."

"You share…"

"Pain." He swallowed tightly. "We never bonded, and she was in love with Adam long before I ever had the chance to persuade her otherwise."

"Did you love her?"

"Not the way I love you. And that's the truth of it, Destiny. She was chosen for me, but I chose you. As much as I am honor bound to protect and look after her, I would have abandoned my duties to have a life with you, if that was the only way it could be."

He couldn't explain the panic welling inside of him. With every word he feared his confession might scare her away.

"Annalise is like a sister to me. She loves my brother. I have no interest—" Her hand closed over his fist.

"It's okay, Cain. I trust you."

His stare jerked to hers and she smiled, glancing back at the road. "I thought you didn't trust anyone."

She smiled. "You're the exception to the rule."

If it was possible, he loved her more than he had a moment ago. His fist opened and their fingers laced together. Her trust was a precious gift and he would value it always.

"So if I feed, will my body change?"

"I hope not too much."

Her hand squeezed his. "I could kiss you for that answer."

"I'll remind you of that later."

"Please do."

When they arrived at the farm, Cain was anxious to take her to bed, but his siblings wanted to welcome her properly, so Larissa insisted on having the family over for dinner. Everyone attended but his mother and father.

"She couldn't pull herself away for one hour?" Cain asked when Adam announced she wasn't coming.

"Father's gotten worse," Adam explained. "She's afraid to leave his side."

Rather than sulk, he took a moment to visit his parents and saw right away what Adam had implied. While his father's vitals remained intact, his overall health had gotten progressively worse. Breath rattled in his lungs with each wheezed inhalation, and his face seemed frozen in a mask of agony. Through the entire short visit, his mother clenched his father's hand and cried.

"She needs to get out of that room," Cain told his siblings the moment he returned to Adam and Anna's. "The skin is practically hanging off her bones. She looks almost as sickly as him."

"She barely feeds and when she does, she passes most of her nourishment to him by opening her vein. It's the only way she can get him to eat," Anna explained.

Gracie had little to say on their father's condition, and Cain sensed she didn't condone their mother's sacrifices. Their kind valued forgiveness, and the fact that Gracie could not bring herself to forgive their father was likely costing her more than it would ever cost him.

"How long can Mother go on this way?"

Adam sighed. "Knowing her, forever. Or as long as he survives."

"Our biggest concern right now," Anna said, "is Jaden. He's severely neglected. Your mother feeds him and dresses him, but she spends more time caring for your father. It's not healthy. The child cries and tugs at her apron, but Abilene is too lost in her own grief to mother him."

Cain looked at Adam. "And I suppose you feel this falls under family law and it's not our place to intervene."

Adam's lips pressed tight, and Anna scoffed. "Of course he does. I, on the other hand, think he has a duty to protect his baby brother. You all do."

Cain drew back, digesting her request and wondering how they could possibly work around one of The Order's most guarded laws. It wasn't likely. The best solution would be to help their mother come around and remind her that she has responsibilities outside of looking after their father.

Cain hated witches and wished his father never involved them in their life. "We need to put more pressure on the plebe. Only she knows what her aunt did to him. She could reverse it."

"She says she can't. Blood magick ties a spell to a specific witch and her aunt's gone."

"Um, can someone catch me up?" Destiny said, reminding his siblings of her presence and that this was supposed to be a celebratory dinner. "There are witches? Like, real ones capable of real magic? Broomsticks and all?"

Cain looped an arm around her shoulders and pulled her close, kissing her temple. "Witches are nasty little manipulators and never to be trusted."

"They don't like our kind," Anna explained. "Something about immortality going against the laws of nature." She rolled her eyes and waved away such nonsense. "Gracie killed one."

"*Anna!*" Gracie snapped. "Why would you tell her that?"

"Well, I didn't want her to be afraid of them. We're way tougher."

"You'll have to excuse my wife," Adam said. "She forgets herself from time to time."

Anna shoved Adam. "No, I don't. I know exactly who I am, just as Destiny should know who she is. Look," she faced Destiny. "I know this is totally overwhelming, and then they throw the whole Amish thing into the mix, but it's really not that bad. You're never tired. There's no such thing as struggling to open a pickle jar. And the sex is…" She glanced at Cain. "Well, I'm sure you know. You just have to go into it with an open mind. Every day is a new adventure. Our males are not like other men. They're overbearing and arrogant, but they don't do anything halfway. I have no doubt that Cain will love you more than you ever imagined possible. Just remember two things." She held up two fingers. "You choose to be here, and they absolutely can make a non-electric water heater out of copper coils and coal."

"The secret's out now, Adam." Cain laughed at his brother's dismay, finding Annalise's brazen personality the perfect medicine for his tightly wound twin. "You're one cold shower away from divorce according to how your wife tells it."

"What about Jaden?" Gracie asked, not sharing their levity. "Grandmother and Grandfather have offered to take him, but Mother is reluctant to surrender him to their care."

"We must respect family law, Gracie." Adam patted her hand to offer comfort. "So long as Father cannot communicate, Mother's word is final."

Destiny's brows lifted and Anna scoffed. "That's another thing. Male chauvinism is alive and well on the farm, especially with the older immortals."

Destiny frowned at Cain and he held up his hands in surrender. "I'm nothing like The Elders. Trust me. Half The Council despises me and the other half thinks I'm a progressive lost cause who should've been excommunicated years ago."

"So you're the Hans Ramoray."

Annalise snorted into her drink. "Oh, my God, did you just quote *Friends*? Are you talking about Joey's evil twin?"

"Yes!" Destiny laughed. "I guess Adam's the Drake."

"Oh, he's a total Drake!"

As Annalise and Destiny laughed over some mortal joke he and his siblings could only observe as outsiders, he realized that Anna would be a great ally to Destiny. It was an unexpected turn of events that pleased him very much.

Glancing at his brother, Adam appeared equally mesmerized by the women. He sensed his stare and turned. Cain gave a slight nod, letting his brother know that they were going to be just fine. This outcome was better than any expectation either of them considered.

Adam pulled Annalise into his arms and covered her mouth as he kissed her cheek. "That's enough out of you. It's not nice to make fun of your husband. You'll bruise my ego and give Destiny the wrong impression."

They enjoyed a delicious supper and laughed a lot. Despite their worry for their parents, the night had been a joyous one. When the last dish was cleared and everyone said goodnight, he pulled Destiny close and nuzzled her throat.

They walked under a moonlit sky. The air was warm and the farm was quiet.

"It's so beautiful here."

He laced his fingers with hers. "You're beautiful."

She giggled. "Where are we sleeping?"

"Are you in a rush to sleep?"

"No." She glanced at him. "But I'd like you to take me to bed, wherever that is."

"I'm staying at Larissa's until the house is finished. I hoped to have it done in the next few days, but I just learned I need to build a hot water heater."

She laughed. "So we're going to live at your parents'?"

Cain wasn't sure if his parents would return to the house where they suffered so much. He supposed his father would find the most care with his parents and wife under one roof. And perhaps his mother wanted him to have this time to settle down. "Gracie enjoys living with Anna and Adam. And my mother is content to stay at my grandparents. I could build us a different home, but there is a perfectly good one available. I could have the water heater installed by next week. Would that suit your needs?"

She hugged him, her lips kissing up his throat until she bit his earlobe. "That suits my needs very much."

His body hardened as his mouth found hers. She softened under his touch, always so malleable and yielding to his wants. As his need grew, his grip tightened.

She glanced up into his eyes and broke the kiss, her breath hitching. "Cain, look."

He followed her stare to the stars and grinned. A meteor shower streaked the sky as comets rained overhead. "You did that."

She looked at him in confusion. "Me?"

"It's what you do to me. When we were apart, my sorrow was so inescapable it rained for months on end. But now that I have you, the sky is clear."

She looked up as more falling stars streaked the sky. "It's incredible."

He took her hand and walked her toward the house. "I'll show you incredible."

He led her upstairs to the guest room he'd been using, toppling her soft body to the bed the moment he shut the door. Kissing every curve and loving every inch of her, he took her to places that had her calling for God and speaking in Portuguese tongues.

Afterward, he held her in his arms. "Do you know you think in Portuguese?"

"I do?" She cocked her head. "I suppose you're right. But sometimes I mix it up."

"That's why I can't compel you. But eventually you'll teach me the language and then I'll turn you into my love slave," he teased.

She lifted on her elbows and looked at him. "Can you compel other people?"

"Mortals."

"Well, maybe it's not the language but my immortal blood stopping you."

He considered that for a moment. "No, that wouldn't stop me. I'm older and more powerful. Plus, I can compel Dane."

"Dane Foster, the orphan?"

Cain nodded. "He's like you."

"Really? Do you think he'll talk with me?"

He grabbed her hip and pulled her back to his chest. "If you're not jamming a microphone in his face, I'm sure he'd give you a few minutes of his time."

"My reporting days are over."

"Will you miss it?"

She thought about the investigative part of the job she liked, but then thought of all the other parts she didn't like. The endless grooming and primping, the dieting, the publicity and marketing, the competitive nature of working for a broadcast network where everyone is always after their co-worker's job... "I think I'm okay with letting it go. I'm going to do what Annalise suggested and lean into this new adventure. I'm ready to start the next chapter of my life."

He kissed her head and she sighed, lowering her cheek to rest over his heartbeat. When she licked his chest, he groaned, his body hardening for her again. "Let me help you." He sliced a gash in his chest with his nail. "Try it."

She looked down at the blood and back to him, her eyes unsure. "I'm afraid I'll get sick."

"You won't get sick. Try it once, and if you don't like it, I won't bring it up again."

She hesitated but slowly lowered her mouth, her big brown eyes never leaving him. A satisfied moan rumbled in his chest the moment her tongue touched his flesh. Sifting his hand into her hair, he pressed her closer.

"Open your mouth a little more. That's it." Her lips closed over his muscle as she softly pulled. "Now swallow. Let it go down your throat."

A curious moan escaped her and she sucked harder, her fingers kneading into his skin as she drank more.

"That's it. Take from me everything you need."

His fingers traced down her spine as he kept a fist locked tightly in her hair. He reached between her thighs and found her drenched. Teasing her sex, she opened for him, and he fed his fingers slowly into her, gliding and exploring, not stopping until she cried out against his chest and came in the palm of his hand.

She gasped and panted, his blood coating the tips of her teeth as the scent of her lust filled the air. He gently ran his fingers through her hair. "You like it." She pleased him very much.

"Why is that so good?"

"Because your body wants it." He toppled her to her back and kissed her deeply, tasting the lingering richness of his blood. "And I want your body." He slid his erection through her slick folds and sank into her heat.

Her body caught fire. Thrusting hard, he released his scent and marked her so that there would be no mistaking his claim.

When she playfully bit at his neck, he suspected she wanted more. Slicing open his vein, he cupped her head and pulled her close. "Drink."

She latched on and he bucked into her. Her nails scraped down his back and through his hair. She was wild and uninhibited and he absolutely loved it.

He buried his length inside of her, forcing her to take every last inch of him as he held himself deep. Her full lips sucked on his flesh, drawing pleasure with every pull.

She arched back and gasped. "I feel drunk. Can blood do that?"

"It can be intoxicating under the right circumstances."

"I didn't expect it to be like this."

He stroked in and out of her, slowly, savoring every delightful quiver they shared. "What do you mean?"

"It tastes wild and earthy." She blushed. "And so incredibly... *Cain.*"

"I have other things you can taste."

"Oh?" she lifted a bow, her dark eyes full of intrigue.

"Let me show you."

Withdrawing from her heat, he rose on his knees. "Open your mouth."

She glanced up at him, a smirk hidden in the corner of her mouth, and did as she was told. He fed his cock past her lips, not stopping until he reached the back of her throat.

"You have no idea how many times I fantasized about having you like this, freely, without haste or worry." Waves of pleasure touched places he never felt before. It was more than chemistry. It was the comfort of love, the security of trust, and the relief of finding hope again.

When she pulled him closer, she finished him, swallowing everything he offered and leaving him pleasantly satisfied.

"You're right," she said, curling into his side. "I like when you take control in bed."

He pulled her close and kissed her head. "I like when you give me control." He smiled against her hair. "You please me very much, Destiny." She slipped out of bed and he sat up. "What are you doing?"

"I feel like I had a B-12 shot. I have all this energy." She searched the room. "Why don't you guys have mirrors? Do I look different?" She couldn't stand still.

"You look the same."

"What?" She slouched. "I'm supposed to be skinny."

He sighed. "You're perfect the way you are. Now quit dissecting yourself, and come back to bed."

"There has to be some change. I can feel it. My senses are on high alert. I think I can actually feel my hair and fingernails growing." She examined a hank of hair. "Does this look glossier to you? God, even the air feels crisper."

"Destiny, come back to bed."

She stilled and blushed. Her smile turned shy then she rushed to the bed and kissed him, giggling when he flipped her to her back and took back control.

Never before had he felt so light and unrestrained. He had finally found someone with whom he could be himself. A love, unmatched by anything he'd felt before.

Anna might have his eternal loyalty, but Destiny had his future. She had his heart.

Pulling her closer, he held her to his heart, pressing soft kisses into her wild hair. If only she knew everything she was to him. His sanity, his salvation, his hope that he was not lost. Entwined as one, they drifted off to sleep, entranced by the soft beat of each other's heart.

Several hours later, a loud crash woke him from a dead sleep. A clatter sounded from the floor below, and a door slammed. Eleazar's voice shouted for Larissa to stay upstairs.

"What's going on?" Destiny startled, her eyes barely open and her curls strewn across her face.

Cain sprung to his feet, animal instinct taking over as he stared protectively at the half-mortal in his bed. All he could see in that moment was her fragility in the face of some unknown threat. "Stay here and don't open the door for anyone."

"What? You're leaving me—"

"Do as I say, Destiny."

She abruptly drew back. "Don't order me like I'm a steak."

More banging and thunderous shouting spread from below and he growled. "Stubborn female, I'm trying to protect you!" He caught her shoulders and pushed her back into the bed. "Do you know what you are to me?" his voice broke as he understood then in that moment exactly what she was. She was his anchor, holding him to this life and a purpose, but also his greatest weakness.

His vision blurred as he stared down at her, so delicately human with only a questionable percentage of immortal blood in her veins. "I need you, Destiny. I need you to stay safe and whole and with me, do you understand."

Something in her dark stare softened and she cupped her palm to his jaw. "I love you, too, Cain."

He pressed his forehead to hers, and the walls shook as something crashed hard into the house below. He was needed elsewhere, but loathed to leave her side, terrified to leave her unprotected for even a moment.

"Go," she whispered, pressing a kiss to his lips. "I promise I won't move."

Relieved by her agreement, he forced himself to let her go. "I'll be quick."

He kissed her and rushed downstairs, following the crush of male voices through the safe house toward the holding cells where Cybil was. His heart hammered as he worried something might be wrong when the men shouted and another screamed.

He raced down the dark corridor, spotting a mob of males. Cybil screamed and shook the bars of her cell hard enough to send plaster falling to the floor.

"What's going on?"

"Cain, stay back!" Eleazar yelled.

Cain jerked to a halt and looked at Cybil. Her eyes flashed, and she bared her fangs at him as tension exploded in the air. She clung to the bars, hanging and shaking them like a caged animal.

"He's going to kill her," the witch taunted. "They're going to kill all of you."

"Shut your mouth," Cain snapped, and the witch laughed.

A loud bang cut through the chaos as a shotgun went off.

Cybil stilled and the men rushed into the adjacent cell. She dropped from the bars, and tipped her head back, all the tension leaving her body at once.

The men rushed out of the neighboring cell and quickly bolted the lock. An awful snarl ripped from the bleeding animal on the floor. Not an animal. A male, filthy with blood and mud and leaves tangled in his hair. Rabid, the beast twisted and snapped, foam forming in its beard. It was then Cain recognized the male as his long lost uncle.

Isaiah sprung to his feet, landing in a crouch, prepared to lunge at the bars, but suddenly stilled. Eyes shut, he lifted his chin and scented the air. A rumbling purr emitted from his chest as he bared his fangs, his neck slowly twisting until he looked at the wall separating him from Cybil's cell.

She also stared at the wall with blood-red eyes. Did she know this was the creature that killed her mother? Did she recognize him? Did she remember?

Isaiah panted and stared at the wall, blood staining one fang, with his eyes so darkly red they appeared black.

"You're all going to die, and I'm going to watch," the witch promised.

No one paid her any mind. The men watched Isaiah, but Cain's attention remained on Cybil. She stepped closer to the wall, her narrow fingers curling around the bars as she closed her eyes and breathed deep, as if scenting the beast in the next cell.

She pressed her cheek to the stone wall, her body loose and her youthful face serene. Her fragmented mind permanently disturbed.

Her lips curved with a malevolent grin as her chin lowered and her blood-red eyes opened. Cain's breath held as something unmistakably intentional flashed in her focused stare, alerting him that she was still in there. Then she spoke his name, *"Isaaaaiahhhhhh."*

TO BE CONTINUED...

Want more edgy romance from Lydia Michaels?
Read Immortal Bastard now!

She gasped as he shoved into her body in one fluid motion, deep and hard, giving her no chance to adjust to his massive size.

"Jesus."

His grunt of satisfaction spoke of sheer arrogance. His hands gripped her hips, holding her in place as if he wanted her to experience all of him—his size, his strength, his complete possession of her in that moment. She'd never felt so full. His palm coasted up her spine and fisted in her hair.

"I have you now, little one."

Read Immortal Bastard next!

Lydia Michaels has a gift for you! Subscribe to her mailing list and receive 7 FREE books!
Click here to stuff your Kindle with freebies!

Do you follow LYDIA?
TikTok @LydiaMichaels
Instagram @lydia_michaels_books
Facebook @LydiaMichaels
Goodreads
BookBub

Show Your LOVE
*If you enjoyed this book, please don't forget to
leave a review.*

ALSO BY LYDIA MICHAELS

BOOKS BY SERIES

Many First in series books are FREE

Grab them here!

Free Books Here!

MCCULLOUGH MOUNTAIN

Almost Priest *

Beautiful Distraction

Irish Rogue

British Professor

Broken Man

Controlled Chaos

Hard Fix

Intentional Risk

JASPER FALLS

Wake My Heart *

The Best Man

Love Me Nots

Pining For You

My Funny Valentine

Side Squeeze

CALAMITY RAYNE

Calamity Rayne Gets a Life *

Calamity Rayne Back Again

Calamity Rayne Gets Hitched

BONUS: Calamity Rayne Veiled & Railed

Calamity Rayne Over the Moon

Calamity Rayne Knocked Up

THE SURRENDER TRILOGY

Falling In

BreakingOut

Coming Home

Ruthless Billionaires

One Billion Secrets *

Two Billion Enemies

MASTERMIND
Blind
Untied

NEW CASTLE
First Comes Love *
If I Fall
Shattered Vows

ADDICTED TO YOU
Crush *
Bang
Throb

THE ORDER OF VAMPIRES
Original Sin *
Dark Exodus
Prodigal Son
Immortal Bastard
Primal Kill
Blood Moon

STAND ALONES

La Vie en Rose

Simple Man

Sugar

Breaking Perfect

Hurt

Protege

ABOUT THE AUTHOR

To receive Lydia's Newsletter and 7 FREE Books, click HERE !

Free Books Here!

Lydia Michaels is the bestselling and award-winning author of more than forty novels. She writes heart-clenching, unpredictable romance with dark elements and high heat. Her work is character-driven and bursting with broken heroes and badass females. With a sweet spot for overbearing, territorial types, her deeply emotional books are spicy, emotionally satisfying, and guaranteed to leave readers with many book hangovers.

Lydia is the consecutive winner of the *2018 & 2019 Author of the Year Award* from *Happenings Media* and the recipient of the *2014 Best Author Award* from the Courier Times. She has been featured by *USA Today, Romantic Times Magazine,* the *Women in Publishing Summit,* and more.

Michaels started her author career in 2007, becoming a recognized presence and advocate within the publishing industry. She is the CEO of LMC Consulting, a certified author coach specializing in character and plot development, and the founder of the *East Coast Author Convention,* the *Behind the Keys Author Retreat,* and www.LydiaMichaelsBooks.com.

She is happily married to her childhood sweetheart. Her favorite things include cooking Italian cuisine, hosting extravagant dinner parties, sipping espresso martinis, listening to her husband play piano, and escaping to her coastal home on the Jersey Shore. She's an LGBTQ ally, a BLM supporter, a firm believer that the patriarchy must end (women's rights are human rights), and an advocate for pediatric cancer research.

LYDIA

Follow Lydia Michaels on social media!
Facebook | Instagram | TikTok

ACKNOWLEDGEMENT

So much work goes into a book that it would be impossible for authors to make it to "the end" alone. I'd like to acknowledge and thank my amazing beta team for always having my back and keeping me on my toes. Loren, Perrin, Darcy, and Claire, I would be lost without you! Special thanks to Daniela G. for sharing her Brazilian background and keeping us entertained with her incredibly skilled Portuguese tongue (wink)!

I'd also like to tip my hat to the original book club girls that inspired the characters of Destiny, Brenda, Camilla, and Rochelle. When I think of where we were and where we are now, I'm filled with warmth and pride—amazed that these original plot lines of mine have stood the test of time. I guess it's true what they say, good stories are immortal.

And, finally, I'm especially grateful for Ivone S. who emphatically claimed Cain as her own when he first came into my imagination almost twenty years ago. Without Ivone, there would be no Destiny. Without the support of so many people, there might not have been a Lydia. Thank you. I'm so thrilled to finally share these characters and their stories with the world!

THANK YOU FOR YOUR REVIEW!

Reviews help authors so much! If you left a review for this book, I greatly appreciate it!
Thank you,
Lydia

Click here to leave your review!